Holy Denver

Also by Florence Wetzel:

Perry Robinson: The Traveler
Madeline: A Novel of Love, Buddhism, and Hoboken
Mrs. Papadakis and Aspasia: Two Novels
Dashiki: A Jazz Mystery
Elvis in the Morning: Poems and Tales

Holy Denver

A Novel

FLORENCE WETZEL

HOLY DENVER
A NOVEL

This is a work of fiction. All of the characters, names, incidents, organizations, and dialogue in this novel are either the products of the author's imagination or are used fictitiously.

iUniverse books may be ordered through booksellers or by contacting:

iUniverse
1663 Liberty Drive
Bloomington, IN 47403
www.iuniverse.com
1-800-Authors (1-800-288-4677)

ISBN: 978-1-4917-5703-1 (sc)
ISBN: 978-1-4917-5704-8 (e)

Printed in the United States of America.

iUniverse rev. date: 1/09/2015

Contents

Part 1 Before

1. Down in the World 1
2. Big Snooze 15
3. Lunch in Pieces 25
4. Lowest of the Low 36
5. Too Clever 49
6. Thick Slice of Crazy 61
7. E to Shining E 82
8. Moms Gone Wild 95
9. Worth Talking To 108
10. The Goof of Terror 126

Part 2 After

1. The Necessity of Shame 137
2. Start Small 172
3. Columbine Is a Flower 198
4. One Heart 207
5. Softest Creature in the World 229
6. I Don't Have Any Words 243
7. Mad Denver Afternoon 255

Acknowledgments 267
Selected Bibliography 269

This book is dedicated to Flora Jane Sugarman:
niece, friend, inspiration

Someone who has acted carelessly
But later becomes careful and attentive
Is as beautiful as the bright moon emerging from the clouds

Nagarjuna, *Letter to a Friend*

But oh when I was in Colorado they sang sad songs about Columbine

Jack Kerouac, *Visions of Cody*

Part 1

Before

1. Down in the World

My name is Elizabeth Zwelland. Although I come from a family of poets—my mom, my dad, my three stepmothers, even my little sister—I've never written fiction or memoir in my life. But now I have a story that I would really like to tell. I'm a bit ashamed to tell it, actually, but that's probably exactly why I should.

I am thirty-six years old. I'm tall, five foot ten, long legged, thin but not curvy. I have straight, glossy black hair that falls just past my shoulders. I have green eyes, an olive complexion, even features, and heavy, straight eyebrows. People usually call me striking, sometimes beautiful. Rarely pretty.

I live in Denver, Colorado. I used to live in Manhattan, but due to the financial holocaust in the last months of 2008, I lost my job as an editor and I lost my apartment, so I had to come out West because this is where my father lives. I did not want to leave Manhattan, and I most certainly did not want to move into my father's fancy Queen Anne house in Boulder, Colorado.

I started looking for a new job the day after I arrived. I contacted every publisher on the Colorado Front Range, which is what people here call the line of communities hugging the Rocky Mountains, from Fort Collins up north all the way down to Pueblo in the south. There are more publishers out here than you might imagine, and trust me, I contacted them all, even the ones for Christian books and knitting guides. But, as you know, at that time all the jobs had vanished. None of the publishers I contacted had openings—many had just fired 20 to 30 percent of their staff, and the rest had hiring freezes. I didn't get a real interview anywhere; I just spoke on the phone to sad, frantic people, all of whom told me no.

By spring 2009 I was getting quite desperate, not just because the little money I had was running out, but because I was suffocating in my father's house. Something had to give. I finally accepted the fact that I might have to change industries, and I started looking wistfully at the cashiers at Whole Foods and wondering what their discount was. Then I saw an ad in Craigslist for a part-time job at Quill & Ink, the large independent bookstore in downtown Denver.

I got the job, to my surprise. There were dozens of people at the initial cattle call, dozens, everyone looking as desperate as I felt. But certainly no one had my credentials, and although I was grossly overqualified, I clearly knew books and had a love for them. So in June 2009 I moved to Denver and started my new job. From day one it was clear to me that I hated working retail, and after three months that impression was set in stone.

Which is a good place to begin my story. It was mid-September 2009, and I was sitting on a bench on the 16th Street Mall in lower downtown Denver, also known as LoDo. It was almost nine thirty in the morning, and downtown was coming to life around me. I was staring at the pink-brick building across the street—one of those massive buildings from the late 1890s that you can still find in downtown Denver—and I was steeling myself to go inside and start my day at work.

As I sat there, a thought came to me that often passed through my mind in those days: *I have come down in the world.* A year before I was working in Manhattan, my heels clicking eagerly up the stone steps of the elegant 1890s brownstone on West Tenth Street that housed Blue Heron Books. No matter how tired I was or what drama awaited me with one of our authors, I was almost always excited to get dressed up and go to work, thrilled to be part of such a prestigious publisher with such a rich literary history.

And now? Now I lived in a cow town, working part-time in retail and making eight dollars an hour, wearing jeans and a long-sleeved T-shirt and thick-soled black sneakers. Worst of all, a name tag. But no matter how much I wanted to be in Manhattan, no matter how much I wanted to be flying up the brownstone steps to Blue Heron Books, it would never happen again. My old job was gone, my apartment was gone, and that was that. *I have come down in the world.*

I looked up 16th Street, the long street that runs through downtown Denver, and I lifted my eyes to the Clocktower, a tall and skinny blonde-brick building with a clock near the top of each of its four sides. Nine thirty. Time to go in.

I rose and looked both ways on 16th Street, keeping an eye out for the Mall Ride, the free bus shuttle that runs up and down 16th Street all day and almost all night. Getting hit by the Mall Ride would be a good excuse to miss work, but it wasn't a sensible long-term plan. I crossed 16th Street, and with a heavy heart I entered Quill & Ink.

If I hadn't been going there to work, I would have been happy to enter Quill & Ink. In fact I did love the store the dozen or so times I went there over the years, usually with one of my stepmothers. Once in my late twenties my flight back East was cancelled due to a snowstorm, and since I was staying a block away at the Oxford Hotel I spent an entire afternoon and evening at the bookstore. The store has two floors, the bottom one a cavernous space with brick walls, worn wooden floors, and high ceilings with exposed wooden beams and fat, snaking silver air-ducts. The bookshelves are made of wood and polished to a high sheen, and there are cozy chairs and mismatching sofas throughout the store, as well as wooden tables of all sizes. The store smells like wood and coffee and citrus cleanser, and altogether it's a warm, comforting environment. Unless, of course, you worked there against your will.

The store had been open several hours when I walked in, and there were already a fair number of customers, reading quietly on the sofas and easy chairs, working on laptops in the seating area in front of the café, or just browsing the shelves and display tables. Q&I opens at six thirty, which is unusual for a retail store, but since there is a café and since the store is only two blocks from Market Street Station, our manager wisely decided to open a few hours earlier so we could be available to commuters.

The café isn't big, but it offers a lot of readymade food, and of course everyone needs coffee. There is a glass refrigerator for cold drinks and a glass display case filled with pastries from Watercourse Foods and sandwiches from Udi's, both local businesses. The front counter is jam-packed with pens, mugs, bookmarks, and Chocolove chocolate bars, which are made in Boulder. There are also bags of candy, such as gummy bears and chocolate-covered espresso beans, all bearing a gold sticker with the Q&I avatar, a gnome-ish creature in a pointy hat who is bent over a desk and writing in a large book with, you guessed it, a lush quill and a fat pot of ink.

On the wall behind the counter is a large green chalkboard with the drink menu written in various shades of bright chalk. There's also a drawing of the Q&I gnome, and at the bottom you can always find the weekly Jack Kerouac quote, supplied by Hadley Barr, the café manager. That day the quote was:

NOW I COULD SEE DENVER LOOMING AHEAD OF ME
LIKE THE PROMISED LAND
JACK KEROUAC, *ON THE ROAD*

Working solo at the café that morning was Hadley Barr himself. What can I tell you about Hadley Barr? He's about my age, at least six foot two, skinny and gangly, with a mop of curly brown hair, a beak nose, and expressive brown eyes that are definitely his best feature. That morning when I walked in, I saw him talking animatedly to a customer. Suddenly he threw his head back, and the café—nay, the store—was filled with his distinctive laugh: "Ha HA ha!"

I walked up to the counter to get my morning coffee, and when Hadley Barr saw me his eyes lit up. Which was the other thing to know about Hadley Barr: he had some kind of fixation on me. I wouldn't call it a crush, because it had more to do with my dad than with me. The first time Hadley saw my name on my time card, he made a beeline for me, and he has been making a beeline ever since.

I didn't particularly like Hadley Barr. I didn't like his beelines, I didn't like his laugh, and I didn't like his obsession with Beat poets, which included my dad. I especially didn't know what to make of his bizarre personal history, which he cheerfully told me in the break room during my second day at work. Apparently Hadley had been trained as a pharmacist, and during his twenties he worked in a drugstore in his hometown of Greeley, Colorado. He became addicted to opium suppositories, stole from the store, got arrested, and then spent six months in rehab. I wasn't put off by the story; I was more puzzled by Hadley's need to tell it to a virtual stranger. This combined with his eager questions about my dad made me wary of him, and I always kept him at arms' length.

But I still needed coffee, and if I wanted to use my store discount, I had to go to the café. Also, as café manager Hadley was allowed to dispose of outdated food as he wished, and he often wished to give it to me. I was so poor that it wasn't a matter of wanting the food: I needed it. In fact my breakfast at home that morning was a cup of tea and a three-day-old bear claw supplied by Hadley.

"Elizabeth Zwelland!" he said, saluting me as he often did. "Good morning to you!"

"Hi, Hadley."

"You look ravishing, as always."

I knit my brow. "I'm wearing jeans and a T-shirt, Hadley."

"Ah, but it's the way you wear them! That black T-shirt, for instance, is very becoming with your hair and skin color."

I rolled my eyes. I wasn't in the mood.

"So, Elizabeth Zwelland, I have good news for you."

"What's that?"

"Just before you came in, a customer asked for a decaf latte, and I accidentally made a regular. Whoops! I saved it for you." Hadley produced a large paper cup with a black plastic lid and a Q&I–gnome imprint. Beaming, he set the latte on the counter.

I swallowed a smile. "Thanks, Hadley." Lattes were my weakness. They were also out of my budget, as rare a treat as taking the bus home from work.

Of course the invitation came next. Nothing was free. "So tonight a few of us are heading over to the Gypsy House Café for a poetry open mike. Care to join?"

"No, thanks. I've told you a million times, Hadley, I don't like poetry readings."

"Ah, but you should! They're in your blood."

"But I don't. Thanks for the latte, Hadley."

A hipster couple walked up to the counter to order. I wiggled my fingers good-bye and left quickly.

I walked to the back of the store. There is a small hallway with customer restrooms, and every inch of wall space is filled with posters of local events and FOR SALE notices. There's also a door that says EMPLOYEES ONLY, along with a drawing of the Q&I gnome looking menacing. I opened the door and stepped into a bright-yellow hallway decorated with framed posters of book covers. The hallway has several doors as well as an elevator. The doors lead to the manager's office, the break room, the receiving room, and the basement, an enormous room that's poorly lit and has many, many spiders—Hadley took me down there once. Each door has a sign that includes the Q&I gnome; for the break-room sign, he is leaning against a mushroom, smoking a pipe and reading a book.

I opened the break-room door and stepped in. The room is not large, and it has no windows. Hadley called it "The Bunker" after William Burroughs' famous subterranean apartment in New York City (a scary place that I once visited with my mother, but that's another story). There are lockers alongside one wall, and two battered couches against the others.

In the middle of the room is a wooden table with scratches and circular marks from glasses, along with several mismatching wooden chairs. There's a noisy avocado-colored refrigerator that's usually stuffed to the brim, and a large garbage can that emits a smell of old food. Framed posters fill the bright blue walls, and there are books and magazines everywhere, most with their covers torn off or some other noticeable damage. The cleaning staff tidied the break room weekly, but like a jungle the mess quickly returned. I think because we were all so focused on keeping the sales floor immaculate, it was a relief to have a space that we could pretty much ignore.

The only person in the room was Ruby, sitting at the table and drinking a cup of tea. I said hello, then I went to my locker and put my sweater and navy-blue knapsack inside. The dreaded object, my name tag, was sitting on a small shelf near the top, but I always waited until the last possible moment to put it on. I wedged my lunch bag into the refrigerator, then sat down on the purple couch. I flipped off the lid of my latte and took my first sip of coffee for the day. I closed my eyes and enjoyed the feeling of caffeine hitting my nervous system. The Q&I espresso beans are excellent, a Costa Rican blend that's rich and strong. The coffee always helped; I liked to get to work at least a half hour early so I could have time to drink a cup and sink into the store.

I slowly and steadily worked on my latte, which I needed to finish by ten—no beverages on the sales floor, at least for employees. I didn't speak to Ruby. I never spoke to Ruby, if I could help it. Ruby had to be in her early sixties, maybe late fifties. She was a short, dumpy woman, not heavy but with rolls of fat in all the wrong places. Her misplaced fat was exacerbated by her wardrobe, which consisted of polyester pantsuits and crewneck shirts in garish shades like lemon, lime green, and violet. That day it was fuchsia, both the pantsuit and the crewneck. She had dead-white skin, black hair that was badly dyed and cut—a blatant do-it-yourself job—and poorly applied mascara that always found its way under her eyes by the end of the day. I may have been poor, but Ruby looked poor. She also exuded a faint smell of alcohol, specifically gin. In short, she was a mess.

I couldn't understand what Ruby was doing at Q&I since she clearly could not pull her weight. According to London, who was my only friend at the store, Ruby was an inheritance from the previous manager, a jovial redhead named Joanne. Ruby only worked on simple tasks, basic things like dusting tables, or polishing the miles of wooden shelving, or sticking price tags on tins of mints decorated with drawings of famous authors, including—to Hadley's delight—Jack Kerouac. But no matter the job, Ruby was easily perplexed, and I often caught her sitting on the floor or at a table with her latest task strewn around her in a sea of confusion. London thought Ruby had ADD or maybe some kind of brain damage, but whatever the case, she was even more out of place at Q&I than I was.

I was sipping my latte, feeling a lead weight of despair in my stomach at the thought of my impending shift, when I heard Ruby's quavering voice. "I saw you yesterday. From behind."

I never talked to Ruby, but Ruby sometimes talked to me. As usual, I wasn't in the mood. "Really," I said.

"Yep." She turned and looked at me. "At King Soopers. The one on Ninth and Downing."

"Oh. Probably."

"You live at Ninth and Sherman, right?"

"That's right."

"I heard you tell someone that. I don't live too far from there. I'm at Tenth and Emerson."

"Really." I picked up a magazine, any magazine, then opened it and laid it across my knees.

As usual, Ruby didn't get the hint. "They have great sales there. Especially if you have a King Soopers card. Do you have a King Soopers card?"

Of course I had a King Soopers card. If it wasn't for the bright-yellow sale stickers all over the store, I couldn't have survived on my tiny salary. I would have preferred to shop at the Whole Foods close by my apartment, but I simply couldn't afford it.

"Yes," I said tersely. "I have a King Soopers card."

"I like them better than Whole Foods," Ruby went on. "Even though Whole Foods is a little closer to me. Do you know what Hadley calls Whole Foods?"

"Whole Paycheck."

"That's right. Isn't that funny? Hadley's funny. He's a nice boy. He reminds me of my son."

You never, ever wanted to be caught in the break room when Ruby started talking about her son. You couldn't avoid it or anticipate it, because anything might cause her to broach the subject. You could be talking about a solar eclipse, your favorite wine, or Stieg Larsson, and inevitably Ruby brought the discussion around to her son, Jaime, who lived in northern Colorado. I said absolutely nothing as she talked about Jaime's new dirt bike; I just stared fiercely at a photo of a fiercely pouting Angelina Jolie. Bad enough that I was stuck working in a bookstore, bad enough that I had a coworker like Ruby, but couldn't I even have a moment of quiet so I could sip my latte in peace?

The door opened. I looked up, and my face brightened: London. Thank God; she would save me from Ruby. She always did.

Of all the people at Quill & Ink, London was the only one I considered a friend. I had more in common with her than anyone else there. Like me, London was in Denver purely by accident. She had worked for a swank interior-design company in LA, and when they decided to open a branch in Denver, London came out as second in command. At first the firm flourished, designing pricey interiors for Denver's elite—a combination of politicians, real estate moguls, and players from the Broncos and Nuggets. But when the economy tanked, the company closed its fancy LoDo office as well as its main hub in LA. London, who had shopped regularly at Q&I for her clients, was desperate enough to put in an application, and she was hired a few months before me.

London was an attractive woman in her early forties, tall like me but much thinner—one might even say she was too thin. She had a mane of thick golden-brown hair, narrow eyes, high cheekbones, a large mobile mouth, and a dark tan that definitely was not natural. In certain lights, you could see a map of light lines all over her face. London always smelled of fancy perfume, and she always looked stylish, even though she worked retail and had a retail salary. She was one of those people with a flair for layering clothes and tying scarves, and instead of wearing jeans like the rest of us at Q&I, she always wore black leggings that clung to her skinny legs.

I perked up and said, "Hi, London."

"Hey." She draped herself on the floral-patterned couch and put her feet—clad in stylish black loafers—on one of the mismatched wooden chairs. That day she wore a loose gold shirt over skinny brown and white tank tops, a thin black-and-gold scarf arranged artfully around her neck, thick gold hoops, and several gold necklaces. And black leggings, of course.

"How's it going?" I asked.

"Oh, another day in dinky Denver. My new loft-mate moved in last night. I converted that big closet into a bedroom, and I'm charging him seven hundred dollars a month."

"Nice," I laughed. I had heard a great deal about London's loft on Seventeenth and Champa, but she hadn't yet invited me there.

"He's a twenty-two-year-old grad student from Texas, what does he know? Hey, Ruby," London said loudly. "What's up?"

"Nothing," Ruby said quietly, looking down at her tea.

"Nothing?" London said, throwing me a wink. "Nothing at all?"

"Ruby was just telling me that Hadley reminds her of her son," I said.

"Is that so? How's that, Ruby?"

"How's what?" Ruby said slowly.

"How is it that Hadley reminds you of your son?"

Ruby swallowed. "Oh—you know."

"No, I don't know. That's why I'm asking you, Ruby. So tell me: How does Hadley remind you of your son?"

"He—well, they're both friendly."

"Is that so? Ruby, if your son is so friendly, why haven't I ever met him? I've been working here almost six months, and I've never even seen him."

"He lives in Craig," Ruby said quietly.

"Craig isn't so far away. Elizabeth, is Craig far from here?"

"Oh, God, don't ask me," I said, playing along. "It's by the Wyoming border, right? Not *so* far."

"It's far," Ruby said, her voice barely above a whisper.

London shrugged. "Well, seems to me if he really wanted to come to Denver and see his mom, he would. Don't you think so, Elizabeth?"

"Seems logical," I said.

Ruby took a nervous sip of tea.

"Aw, Ruby," London said. "I'm only kidding you! I'm sure your son loves you. I'm sure he's not ashamed of you or anything."

Ruby stood up abruptly, knocking into the table. With trembling hands, she found her time card, punched out, then fumbled with the doorknob and walked out.

"Oh my God," London said, stretching out like a big, thin cat. "When is Hilda going to fire that deadweight? I spend half my time cleaning up her messes."

"Oh, I know," I agreed. "Me, too." Which wasn't actually true. London organized the window and in-store displays, and so she often had to work with Ruby, whereas all I ever did was shelve.

"This morning I walked into the bathroom, and I could tell right away she'd been in there. That distinctive Ruby smell, half-alcohol and half-shit." London pushed aside her glossy mane of hair. "God, I can't wait to get out of this place. I went to a networking event last night, and I must have handed my card out to at least fifty people."

I had seen London's card: it was gold with elegant black font and a line drawing of the Tower of London. "Maybe something will turn up," I said.

"Or maybe not. When the economic shit hits the fan, who needs an interior decorator? For that matter, who needs books? I can't believe this place is still in business."

The break-room door opened, and Hilda, our manager, walked in. "Hilda," London said, sitting up slightly. "I was just saying to Elizabeth, how the hell are you keeping this place going in the middle of an economic nightmare?"

Hilda laughed. She was a pretty big-boned Hispanic woman in her late twenties, with creamy light-brown skin, long glossy black hair, generous lips, and chocolaty brown eyes. She put some outdated magazines without covers on the center table and said teasingly, "London, I'm not keeping this place open. Our Lady of Guadalupe is."

London laughed. I said nothing and flipped a page of my magazine. Although London frequently disparaged Hilda in private, London was a bit of an ass-kisser whenever Hilda was actually in the room. I've never been good at ass-kissing.

Hilda leaned against the wall. "It is a miracle we're still open, though. It's all about loyal customers."

London nodded, as if she agreed or even cared.

I flipped another page of my magazine. I didn't dislike Hilda, particularly. I just thought she was rather provincial. I knew that she had been at Q&I for almost ten years; she had gotten a part-time job at the store when she was a student at CU Denver, and over the years she was promoted to supervisor, then assistant manager, and finally store manager. I also knew that she was from Limon, a town in Colorado that I had never heard of. When I asked London where it was, she said, "It's Jack Nowhere, that's where it is."

Hilda took me to lunch on my first day at Q&I, and I remember her telling me that she was eighteen when she came to the "big city." I gave a snort of laughter, and she looked at me curiously. Later when we were discussing my years in Manhattan, she told me in all seriousness, "My dream is to go to New York City one day and go to the big library and pat the lions on the head." So that gives you a sense of where she was coming from.

But despite her provincial upbringing, Hilda was an excellent manager. Her parents had a grocery store back in Limon where she had worked since she was small, and as a result she had a knack for retail. She was particularly good with customers—she actually seemed to like them. She also loved books and was an avid reader, and she was definitely the hardest worker in the store. She even helped out at the front register and in the café, which everyone appreciated since we were more or less a skeleton crew, only a handful of full-timers supplemented with part-timers like London and me.

Hilda also kept close track of the industry through various trade publications, and she was always coming up with new ideas to keep the store vital. It was Hilda who expanded the store's hours, Hilda who created a Q&I coffee brand, Hilda who doubled the floor space for nonbook merchandise. She beefed up the Spanish book section, started a Facebook page, reached out to schools, expanded the café merch, inaugurated a weekly eBook tutorial, and doubled the amount of in-store events. I don't know what Our Lady of Guadalupe was doing, but Hilda worked her butt off every single day.

But although I had a lot of respect for Hilda, I couldn't really relate to her, and she was never as friendly to me as she was when I first started. Still, we got along pretty well, and she had liked my work at the store enough to give me ten more hours a week.

"So, Hilda, how was your day off?" London asked.

"Oh, I had so much fun! My boyfriend's cousins came to visit from Arizona, and we did the Banjo Billy Bus Tour."

"What's that?" London asked.

"You don't know about Banjo Billy? It's awesome."

"I know Banjo Billy," I said. "It's that annoying bus that's decked out to look like a hillbilly shack."

"Oh, that!" London said. "The one with the wood on the side and the tin roof? I always wondered what that was."

"They have a tour in Boulder, too," I said. "It's really annoying—they pass by my apartment building twice a day. They always make these weird beeps, like duck quacks and wolf whistles."

"It's great," Hilda said. "You go all over Denver and hear all these funky history facts. I love it. You should try it, Elizabeth—it's fun."

"No, thanks," I said. "I can't ever imagine myself doing something like that."

Hilda looked at me curiously, just as she had at lunch on my first day, tilting her head and pursing her lips slightly.

"Well," London said. "Break's over."

I sighed and put my magazine on the towering stack on the central table. "Time to punch in."

"Elizabeth," Hilda said. "After you punch in, go see Rebecca for your assignment. She's in receiving."

My stomach tightened a little. I never liked dealing with Rebecca, but since she was assistant manager I didn't have much choice. I downed the last drops of my latte, then went to my locker and pinned the odious name-tag on my T-shirt. It was light green with black letters and had, of course, a drawing of the Q&I gnome. Then I found my time card at the bottom of the long metal rack next to the time clock and punched in: 9:59.

I left the break room and crossed the hall to the door marked RECEIVING, which had a drawing of the Q&I gnome surrounded by towering stacks of books. The receiving room is a large rectangular space filled with tall green-metal shelves, all neatly labeled and brimming with books, and a rolling steel door that opens onto an alley so trucks can back up there. Next to the receiving scanner and computer were dozens of boxes of all sizes, and slicing open a box with an X-acto knife was Hector, the Q&I receiving manager. A short middle-aged Hispanic man with bulging muscles, Hector always wore jeans and a crisp white T-shirt that somehow remained spotless even after a long day at work. He took a few books out of the box and ran them over the scanner while simultaneously listening to Rebecca, who was standing with her back to the door, talking rapidly and flapping her hands as she always did when she was in the middle of one of her overlong stories.

I walked up to them. "Hi, Hector. Rebecca, Hilda asked me to see you."

Rebecca turned her head and looked at me, a slight frown between her eyebrows. She didn't like me, and I knew exactly why. On my first day at Q&I, I arrived at nine, filled out paperwork with Hilda, got my name tag and locker, and then was handed over to Rebecca's care. She started by giving me a tour of the store, and as I followed her around and listened to her explain the shelving system, my mood was black, and my feet felt like they were filled with lead. I spent the rest of the day shelving, and when Rebecca came over at the end of my shift and asked me how I was doing, a surprising thing happened: I burst into tears. I'm not a big crier, not at all, but I think it was only at the end of my first full day of working retail that I became aware of the hours of drudgery that lay before me. And very aware, once again, that my old life was gone forever.

Rebecca took me out to Rio Grande for a drink. I rarely drink, but I had a few strawberry margaritas that evening, and I ended up telling Rebecca all about Blue Heron Books and my boss, Mr. Dove, and my coworkers Hansika and Gerard and Eileen. I got a little maudlin, frankly. Rebecca listened carefully, and at the end of the evening she told me not to worry: everyone at Q&I was great, they'd all help me through this hard time, I'd make plenty of friends in Denver—and that she, in fact, was my friend. We hugged, and believe me, I'm not a big hugger.

The next morning I woke up and felt like an idiot. Rebecca wasn't my friend; I could never be friends with someone like her. She wasn't a bad person, but she was another one of those people from some godforsaken corner of Colorado who didn't have a clue. Rebecca was from a town named, of all things, Dinosaur. Can you imagine? *Dinosaur.* She was in her late twenties, a big boxy girl who wore high-waisted dark jeans, flannel shirts, thick-soled white sneakers, and a unicorn necklace. She had pale skin, wire-frame glasses, long brown hair, and, worst, slightly buck teeth. London called her "Rebucky"; London had a nickname for everyone.

When I went into work the next day, I was happy to see that Rebecca was off the schedule and we weren't due to work together for another two days. During that time I met London, with whom I had so much more in common. We started talking whenever we were together in the break room, and during working hours we often snuck off for small chats in the far corners of the store. In fact, I was with London the next time I saw Rebecca: London and I were standing at the café getting our morning coffee from Hadley when Rebecca walked into the store. Seeing me, she rushed over eagerly, awkward in her jeans and big white sneakers, her buck-toothed mouth in a big grin. I gave her a small smile, then turned my attention fully to London.

Rebecca tried to engage me a few times after that, but I always kept our talks short and steered them back to work, and I never accepted her invitations to go out for a drink. After about two weeks she gave up, to my relief, and her attitude changed to hurt anger. Which was ridiculous—a talk over margaritas doesn't mean someone is your friend. Then her hurt anger turned to coldness, and I soon noticed that she always gave me the worst possible assignments.

Like that day. "Elizabeth, I have you in the Wedding section. You can start by organizing the wedding books back here in receiving. Hector hasn't had a chance to get to them, and they're a bit of a mess."

"All right," I said neutrally. Everyone knew the Wedding section was a nightmare, full of oversized books that were unwieldy and hard to fit onto the shelves. The books were boring, too.

"That'll take you a few hours. When you're done, come find me for your next assignment."

"OK."

I went to the front of the receiving room and grabbed one of the green shelving carts lined up by the door; they were larger than the silver carts, which weren't big enough for the bulky wedding books. I tipped the cart on its back wheels and rolled it to the far corner of the room where Hector kept the wedding books. I was dismayed to see the two shelves marked WEDDING overflowing with books, as well as a half-dozen boxes on the floor, open but not emptied. Where were all these books going to fit? I sighed.

Like I said: drudgery.

2. Big Snooze

I spent the next hour in the receiving room. I laid paper towels on the floor, unpacked all the boxes, and put the books in neat piles. I took all the books off the shelves, adding them to the piles when they matched, which they often did, and making new piles when they didn't. When the shelves were empty, I took paper towels and a spray bottle of citrus cleaner (another Hilda innovation; she said it made the store smell better than the usual chemical sprays), and I cleaned off the dusty shelves. I filled my cart with a few books from each pile and put the rest on the shelves. I tipped the heavy cart back so I could move it, then I went out into the hall and took the creaky old elevator up to the second floor.

The Wedding section is in the far corner by a big window overlooking the 16th Street Mall, so I negotiated my cart over the dark-green carpet that covers the second floor. Luckily the shelves were pretty empty; I put all the books on the shelves, organizing them alphabetically by author and turning a few of the newer titles so their covers faced the customers.

The work was terribly boring, but it was not hard by any means, and it was peaceful work that didn't involve customers. Working as a proofreader, then a copyeditor, then an editor at Blue Heron had suited me perfectly: it was quiet work that I mostly did alone, and that's what I loved best, being alone with words. At Q&I, I wasn't working with words, but at least I was on my own. There were information desks located on each floor, and one or two cashiers on the main floor, so the only thing I did all day, every day, was shelve. Usually I was on the second floor, which was generally pretty quiet, although things always got a little busier around lunchtime.

The good thing about shelving is that you need to handle the books, so you don't appear to be goofing off if you take a few moments to read the back covers. Depending on the section of the store I was in, I could almost find myself—well, definitely not happy. Content, maybe. Those quick interludes of reading soothed me, and they helped me forget where I was and why I was there.

The Wedding section, however, was a big snooze. I wasn't one of those little girls (or grown women) who spent hours picturing themselves walking down the aisle in a poofy white dress. I wondered about this now and then: Did I have some sort of gene missing? I have had three serious boyfriends in my life—one in college, one during my first year out of college, and the last and longest in my midtwenties. The third guy was the only one I thought about marrying; I was actually about to move in with him, and he had even bought extra shelves to accommodate my many books. But we broke up in the fall of 2001. And I sold my books before I came out West in order to raise money.

By the time I was done with the Wedding section it was gleaming, beautifully organized with at least one copy of each title on the shelves. I felt a sense of accomplishment, I suppose, and a flicker of pride when Hilda passed by and said, "Nice work, Elizabeth!" Hilda was big on giving positive feedback and making sure everyone felt appreciated. However it was completely meaningless for me to get positive feedback about such a menial task, a task anyone could do.

Well, not anyone. As I negotiated my cart back to the elevator, I saw Ruby in front of the Denver History section, a freestanding bookshelf that faced the wide staircase that led to the first floor. She had clearly been instructed to dust and clean the shelves, but she had nonetheless managed to make a mess, the brightly colored duster and the spray bottle and rag in a pile on the carpet, the books spread out haphazardly, and Ruby's face a twist of confusion. Juniper, the heavyset middle-aged black woman who worked the second-floor information desk during the day, was at Ruby's side helping her sort out the mess, which struck me as a colossal waste of time and manpower.

Hilda's weakness as a manager, I mused as I pushed my empty cart onto the elevator, was that she was incapable of firing anyone. She felt that everyone could be rehabilitated, even Fat Bob, a cashier who had been stealing books and selling them on eBay and Amazon, and sometimes locally to Capitol Hill Books. Which is where he got busted by Rebecca when she happened to stop by during one of his sales.

The store also employed a creepy lady named Stacie with a blonde-white crew cut. It was weird enough that Stacie wore the same camouflage jumpsuit day in and day out, but she also wore a khaki eye-patch and chewed a toothpick all day long. Stacie spoke in utterances of no more than three words—London and I had counted—which made it impossible to have any kind of real conversation with her. Worst of all for the store, she suffered from debilitating migraines and seemed to spend at least half of every shift in the break room on the flower-patterned couch. I always stayed clear of Stacie.

But the biggest liability was Ruby, with her obvious drinking problem and her inability to complete even the most basic tasks. She had no business whatsoever working in a bookstore, where all she ever did was create a mess on the selling floor.

If Hilda had any guts, I mused, she would fire Fat Bob, Stacie, and Ruby. Keeping them on was probably some kind of religious thing with her. I don't think Hilda was kidding when she told London that Q&I was still afloat because of Guadalupe. I wasn't entirely sure who Our Lady of Guadalupe was—I knew she was a Hispanic Virgin Mary with a colorful dress, but that was about it. Hilda has a big statue of Guadalupe in her office (too big, London and I agreed), and every day she wore a necklace with a colorful medallion of Guadalupe. Religion clouds people's logic, I always thought, and if Hilda was in fact keeping employees on as some kind of religious project, that simply confirmed my belief.

Back in the receiving room, I asked Hector if he had seen Rebecca.

"She went out to lunch with Hilda. She told me to tell you to finish that cart by the water cooler. Stacie was in the middle of shelving, but she had to go lay down."

"Toothpick get caught in her throat?" I asked.

Hector waggled a finger at me. "Now, Miss E, be nice. Stacie's got issues."

She sure does, I thought. I went over to Stacie's barely touched cart and knelt down to look at the spines. Fiction! My favorite.

The Fiction section is on the side of the building facing Wynkoop Street, and at that time of day the tall, thin windows between the shelves poured in gentle sunshine. Fiction was the easiest section to shelve because the books didn't vary much in size and you didn't have to worry about endless subdivisions, like in the History section. The only thing you needed to know was the alphabet.

I love novels. I can't even begin to count how many books I've read in my life, but I was familiar with most of the authors in the fiction section, and the ones I didn't know I made it my business—my pleasure—to find out. Even with our 30 percent discount, books were still too expensive for me, so whenever I found a new writer I added their name to my mental list, and eventually I would stop at the main branch of the Denver Public Library and take out one of the author's books. So I was always happiest working in the Fiction section, although Rebecca rarely put me there, probably out of spite.

The afternoon was quiet. The easy chairs were filled with people reading, or sometimes sleeping. A few customers browsed in Fiction, but mainly they strode purposely to a shelf, found their book, and then left. I worked in a mellow bubble, on my own with the books.

I took my time with each book, reading the back cover, looking at the author photo, noting who had written the blurbs. I was intensely interested in all parts of the books, from the words to the graphics. During Blue Heron's editorial meetings, it always amazed me when the core staff—Mr. Dove, owner and editor in chief; Hansika, the senior editor and my friend; and Gerard, our graphics wizard and also my friend—discussed book design, knowledgably dissecting minute details of color and font. I could always offer some innocuous comment to keep myself in the game, but mostly I listened to their verbal volleying and soaked up their knowledge.

In fact, there was one of our books on my cart: *In the Playroom* by Charlotte Plessing. Blue Heron Books were always top quality, in terms of content but also visually and tactiley. It had to do with the unusual color schemes as well as the quality of the paper and the cardboard cover stock. Charlotte's book, for example, was a vibrant gray with a graceful black font and a simple design, just a brown teddy bear leaning against a red-and-yellow ball. The teddy bear–ball motif was repeated on the spine and in the right-hand corner of the back cover. Simple, but there was something classic and elegant about it, like all Blue Heron's books. The books even smelled good: each time we published a new book and received a box of the first printing, Mr. Dove would take out a copy, ruffle the pages under his nose, breathe in deeply and say, "Ahhhh!"

Mr. Dove. I loved him. And I loved this book, even though it had been a major ordeal for Hansika and me to wrest it from the author, a notorious perfectionist who would, if she could, hold on to her books for eternity, changing commas to semicolons, then changing them back again. Mr. Dove always preferred to stay out of the messier aspects of author relations, but we finally had to appeal to him about this project. I remember Mr. Dove picked up the phone, and in his crisp, Columbia Class of 1966 voice, informed Charlotte that Hansika and I would be coming over that afternoon in order to pick up the manuscript. He listened to Charlotte's pleas, which we could hear from across his massive oak desk. Finally Mr. Dove declared, "Charlotte, by this stage of the game, you and I both know that books are never finished, they are only abandoned. My girls will be by at four o'clock sharp to remove the manuscript from your hands. Preferably without force. Good day."

The book was perfect, of course, the prose immaculate and sparse, with Charlotte's distinctive lilting rhythm. I remember Hansika and me sitting side by side in the couch in her office, eagerly reading the manuscript until two a.m. on a Friday night.

Hansika. Where was Hansika? After the company went bust, I had to leave Manhattan so quickly. I know Hansika was planning to move into her brother's place in Brooklyn if she didn't get another job, but I'm not sure if she did. I only had her Blue Heron e-mail, which had become defunct, and although I did have her cell number, I didn't have my cell anymore—I couldn't afford it. So if Hansika had tried to call me, there was no way of knowing.

But if I was perfectly honest with myself, my lack of a cell phone was just an excuse. I could have used my dad's landline to call Hansika, or even my stepmother Jasmine's cell. The truth was that talking to Hansika would be painful; it would be a raw reminder of everything I had lost. Also I felt ashamed. At first I was ashamed because I was unemployed, and then I was ashamed because I was working part-time at a bookstore. I had come down in the world, and I was too proud to let everyone back East know about it.

I missed Hansika. Every day. I think Hansika was the best friend I'd ever had, even though we mostly saw each other at work—but then, we both worked at least fifty hours a week so we saw each other quite a lot. We thought alike in so many ways, despite our completely different backgrounds. I was raised in fractured third-generation Beat households in both Colorado and suburban New Jersey, whereas Hansika grew up in Queens with a tight-knit Indian family that ran a restaurant and lived in an apartment right above it.

We didn't look alike, either. In Hindi, the name "Hansika" means "small swan," but Hansika was not at all swan-like. I always thought she resembled a James Bond villain: she was short, waif thin, and she always wore the same outfit—black jeans, a tight black cardigan, black Doc Martens boots, and a white Oxford shirt buttoned to the neck. She had stylish glasses with heavy black rectangular frames, and her shiny black hair was short and cropped close to her head. She also wore black gloves, and that was because there was something wrong with Hansika's left hand. I think it was a birth defect, but she never mentioned it and I never asked. Sometimes at the end of an extremely long day—longer than our usual long days—I would walk by her office and see her massaging thick white cream into the hand. I only caught a glimpse of it here and there; it was just a nub, pink and shiny, with no real fingers to speak of.

It couldn't have been easy growing up in Queens with a deformity like that. Once when Gerard was talking about going to his ten-year high school reunion, he asked Hansika and me if we had gone to ours. "No way," I snorted. As for Hansika, she folded her arms and said calmly, "As far as I'm concerned, all those people can go burn in hell." Gerard and I exchanged a look, and I don't recall either of us mentioning high school to Hansika again.

I sometimes wondered why Hansika wore two gloves, since her right hand was fine. Perhaps she thought that wearing two gloves all the time was slightly less weird than wearing one. I don't know; as I said, we never talked about it. Her deformity certainly didn't interfere with her work. Hansika was the fastest one-handed typist I ever saw—actually, the only one-handed typist I ever saw. She found uses for the little hand; I think she must have stuffed the fingers of the glove with cotton, because she often held manuscript pages between the fingers, or used the whole glove as a paperweight.

Hansika was always a bit of a mystery. Over the years we grew quite close, but she was never one for exchanging girly confidences. To this day, I'm not sure about Hansika's sexual orientation. She may have been, as John Irving put it in *A Prayer for Owen Meany,* a nonpracticing homosexual, but I often suspected that she had feelings for Gerard, who was a short, handsome fellow with bright red-gold hair and glasses with black rectangular frames almost identical to hers.

The main thing to know about Hansika is that she is smart as a whip. She is a marvelous editor with a knack for dealing with authors, and I never met anyone with a better vocabulary, not even Mr. Dove. She has a deep love of books, just like me. She worships Simone de Beauvoir, just like me. She even went to Barnard College, just like me (Mr. Dove loved his Barnard girls), although she graduated four years ahead of me so we weren't there at the same time.

Hansika. I used to work every day with someone of her quality, not to mention Mr. Dove, Gerard, and Eileen (Mr. Dove's executive assistant and long-term mistress, and a Barnard girl as well). Not to mention our authors, who were all so talented and impressive, and our slew of eager interns from Barnard and Columbia. Everyone was smart, verbal, and well educated. At Q&I, however, I was working with ADD Ruby, Stacie and her eye patch, Fat Bob the thief, Hadley the former opium-suppository addict, and Rebecca from Dinosaur.

Like I said: I have come down in the world.

I put Charlotte Plessing's book on the shelf between Sylvia Plath and Edgar Allen Poe. Thinking about Blue Heron and Hansika just made me sad. And angry. Who am I angry at? I wondered as I picked up William Faulkner's *As I Lay Dying.* Where should the finger be pointed?

Mr. Dove, maybe. Mr. Dove, probably.

I first met him in 1997. I was twenty-four years old and working for a literary agent on the Upper West Side. A stunning first novel had fallen into our hands, and my boss said, "I know the perfect home for this: Blue Heron Books. That gives us an excuse to go out to lunch with Donald Dove. He's a literary legend."

We met Mr. Dove at Café des Artistes, an exclusive restaurant on West Sixty-Seventh Street. Mr. Dove was in his late fifties then, a small man, dapper and elegant, with bright brown eyes, a thick tweed jacket, and a sparse but carefully tended comb-over. His most distinctive feature was his voice, which was sonorous and sculpted, half–Ivy League and half-English. His voice was particularly remarkable given that he had grown up in the Bronx, but his time at Columbia College and his years on the New York City literary scene had polished him to a highly cultivated sheen, and marrying an obscenely wealthy woman on the Social Register hadn't hurt.

I was utterly charmed by Mr. Dove, who had beautiful manners and a wealth of self-deprecating tales about his encounters with literary giants. We had a wonderful lunch, which included him agreeing to read our novel. At the end of the meal my boss excused herself to use the bathroom, and the moment she was out of earshot Mr. Dove leaned forward and said, "We could use a bright Barnard girl like you on our staff. Any interest in jumping ship?"

Three weeks later, I was Blue Heron's proofreader and jack-of-all-trades. Hansika was assistant editor then, and over the next eleven years we both moved up. I learned so much from Mr. Dove and Hansika, and I fell in love with Blue Heron Books. We were renowned for publishing fiction of the absolute highest quality; we had about forty authors altogether and published about a dozen books a year, each one swaddled as tenderly as a newborn baby. Our books didn't always sell particularly well, but they were generally well received, and over the years a handful made *The New York Times* bestseller list.

But no matter the sales, Mr. Dove was always generous when it came to the company, whether it was the quality of the books, the author advances, or the staff salaries. He could afford to be generous, because he was funding the company with his wife's fortune. Not that she was involved in the company, and in fact I rarely saw her; she was more or less a ghostly presence on the phone, her voice dripping diamonds and Fifth Avenue. They had one daughter, who lived with her husband and two children in Short Hills, a fancy New Jersey suburb. Mrs. Dove seemed to spend most of her time there and not in their apartment on Fifth Avenue, which was located across from the Metropolitan Museum of Art.

Anyway. Charming as Mr. Dove was, intuitive as he was about literature, blessed as he was by an instinctive gift for the English language, he was not a fan of the computer age. Eileen once told me that in the eighties, the staff threatened to quit unless Mr. Dove bought them computers. He finally gave in, but he himself never used one. "I choose not to," he said simply. And forget eBooks: Hansika read *Publishers Weekly* cover to cover each week and so she smelled the change before it came, but whenever she tried to broach the subject with Mr. Dove, he would always brush her off. "Nothing will ever come of that. Horrid! Who wants to read a book on a slab of plastic? No, my dear, it won't ever happen."

But that's not why we crashed, although it certainly didn't help, given that our catalog was never available as eBooks and so we lost all those sales. No, the problem was that Mr. Dove had been funding the company with his private money, and his private money was invested with a certain Bernie Madoff, who as it turns out was also funding his company with Mr. Dove's private money. I remember glancing at the headlines as I came into work in mid-December 2008. I didn't know what a Ponzi scheme was, just that a lot of people had lost a lot of money. When I walked into work—happy, eager, ready to dig into Charlotte Plessing's latest novel, which we had wrested from her the previous day—everyone was in Mr. Dove's office, and his head was in his hands.

A week later, we were all gone. Poof! Finished, over.

I shelved Faulkner, then picked up Flannery O'Connor's *A Good Man Is Hard to Find,* one of my favorites. I had grown to really love Mr. Dove, and over the years he had become like a father to me. I didn't care about his odd marriage or the fact that his assistant was his mistress. I didn't care about his Ivy League snootiness and his more-than-occasional name dropping. I loved his passion for words and literature, his commitment to mentoring his staff, and his generous heart.

Best of all, Mr. Dove didn't give a damn about my father. Having a famous parent is like a shield between you and the rest of the world: it's often hard for people to see me because when they look at me, all they see is my dad. Not that everyone in the world knows who my dad is, but in the circles I've been part of—the Barnard College English department, the New York City literary world, and now the bookstore—people knew his name, and that name made them see me through a distorted lens.

But never Mr. Dove. Two days after the lunch at Café des Artistes, I went to the Blue Heron offices for a formal interview. Mr. Dove and I chatted merrily about books in his wood-paneled office, which was full of museum-quality artwork and overlooked a charming garden. We ate elegant butter cookies dotted with tiny chocolate chips and drank aromatic Darjeeling tea that Eileen brought to us in a rose-patterned tea service.

Eventually Mr. Dove picked up my résumé and read it over. "Zwelland . . . Zwelland. Are you by any chance related to—"

"Yes," I said. "I'm his daughter. And her daughter. And her stepdaughter."

Mr. Dove looked pained. "I must say, I loathe the Beats. Every last one of them. Particularly Jack Kerouac." He closed his eyes and shuddered. "The English language was not safe in that man's hands. Well, we certainly won't hold your family against you. I suppose it means that you're used to dealing with writers, who can be a rather temperamental lot. However it makes me wonder: Are you a writer yourself? I don't find that frustrated writers make good editors, which is of course what we plan to do with you eventually, after subjecting you to years of grueling proofreading and copyediting."

"I don't write," I said truthfully. "But I love words."

"Ah, perfect. Hansika is the same. It's like being a music lover: you can't play an instrument, but you can't live without it."

"Exactly," I smiled.

And now? I wondered as I nestled Flannery O'Connor between Patrick O'Brian and Tawni O'Dell. Now what was Mr. Dove doing? On our last day in the office he had chest pains, and since his fancy Fifth Avenue apartment was about to be put up for sale, his daughter drove in from New Jersey to bring him back to her house. I liked to think of him propped up in bed, reading Flaubert while sipping Darjeeling from his rose-patterned tea service—unless of course he had to sell that as well.

3. Lunch in Pieces

At last it was time for my forty-five-minute lunch break. I still had more fiction to shelve, so I took my unfinished cart back to the receiving room and left a piece of paper with my name on top—Hilda didn't like the sales floor cluttered with carts. I went into the break room and punched out. At Blue Heron we generally ordered in lunch and ate at our desks, and most every day I took a walk around the neighborhood to stretch my legs, usually passing through Washington Square Park. I loved Greenwich Village, and it was always a joy to ramble around the backstreets and look at the stately brownstones and eclectic shops. But now I worked retail, and lunchtime was mostly an opportunity to get off my feet.

There were two people in the break room: Stacie on the flower-patterned couch and Hadley at the wooden table, eating from a complicated array of plastic containers. I took my peanut butter sandwich out of the refrigerator and sat down at the table. I wanted a quiet, peaceful break, but the chances were extremely slim. I wasn't worried about Stacie—she might as well have been a piece of furniture, lying there with an arm flung over her head, her one eye closed, and that incomprehensible toothpick jutting out of her mouth. Like I said, I always gave Stacie a wide berth. But Hadley loved to talk, and I knew he would chatter throughout my entire break.

"Elizabeth Zwelland!" he said, a gleam in his eye. He dunked a spear of cucumber into a container of hummus, then wedged the whole thing into his mouth. "How's your morning going?"

"Nothing special," I said, unwrapping my sandwich. "Same as always."

"You really should come to the poetry reading tonight, Elizabeth. It'll be fun. Bob's unveiling a new poem—it's an homage to the Lord of the Rings trilogy."

"No, thanks."

"Well, if you change your mind . . . Hey, I was behind your building yesterday."

"Really."

"Yep. My neighbor had a friend visiting from out of town, and I took them on my unofficial Denver Beat Tour. We went to the Colburn Hotel on Grant, and then we had a drink at Charlie Brown's next door. The Colburn is where Neal Cassady met Carolyn Cassady—did you know that? Ginsberg stayed there, too. They all used to drink at Charlie Brown's, including Jack when he was in town."

In my dad's living room, he has a photo of me as a little girl sitting on Allen Ginsberg's lap. If Hadley had known that, he would probably have asked me to marry him. "You told me all this before," I said.

"And those places are all like one block from you!"

"I don't care, Hadley. I really don't."

"But you should! First of all because of your dad and the lineage, but second 'cause it's part of Denver history. The whole point of *On the Road* was Kerouac coming out West to see Neal in Denver. *On the Road* is where he uses the phrase 'Holy Denver.'"

I laughed. "What on earth is holy about Denver?"

"Don't you see? Everything's holy! That was Jack's whole point."

"If everything is holy, why was he an alcoholic who drank himself to death?"

"Things got dark for Jack, I'm not saying they didn't. But even at the end he was painting angels and the Buddha. You can be an alcoholic and still be a saint."

I exhaled loudly. "I don't know every detail of Kerouac and Cassady's lives, Hadley, nor do I want to. What I do see are two self-destructive narcissistic men who didn't want to grow up, and who left a string of women and children to fend for themselves. That's what I see. I don't find them admirable at all. Cassady didn't even write or produce anything worthwhile, except his children. Neal Cassady was just a charming con man."

Hadley shook his head vigorously. "That's not true! He was very intelligent. When he was a teenager he used to go to the Denver Public Library—the old building, not the one on Broadway—and he used to read voraciously. He wrote a third of his autobiography, and there was that famous letter he wrote, the Joan Anderson letter, which totally changed Kerouac's writing style, although unfortunately Kerouac lent it to Ginsberg, who unfortunately lent it to someone else who lost it. So it's not true that—"

"Hadley," I interrupted him. "I don't care. I really, really don't care. I don't want to talk about the Beats. I just want to eat my lunch in peace."

"But your dad—"

I looked at him wearily. "Hadley, you know nothing about my dad."

"You don't get along? I mean, you never talk about him."

I took another bite of my sandwich.

Hadley leaned over the table. He put his chin in his palms, his elbows awkwardly splayed amid his containers. "You know, Elizabeth, I think you're interesting. We should go out sometime. Sometime soon."

That was, what, the tenth time Hadley Barr had asked me out? The twentieth? I had lost count. "No, Hadley. I don't want to go out with you."

He shrugged cheerfully. "Okeydoke. But I think one day you'll change your mind."

"I sincerely doubt that." I rolled up the plastic wrap from my sandwich and put it in the smelly garbage can. I went to my locker and took a book out of my knapsack: *She Came to Stay* by Simone de Beauvoir. Along with Jane Austen, Simone de Beauvoir was my literary comfort food—her journals, her letters, her memoirs, and most of all her novels. Her prose was achingly pristine and her point of view so incisive, and her characters said fabulous things like, "Your plasticity is so perfect." I also admired de Beauvoir herself: she was so brilliant and hardworking, and she had the courage to carve out her own lifestyle, living in hotels and writing in cafés instead of being tied down by a husband and children.

I sat down on the purple couch. Unfortunately Stacie was on the other couch, which was long enough for me to lie down on and elevate my feet, whereas the purple couch was about half the size. At least I could get my feet off the ground; I took off my sneakers and swung my feet onto the soft cushions. Then I opened my book and put it on my lap.

"Simone de Beauvoir again," Hadley said, putting his hands on his head and leaning back in his chair. "I don't know why you like her so much."

I looked at him. "I bet you don't."

"I always thought she was kind of mean. Her and Sartre used to chew people up and spit them out."

I ignored him.

"Did you ever read that book by one of their former lovers? De Beauvoir was horrible to her."

"I don't know what book you mean," I said, not taking my eyes off the page. Actually I knew exactly what book he meant, and I had even read it: *A Disgraceful Affair* by Bianca Lamblin. I have to say, I was impressed that Hadley even knew about it.

"Oh well," he said merrily. "Who am I to destroy your literary heroes? Are you ready for book club tomorrow afternoon?"

Another one of Hilda's initiatives was employee book clubs. Our events manager—an energetic, middle-aged woman named Hope, who I rarely saw since she mostly worked evenings—ran several book clubs for our customers, but we also had a few strictly in-house ones. I went every month, but not because I was eager to hear what my fellow employees thought about books. I attended because everyone who participated got a fifteen-dollar coupon for the café. The café credit was very shrewd on Hilda's part: I always spent my fifteen dollars on food, but most people spent it on coffee, and Hadley told me that coffee has the biggest mark-up in the store—a latte costs about thirty-five cents to make, but sells for almost four dollars. So the café didn't really lose any money with the coupons, and the clubs got the employees buying books and talking about them.

Hilda ran a club on South American literature, Hadley ran one on the Beats, and Rebecca ran one on the short novel. South American literature is not one of my favorite genres and I could care less about the Beats, so despite my aversion to Rebecca—and her aversion to me—I was in her club.

"What's your book this time?" Hadley asked, although I knew he knew. In fact, there was a big notice right above the time clock.

"*Washington Square* by Henry James," I said.

"Did you like it?"

"I've read it before. It's excellent. It's more readable than most of his longer works, especially the ones he wrote—actually, dictated—later in life."

"Yeah, some of his sentences are like black holes. Well!" Hadley announced, gathering up his containers. "Break's over. Don't forget about the poetry reading tonight."

"Hadley! I'm not going."

"You say that now, but who knows, you might get a wild hair."

I knit my brow. "Get a what?"

"Get a wild hair! You never heard that expression?"

"No."

"It means like a sudden impulse."

I nodded. It must be another one of those Colorado things.

Hadley had just tucked his containers in his locker when London came in with a sandwich from the café. I smiled and put down my book. I was always happy when her break overlapped mine.

"Greetings, LA woman!" Hadley declared, saluting her.

London looked at him drily. "Hadley, the café's out of egg salad. Go make some."

"Ah, a cheerful burst of sunshine as always! But as you know, Tower of London, our egg salad is not made here, but rather is provided by Udi's."

"Whatever," she said. "Just go anywhere other than here."

"See you lovely ladies later!" Hadley punched out, bowed deeply, and left the break room.

London sat at the table and put down a napkin and her sandwich. She looked at Stacie and rolled her eyes; I rolled mine back. We were in complete agreement about Stacie.

"Poor you, sharing your break with Mr. Big Nose." Which was London's nickname for Hadley.

"I just ignore him. How's your day going?"

"It's all right," she said. She unwrapped her sandwich and started tearing off the crusts as she always did. "I was redoing the business-section display, and some guy came over to look at résumé books. We started talking, and he goes on and on about how he could never live anywhere but Colorado, blah blah blah, wasn't I glad to get away from LA and all that smog." She shook her head. "I told him that the only reason I left LA was because my boss promised I'd spend two years in Denver, and then I'd come back to a raise and a better title. I didn't expect the whole company to tank."

I sighed. "I know how that is."

"And you know, I realized something. If you're a wildly ambitious person, you're not going to be living in Denver. If you want to make your mark on the world, you've got to live in a real city, like LA or San Francisco."

"Or New York or DC."

"Exactly. So that's why this city is so excruciatingly slow—if anyone was really anyone, they wouldn't be here."

"I saw a billboard the other day that said: DENVER—FROM COW TOWN TO ART TOWN."

London snorted. "That's bullshit. There's no real artists here. Not unless you count Fat Bob and his Hobbit poems."

Suddenly Stacie sat up. She was an unsettling sight with her shock of white-blond hair, her khaki eye-patch, and that ever-present toothpick. She rose off the couch and left the room, not once glancing at London or me. I immediately moved to the flower-patterned couch, where I stretched out full-length and elevated my feet.

"What a freak," London said.

"I had to finish her cart this morning. That happens almost every time I work."

"You know, if I laid down every time I felt like it, I'd be back here all day, too. She must be related to the owners. That's the only reason I can think of why she's still here."

"Must be. What time are you here till?"

"Five."

"I'm here till six. Do you want to take that rain check tonight?"

Finally, after talking about it for weeks, London and I were going to hang out together outside of work. We were supposed to go out the previous week, but London canceled at the last minute due to a headache.

"Oh, Elizabeth, I'm so tired after all that networking last night! Maybe this weekend."

"I'll be in Boulder all weekend with my little sister."

"Lucky you," she said drily.

"Oh no, it'll be fun. She's a great kid."

"I'm not a big fan of kids."

"Well, my sister's different. Even you would like her."

"I doubt it."

I smiled, but I felt a little hurt.

"So tomorrow we have the exquisite torture of book club," London said, tearing the crust from the next triangle of her sandwich. I tried not to look at her hands; in contrast to the rest of her, which was so flawlessly put together, London's hands were red and chapped, a different color altogether from her otherwise tanned skin.

"Indeed we do. Did you read the book?"

"Of course not. I'll check SparkNotes online tonight."

As a book lover, I found that a little shocking. And frankly unethical, given that we were getting paid to read, even if it was only café credit. But I didn't say anything—I was always a little afraid to cross London and find myself at the receiving end of her biting wit.

"It's a really good book," I said mildly. "I'm sure you'll like it."

"Give me a summary now. Fifty words or less. That'll help me tomorrow."

"OK. The book is set in the nineteenth century in New York City. The main characters live in Washington Square, which nowadays we think of as an older neighborhood, but then it was considered cutting-edge because most of Manhattan was still farmland at that point, and—"

"Elizabeth!" she laughed. "TMI! Fifty words or less."

"Sorry. It's the English major in me. All right—a girl named Catherine Sloper is the only child of a rich doctor. She's a good person but she's socially awkward and not very pretty, and her father is ashamed of her. She gets involved with a handsome young man who her father thinks is a fortune hunter. She has two aunts, and the one named Lavinia tries to—"

"Still too much!" London said. "Never mind, I'll check out SparkNotes tonight."

"Sorry," I laughed.

"Anyway, no matter how little I know, it'll still be more than Ruby."

"That's for sure." Ruby was a disaster at book club, and it was all London and I could do not to howl with laughter at her non sequiturs and irrelevant questions.

London and I chatted about this and that, and soon it was time for me to punch back in. "Well," I sighed, rising from the couch. "Back to the grind."

"Have fun."

"If you change your mind about hanging out, let me know. I'm here till six."

"Thanks, Elizabeth, but like I said, I'm so tired. Networking is exhausting."

"I'm sure. See you on the floor."

I went back to receiving to retrieve my cart, and I saw that Hector had filled it to the brim with more books. "Thanks a lot!" I called out to him. He laughed and gave me a wink.

Hector had piled my cart with books from the Religion section, which was right next to Fiction. I had shelved about a dozen books when I came to a gift book on yoga, which belonged downstairs in a display next to the cash register. I tucked my cart in a corner and went down to the cashier's station in the center of the first floor. Fat Bob—tall with a brown crew-cut, heavily bespectacled, and yes, quite fat—was working the register, and Stacie was assisting him, bagging books for customers. Again, a colossal waste of resources: a bookstore isn't like a grocery store where bagging takes time, and you certainly didn't need two people to do it.

Back upstairs, the rest of the afternoon slipped away quietly. I thought about London's comment that really ambitious people lived in big cities. Denver was just so slow and middle of nowhere. Boulder was just as backward, but Boulder thought it was special, particularly people like my dad and all his groovy literary friends. I so preferred the New York City literary world. I was only on the fringes of that scene, but even so it was better than the hippie chaos in Boulder that passed for—

"Excuse me."

I looked up. A customer. A bony middle-aged woman with wire-frame glasses, frizzy gray-brown hair, a green Q&I tote bag, and an earnest expression. What London would call a perma-spinster.

"Yes?" I said.

"Can you help me? I have a question."

"Actually, you need to go to the information desk if you have any questions."

"She has a line of two people."

"There's another information desk downstairs," I said, turning to my cart.

"But I have a question about a religion book, and you're right here."

"But I don't know as much as they do, and they have computers to look things up."

"Please. It's just a simple question. It'll only take a moment."

I sighed. "What?"

"Well, I want to get a copy of *The Tibetan Book of the Dead.* The only trouble is, I found two translations, and I can't tell which one is better. Here." She handed me two books, one with a blue cover and Tibetan iconography, and one with a green cover and Tibetan iconography.

"I have no idea," I said. "I've never read either of them." I tried to pass the books right back to her, but she wouldn't take them.

"But couldn't you just take a look and tell me which one is better?"

"What do you mean by 'better'?"

"More accurate."

I sighed heavily. I glanced over the translators' biographies on the back covers. "Both these translations are by Tibetan scholars who have published a number of other books. I'm sure you can't go wrong with either one."

"But which one has better language?"

I looked at her steadily. "What do you mean by 'better language'?"

"I don't know. More accurate language, I guess."

"Ma'am," I said sharply. "Given that both these books are by eminent scholars, the translations are definitely accurate. However, I'm sure that each one has their own literary style, which you can ascertain if you simply open up each book and read a paragraph or two."

She blinked. "You don't have to take that tone with me."

"I'm not taking a tone. I'm just telling you something that seems really obvious."

"I'm just asking you for help."

"You want help? Fine." I opened up one of the books in the middle and glanced at the pages, then opened up the other and did the same. "This one," I said, handing her the book with the blue cover. "This one is better."

"But you didn't really read it."

"I speed-read."

She tightened her lips. "You haven't been very helpful."

"Ma'am, what would you like me to do, sit down and read each book? You're asking too much."

"I've shopped in this store for ten years, and I've never encountered anyone like you."

"I'm just telling you the truth. You're asking me to make a decision for you that you need to make for yourself."

"Can I have the other book back?"

"Certainly." I handed her the book with the green cover, and she stormed away.

I rolled my eyes and went back to my cart. I had never worked retail before, and I was constantly amazed by how foolish people were. I had shopped in bookstores practically my whole life, and I had never needed anyone to hold my hand through a purchase.

I finished my cart and brought it back to receiving. I had forty-five minutes left on my shift, so I went to find Rebecca to ask her what I should do. I found her in the Travel section with Ruby, both on the floor surrounded by Lonely Planet books. Hardly meeting my eye, Rebecca told me to walk around the second floor and straighten up. So for rest of my shift I wandered aimlessly, collecting stray books, neatening up the shelves, throwing away empty coffee cups. One day when I was straightening up I found an unused condom in the Science Fiction section, and a few weeks before London had found a syringe in Humor, but tidying up was not usually so eventful.

My last task was putting a stack of reshelves on the cart next to the information desk. Juniper was on duty, humming to herself and typing into her computer. In addition to helping customers in real time, she handled online queries whenever she got a free moment. I got a kick out of Juniper; she was a fashion shape-shifter, with a different look each day. That day was a Black Panther theme, complete with a huge afro wig, brightly colored dashiki, bell-bottom jeans, and big gold earrings in the shape of raised fists.

"Here's some reshelves," I said, placing the books carefully on the cart next to her desk, then arranging them by size. "There's not too many today."

"Thanks." Then she laughed. "Hey, Slim, what on earth did you say to that *Tibetan Book of the Dead* lady? She was practically in tears."

"Oh my God. She couldn't decide which book to buy, and she wanted me to decide for her."

"Some people need that."

"Well, then I did decide, and she didn't like that, either."

Juniper nodded knowingly. "Customers," she said.

"That's right, customers. I don't know how you do it all day, Juniper."

"I do it with the Lord's grace, Slim. I do it with the Lord's grace."

Juniper had two favorite topics: the Lord and her surprisingly active sex life. She was always ready to discuss each one in excruciating detail. London called Juniper "TMI Queen," and it was true, whether Juniper was relating a dream about Jesus or the previous night's hot date—and Juniper's dates were always hot. During my second week at Q&I, Juniper cornered me in the Film section and delivered an impassioned speech about the need to make Jesus Christ my personal savior, and since then I kept our conversations as short as possible.

"Well, I'm off," I said. "See you tomorrow."

"If the Lord is willing, I'll see you then."

I smiled noncommittally and headed downstairs to the break room to punch out. I must say, the whole Christian thing in Colorado weirded me out a little. I never met one person in Manhattan who identified themselves as a Christian. A Presbyterian maybe, or perhaps a Catholic, whereas people in Colorado seemed to tell you within the first five minutes that they were Christians. I mentioned this to London once, and she agreed. "They're all a bunch of freaks," she said.

I punched out. Hooray! Another day of drudgery was finished. I opened my locker and took off my name tag, put on my sweater and knapsack, then headed to the front door. I was passing by the café when Bree, a tiny pale woman in her early twenties with a full range of tattoos and piercings, called out, "Elizabeth, I have something for you."

I stopped, and she handed me a white bag with MS. EZ written on the front, along with a sketch of a demented-looking Q&I gnome. "It's from Hadley," Bree said.

"Thanks," I replied. I didn't have to look inside to know that it was a cache of just-expired Udi's sandwiches. I put the bag in my knapsack and waved bye to Bree. It was nice of Hadley to think of me and I did truly appreciate it, but I still wasn't going to date him.

4. Lowest of the Low

I walked out the door onto Wynkoop Street. It was a lovely September evening, still light out, the air slightly crisp with cold. My feet were killing me, and how I would have loved to get the 0 bus behind Market Street Station, which dropped me off a few blocks from my apartment building. But the bus cost two dollars, so I only took it during rainstorms, which had happened exactly twice in my three months at Q&I.

As I walked up 16th Street to catch the Mall Ride on the corner, I wondered about my feet and why they hurt so much. My first day at Q&I, I wore black leather loafers with a modest heel, perhaps an inch at most. At our lunch that day, Hilda had gently suggested that I switch to sneakers because it would be easier on my feet. "There's no dress code at Q&I," she said, "so it's fine to wear jeans and sneakers." I had noticed during my interview how casually everyone at Q&I dressed, and I had put it down to Western redneck-ism—everywhere's a rodeo! But by the end of my first day, my feet were sore and swollen, and I winced constantly on my walk home. The next day I bought a pair of cheap black sneakers with thick soles, and from then on I wore jeans and sneakers like everyone else. I had always prided myself on being a stylish dresser, but that was barely possible in my new life, what with the nature of my job and my low salary. Also my old wardrobe was gone: I had sold most of it to a secondhand store in Manhattan before I left, raising four hundred dollars in the process.

London was the sole employee at Q&I who didn't seem to have a problem with footwear, I mused as I approached the Mall Ride stop. She wore elegant black loafers that must have cost a fortune, a remnant from her high-salary days, and as a result she was the only one in the store who looked halfway presentable.

Just as I was thinking of London, I glanced into Dixons, the big bar and restaurant on the corner of Wazee and Sixteenth Street, and I saw her sitting with a group by one of the large plate-glass windows. At first I wasn't sure it was London—her hair was swept into a glamorous updo, and she was talking animatedly with a woman with long blonde hair who was sitting on her right. The woman was a classic example of rich Colorado: she had a bronzy tan, chunky silver-and-turquoise jewelry, an exquisite macramé top, and—I couldn't see her from the waist down, but I didn't have to—high-end jeans and superfancy cowboy boots with elaborate stitching. If anyone in Manhattan dressed like that, they would be laughed out of town, but in Colorado this kind of getup was considered chic. No one at Q&I dressed like that, but some of our customers did, the kind of people who have a loft in LoDo and a house in Aspen or Vail.

I was surprised to see London since she had seemed dead-set on going home after her shift, but maybe a networking opportunity had come up. I thought about stopping in and saying hello, but then the Mall Ride pulled up and I decided to just go home. If London was doing business, it wouldn't be a good idea to interrupt.

The Mall Ride opened its doors, and I hopped on. The 16th Street Mall is the heart of Denver: it's a long thin street that starts a block from Q&I at Union Station, and runs about twenty blocks all the way up to Civic Center Station. Cars and bicycles are not permitted, so the Mall Ride is the only transportation, other than walking. The Mall Ride is a fleet of clanging white buses that shimmy up the narrow streets that flank the central islands, strips of land that have a life of their own, with benches, sculptures, food carts, potted plants, and even a few life-size plastic cows.

Shockingly—to me, at least—the Mall Ride doesn't cost a cent, and you can jump on and off during the course of the day as many times as your heart desires. This makes it the most democratic transportation system I have ever used. In Manhattan, for instance, homeless people don't have enough money to take the subway, and wealthy people have enough money to avoid it. But everyone takes the Mall Ride in Denver, and you never knew who you might find next to you. That evening I was surrounded by a wide-ranging gaggle of humanity: a fragile old man in a red beret, two tough Hispanic guys talking about jail, giggly East High girls, a Native American man in a cowboy hat, a businessman in a sharp suit talking on his cell, a dude of indeterminate age with meth mouth, a tourist couple fumbling with a map, a homeless woman who smelled so bad I had to breathe through my mouth when she passed—in other words, everyone.

I sank into a corner seat in the back, which allowed me to rest my feet. I stared out the window, tired and drained. Then a few blocks up, I suddenly saw a familiar face: the Wolf Man, sitting on a bench in front of a pharmacy. He was an older man, grizzled and thin but clean, wearing as usual one of those wool hats designed to look like an animal's head—in his case, a wolf. He also as usual carried a stuffed-animal wolf, a little gray beast with a black nose, alert ears, and bright blue eyes. The Wolf Man had brilliant blue eyes as well, but he always looked slightly lost. If I had to guess, I would say he was one of those people who had a bad acid trip in the 60s and never came all the way back. He was at Q&I every morning when the doors opened at six thirty, and he sat for several hours in one of the easy chairs, stroking his little wolf on the head or staring blankly at the space in front of him. Once London complained about him at a staff meeting, but Hilda said he was harmless and we should just leave him alone. I know that Hadley and Bree gave him free coffee, because he always had a cup by his side.

Before I knew it we were at Tremont Place, and there they were. I'll never forget the first time I saw them: it was like getting a sad slap in the face. Downtown Denver is a mix of old buildings and new. The old buildings, like the one housing Q&I, are sometimes as big as half a block and are usually made from large red or white stone, often with fading old-timey signs such as DUPLERS FURS or THE MOREY MERCANTILE CO. There are also many modern buildings—a handful of skyscrapers, a few squat office buildings, some indoor shopping centers, and the large Denver Pavilion mall complex. On the corner of Sixteenth and Tremont Place, there are two buildings, no more than thirty stories high, covered with slabs of dark-gray mirror. In front of the buildings there is a landscaped plaza and a large silver sign on the sidewalk that boldly proclaims: WORLD TRADE CENTER. I could hardly believe my eyes the first time I saw that sign, and whenever I saw the buildings and the sign on my commute—if my attention wasn't caught by something else, or if I hadn't remembered to avert my head—I felt that same sad slap once again.

I rode the Mall Ride to Civic Center Station, the final stop at the eastern end, and got off with the rest of Denver. I went up a concrete staircase and entered the Sketchy Park. A triangular area built on top of the relatively small Civic Center Station, it's a tiny park that's really just a concrete plaza with a few benches, along with some trees and small grassy areas enclosed by low iron fences. As usual, small groups of people were gathered here and there. I smelt wafts of marijuana smoke, and out of the corner of my eye I saw two people in hoodies passing something quickly. I'm sure this was originally envisioned as a nice place to rest before catching a bus, but whatever the original plan, the reality was that the little park marked the beginnings of Colfax Street, which Hadley Barr told me was once called "the longest, wickedest street in America" by *Playboy* magazine.

The Sketchy Park is thankfully small, so it only took a minute to stride through and arrive at the busy intersection of Colfax and Lincoln. Diagonally across from me was the Colorado State Capitol Building, an imposing white-marble structure on a small hill, topped by a shining gold dome. I crossed over and walked up steep red-stone steps to the front of the Capitol Building, then I walked up the building's main steps and turned around to see the view. In front of me was the sweeping green lawn of Civic Center Park, and across the park was the Denver City & County Building, an imposing semicircle of white marble. When I told my dad I was moving to Denver, he quoted some lines from one of Allen Ginsberg's poems:

> Denver! Denver! we'll return
> roaring across the City & County Building lawn

Towering above the park and the buildings are the Rocky Mountains. The mountain range stretches across the horizon like a ragged jewel, and depending on the weather and time of day, the mountains vary from vividly detailed to foggily mysterious. That evening they were bathed in the pink-orange light of the setting sun, with a stretch of silvery snow glinting from the peaks and deep purple pockets in between.

I have always had a special place in my heart for mountains. I don't have too many memories of my first years in Colorado—my mom and I moved to New Jersey when I was five—but I always remembered the mountains. I also recalled the thin, light air. Denver is, famously, a mile high, and the air truly is different. The altitude makes some people ill, but it seems to suit me, which may also be a holdover from childhood.

I descended the Capitol Building steps and turned left toward Sherman Street. This was the last stretch of my walk, only five blocks, but my feet were so swollen it might as well have been a mile. Sherman is mostly a residential street, with a few dozen Art Deco buildings from the thirties. An exception is a red-brick, three-building modern construction called THE JACK KEROUAC. This, incidentally, is where Hadley Barr lives. The front of the building has a few Kerouac quotes painted on the brick, including:

> AND HERE I AM IN COLORADO!
> I KEPT THINKING GLEEFULLY.
> DAMN! DAMN! DAMN!

As I walked by, I could just see the blown-up photos of Kerouac in the lobby, including the famous shot of him and Neal Cassady standing side by side with their arms around each other's shoulders, looking like twins.

When I first came to this part of town to find an apartment, I found it odd to see a building with a name, much less THE JACK KEROUAC. But in this older, nonsuburban part of Denver, many of the buildings have names. In fact the next block of Sherman is known as Poets Row. The buildings on this block are all named after writers and poets, such as THE THOMAS CARLYLE, THE EMILY DICKINSON, THE NATHANIEL HAWTHORNE. It is a quiet, charming street, but whenever I was on the last stretch of my walk home, my feet hurt so much that the charm was impossible to take in.

After passing a few more stately apartment buildings, I arrived at my building on the corner of Ninth and Sherman, which also has its name on the front: THE SWISS ARMS. A three-story cream building with a central portion and two wings, it has dormer windows, Elizabethan half-timbering, a central red-brick courtyard with immaculate shrubbery and a white stone well in the middle. In a street full of charming buildings, the Swiss Arms is unique.

You might be wondering how I managed to get such a nice apartment on my salary. Well, the building is nice, but my apartment was not. The day after I got the job at Q&I, I came down to Denver to find a place to live. Jasmine, who is my second stepmother, knew about Poets Row because a former student of hers used to live there. Jasmine called the woman for advice, and the woman said that there were several management companies right on Poets Row, so all I had to do was go down to Denver and see what was available.

That was a sad day. On the bus into Denver, and then on the Mall Ride, and then on my walk to Poets Row, I kept thinking of my old apartment in Manhattan, a small but beautiful one-bedroom on Morton Street, just a short walk from Blue Heron Books. Not long after I started at Blue Heron, Mr. Dove called me into his office and said that he and his wife owned a building in the neighborhood, and since one of their tenants was moving out, might I be interested in moving in? We walked over at lunchtime to see the place, and I fell in love immediately. The apartment was a little jewel, with high ceilings, elaborate molding, and a fireplace, as well as a tiny garden with a cherry tree right outside my window. Rent was high, but so what? Everyone I knew in Manhattan spent most of their salary on rent. I ended up living there almost eleven years, but once I lost my job I couldn't afford it, and anyway Mr. Dove and his wife had to sell the building in order to raise money.

Living at my dad's was one thing, but getting my own apartment in Denver seemed to make this loss even more final. It would also cement my place in Denver and in Colorado, where I did not want to be. But I had to do it; I couldn't live with my dad one moment longer.

The first management company I went to was closed for lunch, but the next one was open, and Pat, the woman who worked there, was very nice. A short, older woman with bright blonde hair and many gold rings, she was intrigued about my comedown in the world, especially the Bernie Madoff element. However her brow knit when I told her my hourly salary. She took out a calculator and rapidly punched in numbers: she told me that since I was getting eight dollars an hour and working at most thirty hours a week, and then losing 20 percent to taxes, I had a monthly income of about $760.

"Here's how I see it," she told me. "For that price, you can get a bigger apartment in one of our less fancy buildings, or a small apartment in one of our showpieces. What do you prefer?"

"Can I see both?" I asked.

Two blocks from Poets Row, she showed me a drab one-bedroom in a drab modern building. No Art Deco touches, no building name, plus a smell of sick old people in the hallways. My stomach sank. We saw another apartment in a similar building down the street, this time with green walls the color of baby puke. I felt so disheartened I started to tear up. Then Pat said, "We have a basement studio in the Swiss Arms. It's not fancy, but it's one of our least expensive units. The building is gorgeous; it was built in 1921, and there's nothing else like it in all of Denver."

Long story short, I loved the building. My stomach dropped when I saw the tiny studio, but at $450 a month (all utilities included, plus free air-conditioning from the building's swamp cooler), it was all I could afford.

Pat approved my application that afternoon, and my two suitcases and I moved in the next day.

The sight of the building always cheered me up, at least a little bit. Then as I was walking up the steps to the courtyard, my thoughts were interrupted by a loud sound: QUACK! QUACK!

I turned around quickly, but I already knew what it was. Rounding the corner of Ninth Avenue was a hillbilly shack on wheels, with wooden siding, a tin roof, and jaunty red-and-yellow lettering declaring BANJO BILLY'S BUS TOURS. It was a mild evening, so the tourists had their windows wide open, and a few were leaning out. When they saw me scowl at them, they called out, "Yee-haw!" Then the bus driver honked again, this time a horse whinny: NEIGH! NEIGH!

I shook my head. The only bad thing about the Swiss Arms was that the Banjo Billy tour bus passed by twice a day, and occasionally in the evening if someone had rented the bus for a private party. If the bus was quiet I wouldn't have minded, but they always beeped at me, probably because I looked so unhappy to see them.

I took out my Jane Austen key ring that I got from the clearance table at Q&I and opened the door. The wooden mailboxes were on the right; I opened my box and took out my lone piece of mail, a menu from a local Thai restaurant.

As I was shutting my mailbox, I noticed that a few tenants had left mail on top of the boxes so the postman could collect it the next day. This struck me as incredibly naive; no one in Manhattan would ever do such a thing. What if someone took their mail? What if someone stole their identity? Sometimes it seemed like no one out West had any street smarts.

In a perfect world, I would have ascended the stairs. I would have walked down the long, hushed hallway carpeted in a gold-and-brown floral design, inhaling the building's pleasing scent of vanilla and polished wood. Then I would have entered my lovely one-bedroom apartment. I knew what the apartments looked like, because once Pat showed me a few empty ones: they all had high ceilings, tall windows, dark wooden floors and doors, and old-fashioned touches like glass doorknobs.

But alas, it wasn't a perfect world. So instead of going upstairs to my finely appointed one bedroom, I went downstairs to my basement studio.

My stomach sank with each step. People my age don't often talk about retirement, but when they do they usually say something like, "I don't want to end up living in a basement studio eating cat food." I wasn't so poor that I was eating cat food, but there I was, lowest of the low, living in a basement studio. I imagined that Ruby lived in a similar situation, although probably in a crummier building, like the first ones Pat had shown me.

The basement was composed of the boiler room, the laundry room, dozens of storage units, and three apartments. There was no carpeting, and the ceilings were lower than the rest of the building, with snaking black pipes, some so low I had to duck my head to pass. The building smelled different as well; there was a damp musty odor, and sometimes at work I caught a whiff of it on my clothes.

I was just putting my key in the lock when my neighbor Trixie's door opened. A brunette woman in a business suit walked out, followed by Trixie, a pretty, leggy redhead with an erect carriage who was in her early forties or maybe late thirties. Trixie gave the woman a hug and said cheerfully, "See you next week!"

I waved at Trixie. She smiled and waved at me, then she went back into her apartment.

Before I moved in, I had asked Pat about my fellow basement dwellers. She said, "On one side you have Trixie. She's a nice person and she's like you, she lost her job and needs low rent. And on the other side—well, don't worry. He's harmless." Which didn't do much to inspire confidence. After living at the Swiss Arms for three months, I still hadn't seen this mysterious tenant; I just heard his odd snufflings and shufflings whenever he passed by my door.

I didn't know Trixie well, but I liked her. She came from Boston, so she had a little more snap than most people I had met in Colorado. When I first moved in, she knocked on my door and introduced herself. She told me that she used to dance with the Boston Ballet, but in her midtwenties she blew out her knee and went back to school to become a masseuse. She said that she often saw clients in her apartment, and she hoped that I wouldn't be bothered by the people coming in and out. I told her it was no problem, and then she said, "Oh, I'm so glad. Listen, if you ever need anything, I'm here. Don't hesitate to knock." Which was nice of her. But I often went for days without seeing Trixie, and I never heard a peep from her apartment or the Snuffler next door because the walls between our apartments were so thick. When Trixie and I did see each other we always said hi, and sometimes we had a little chat, but I got the sense that she wanted her space, and I definitely wanted mine.

Not that I had much of it. I opened my dark wooden door with the metal letters B2 on the front, and I walked into my studio. "It's cozy," Pat had told me as she opened the door, but I knew that "cozy" was real-estate parlance for "tiny." Indeed it was tiny, about twelve-feet wide and fifteen-feet long, with a surprisingly large bathroom and closet. The walls were a bright lemon-yellow; Pat told me that the rest of the apartments at the Swiss Arms had cream walls, but when a former tenant asked to paint the studio, the management agreed because it made the space more cheery. So the studio wasn't depressing, but it was small and functional, and the only reason to live there was if you couldn't afford anything else. Which I couldn't.

I turned on the light switch for the overhead globe. On my left was a bright-red, drop-leaf wooden table with two chairs, a leftover from the previous tenant. I put my keys in the ceramic dish full of change in the center of the table, then unpacked my knapsack, putting *She Came to Stay* on top of my beloved Jane Austen omnibus. To my right was a side table and a twin bed that doubled as my couch, and in front of me was the kitchen, which consisted of the tiniest stove on earth in one corner, the tiniest refrigerator on earth in the other, and counter space and drawers in between. Above the kitchen sink was the studio's lone window. It was thankfully wide, but it had thick black bars, which were necessary and which I hated. I was so paranoid of people looking in from the sidewalk that I always kept the wide Venetian blinds drawn, but light was still seeping in from the last rays of the sunset, and during the day the studio was often quite bright.

In the spirit of the lemon-yellow walls and bright-red table that I had inherited, I had filled the apartment with cheerful colors. Over the previous three months, the little disposable income I had went toward purchasing a multicolored striped rug, a white duvet, turquoise throw pillows, festive flower-patterned plates and mugs, and red plastic frames for my sister's vivid artwork, which hung in a neat line on each wall. My stepmother Jasmine had offered to drive in some things from Boulder, but I was too ashamed to let her and my sister see the tiny studio, so I declined.

I changed into my favorite pajamas, dark-green flannel with white frogs, an old birthday present from Hansika. I took an egg-salad sandwich out of Hadley's bag and put it on the table. Then I did what I always did after work: I went into the bathroom and got a towel, a container of Epsom salts, and a pink plastic basin (only $1.99 at King Soopers). I laid the towel on the floor, filled the basin with hot water and a cup of Epsom salts, nudged off my socks with my toes, and then—ahhh! I sank my feet into the hot, soothing water.

I slowly ate my egg salad as I soaked. Thank goodness for Hadley, otherwise it would have been peanut butter again. I didn't like to cook, which was something I inherited from my mother, so my food options were generally rather limited. In Manhattan I almost always ate out, or picked up a deli sandwich or Chinese food on my way home from work. I had yet to find good, cheap Chinese takeout in Denver, which was a shame because I could live off a large order of Chinese food for several days.

I finished my sandwich, then wiggled my feet around. Better, but the water was still warm so there was no point in moving. Sitting there in my tiny, vaguely smelly basement studio with bars on the window, I felt a strong wave of despair. Yes, I was lucky: I had a job, I had no debt, and I no longer had to live with my father. But I felt so unhappy. My life had transformed from a colorful adventure—albeit of a quiet, literary kind—to sheer drudgery and poverty. I felt my eyes fill with tears and I cried, just a little, as I did on most nights.

The problem was that I couldn't really see a way out. It was almost a year since the economy collapsed, and things were not any better. Hilda always left her issues of *Publishers Weekly* in the break room, and just a glance here and there told me how much trouble the publishing industry was in. At our staff meetings, Hilda encouraged us to look at this period as a time of transition, and therefore a time of opportunity—I never met anyone as excited about eBooks as Hilda. But I didn't see things that way. The publishing world I knew, the industry I loved, was dying. Even the bookstore was in danger: How long could Hilda possibly keep it going, what with all the online stores offering the same products for so much less?

I doubted I would ever work in publishing again, and this saddened me to the core of my heart. I was stuck. The best I could hope for was that one of the small Colorado publishers would eventually have an opening. Yet I knew I couldn't count on that. The most realistic hope for me was becoming full-time at Q&I, which meant I would make more money and get health insurance. It would also mean that I could get a cell phone and replace my laptop, which had died after I moved to Colorado, perhaps unable to adjust to the high altitude.

I shifted in my seat and moved my feet in the water. When I was hired, I told Hilda that I wanted to be full-time. She told me that it was her policy to hire people part-time, and then if things were going well after three months, she would bump them up to full-time if she had the hours. I worked twenty hours a week during my first two weeks at Q&I, but then one of the part-timers quit so Hilda gave me ten more hours. I was almost at my three-month anniversary, and I had high hopes of becoming full-time. But how sad to want to work more at a job you didn't like.

I considered, as I often did, the possibility of finding another part-time job. I noticed people on the 16th Street Mall holding up big signs for restaurants; it looked easy, and I always saw ads for those jobs on Craigslist. But then I'd be on my feet even more, and let's face it, that was a pretty humiliating line of work. It also didn't make sense for me to get another part-time job because my schedule at Q&I varied so much, and I needed to be available for whatever shifts I was offered. To get more hours, I needed to be flawless: I was never late, I never called in sick, and I worked my butt off. You never found me lying on the couch in the break room when I was supposed to be on the floor.

My lone window had turned completely dark. I looked over at the purple clock on my side table: eight thirty. I gingerly took my feet out of the basin and put them on the orange towel, leaning over to dry them thoroughly. I tidied up the room, then I went into the bathroom for my pedicure supplies, which included a bottle of shiny red nail polish ($1.69 at King Soopers). I sat on the couch-bed and snapped on the lamp on the side table. I cleaned off my toenails with a cotton ball soaked in nail-polish remover, then I carefully stroked little swatches of fiery red onto my toenails.

One of my favorite things in life is getting a pedicure. Hansika introduced me to them when I was still new at Blue Heron. We had just sent a book off to the printer, and as soon as the files were out the door, Hansika turned to me and said, "Pedicure?"

I laughed. "Really? I've never had one."

She raised her eyebrows. "We need to change that. At once."

We walked over to a nail spa on Seventh Avenue, and within five minutes my feet were soaking in hot soapy water, and a Korean woman was vigorously scrubbing my ragged heels. After clipping and cleaning and more scrubbing, topped off by a blissful calf massage with rose-scented lotion, she painstakingly painted my nails blood-red. When she was done, I looked at my feet in awe: it was safe to say they had never looked so good. I glanced over at Hansika; her nails were a light pink, delicate as a seashell, and I was surprised to see how beautiful her feet were, white and arched and finely formed.

That became our tradition, or rather I became part of Hansika's tradition: approve final files for a book, then get a pedicure. Blue Heron published about twelve books a year, so it was a monthly treat that I looked forward to. Hansika and I rarely spoke as we sat perched on our pedicure thrones, but we always had coffee afterward, or if it was late enough, Indian food at Baluchi's.

In my new life, however, pedicures were a luxury I could not afford, along with books, hair salons, nice clothes, and daily lattes.

I had just stroked on my second layer of polish when I heard a noise in the hallway, a strange muffled snuffling, as if someone had a bad cold but was reluctant to blow their nose. That could only mean one thing: the Snuffler was home. For me the noise was a relief because it meant that the Snuffler was still alive. He was clearly one of those people who would lie dead in their apartments for weeks until a neighbor—in this case, me—noticed a bad smell. I always took a deep whiff when I passed the Snuffler's door, and I listened for his phlegmy breath whenever I heard footsteps passing my studio. I was always happy to hear that he was still alive, because it meant I didn't have to worry about him for at least another twenty-four hours.

As my final coat of polish dried, I contemplated the mystery of the Snuffler. We never bumped into each other in the hallway, but I would sometimes see his door close when I left my apartment, which made me suspect that he listened at the door before emerging from his lair, deliberately avoiding an encounter with me. I think he even did his laundry in the middle of the night, because once when I was having a bout of insomnia I heard his door open and close, heard him shuffle away, then shuffle back about ten minutes later.

Clearly the Snuffler had something to hide, but what it was, I had no idea. Pat had said he was harmless, but I wasn't 100 percent sure she was right. I asked Trixie about him during one of our brief chats. She told me that she had only seen him once, and that was from behind.

"I called out 'Hello,' but he didn't turn around," she told me as we stood in her doorway. "He was a wearing a gray T-shirt with black letters. Do you know what it said?"

"I shudder to think."

"It said: LOSING FAITH IN HUMANITY ONE PERSON AT A TIME."

"Oh my God—he's the next Unabomber."

"That's what I think, but Pat swears he's a nice old guy. He's lived here thirty years, you know. Like the lady who had my place. Pat said the lady was a packrat who took the stuff people left by the dumpster when they moved." Trixie's apartment was about five times the size of mine, so being a packrat was actually possible. "Pat said that when they cleaned out the apartment after the lady died, they found two dozen brooms and over three hundred dishes. But at least she died in the hospital and not here."

"At least," I agreed.

I took Trixie's story about the hoarder as a cautionary tale, just as I took the Snuffler as one. I didn't know what my future held, but I didn't want to end up as the Female Snuffler, still in the basement studio decades later, the kind of person other people talk about in doorways in hushed tones. As I cleaned up my pedicure supplies, I vowed to work hard so I could become full-time at Q&I and create a better life for myself. I also needed to start checking the help wanted ads on Craigslist, in case of the wildly remote possibility that a publishing job opened up. Q&I and the studio were my current life, but they could not, would not, be my life forever.

I brushed my hair and teeth, then rubbed coconut oil (on sale for only $2.99 at King Soopers) into my face and neck, a beauty trick my stepmother Jasmine taught me. I set my alarm for six; the next day I had an early shift. I turned off the overhead light and tucked myself into bed, reading from *She Came to Stay* until my eyes grew heavy. I put the book on the side table, turned off the lamp, and fell deeply asleep.

5. Too Clever

At quarter to three the next day, my aching feet and I were seated in the Q&I event room, ready for the Short Novel Book Club. The event room is on the second floor; it's quite a big space, with a small stage in front, rows of folding chairs, and large windows overlooking the alley behind the store. The walls have dark wood paneling and are decorated with framed photos of writers, most of whom had visited the store and autographed their pictures.

The book groups met in the space in back by the windows. Fat Bob and I were scheduled to set up for the club at two thirty, and we quickly moved two tables together and surrounded them with folding chairs. Fat Bob went to the café to help Bree bring up the snacks, so I was blessedly alone for a few minutes. I sat down, took off my sneakers, and massaged my swollen feet. The day had gone quickly, the store quiet in the morning and busy midday. My break had been peaceful; Stacie had not been on the flower-patterned couch, so I was able to lie down and elevate my feet. I had eaten Hadley's expired sandwiches for breakfast and lunch, and my dinner plan was to fill up on book-club food, and also grab a sandwich for breakfast the next day.

I had the upcoming weekend off—a miracle in retail—so the next day after breakfast I was going up to Boulder to see my sister, Emma; my stepmother Jasmine; and, by default, my dad. I was looking forward to seeing Emma and Jasmine. It was always nice to get away from my studio and stay in their charming house and eat Jasmine's delicious cooking.

I heard a noise and looked up. Fat Bob and Bree were entering the room, Fat Bob laden with a tray filled with Udi's sandwiches and Watercourse pastries—all at least a day old, for sure, but better than nothing. Bree carried two plastic pitchers, one filled with ice tea and one filled with lemonade, and she had plastic cups and napkins tucked under her elbows. I helped them arrange the food on the table, which wasn't easy because the two tables were mismatched, one about an inch taller than the other, but we finally distributed everything within easy reach of everyone.

Fat Bob and I laid our copies of *Washington Square* on the tables, and Bree put a hand to her mouth. "Oh, shit—I forgot my book in the café."

"I'll get it for you," Fat Bob volunteered. Fat Bob's crush on Bree was common knowledge in the store.

Bree protested, but Fat Bob was already on his feet and lumbering toward the door. "Thanks, Bob!" she called after him.

The moment Fat Bob was gone, Bree turned eagerly to me. She was a tiny thing, five feet at most, with short blonde hair, a diamond nose ring, multiple earrings in both lobes, and a host of colorful tattoos running up her arms, with another on her chest peeking up over her black T-shirt. I had pegged Bree as a Beat Book Club person, so I was surprised when she turned up at the Short Novel Book Club, and even more surprised by her intelligent comments and passion for good writing. Hadley later told me that Bree had been an English major and was a writer herself, so that explained it. Still, all the piercings and tattoos made me doubt that she was someone I would ever befriend.

"Elizabeth, I'm so glad to have a moment alone with you! I never seem to have my break at the same time as you, and I've been wanting to speak to you."

"What's up?" I said, drawing a foot into my hand and rubbing it.

"Well—I don't know if Hadley mentioned it, but I'm a writer."

"He did tell me that. What do you write?"

"I wrote short stories for years, and then when I graduated from CU Denver two years ago, I started working on a novel."

"That's great," I said, switching to the other foot.

"The thing is, I'm almost done, and I was hoping I could get some advice from you. Hadley said you worked at Blue Heron Books? I love their books."

My stomach sank. "Well, I did work for them. They closed up last December."

"I heard about that. I'm sorry. I was thinking, though, that maybe you could give me a sense of how the whole submission process works? I don't know anything about the New York publishing world."

I sighed. I had nothing against Bree, but it had been a long day, and the demise of Blue Heron Books and the upheaval in the publishing industry was not what I wanted to talk about just then. So I told her exactly that.

"Bree, it's the end of my shift, and I'm pretty exhausted. Can we maybe talk about this another time?"

She blinked. "Oh. Sure. Sure, anytime. Just it's so hard for me to get a moment alone with you—like I said, we don't seem to have breaks together, and you're always out the door once your shift is up."

"Isn't everyone?"

"Well—no, not everyone."

Fat Bob came in then, proudly bearing Bree's book. They started talking, and I poured an ice tea and helped myself to a tuna fish sandwich on a ciabatta roll. I leafed idly through *Washington Square,* ignoring Fat Bob and Bree's conversation about the movie *Inglourious Basterds,* which they had both seen recently.

Gradually everyone else drifted in. Getting a chunk of the staff together for the Short Novel Book Club once a month at 3 p.m. was a scheduling task that Hilda always managed to conjure: most of us worked the early shift, so all we had to do was stick around another hour, and everyone else started their shift when the book club was over. It seemed like a lot of juggling just for a book club, but Hilda felt that the club bonded the staff and improved our knowledge of literature. I wasn't too sure about the bonding, and I seriously doubted whether anyone's knowledge of literature was vastly improved. I was there for the fifteen-dollar café coupon that would show up in my next pay envelope—otherwise, I wouldn't have bothered. London of course felt the same way I did. She was the last one to enter, and as she slipped into the seat next to me, she shot me a quick eye roll.

Finally everyone was settled around the tables, with their book and a drink and a sandwich or pastry in front of them. We were a motley crew: me, London, Rebecca, Juniper, Fat Bob, Bree, Stacie, and Ruby, who that day wore a tangerine pantsuit and a yellow crewneck top. Rebecca was in charge, which she really seemed to enjoy. To her credit, she did put a lot of work into the club; her copy of *Washington Square* was well thumbed and full of small yellow Post-It notes.

"Hello!" Rebecca said, clapping her hands together, eyes shining. "Glad everyone could make it. I see we all have our books. So tell me, did you like it? What did you think?"

"I loved it," Bree said. "I thought it was brilliant."

"Brilliant," Rebecca said. "Why?"

"Well, the characters are so well drawn, and he—James—creates a whole world that just feels so vivid. He really gets into the character's emotions. It's very touching; it's sad."

"It was sad," Ruby said.

London gave a small snort disguised as a cough, and I shifted in my seat. There it was once again: Ruby's parroting and non sequiturs. Then to top it off, Ruby picked up her pen and scribbled furiously in her notebook, a brightly striped book that I recognized from the clearance table. London and I had many laughs over Ruby's notebook, which we were convinced was filled with aimless scribbles and not a single literary insight. We wondered if Ruby even read any of the book-club selections, and London even suspected that Ruby was illiterate. I didn't think that Ruby was illiterate, but I doubted she had been able to follow James' circuitous sentences—I had trouble with some of them myself.

No one else seemed to notice how funny it was. They all looked at Ruby seriously, nodding thoughtfully at her noncomment. At least Stacie, the other blatantly odd person at the table, never said a word. Her book always looked genuinely worn and she always listened intently, but she just chewed on her toothpick and kept absolutely silent.

"Anyone else?" Rebecca asked.

"I felt sorry for Catherine," Fat Bob said.

"Why?"

"Well, she was a victim. Morris and her aunt Lavinia both used her for their own ends."

"Her father, too," Bree said.

"Yes, her father," Ruby repeated.

"Victim!" London snorted. "That's such a copout."

"So this is an interesting point," Rebecca said eagerly. "What options did Catherine really have, given the society she was born into? She wants to marry Morris, but her father doesn't want her to, and he even takes her to Europe for a whole year to make her change her mind. Then when that doesn't work, her father blackmails her by saying that if she marries Morris, she won't get a cent of the family fortune. Which makes Morris leave."

"I just think the whole victim thing is bullshit," London said. "People throw that word around all the time these days."

If I was honest, London offered up quite a few non sequiturs herself, probably because she never read the books. Her remarks were always slightly off center, but since she was so emphatic and appeared so confident, no one ever dared to contradict her.

"I'll tell you what I think," Juniper said. She was in her librarian mode, wearing a brown corduroy jumper that strained across her ample chest, a white button-up shirt, hair greased and pulled back in a tidy bun, and a pair of empty black frames perched on her nose. "The trouble with these people is, they don't walk with the Lord. I did not see the word 'Jesus' in this book one time. Not one time."

"OK," Rebecca said. "Juniper is bringing up another important point. What *is* their moral code? What are the values that the Slopers live by?"

I had to speak up sooner or later, so I said, "I don't know if they live by a moral code so much as a social code. If they have any god, or set of guidelines, it's the rigid societal structure that they're part of."

"I agree with Elizabeth," Fat Bob said. "Money is their god. Money and societal status. Just like in Edith Wharton's books."

Fat Bob always managed to surprise me. Apparently he didn't just steal books, he also read them.

"But even more than all that," Bree said, "her father values intelligence over goodness. There's that one comment he makes early in the book. Something about being clever versus being good—wait," she said, ruffling through the book. "I'll find it."

"I marked it," Rebecca said. "Here it is, on the bottom of page 10 in the Modern Library edition, which is what most of you have." She tilted her voice slightly upward and read:

> "Try and make a clever woman of her, Lavinia; I should like her to be a clever woman."
>
> Mrs. Penniman, at this, looked thoughtful a moment. "My dear Austin," she then inquired, "do you think it is better to be clever than to be good?"
>
> "Good for what?" asked the doctor. "You are good for nothing unless you are clever."

"That's what I'm talkin' about," Juniper said. "They don't care about bein' good."

"I agree with Juniper," Bree said. "Because I think what's implied is that if you're clever, you can get the things that this society values—a fancy address, social standing, a good marriage."

"So what does everyone think?" Rebecca asked. "Is it more important to be good, or is it more important to be clever?"

"Isn't that what the whole book is about?" Fat Bob said. "Catherine is too good, and her father is too clever."

"Morris is too clever, too," Rebecca said. "There's a line about that somewhere. Hold on a second, I think it's—right, page 34. Catherine is talking to Morris' cousin, and they're talking about Morris:

> "I suppose you can't be too clever," said Catherine, still with humility.
>
> "I don't know. I know some people that call my cousin too clever."

"Who's 'my cousin'?" Ruby asked.

London snorted, and I suppressed a smile. Rebecca knit her brow and gave us a look, then said, "Here 'my cousin' refers to Morris Townsend. Remember how Catherine meets Morris? He's the cousin of Arthur Townsend, and he's marrying Catherine's cousin, Marion Almond."

"But he's not Catherine's cousin?" Ruby said, her face twisted with bewilderment.

"No. Think of it this way: Marion Almond and Arthur Townsend are getting married. They introduce their cousins, Catherine Sloper and Morris Townsend. See?"

Ruby said, "I see." Although clearly she did not. Then she bent her head and wrote furiously in her notebook.

London snorted again, and this time I couldn't help but laugh out loud. Again Rebecca shot us a look. "All right," she said. "Let's talk a bit about James' writing style. What did everyone think? Last month we read Hemingway, and this is a whole other kind of language, right?"

"I liked it," Juniper declared. "It's majestic."

"This book is actually much more accessible than some of James' later novels," I said. "Sometimes his sentences go on forever, and it can be hard to make sense of them."

"Didn't he dictate those later books?" Fat Bob asked. "That might explain some of his wordiness."

I looked at Fat Bob curiously. "Yes, he did dictate them. He edited the later drafts, but the first drafts were always dictated."

"But he can also write so simply and beautifully," Bree said. "I marked a passage early on that I really liked. Here it is, page 19; I'll read it:

> I know not whether it is owing to the tenderness of early associations, but this portion of New York appears to many persons the most delectable. It has a kind of established repose which is not of frequent occurrence in other quarters of the long, shrill city.

"That's nice, Bree," Rebecca said. "I really like the word 'delectable.' It's not what you'd expect when describing a city."

"I'm sure Elizabeth has been to Washington Square," Bree said shyly. "Is it delectable?"

I blinked. I hadn't anticipated being put on the spot like that. I let my mind flash on Washington Square Park, the white marble arch, the large leafy trees, and the gorgeous row of brownstones that lined the north end of the park. There were also plenty of homeless people and blatant drug dealing, but I somehow never thought of it as a sketchy park. Once, just once, I went inside one of those brownstones: A Blue Heron author was staying with a friend, and I had to pick him up for a reading at the 92nd Street Y. I had a quick glimpse of elegant pale-green wallpaper, a shiny wooden banister, an exquisite Oriental rug, and several Picassos lining the walls.

"Yes," I said briefly. "It's delectable."

"Delectable," Ruby said, scribbling in her notebook.

"So," Rebecca said. "Let's talk about specific characters. Who were your favorite characters, and who were your least favorite?"

"I really, really disliked Dr. Sloper," Bree said. "I disliked him more than Morris. He can't love Catherine for herself because she's not pretty or clever, so he can't imagine anyone else loving her."

"He didn't seem mean to me," London said. "He just seemed practical."

Bree wrinkled her nose. "I don't think it's practical not to love your own daughter. There are plenty of people in this book who do love Catherine for herself."

"Her aunt Mrs. Almond, she loved her," Juniper said. "I liked her."

"I liked Mrs. Almond, too, Juniper," Rebecca said. "Remember toward the end of the book when James says that Catherine got several offers of marriage when she was older, and how one of those men genuinely loved her?"

"Exactly," Bree said. "I think Dr. Sloper was a terrible snob, and he destroyed his daughter's happiness."

"Fair enough," Rebecca said. "But do you think that Dr. Sloper was wrong about Morris? Morris was definitely a fortune hunter; I think James makes that pretty clear."

"To me the problem is not so much that Dr. Sloper doesn't like Morris," I said. "The problem is that Dr. Sloper doesn't like Catherine. Which she eventually figures out."

"Right," Bree said. "Dr. Sloper doesn't like her, and so he doesn't take her feelings into account. He just toys with her."

"So when does Catherine finally understand her father's true feelings for her?" Rebecca asked.

"It's when she's back from Europe, and she's talking with Morris," I said.

Rebecca nodded primly and started leafing through her book. Even during book club, she treated me with a distinct chill. "Here it is," she said at last. "Page 181. I won't read the whole thing. This is Catherine speaking, and Morris answering:

> "You can tell when a person speaks to you as if—as if—"
>
> "As if what?"
>
> "As if they despised you!" said Catherine passionately.

"But it's not just that he doesn't like her," Juniper chimed in. "The man bullies everyone. I think he's sexually frustrated—he lost his wife when Catherine was born, he's got no lady friend in his life, and he takes it out on Catherine. That man needs to go on a date."

Fat Bob said, "I think Juniper is right about him being a bully. There's this passage where he says how he knows that Catherine and Aunt Lavinia are afraid of him. It's on page 90:

> "I suspect—"

"Who's speaking?" Rebecca asked.

"Um—let's see. It's Mrs. Almond talking to Dr. Sloper. She says:

> "I suspect she will be careful; for she is at bottom very much afraid of you."
>
> "They are both afraid of me, harmless as I am," the doctor answered. "And it is on that that I build—on the salutary terror I inspire."

Fat Bob raised his head. "I looked up 'salutary.' It means something healthy or beneficial."

"Good," Rebecca said. "Thanks for checking."

"What an a-hole," Juniper said, shaking her head.

"Can you spell that word?" Ruby asked.

Rebecca spelled out "salutary," and Ruby carefully wrote each letter in her notebook. "All right then," Rebecca said. "So no one likes Dr. Sloper. What about Morris?"

"He's a skeeve," Fat Bob said.

"I agree," Bree said. "All he cared about was Catherine's money. When he found out that Catherine wouldn't be getting her father's money on top of the money she already had, that's when he broke it off. He was greedy and lazy and cruel."

"But what about Catherine?" Rebecca asked. "Why didn't she see all this?"

"I'll tell you why," Juniper said. "Sex. Sex makes people stupid."

"But they don't actually have sex," Bree said.

"Maybe not, but he kissed her, and all that blushing she was doin'—this book is about sex."

"And money," I said. "And misplaced loyalty."

"Loyalty," Ruby repeated.

"I think Juniper is on to something," Rebecca said. "Remember how James is always saying how handsome Morris is, and how strongly Catherine is affected by him? Even Dr. Sloper admits that Morris is handsome. He's good-looking, so women fall for him. And because he's a selfish person, he uses his good looks to take advantage of people. There's this great passage on page 98, where Dr. Sloper is talking to Morris' sister:

> "He is very good-looking," said Mrs. Montgomery.
>
> The doctor eyed her a moment. "You women are all the same! But the type to which your brother belongs was made to be the ruin of you, and you were made to

> be its handmaids and victims. The sign of the type in question is the determination—sometimes terrible in its quiet intensity—to accept nothing of life but its pleasures, and to secure these pleasures chiefly by the aid of your complaisant sex."

I started. Although I had read the passage the previous week and been struck by it, I suddenly realized that it was a perfect description of my father.

"Elizabeth?" Rebecca said. "You look like you want to say something."

"Um. Yes—this reminds me of Neal Cassady and Jack Kerouac. What I know of them."

Bree laughed. "Don't let Hadley hear you say that!"

"So the point is," Rebecca said, "this is the type of man that Morris is, but Catherine doesn't see it. Why?"

"It's just what we were saying before," Fat Bob said. "Morris is too clever, and Catherine is too good."

"I love that one passage about her," Bree said. "Although it makes me sad. It's at the beginning of the book . . . here, on page 15." She cleared her throat and read:

> But she was irresponsive because she was shy, uncomfortably, painfully shy. This was not always understood, and she sometimes produced an impression of insensibility. In reality, she was the softest creature in the world.

I was surprised to see that Bree had tears in her eyes. "Something about that passage," she said. "It's really touching."

London laughed. "It makes her sound like some sea creature without a shell."

Bree looked at London steadily. "I think it's beautiful."

"But it's not all Catherine's fault," Juniper said. "She also had that meddlesome Aunt Lavinia. That woman was always up in Catherine's business."

We discussed Aunt Lavinia in depth, then we spent the rest of the time dissecting the ending and trying to figure out why Catherine never married. As Fat Bob gave a passionate soliloquy about Catherine's loyalty,

I took an egg-salad sandwich from the tray and put it in front of me on a fresh napkin. When book club was over, I would wrap it up and put it in my knapsack.

Rebecca spent the last five minutes attempting to unravel Ruby's confusion about the ending. The ending *was* genuinely confusing, Rebecca said, because James never tells the reader exactly what's going on in Catherine's mind. Ruby could not grasp this, no matter how many words she repeated or how often she wrote in her notebook. London kept kicking me under the table, but thankfully book club ended before I burst into laughter.

Rebecca thanked us all for coming, then she said, "The book for next time is *St. Mawr* by D. H. Lawrence. We should get copies here early next week; I'll leave a note in the break room. Thanks again, everyone! Great discussion."

Juniper and Stacie left the room quickly so they could start their shifts. Rebecca, Fat Bob, and Bree gathered up the remaining food and the empty pitchers, still talking about the book as they slowly made their way out of the room. That left me, London, and Ruby, who was stuffing her book and notebook in her ungainly white plastic purse. London also had to start her shift, but she didn't seem to be in any hurry.

"Hey, Ruby," London said. "That's quite a lot of notes you took. Do you read them over later?"

Ruby mumbled something.

"What?" London said. "I didn't hear you."

Ruby glanced at London, her blue eyes tremulous. "I said no, I don't."

"Why do you take notes if you don't read them afterward? What's the point?"

Ruby looked close to tears. She grabbed her purse and ran out of the room.

London rolled her eyes at me. I smiled and said, "I'm going home now. It's been a long day."

"Yeah, well, mine's just starting. I can't believe you have both Saturday and Sunday off! How did you manage that?"

"Well," I said, wrapping up the sandwich and putting it in my knapsack. "I asked Hilda a few weeks ago if I could work an early shift on Saturday and have Sunday off so I could babysit my sister, and she ended up giving me the whole weekend off. I haven't been late or sick once since I started, so maybe she's throwing me a bone."

"Or maybe Guadalupe told her to do it." We laughed. "Hey, did everything work out with your sister's birthday party next week? Do you need to switch?"

Emma was having her ninth birthday party a week from Sunday, a momentous event that I could not possibly miss. "No, I'm good. I'm closing Saturday night but I have all day Sunday off, so I'm covered."

"You'll be full-time soon," London said as we walked out of the event room and into the rest of the store. "Then you'll have a little more seniority with the schedule and you won't have to worry about this kind of thing."

"Well, you've been here longer than me, so they'll give it to you first."

"I don't want it," London declared. "I hate being here, and I'm still holding out hope that my networking will pay off. I've kissed so much ass around this town, it's a wonder my lips haven't worn off."

I was about to ask London if she was networking at Dixons the previous night, but I held back. I didn't want her to think I was spying on her.

"Something will work out eventually," I said. "Unless the economy crashes again."

"Is it possible for it to crash any more than it already has?"

I laughed. "Anything's possible."

"That's what I like about you, Elizabeth," London said as we descended the staircase to the first floor. "You're bitter, just like me."

6. Thick Slice of Crazy

The next day—a brilliant autumn Saturday—I was on the 10 a.m. express bus to Boulder. I caught the bus at Market Street Station, just two blocks from Quill & Ink. It was absolutely delicious to know that I wouldn't have to step foot in that place for two whole days.

As I stepped onto the bus and put my money in the fare box, I immediately recognized the driver. He was the weird guy who always talked to the passengers, delivering a steady stream of chatter about traffic and stupid drivers and what happened on his shift the previous day. I usually like to sit in one of the front seats so I can look through the large front window, but because of him I took a seat on the right about halfway back. I brushed off my seat before I sat down, then I settled in and stared out the window as the bus roared off.

Boulder. Time to see my dad and Stepmother Two, aka Jasmine. Hopefully not Stepmother One, but you never knew. Most of all, it was time to see my sister, Emma.

The history is tangled. My dad and my mom met at University of Colorado in Boulder in the late sixties. They both came from the East Coast—my dad from Baltimore, my mom from New Jersey—and they both had an adventurous spirit, a desire to go West and reinvent themselves. In those days Boulder was a sleepy college town, with nothing in the long stretch of land between Denver and Boulder except farms and fields full of prairie dogs. At least that's what my dad says. Not that you ever wanted to get him on a nostalgia jag, because implicit in my dad's reminiscences was the unstated conviction that having seen that different, better time, he was superior to you. As usual.

But I digress. Both my parents were English majors at CU Boulder, and both wanted to be writers. My dad wanted to write novels like Norman Mailer, and my mother wanted to write poems like Anne Sexton. According to my mom's very occasional recollections from that time, my dad was hopelessly square. She was the one who got him into poetry and the Beats, she was the one who handed him a copy of Allen Ginsberg's poem "Howl," and she was the one who told him he couldn't live one more day without reading Jack Kerouac's *The Subterraneans,* a short novel more poetry than prose. My dad claims that none of this is true, that in fact he was the one who turned my mom on to the Beats. I tend to believe my mom, but those two could disagree about anything and everything, which they did right up to my mom's death.

In 1970, Boulder experienced a sea change: Chögyam Trungpa Rinpoche came to town. A high-ranking Tibetan Buddhist teacher who escaped from Tibet in 1959, he lived first in England and Scotland and then came over to America, where he embraced the counterculture scene. He established himself in Boulder and quickly attracted a community of seekers and artists and poets, including the great Allen Ginsberg. My mom dragged my dad to a talk by Trungpa at his house in Four Mile Canyon, and they were immediately hooked, not so much by Tibetan Buddhism—in fact, among my dad and his many wives, only Jasmine is a dedicated practitioner—but by the energy and excitement that Trungpa generated, as well as all the notable poets that he attracted.

At first Trungpa taught at CU Boulder, where both my parents studied with him, then in 1974 he established Naropa Institute, a summer writing workshop that eventually grew into Naropa University, which includes the Jack Kerouac School of Disembodied Poetics, the famous writing program established by Allen Ginsberg and Anne Waldman. My parents were on the ground floor of Naropa, and Allen Ginsberg was a mentor and friend to both of them. My mom and dad were seen as the literary future, the third generation of Beats, if you will. Each of them wrote reams of poetry and published regularly in small literary magazines and chapbooks, and they also began to establish themselves as teachers. It must have been a heady time: all those writers gathered in this beautiful town underneath the mountains, and at their center the mysterious, outrageous Tibetan rinpoche.

Then my mom got pregnant with me, and hippie values notwithstanding, my mom and dad got married. Their wedding photos are a sight to see: Trungpa Rinpoche officiated, Allen Ginsberg was their best man, Diane di Prima the maid of honor. Everyone was barefoot with joints in their hands, my mom was sizably pregnant in a flowing white dress, and my dad wore jeans and a dashiki with, even then, his shirt low enough to reveal a mass of chest hair. I was born three months later on July 27, 1973. My mom named me after her favorite literary heroine, Elizabeth Bennet of *Pride and Prejudice.*

According to my mom—or my mom's poems, anyway—my dad had always cheated on her. Always, starting a month after she moved into his funky house on Walnut Street. Yet what really drove them apart was me. My dad didn't like being a dad. He didn't like me crying when he was trying to write, he didn't like keeping quiet when I was napping, and he didn't like being financially encumbered by a child at the tender age of twenty-four. Again, I know all this from my mother's poems—to me she maintained a bitter silence about my dad, punctuated by the occasional cryptic comment.

I also know this from my dad's poems, but the picture he paints is considerably different, and involves my mom getting pregnant behind his back in order to trap him in a jail of domesticity. Even Sylvia Plath would have blushed at his honesty about how much he loathed raising a child. Both my parents often mention me by name in their poems, including my dad's wince-worthy lines:

> Elizabeth Elizabeth Elizabeth!
> You cry cry cry eat eat eat shit shit shit

None of my dad's affairs were serious, apparently, so my mom turned a blind eye and did her best to raise me, write poems, and teach a few classes at Naropa. Then Stepmother One entered the scene. She came to Boulder to attend the Naropa Summer Writing Program and ended up moving there altogether. A moony poet girl with long blonde hair and large blue eyes, she was one of my mother's students, and she and my mother became fast friends. Practically every day Stepmother One was at our house, drinking tea and talking poetry with my mom. It took months before my mom understood that Stepmother One was actually there because she hoped to see my dad, and a few more months before my mom realized that my dad and Stepmother One were carrying on a torrid affair.

Stepmother One was only a few years younger than my mom, but since she was unencumbered by motherhood, she offered my dad a lifestyle he yearned for. His old lifestyle, actually. The affair grew serious, so serious that my dad was seen more often with Stepmother One than with my mom—even then my dad loved being out in public, making a late entrance with a beautiful young woman on his arm.

Finally my mother had enough. She gave my dad an ultimatum: me or her.

My dad said: her.

I was only five, but I was a sensitive child, and I had known for a long time that things were amiss. The atmosphere in our house was off kilter; there was always a simmering something just under the surface. My mother wasn't a yeller; she fell on the silent suffering end of the spectrum, so the house was often pregnant with angry stillness. I only recall one fight: my parents had brought me to a hippie Naropa party up in Nederland, a mountain town famous for Caribou Studios and its tolerance of marijuana (and nowadays famous for having a cryogenically frozen corpse, but let's not go there). I recall a hazardous trip down the mountains at night, my father driving fast and furious, and my mother spitting out a stream of low, harsh words. Probably Stepmother One had been at the party, and probably there was some kind of public or private scene. All I remember about that party was joining a few other kids in a barn to watch a mother cat nurse five kittens, the first time I had ever seen that.

Not long after, my mom packed me up and we moved to New Jersey. I never got a real explanation, just one day my mom told me that we were going on a trip. It was a trip, however, that never ended. We moved into my grandmother's apartment, a big musty place with dozens of china figures, mostly creepy children that I later found out were Hummels. My mom got a teaching job at the local high school, and then we moved into our own place, a tiny rundown house a block from downtown. I must have asked my mom about Colorado and my dad, but I think I figured out for myself that we weren't going back and, as children do, I went on with the life in front of me.

The other big change was my mom's hair. My mother was not a great beauty; she had a plain, open face, and she was short and not very curvy. But she had gorgeous hair, soft gold-red curls that reached almost to her waist. The day before we left Boulder she chopped it all off into a sort of misaligned pageboy, and she never grew it back.

My mom's drinking was always at the periphery of my consciousness. In those early days, she saved it for when I went to bed. In the evenings I would sit with her at the kitchen table, doing my homework or reading while she graded papers and prepared for her classes the next day. Those were the best times with my mom, both of us quiet and peaceful, me occasionally breaking the silence to ask a question or look up a word in the thick dictionary that never left the kitchen table. However in the mornings I found evidence of her life after I went to bed: the kitchen table would be strewn with open books, yellow legal pads, capless pens, her reading glasses, and an empty tumbler with a distinctive, bitter smell. I never saw a bottle, mostly because I was not yet tall enough to access the upper cabinets, but the tart, medicinal smell of gin was a constant during those mornings. I would push the books aside and make a little place for my bowl of cereal, that acrid scent in my nose the entire time I was eating. My mom would eventually stumble downstairs, gulp down two cups of coffee in rapid succession, then drive me to school and head over to the high school. In those years she was always functional, but she always drank.

That's also when my mom was working on *The Insect Poems.* She was already a well-known poet with numerous publications, but that book made her name. What she was doing every night was reading deeply about insects and making notes that she slowly turned into poems. It took her years to finish the book, but all along the poems were getting published in literary magazines, including *The New Yorker.* Some of the poems concerned mating habits, such as the one about the robber fly, a predatory insect that often had trouble distinguishing who was a partner and who was prey. But my mom's favorite subject was parasitic behavior. It turns out that insects have myriad sneaky ways of taking other insects' territory, such as the psithyrus genera of bumblebees, which enter the nest of Bombus bees and dominate the worker bees and the original queen. The invading queen kills the eggs of the original queen, and quite often kills the original queen as well.

You didn't have to be a genius to figure out the metaphors. I usually read whatever my mom had left lying on the kitchen table in the morning, as well as the complete poems when they came out in magazines. Once when I was around ten, I asked her, "Mommy, are these poems about Daddy?" She looked at me dryly, her mouth in an angry twist, but she never answered my question.

To this day, I have mixed feelings about those poems. My mom always wrote about the most horrific examples of insect behavior, but not all insects are vicious. And in a way the poems seem obvious to me: insects are not people, and you can't expect them to exchange shy glances or go for candlelit dinners. But my mom's point was that people—read, my dad and Stepmother One—can be just as mechanical and cruel when getting their needs met.

Where was my dad all that time? Back in Boulder, married to Stepmother One (for health-insurance purposes, I later found out), and publishing his own poems, which alternated between furious screeds that derided my mother and described the fallout from their marriage, and no-holds-barred descriptions of the mystical love and transcendent sex life he shared with Stepmother One. If you want to read poetry about nature, political events, or philosophical ideas, don't bother with my dad's books. However, if you're interested in every detail of my dad's bodily functions and emotional life, please be my guest. My dad finds himself endlessly fascinating, and the odd thing is that many other people find him fascinating as well. I admit he has a powerful way with words—his poems have an energy and drive that practically leap off the page—but his subject matter is relentlessly self-focused.

On top of all that, Stepmother One was writing poems too, also about the numinous relationship she shared with my father and their marvelous, mind-blowing, not-to-be-believed sex life. They even used to do readings together where they read their highly charged poems (my dad in the featured slot, of course), legendary events that are still talked and written about among the Naropa-Beat community. Stepmother One also wrote a fair share of poems about my mom, mostly concerned with my mom's demands for child support, which cast an annoying shadow on Stepmother One's blissful lifestyle. I'm sure my mom read those poems, and I'm sure my mom wished she was a big hairy spider that could immobilize Stepmother One in a web and eat her bit by bit. Alas, that was not to be. My dad and Stepmother One continued their sycophantic relationship and ascended to literary heights, while my mom kept up her bitter vigil in our kitchen night after night, slowly crafting her masterpiece one poem at a time.

My dad phoned on occasion, and he always sent me birthday and Christmas presents, but I didn't actually see him again until I was twelve. My mom had been invited to teach at the Bread Loaf Writers' Conference in Vermont in mid-August, and she had also been awarded a residency at Yaddo for July. My grandmother had died of cirrhosis a few years earlier, so there was no one to look after me other than my dad, and after a tense late-night phone call that I could hear from my room, my dad agreed that I could spend the summer in Boulder.

It was an odd summer. I had not seen my dad for seven years, and by that time I had learned to live without him. He was like a stranger to me, plus he was living in a new house with a woman I didn't know. I vaguely remembered Stepmother One as one of the adults roaming through our house when I was little, but not much more. I'm sure I was like a stranger to him, too; the five-year-old he had known was now twelve years old, tall, rail-thin, and hopelessly introverted, with long hair in her face and more books than clothes in her suitcase.

The day I arrived was also my dad's birthday, and Stepmother One had planned a huge party, which was also ostensibly for me. Even as a child I was uncomfortable in large groups, probably a result of so many solitary years with my mom, and I was overwhelmed by the noise and the laughter and the press of people. I was particularly overwhelmed by my dad, who was loud and brash and wearing a low-cut dashiki that revealed his flowing chest hair, talking a mile a minute with a large glass of liquor sloshing in one hand and a burning joint in the other.

After the cake was served, I escaped upstairs and spent most of the party reading in my room. When I came down later for a second piece of cake, I glanced out the window and saw my dad on the porch, passionately kissing someone who was most definitely not Stepmother One. I was shocked for a moment, but only for a moment. Then I took my piece of cake and retreated back to my room and my book.

I didn't see my dad much that summer, which was something he had warned me about: "I'm happy you're here, of course, but I can't put my life on hold. I'm too important to too many people." The Naropa Summer Writing Program was in full swing when I was there, and my dad was involved both as a teacher and an organizer. Back in those days all the major Beats were still alive (with the exception of Kerouac and Cassady, who had both died at the end of the sixties), so the program was full of luminaries such as Allen Ginsberg, William Burroughs, Gregory Corso, Amiri Baraka, Ken Kesey, Anne Waldman, Diane di Prima, even Norman Mailer.

All those people were in and out of our house during the summer, with Allen and his partner, Peter Orlovsky, the most frequent visitors. When someone famous came over, Stepmother One would drag me away from my room and my reading, and force me to spend an awkward hour in the company of whoever it was. I liked Allen and Peter, and the women poets were always kind to me, but I was unsure of everyone else, not to mention flat-out scared of Burroughs and Corso. I protested each time, but Stepmother One never took no for an answer. She would always hiss at me, "These are great writers! Not all little girls are as lucky as you." Yet I only felt lucky when I was back upstairs in my room, eating Hershey Kisses and reading, occasionally looking at the glorious view of the Flatirons right outside my window.

One evening Stepmother One demanded that I attend a panel discussion with Allen, Burroughs, and Corso that my dad was moderating. It was an excruciating event, which was made even more intolerable by Stepmother One's insistence that I wear a dress, a weird brown Indian shift that she had bought especially for the occasion. My dad has photos from that evening in his living room, and to describe my expression as sullen would be an understatement. It was that night, sitting in the front row watching my dad on stage, seeing his posing, his ass-kissing, and his self-satisfaction, that I had a clear and distinct thought: My dad is an asshole.

I looked over at Stepmother One. Didn't she see it? But no, she sat there in a bright orange sari and gladiator sandals and big silver earrings like chandeliers, her thick honey-blonde hair flowing down her back, watching my dad with moist, glowing eyes, her hands stroking each other on her lap, which I thought was creepy. I remember having a mean thought that I should tell her about my dad kissing someone else on the porch, but I held my tongue. Even at twelve years old, I knew that she would be madder at me than at him.

That realization—my dad is an asshole—deepened as the summer progressed, and quite frankly it's never really gone away. How could it? My dad has always lived in his own self-enclosed bubble constructed of mirrors, and all he could ever see—all he ever wanted to see—was himself. I was never a child to make a nuisance of myself, and I think he was relieved that I didn't seem to need him. He was never there, anyway. Even after the Naropa Summer Writing Program ended, he had other obligations and a constant string of poetic emergencies. Usually when I saw him he was running out the door, leather satchel spilling over with books and papers, talking a mile a minute over his shoulder. After a while I got used to his continual exits, and generally speaking it was a relief to have him gone. Certainly it was quieter.

But it wasn't a bad summer, nor were all the summers that followed. I loved my dad's new home—a fancy old house on Mapleton Street, full of stained-glass windows and mysterious nooks—and I loved my room.

My dad was never mean to me, and he made sure I had a bicycle and my own library card. I spoke to Stepmother One just enough to give her the impression that we were building a relationship, but not enough to be disloyal to my mom. Mostly I was on my own, which is what I was used to, and which I preferred.

When I returned to New Jersey at the beginning of September, I quickly realized that my mom had changed. It wasn't until she died and I went through her papers that I pieced everything together, but the upshot is that in the early to mideighties, my mom carried on an affair with a famous poet—a famous married poet, so I won't out him here. My mom had hoped he would leave his wife for her, but that summer at Yaddo, where he also had a fellowship, he broke up with her. She never mentioned a word of this to me at the time, but suddenly the thin membrane that separated her drinking from the rest of her life vanished. She wasn't drinking all day long—that came later, once I left for college—but now the first thing she did when she came home in the afternoon was grab a glass, a few ice cubes, a bottle of tonic water, and a large bottle of gin, which was no longer hidden but instead occupied a treasured place on top of the refrigerator. She still made dinner, still graded papers, still wrote poems, but that glass never left her side from four p.m. to whenever it was she finally passed out.

My response to this was to avoid my home. I became an avid babysitter, and as soon as I got my working papers at age sixteen, I got a part-time job at Burger King two blocks from our house. I also got involved in afterschool activities, particularly the literary magazine. My closest friend was Helena Papadopoulos, a pale Greek girl with a mop of curly black hair, and I used to eat dinner at her house several nights a week. Her mother was a junior high-school teacher, and through the grapevine she surely knew what was going on with my mom. Mrs. Papadopoulos always paid a lot of attention to me: she asked about my schoolwork and my Burger King job, and she complimented me on my burgeoning looks—I had shot up to five ten, developed hips, and stopped wearing my hair in my face. She also bought me my first bras, taking me along on a shopping trip with her and Helena and casually buying me three white-lace bras with a rosebud between the cups. I wore those bras for years, until finally they fell apart.

Not long after my mom returned from her summer at Yaddo and Bread Loaf, she sold *The Insect Poems* to a large publisher. Few people make money from poetry, but my mom was lucky: she met an editor at Bread Loaf who loved her work and who had just been given an imprint at Random House to publish a line of women-oriented books. The editor was clever and the marketing good; they fully exploited my mom's link to my dad, now quite a famous poet himself, and they positioned my mom as a new feminist voice.

The poems were quite gruesome, but they resonated with people. The metaphors of insect habits were accessible, and they have proved fertile ground for academics, scholars, and feminist writers to this day. Most of all, my mom was an incredible writer. Her language was crisp and clear, with not an extraneous word or punctuation mark to be found. It also didn't hurt that Allen Ginsberg wrote the introduction, and that the book had blurbs from William Burroughs, Gary Snyder, and Maya Angelou.

The first check for $2,500 arrived a few weeks after my mom signed the contract. My mom paid a slew of outstanding bills, bought a new refrigerator, and got our treacherous front walk fixed. The next check for $2,500 arrived soon after the book was published, and when I arrived home from my second summer in Boulder, I was shocked to find a sporty red Mazda in the driveway. As is often the case with sporty red cars, I think it was some sort of desperate attempt at youth: by that time my mom was only in her midthirties, but she looked much older, due partly to her drinking and partly to her utter lack of concern for her appearance. My mom dressed in drab skirts and blouses, and no matter how many times I begged her to grow back her beautiful red-gold hair, she always refused. She didn't just destroy her best asset, she deliberately suppressed it. It's as if my dad cut out my mom's heart when he chose Stepmother One over her, and then when it didn't work out with the married poet, all my mom's romantic dreams died. She never went on dates, and she never mentioned men: she taught and she wrote and she drank.

My mom's success attracted acolytes, a never-ending stream of sincere young women who saw her as the next Sylvia Plath. They came to our house in New Jersey in droves, interviewing my mom for their newspapers and magazines and academic papers, hanging on to her every word as if it was gold. My mom knew a tremendous amount about poetry, the entire Western canon back to Homer, and when she was done talking about her own poems, she would talk about everyone else's. Often when I returned home from a shift at Burger King or dinner at Helena's, I would walk into the kitchen and hear snippets of these interviews, and I saw a new side of my mom that I didn't like, a side that was puffed up and garrulous and drunk. The acolytes never seemed to notice, and they never seemed to mind the drinking. On the contrary, they appeared thrilled to get drunk with my mom, if they could keep up with her, and many mornings I woke to find an acolyte passed out on the couch.

My mom also got invited to read her poetry, often in New York City but many other places as well. I rarely went to any of these readings, but I know she loved doing them, and at least that was one area of her life where she felt fulfilled. She became a mainstay at the Poetry Project at St. Mark's Church in the East Village, and she usually drove up to Manhattan a few times a week to give a reading or teach a workshop or schmooze with other poets. And drink. I spent many uneasy nights listening for the sound of the Mazda bumping into the driveway; I could only fall asleep when I knew she was home in one piece.

All the fame and activity did not blend seamlessly with my mom's day job. She had always been a conscientious teacher, but by the time I entered my senior year of high school, it seemed like I went to school more often than she did. I can't even count the number of times she asked me to call in sick for her because she was too tired or hungover to make it into work. I went to the same school that she worked in, so making those calls was doubly embarrassing for me; I sidestepped the school office as much as I could in order to avoid the school secretary's sympathetic looks.

I began to long for college, for escape. I got into Barnard College in Manhattan due to my strong grades, my high SAT scores, and my work on the literary magazine. I also shamelessly exploited my parents' fame in my application, writing a personal essay that laid on a thick layer of bullshit about the merits of having two literary parents. That's how desperate I was to escape. In any case, I got into Barnard, and the day I left for school—getting a ride with Helena, who had gotten into New York University—I felt nothing but relief.

Not long after I left for college, my mom was fired from her job. That's when her drinking became a full-time occupation, and that's when her debts started to mount. But that's another story altogether.

I continued spending summers in Boulder. I had noticed the mystical glow between my dad and Stepmother One slowly diminishing over the years, but they were still hanging in there, although her poems told me that she knew about his affairs, and his poems told me that he knew she knew. The summer after my sophomore year in college, Stepmother One picked me up at the airport in Denver full of cheer, telling me all about the upcoming Naropa Summer Writing Program, the new poetry book she had coming out in the fall, the success of my dad's *Los Angeles Times* interview with Ken Kesey—everything was coming up roses. Oh, and did my dad tell me? They had taken in a boarder, a lovely poet who had just completed the first year of her masters at Naropa. Her name was Jasmine.

When we walked into the elegant home on Mapleton Street, my dad was sitting at the kitchen table in his bathrobe, drinking tea and chatting with a beautiful young woman, also in her bathrobe. I only needed to take the quickest glance at them to know that they were lovers. I looked at Stepmother One, waiting for her to react, but she just chirped cheerfully, "Look who I found at the airport! Jasmine, meet Elizabeth."

"Hi," Jasmine said shyly, wiping a hand on her faux-silk bathrobe before offering it to me. I shook her warm hand coldly. She was a beauty, no doubt—she had luxurious curly brown hair past her shoulders, huge green eyes with thick black lashes, a heart-shaped face with creamy skin, a full red mouth, and a curvy, unclothed body peeking out of her robe.

"Jasmine's going to be your dad's teaching assistant this summer," Stepmother One said, reaching across the table to grab a piece of my dad's buttered toast. "And she's an incredible poet."

"I just bet she is," I said. "Hi, Dad."

"Hello, Daughter." He looked at me, and I looked at him. Something passed in that look—my scorn, his defiance—and I don't think I looked at him again all summer.

It was probably the worst summer of my life. No, scratch that—it *was* the worst summer of my life. Dad and Jasmine were madly in love, and they did nothing to hide it. They were always looking for opportunities to have sex whenever Stepmother One was out, and I don't know how many times I caught my dad or Jasmine creeping through the upstairs hallway in their bathrobes.

It was a seedy little drama, and I was furious at my dad for putting me in the middle of it. But here's the thing about my dad: he loves triangles. He loves being smack in the middle of high drama, and then feeding off the ensuing chaos. The more of an audience he has, the better. For that particular show, he had Stepmother One and Jasmine and me at home, plus the entire Naropa community the moment he stepped out the door. I went to one public event that year, but the sight of my dad, puffed up and loud, running from Stepmother One to Jasmine to whatever literary celebrity was around—it was too much, and I never joined them all in public again.

As for Stepmother One, that's when our relationship started to deteriorate. I never liked her much, partly because of the pain she had caused my mom, and partly because I thought she was—as Holden Caulfield so succinctly put it—a phony. But that summer, her bitter, controlling side began to emerge. It was weird: after eight summers of benign neglect, she suddenly started grilling me about my activities, and I couldn't make a move without her commenting on it. This was doubly odd because there was no basis for her hovering: the few friends I had were innocuous, I didn't stay out late, I rarely drank, and as for drugs, the adults were the ones leaving roaches all over the house. Finally I realized that she couldn't control my dad, so she focused on controlling me. Yet knowing the reason did nothing to alleviate my feeling of suffocation.

Things came to a head one evening when I was sitting at the thick oak table in the kitchen, eating cereal for dinner—a common practice at home with my mom—and Stepmother One made a sarcastic remark about me missing the lovely dinner she had prepared.

I swallowed my granola and shot her a look. "There was fennel in it. Fennel makes me ill, you know that."

"You could have picked it out. You know, young lady, I don't see you participating much in this household."

Young lady! I rolled my eyes and went back to my cereal.

"Even Jasmine has noticed," Stepmother One continued.

"Oh, has she."

"You know," Stepmother One said, sitting across from me and narrowing her eyes, "you hardly even speak to Jasmine. I get the feeling that you don't like her very much."

"Oh, you do, do you?"

"Yes, I do."

I put my spoon down. "Do you like her?"

"I do, very much. She's a lovely young lady. Such a talented poet! We're lucky to have her here, not just for her rent money, but for her spirit."

I nodded and said nothing.

"You know what I think?" Stepmother One said, folding her arms over her braless chest.

"Tell me. What do you think?"

"I think you're jealous. I think you're jealous of Jasmine living here, and I think you're jealous of how close she is to your dad and how much attention he pays her."

I stared at her. How was it possible that Stepmother One didn't realize what was going on? It always amazed me how women saw my father, the way they distorted their vision so they didn't have to recognize what he truly was. But it wasn't my job to tell Stepmother One. She was a bright lady, and she was going to have to figure this one out all by herself. So I said nothing. I finished my cereal while she watched me with burning eyes, then I got up and walked out of the house, letting the door close with a big fat slam.

I waited with bated breath the rest of the summer, knowing that the whole situation was poised to explode at any moment, and silently hoping it wouldn't happen on my watch. The tension was unbearable, and once again I found myself longing for escape.

About a week before I went back to New York, Allen Ginsberg and Peter Orlovsky stopped by after dinner for a visit. I was dragged down from my room, and my dad insisted that Jasmine read her latest poem to us. The poem concerned a torrid sexual encounter, and the language was similar to my dad's. As Jasmine read, my dad watched her like a puppy dog, and Stepmother One listened with a big smile on her face, ignorant and oblivious. I looked over at Allen, who was listening intently, nodding his head and staring at the carpet.

When the poem started describing intertwining thighs, I was done. I got up and went into the kitchen, where I stood at the back door and looked out into the lush garden and cool Boulder evening. I promised myself then and there that I would not spend another summer in Boulder. I was twenty years old, and I didn't have to put up with my dad's chaos any longer.

I felt a hand on my shoulder. I turned around and saw Allen. I smiled; you couldn't help but love him.

"You all right?" he asked.

I shrugged. He nodded sagely. Allen knew the score: he knew all about my mom and her drinking, and he knew about my dad and his many women.

"You're your own person," he told me. "Just remember that." He gave me a big hug, then went back into the living room.

You know, I always did remember him saying that, and I've thought of it often throughout my life. Allen died a few years later, so as it turned out that was one of the last times I ever saw him.

That was also my last summer in Colorado. I completed my junior year at Barnard, then got a summer job in Manhattan as an assistant to a literary agent. I rented a cheap room in one of the Columbia fraternities on 114th Street, small and roachy and all mine. It was my first summer without my dad or my mom, and I loved it.

One evening there was a knock on my door. "Phone call!" someone yelled cheerfully. I went downstairs to the payphone next to the beer-soaked common room.

"Elizabeth. It's Jill." The voice was quivering and loud.

I frowned. "Jill?"

"Your stepmother!" she yelled.

"But—how did you get my number?"

"Your mom."

"My *mom*? You spoke to my mom?"

"We just got off the phone. Your dad left me. Or kicked me out, I should say!"

"Oh."

"Don't you want to know what happened?" Before I could reply, Stepmother One unleashed a torrential flood of tears and words. I caught about half of what she said: your dad, Jasmine, naked, poems, cheating. However I only really paid attention to two words: your mom.

"Jill," I interrupted her. "You called my mom? How could you? My mom doesn't want to speak to you."

"Oh, Elizabeth! I've always had nothing but respect for your mom. We were friends, once upon a time."

"Yes, I know," I said drily. "I read about that in your poems."

"Well, your mom gave me good advice. She said to stay and fight; she said she ran away, and in retrospect that was a mistake. What do you think?"

"Jill, I would really rather you didn't ask me for relationship advice." I felt a surge of anger, which I had been repressing for years in the interest of keeping the peace. "You know what? Don't call me anymore. And don't call my mom, either!" I hung up the phone with a bang. That was the first and last time I ever slammed down a phone.

The divorce between my dad and Stepmother One dragged out for several years. I didn't visit Boulder once during that time, but I knew about the unfolding drama via occasional phone calls from my dad. I also heard about it from my mom, who was kept up-to-date by friends in Boulder as well as Stepmother One, with whom she had formed an uneasy alliance. The mess started with Stepmother One kicking out Jasmine, continued with my dad kicking out Stepmother One and inviting Jasmine back, and escalated with Stepmother One storming the house one evening and attacking my dad with, of all things, a hardcover volume of *The Chicago Manual of Style.* The police were called, Stepmother One was arrested, and to this day my dad has a scar on his forehead.

The battle went on, but my dad always managed to gain ground, and over the next few years he squeezed Stepmother One out of his life. Turns out the house was in his name so he kept that, and due to some arcane Colorado law he avoided alimony payments. He also succeeded in getting Stepmother One out of Naropa. When all was said and done, Stepmother One had a townhouse in south Boulder, a teaching job at CU Boulder, and two restraining orders. My dad remained exactly as he was, only now he was living with a gorgeous young woman in her twenties. He wrote a book of poems about the experience entitled, I'm sorry to say, *Cock and Bull,* which was a runner-up for the National Book Award. Stepmother One's book about the debacle was called *The Fascist Heart,* and Jasmine's slim inaugural volume was named *Hot and Holy Love.*

In 2000 I was twenty-seven years old. I was working at Blue Heron Books, living in my lovely Greenwich Village apartment, and seriously dating an IT consultant named Max. My life had fallen into place, and as Allen had advised, I was living as my own person.

Then one early spring day, my dad called. *Esquire* magazine had commissioned him to do an interview with Norman Mailer in Mailer's apartment in Brooklyn Heights. The magazine was putting my dad and Jasmine up at the Roosevelt Hotel in Manhattan, and they would be in town for three days altogether. My dad wanted to see me; it had been a long time, he said, seven years, and he wanted me to get reacquainted with Jasmine, who had become such an important part of his life.

Of course when I knocked on their door they were still in bed, although I had purposely arrived a half hour late to avoid such a scenario. Of course they giggled about their naughtiness and promised to meet me in the lobby in fifteen minutes. Of course it took them forty-five. Of course they had their hands all over each other during our dinner at the swanky hotel restaurant. I didn't bother to find out what dessert would be like. As soon as I was done with my entrée, I grabbed my purse and coat and stood. "I have to go," I said.

"Already!" my dad protested. "We haven't even told you our news." He curved a hand over Jasmine's stomach. "We're pregnant. We're getting married this summer. Aren't you happy for us?"

"Delighted. Now if you'll excuse me." I walked out of the restaurant, so angry I must have had steam spurting from my head.

As I stalked down Madison Avenue, I realized that I didn't care so much about the marriage—I had expected it. I didn't care so much about all their groping—I had expected that, too. What really bothered me was that for a man who hadn't seen his daughter in seven years, my dad showed no interest whatsoever in my life. Instead he talked on and on about himself, his poetry and his awards and his plum interview assignment with his old buddy Norman. It was Jasmine who gently asked about my job, my apartment, my boyfriend—but even then, my dad always managed to turn the conversation so it faced him. He didn't even ask about my mom, although her situation had deteriorated alarmingly in recent years. He knew that, and I knew he knew that. I desperately needed his support, but he never even mentioned her name, not once.

The next day I had lunch with Hansika at the Waverly Restaurant, and I told her all about the previous evening. She listened carefully as she ate her omelet, and when I was done she said, "Your dad sounds like an asshole."

Exactly.

Dad and Jasmine had a splashy June wedding. I didn't go, but Jasmine sent me pictures: bare feet, joints, happy smiles, famous poets, Flatirons in the background. Just like the photos of his weddings with my mom and Stepmother One. Also like my mom, Jasmine was sizably pregnant. I didn't care at all.

But as summer progressed, so did Jasmine's pregnancy, and in one of her letters she mentioned how excited she was to finally see "your brother or sister," as she put it. That's when it hit me: I wasn't going to be an only child anymore. Someone else was joining the family, and it wasn't just another stepmother. For the first time in years, I began to think about visiting Boulder.

Emma was born on September 27, 2000. A Libra, the birth announcement declared proudly. I decided to go to Boulder for a long weekend so I could meet her. I was not surprised that my dad was absent most of the time due to the usual unspecified poetic emergencies, but I was stunned by my reaction to Emma. As the novels say, it was love at first sight. When Jasmine—now Stepmother Two—put the fresh-smelling bundle into my arms, my heart burst open. Emma had olive skin and deep green eyes, the same dark Eastern European coloring as my dad and me. And just like me she was born with a full head of thick black hair, which Jasmine had decorated with tiny pink bows. I asked Jasmine why she had chosen the name "Emma," and Jasmine told me shyly that she wanted to give her daughter the name of a Jane Austen heroine, just like me.

I was deeply touched, and after that Jasmine and I got along better—not great, but better. Motherhood seemed to have grounded her, and she started working hard to have a relationship with me. She sent me photos of Emma and regularly updated me on life in Boulder via letters and e-mails. Her letters were increasingly reflective, and she even apologized for behaving so selfishly during her trip to New York with my dad. When my mom died—on September 1, 2001—I spoke to my dad for about ten minutes, but Jasmine and I talked for over an hour. I think that's when I really began to think of Jasmine as a person in her own right, not just as Stepmother Two, and not just an extension of my dad.

Not coincidentally, the same thing was happening to Jasmine. When I visited them in January 2002, the edges of their marriage were clearly unraveling. I saw that although my dad loved Emma in his way, he wasn't happy about sharing Jasmine. I saw how disappointed Jasmine was that my dad was not able to expand his notion of love to include a child. Late at night in the beautiful Queen Anne house, I heard low, tense conversations that were punctuated by Emma's cries. In the mornings my dad looked cross and spoke little, and as Jasmine nursed Emma at the kitchen table, she stared out the window blankly.

The evening before I left, Jasmine cooked a farewell Indian dinner for me. While she chopped and stirred, I sat in the rocking chair holding Emma. The phone rang and it was my dad: he was bailing out of dinner due, once again, to an unstated poetic emergency. Jasmine put down the phone, then burst into tears. Emma looked up at me, her green eyes frightened. She would have been even more scared if she knew about the poetry books my dad and Jasmine were concocting, which concerned the dissolution of their marriage and mentioned Emma often—my dad's book was called *The Betrayal,* and Jasmine's was *Shredded Vows.*

I visited again in the fall, and by that time my dad and Jasmine were barely speaking. Two visits later, Jasmine had moved out. The day I arrived, I had lunch with my dad at the Kitchen in downtown Boulder, and as soon as he left to go teach, I hightailed it to Jasmine and Emma's new house on

Grove Street. As I sat in the small pink kitchen drinking coffee, Emma sitting on my lap with her arms twined around my neck, Jasmine filled me in on their new life. Unlike my mom, who ran off to the East Coast when her marriage ended, and unlike Stepmother One, who was pushed off to south Boulder and the University of Colorado, Jasmine stood her ground: she was adamant about staying in central Boulder, determined to hang on to her assistant professorship at Naropa University, and she didn't care one drop about my dad and his (already) new girlfriend. Jasmine told my dad that he had a legal obligation to take care of Emma, and if he wanted to go to court to fight about it, so be it. My dad knew he couldn't defeat Jasmine: unlike Stepmother One, Jasmine had a child by him, and unlike Stepmother One, Jasmine was sane. My dad agreed to pay child support, and he bought Jasmine and Emma a cute little Victorian house in the Goss Grove neighborhood, just a block from the main Naropa campus.

"I no longer have any illusions about your dad," Jasmine told me as she topped off my coffee. "He has officially made the transition from being the love of my life to being the thorn in my side." She paused. "I hope it doesn't shock you to hear me say that."

"I understand," I said. I looked down at Emma; she had fallen asleep, so I decided to speak my mind. "I've never said this to you before, Jasmine, but I think my dad is an asshole."

She snorted. "I'd go further than that. I'd say he's a narcopath."

"What's that?"

"Half-narcissist, half-sociopath. Your dad is completely self-centered, and I really don't think he feels any empathy or guilt. I mean, he maybe has a flicker of shame here and there, but for the most part he never thinks about how his actions affect other people. He's the least introspective person I've ever met."

"In other words, he's an asshole."

She laughed. "Yes. Exactly."

That visit established my routine for all future trips to Boulder: stay with my dad and spend most of my time in Goss Grove with Emma and Jasmine. Naturally my dad took this amiss—not because he wanted to see more of me, but because he thought I was taking Jasmine's side. Which of course I was, but I never said it out loud, so my dad and I managed to forge an uneasy coexistence. I continued to visit regularly, and then in December 2008 the bottom fell out, and I had to move back to Boulder altogether.

☼ ☼ ☼

I sighed, shifting in my seat. The bus was almost in Boulder, and I could see the mountains out the window. One big difference between Denver and Boulder is that the mountains are closer in Boulder. In Denver you need at least a half hour to get to the Rockies, but from certain points in Boulder, you can walk directly onto the trailheads. The mountains are also quite different; the Flatirons in Boulder are five rust-red sheets of rock jutting up from the earth, as if giants had shoved enormous flat stones into the ground. Behind the Flatirons are rolling green mountains, and towering above it all are snow-covered peaks, which that day were breaking through a bank of bright white clouds. It's so beautiful it's almost unreal, a true-life version of Shangri-la. When I was a little girl these were my mountains, and anytime I came back to Boulder I was happy to see them, even though I was not always happy to see the people who lived underneath them.

As we made our way to the center of town, we passed the University of Colorado, a picturesque campus of sandstone buildings with red-slate tiled roofs. To the left was the Hill, a neighborhood of sagging Victorians, restaurants, bars, bookstores, and, a more recent phenomena, medical marijuana stores bearing the telltale green cross. Forgive me for being cynical, but I really doubt there are that many sick people on the Hill. Almost everyone I know in Boulder has their medical-marijuana card, including my dad, who has the constitution of a bull and has rarely been ill a day in his life.

The bus entered downtown Boulder, and I felt my familiar mix of anticipation and dread. I was not fond of Boulder, and if it wasn't for Emma and Jasmine, I would never have gone back. Yet when my life in New York exploded, I had no other option than to move West. My dad, to his credit, invited me to come and stay with him, and he did so without a moment's hesitation. It's just that once I was back, he never had any time for me. As usual.

I do love my dad, I suppose, but I don't like him very much. Everything he does is a thick slice of crazy, and all I ever want to do is separate myself from his chaos. And honestly, although I loved my mom dearly, I felt the same way about her when her drinking got really bad. But I loved Emma, and to my surprise I had become close to Jasmine. I used to think that Jasmine was nice to me out of a sense of duty, but as time went on I realized that she was a genuinely kind person who really did love me, stepmother or not.

Yet despite my disdain for my dad and, sometimes, my mom, there is a certain way that I am without question their daughter: I love literature, and I love words. However, unlike them, I'm able to separate this passion from my personality and my life story. My immense pleasure in doing small things with words (as the great poet Alice Notley once said) was conducted behind the scenes, clean and quiet, while theirs wove hotly among their affairs and hormones and dramas. I like to fix sentences and I like to make them sing; I am not interested in exposing my soul to the world. In that sense I will never, ever be like them, and for that I am grateful.

7. E to Shining E

As the bus pulled into the Boulder Transit Center on Fifteenth and Walnut, I saw Jasmine and Emma standing in the outside waiting area, holding hands and searching the windows of my bus. Emma saw me first, and she immediately started jumping up and down. I smiled and waved furiously. Every human being should have at least one person who jumps for joy at the sight of them.

When I emerged from the bus, Emma ran to me and wrapped her arms around my waist, pushing her head into my solar plexus. "Sister!" she exclaimed.

"Sister!" I exclaimed back, kissing the top of her head.

Jasmine came toward me, and I leaned over so she could kiss me on the cheek. Jasmine is five foot two, and at five ten I tower over her; one day Emma would, too. "Hey there," Jasmine said. "Do you have any bags?"

"It's just me and my knapsack."

"Our names are down at Dushanbe, so by the time we walk over there our table should be ready. Emma," she laughed, putting her hand on Emma's head, which was still snuggled into my middle. "Elizabeth can't walk if you're wrapped around her like that."

"OK." She unwrapped herself and took my hand, then she took Jasmine's hand, and the three of us walked through the small bus terminal to Walnut Street.

Boulder. What can I say about Boulder? If you haven't been there, it's hard to imagine that such a place actually exists. Nothing in Boulder is sketchy or gritty; there's no real sense of danger, although it's probably sensible not to roam the Hill in the wee hours. The Pearl Street Mall is a jewel in the center of town, a quaint pedestrian mall with red-brick walkways, bright shops, thriving trees, interesting sculptures, happy musicians, and charming street performers. There's a movie called *Catch and Release* that's set in Boulder, and as two of the characters walk down the Pearl Street Mall, one of them calls the place "Patagonia Disneyland." It's one of the best descriptions of Boulder I've ever heard, and I always think of it when I'm on the Mall.

As I said, the Boulder of 2009 is a million miles away from the Boulder I knew as a child. Back then Boulder was a sleepy college town full of hippies, whereas now it's a bustling mecca of green innovation, extreme sports, and medical marijuana. I guess the biggest change is that Boulder feels—nay, is—a town for the wealthy, or at least the well-off. It's more or less a bubble of privileged white people, and I defy you to walk down the Pearl Street Mall and find more than a smattering of nonwhite faces. I don't think this was anyone's intention, particularly, but it has certainly turned out that way. As a result the town has—at least to me—a slightly sterile feeling, a sense of smug insularity. My dad is a classic example of a Boulderite: he's lived there for decades, he's convinced it's the best place on earth, and he never says the word "Denver" without a slight shudder. I think he would curl up and die anywhere else.

As someone who was used to New York City, I had a profound shock when I came back to live in Boulder. People are so happy and healthy there it's scary; never before have I encountered people who exercise so much. Often when I was in a coffee shop or perusing things I couldn't afford in a Pearl Street boutique, I would overhear someone in a neon spandex outfit talking about their forty-five-mile bike ride that morning. In Boulder, people run marathons up mountains, they dangle from ropes on sheer rock faces, and they climb 14ers, which means mountains with peaks above fourteen thousand feet, something Colorado has dozens of. People are fit, trim, and rarin' to go. Then there was me, with a predominantly black wardrobe, deadly pale from years of sitting inside marking up manuscripts, with my daily walk to Starbucks my only form of exercise. I felt like I had landed in an alien nation. But Boulder is also where Emma and Jasmine live, and whenever I'm with them I always have a feeling of home.

We crossed Broadway, and as we walked Emma chatted about their visit to the library that morning to see an environmental improv group, with an occasional comment from Jasmine. On our right was the town park with a maze of sidewalks and bicycle paths, the Flatirons looming above. On our left was our destination, the Boulder Dushanbe Teahouse. We passed through the black-iron gates into the Teahouse garden, a wide walkway surrounded by rose bushes, small trees, and sunken patios on each side. Running alongside the right-hand patio was Boulder Creek, a picturesque stream that starts in the Rockies and passes through town.

As we got closer to the gaggle of people waiting by the front door, the stylish hostess opened the door and called out, "Zwelland, table for three!"

Jasmine smiled at us. "Perfect timing."

The Teahouse's main room is a large square with a high ceiling featuring a skylight in the center, long large windows with transparent white curtains, elaborately carved wooden pillars spaced throughout, and white frescos and large abstract drawings painted directly onto the walls. In the center of the room is a raised hexagonal pond in a terracotta base, with statues of graceful dancing females. I tilted my head slightly and looked up at the ceiling, which is a riot of bright colors—red, green, blue, yellow, orange—painted on carved wood in intricate designs. Even with a room full of chattering diners, entering the Dushanbe Teahouse felt like stepping into another world, an elegant, airy oasis.

As we walked to our table, I looked out the windows on the right-hand side of the room, and my eyes fell on a sign on a neighboring building: COLORADO GUNSPORT. Which was a not-so-subtle reminder that despite the healthy, wealthy refinement of Boulder, we were still in Colorado and the Wild West, the Boulder Bubble surrounded by hunters, fundamentalist Christians, and military installations.

We sat down at a square black-iron table on the left-hand side of the room, putting our jackets and bags on the spare chair. I looked at Emma and smiled; she was squirming in her seat, clearly ready to burst. "I have so much to tell you!" she said.

Jasmine picked up the stack of small black menus and passed one to me and one to Emma. "Let's order before you pull out the list, all right?" she said mildly. "Then we can concentrate."

I took the menu and opened it, but I already knew what I wanted. I always got the Basic Breakfast: eggs over medium, potatoes, and a biscuit. And coffee, even though it was a teahouse.

I put down my menu and looked at Emma. She could have been my twin, although almost thirty years younger. She was tall and beanpole thin, with olive skin, green eyes, straight features, heavy brows, and straight black hair, although she wore hers in bangs. If you see pictures of our dad when he was a boy—sans chest hair and extra eighty pounds—he looks just like us. Our dad's ancestors came to America from Eastern Europe over a hundred years ago, but even after decades of the Zwelland DNA mixing with fair-skinned people, we had not changed one drop.

Jasmine was a different sort, more Irish looking with fair skin, cascades of curly brown hair, big green eyes, a heart-shaped face, much shorter and much curvier. Her lusciousness had tempered somewhat with age, but now that she was close to forty I actually thought she was more beautiful than when I first saw her at my dad's kitchen table sixteen years before. Apparently I wasn't the only one who thought so; I noticed the two men at the next table surreptitiously checking her out. Unlike my mom and Stepmother One, who both looked so bitter and dried-up after their divorces from my dad, Jasmine was blooming. But then, she had left him; she was the only one who had.

We ordered our food, and before long the waitress brought over our drinks: Assam tea for Jasmine, hot chocolate for Emma, and a French-press Ethiopian coffee for me. Ah—real, gorgeous coffee, dark brown and rich, with thick cream and brown sugar! The individual French presses were small so I always got two, which was why I ordered the cheapest dish on the menu. I knew that Jasmine would be paying, but I still didn't want to take advantage. Between her job as a Naropa professor and my dad's child support and a bit of help from her parents in Eugene, Oregon, I think Jasmine does just fine, but I know it's not cheap raising a child on your own, particularly in Boulder.

"I have a list for you," Emma told me. "Mommy, can you hand me my backpack?"

Jasmine handed Emma her pink Hello Kitty backpack, from which Emma unearthed a pink Hello Kitty notebook and a purple pen with a plastic Hello Kitty head perched on top. I remember when I first started working at Blue Heron, Hansika and I went out to lunch, and when it was time to pay she pulled out a beaded Hello Kitty change purse, just Hello Kitty's big white head with a red bow by her ear and that unnerving blank stare. I bit my lip to stop from laughing, whereupon Hansika said calmly, "Laugh if you want. You either get Hello Kitty or you don't."

Emma opened her well-worn notebook and read her list out loud. It even had a title:

E to Shining E

1. Famous Peach story turtle
2. Math problems fine
3. Soccer maybe what think?
4. Monopoly Mad Men Futurama
5. Pizza no anchovies please but no peppers
6. Love you happy to see

As we worked our way through our food, Emma unpacked her list. Item 1, "Famous Peach story turtle," referred to Emma's best friend, Peach, who I always called "Famous Peach" because Emma talked about her so much. Apparently Peach was now the proud owner of a turtle, who had a fondness for hiding under the washing machine. "Math problems fine" concerned my most recent visit, when I had helped Emma with her math homework and requested her to tell me how it all turned out, since my math skills were rather rusty. "Soccer maybe what think?" posed Emma's dilemma about trying out for the soccer team. Apparently her gym coach told her she was quite good, but Emma didn't want to do it because she thought playing a sport was not quite her thing. As someone who has always had a strong aversion to team sports of any kind, I thought her decision was quite sound. Items 4 and 5 addressed our plans for the afternoon and evening: "Monopoly Mad Men Futurama" meant we were going to play Monopoly, then watch an episode of *Mad Men,* followed by Emma's favorite cartoon, *Futurama.* "Pizza no anchovies please but no peppers" had to do with our dinner that night and our ongoing negotiations about toppings. The last item, "Love you happy to see"—well, me too.

I listened carefully to Emma while I ate my eggs and drank my ambrosial coffee. One of the only good things about being unemployed and living at my dad's was that I got to spend so much time with Emma. She is a cool little girl. She can be chatty, like she was at lunch that day, but she can also be quite serious, her dark brows drawn and her eyes watchful. Like her mother, Emma is a genuinely kind person, and she also has a tremendous love for animals, not to mention Hello Kitty.

Jasmine is also a good mom. She let Emma talk, adding a gentle word here and there, and when the list was complete she said, "You know, Emma, that list sounds like a poem."

Emma's face brightened. "I could rewrite it and take the numbers out."

"You could. Or you could leave them in. It's OK for poems to have numbers."

Emma nodded seriously. "Or I could leave them in. I want to keep the title."

"I agree," Jasmine said. "The title is wonderful." She winked at me. "Emma definitely has the family word gene."

I nodded. For a long time I had noticed that Emma had a gift with words, and it just got more apparent as she got older.

Emma bounced in her seat. "Tell Elizabeth about Beatrice and what she said."

"Oh!" Jasmine laughed. "Beatrice was over for tea about a week ago, and Emma read her a few poems. Beatrice was very impressed."

Emma beamed. I reached over and put a hand on her head. "How is Beatrice?" I asked Jasmine. Beatrice Woolster was an ancient poet who was one of Jasmine's mentors; Beatrice had actually been Jasmine's teacher before my dad was. I also got the sense that Beatrice was a key factor in Jasmine staying at Naropa after the breakup with my dad.

"She's doing great. We're planning next summer's writing program, and we already have some amazing people lined up." Jasmine checked her watch. "Ooh, we need to get going soon. Emma, why don't you go see how the goldfish are doing?"

Emma took off like a shot, almost bumping into a waitress in the process.

Jasmine turned to me. "I was hoping I could get a word alone with you. I have to warn you about something."

"Dad?"

"Actually, for once it's not about him. Or not much." Jasmine sighed and rolled her eyes. "One of Emma's little friends told her about JonBenét Ramsey."

I grimaced. Boulder's most famous murder, and one of the most notorious forensic botch-ups in the annals of crime. I wasn't in Colorado when it happened, but it was nationwide news for months. "You mean she didn't know about it?"

"Of course not. This is Boulder; no one talks about it. It's not even on Banjo Billy's Bus Tour. You can't blame them, it's such an awful story. Anyway, Emma's pretty obsessed with her. She wants to go to the house."

"Wow. I'm kind of surprised." Emma was not what you would call a morbid child; she was into Hello Kitty, not vampires or zombies.

"I told her no, but I'm sure she's going to ask you." Jasmine looked over at the pond, and I looked, too. Emma was on her knees on the floor, peering into the water. "So if she asks, could you please just say no?"

"Sure. But how much does she actually know about it?"

"Elizabeth, it's the Internet age. Information is free, and you can't hide things from kids anymore. Our computer is in the kitchen and she mostly just plays Club Penguin, but I'm about 100 percent sure she looked it up at her dad's house."

"Did you ask him about it?"

"I tried. He just told me that I was being overdramatic. You know your dad—if a woman doesn't agree with him, or if she presents him with a problem that he can't solve, she's overdramatic."

This was true. My dad was no help whatsoever during my six months of unemployment.

"Here she comes," Jasmine said. "Thanks for your help."

Emma scootched onto her chair, and Jasmine smiled at her. "How are the fish? Are there still four?"

While Emma updated us on the Dushanbe fish, our waitress came over and put the check on the table. Jasmine took her wallet out of her large brown leather purse, and after putting her credit card on the check, she discreetly handed me ten dollars for bus fare. I smiled at her and mouthed, "Thank you." When I moved to Denver, my dad told me he would give me bus fare so I could come back to Boulder whenever I wanted, but he always forgot and I always had to remind him several times, which was humiliating. Finally Jasmine took over. "I just add it to his bill," she told me. I wished I earned enough so that ten dollars didn't make a difference, but unfortunately it really did.

"So here's the plan," Jasmine said. "We go back home, I get ready for the hike and leave, you two have fun. Emma is in bed at nine. Sound good?"

Emma and I looked at each other and nodded. "Where's the hike?" I asked.

"Up Mount Sanitas. This is the group Emma and I belong to, the Moms and Daughters Hiking Celebration. Tonight, though, it's just the moms. We'll hike up, and then we'll have an empowerment ceremony at sunset."

I raised my eyebrows. Jasmine used the term "empowerment ceremony" with no irony whatsoever.

"Then we'll come down and have pizza and beer at one of the mom's houses. But it'll be craft beer, and the pizza will be scratch-made with gluten-free crust and local goat cheese. This is Boulder, after all."

I laughed. That was something else I appreciated about Jasmine: she was utterly enmeshed in the Boulder lifestyle, but she took it with a grain of salt, and she wasn't above poking a little gentle fun now and then.

"We hiked last week," Emma said as the waitress returned with the bill. "We went to Rocky Mountain Natural Park, and we saw marmots."

"Cool," I said. "I love marmots."

"Emma's a good walker," Jasmine said as she signed the credit-card receipt. "She has strong legs. Some of the other girls were really struggling."

Emma looked at me and widened her eyes. "*Peach* was struggling."

"Speaking of walking," Jasmine said, "shall we walk over to the car? I'm parked in the lot out back."

"Sure," I said. "Let's go."

Jasmine and Emma's home in Goss Grove is a miniature Victorian that looks like a gingerbread house. It's three stories tall, painted deep-blue with white trim and topped off by dark-gray shingles. There is a cherry tree in the tiny front yard, and a white-wood fence that has a blue door with a heart-shaped space carved near the top.

Inside the house is equally charming, but space is at a premium: the rooms are always bursting at the seams with furniture and books and backpacks and Emma's many art projects. A child obviously lives here, unlike the museum atmosphere of our dad's home. I always like visiting the little Victorian, and it feels like home—yet I sometimes wonder what will happen if Jasmine remarries, because it's difficult to imagine their home accommodating another adult, much less another child. But although Jasmine is so beautiful, she rarely dates. Perhaps that's where the blowup of her marriage to my dad still affects her the most—she is very, very cautious about men.

I went up to the tiny third-floor attic to drop off my backpack. It is a wee Hobbit room, with slanted walls on each side that form the peak of the roof, and an octagon-shaped stained glass window overlooking the minuscule backyard. There are little doors in each wall that open into jam-packed storage spaces, and the room itself is only big enough for a futon, a meditation cushion, and a small altar with a shiny gold Buddha statue and a photo of Chögyam Trungpa Rinpoche wearing thick black glasses and elaborately embroidered gold robes. This is Jasmine's meditation room, but whenever I visit she willingly turns it over to me and meditates in her room. In fact as I was walking down the narrow dollhouse steps to the second floor, she called out from the bathroom, "Liz"—once in a while she calls me that, and she is the only one who I don't correct—"can you bring my *zafu* with you?"

I went back upstairs for the squishy purple meditation cushion, then came back down and put it on the four-poster bed in her sage-green room. I went down to the living room, where Emma was already setting up the Monopoly board on the low wooden coffee table. As always, she was the dog, I was the car; she was real estate, I was the banker. I brewed a pot of coffee in the little pink kitchen, and then I joined Emma on the floor on the well-worn blue Oriental rug.

We had just started the game when Jasmine came downstairs in her hiking clothes and small backpack. "I'm off. Pizza money is on the kitchen counter, bedtime is nine."

"You told us that already," Emma said as she picked up a Community Chest card.

"Well, I'm telling you again." Jasmine leaned down and kissed Emma on the head, then she kissed my head, too. "Be good," she said. "Have fun!" She gave us a wave and left; a few minutes later we heard her green Subaru drive away.

Emma and I played two games of Monopoly, with each of us winning one. Two-person Monopoly is not ideal, but we somehow made it work. As we played we chatted and laughed, and sometimes fell into easy silences. For me Emma is maybe the best company I've ever had; I never feel self-conscious or on my guard with her. Adults are often scared of silence, but that's where Emma and I started out, with me holding her as a baby and watching her sleep, occasionally dipping my nose into her fuzzy black hair.

At five we ordered pizza. As we drank blueberry Izze sodas and ate slices laden with mushrooms, tomatoes, garlic, and extra cheese, Emma told me more about the hike to Rocky Mountain National Park the previous week. Turns out Peach was not only struggling, but she also threw up. "I didn't want to say that at the Teahouse," Emma said, "because it's a nice restaurant." Apparently another girl got a bee sting, and another had a tantrum that ended up in a complete meltdown.

"Wow," I said. "What do you think happened?"

"I don't know," Emma said as she chewed on a crust. "But that's why the moms are doing a ceremony tonight. They want to clear up the bad energy in the group."

"Is there bad energy in the group?" I asked.

"Not with me and Mommy. We get along with everyone. But sometimes the moms fight, and two of them used to date. They're lesbians," she told me matter-of-factly.

I nodded. When I was Emma's age, I don't think I even knew that word. No one talked about lesbians in New Jersey.

This led to a discussion of kids who had two moms, and kids who had two dads. Emma even told me about an experimental family with two moms and one dad.

"That sounds a little complicated," I said. And a little too close to home. "Are you done?"

"Yep."

"Time for *Mad Men*?"

"Yes!"

"But dishes and cleanup first, right?"

"That's what my mom would say. But my mom's not here."

"Your mom's not here, but the dishes are. We don't want your mom coming home to a dirty kitchen. That would make her sad."

Emma nodded. "Sad, not mad."

We cleaned up, then set the scene for our evening TV fest. There is a small flat-screen TV in the living room wedged between stacks of books, and after turning on a few strategic lamps, I put in the DVD and found the right episode. We snuggled into the fat purple couch under a fuzzy, multicolored afghan, with one of Emma's bony elbows nestled in my stomach. The sun started to go down; I drew the ruby-red curtains, and the living room felt like a warm, colorful cave.

The episode concerned the birth of a baby, a surreal dream, and the Civil Rights movement. I looked at Emma; her eyes were glued to the set, her concentration fierce. I don't imagine there are many eight-year-olds who enjoy *Mad Men,* but once when Jasmine was watching an episode late one evening, Emma had a bad dream and so she came downstairs and curled up with Jasmine on the couch. To Jasmine's surprise, the next evening Emma wanted to watch another episode, and when Jasmine told her no because it was a show for adults, Emma was practically inconsolable. Jasmine gave in, and now Emma had me hooked as well.

As we watched, I wondered several times if Emma really understood any of the plot. As the credits rolled, I asked her, "Did you understand that?"

"I like it," she said simply. "I like the clothes."

We discussed the characters a bit, especially the little girl, Sally Draper. Then we moved on to *Futurama,* another show that Emma had gotten me hooked on. Her favorite character was Leela, the purple-ponytailed, one-eyed sewer mutant, and mine was Doctor Zoidberg, an alien lobster with a Yiddish accent. We watched two episodes, and then I said, "All rightee, missy, time for bed."

Emma's eyes got huge. "But it's only quarter to nine!"

"But your mom wants you in bed by nine. She said it twice."

"Yes, but—"

"Yes, but let's go upstairs. I'm still going to read to you for a while."

We went through the putting-on-pajamas and tooth-brushing ritual with minimum drama. Emma's pajama bottoms were pink with free-floating Hello Kitty heads, and the pink top had one big Hello Kitty head in the middle, complete with a real pink bow. Emma's room was similarly infused with Hello Kitty—duvet, sheets, posters, and Hello Kitty dolls in various costumes, including Hello Kitty as an astronaut, her big head enclosed in a plastic bubble.

As was often the case, Emma's room was catastrophically messy, but I didn't say a word. One of the advantages of being her sister as opposed to her mother is that I don't have to discipline her. After an intensive search in her bedclothes, we found her current book: Nancy Drew number 10, *Password to Larkspur Lane.* The cover showed Nancy—wearing a nifty sleeveless yellow dress, stylish and competent as always—talking to a distressed elderly woman in a wheelchair. I had introduced Emma to old-school Nancy Drew books when I came out West the previous December, and now she was as addicted as I had been at her age.

We lay down together in bed, Emma's head angled on my shoulder so she could follow along. I read two chapters, Emma listening carefully as Nancy tracked down supernatural doings at her friend Helen Corning Archer's lakeside house.

"Another chapter!" Emma said as I closed the book.

"Nope." I looked up at the Hello Kitty clock on the wall, which had a large brown Chococat head in the middle. "It's almost nine thirty."

"Can I ask you something?"

"Sure."

"Do you know about the little girl JonBenét Ramsey?"

Oh, shit. I had completely forgotten Jasmine's warning, and now there it was. "Yes," I said slowly. "Yes, I know about her."

"She lived here in Boulder."

"That's right, she did." I paused. "Who told you about her?"

"A friend."

"Famous Peach?"

Emma shook her head. "Dylan. Boy Dylan." Emma was friends with two children named Dylan, one a boy and one a girl. "He said his parents have friends who live on the same block as she did."

I had never been to see the house, but I knew it was in a nice neighborhood not too far from the Hill. "So what did Boy Dylan say?" I asked.

"He said her parents killed her and put her in the basement."

I nodded. "It's very sad."

"It's *very* sad. She was really pretty. She looked like a doll."

"Yes, she was pretty, wasn't she?"

"Can you take me to the house? Mommy said no, and Daddy said no, and Peach's mom said no."

"Does Peach want to go, too?"

"No. But I asked her mom anyway."

I sighed. "Oh, honey, we can't go. First of all, I don't have a car."

"You could borrow Mommy's. Or we could take a taxi, or a bus."

"And second—well, we don't want to be creepers. Right? If we did that, we'd be creepers."

Emma shook her head. "I'm not a creeper. I just want to go to the house."

"Well—not now. Maybe when you're older."

Emma looked down at her hands. I could tell she was deeply disappointed. It's hard being a kid sometimes; it's hard being so powerless. I felt bad for her, but I had to respect Jasmine's wishes.

"So tomorrow," I changed the subject, "we're going to see Dad, right?"

"Right," she said listlessly.

"Should we maybe try to get him to buy us ice cream?"

She shrugged. "OK."

It frustrated me to see her so unhappy. I wanted to make her feel better, but frankly even if it had been all right with Jasmine, there was no way I was going on an expedition to JonBenét Ramsey's murder site.

I got out of bed and made elaborately fussy tucking-in gestures, which usually made Emma laugh, but not that night. I leaned over and kissed her on the head, and just as I was turning off the light switch (which was, of course, in a Hello Kitty light cover), Emma said, "I say prayers for her. I say the Buddhist prayers that Mommy taught me."

My heart melted. "That's really nice of you."

"Do you think she hears them? I kinda don't think she was a Buddhist."

"Yes," I said firmly. "I'm sure she hears them."

Emma gave me a little smile, then she snuggled onto her side under the duvet. I left the room, leaving the door open a few inches in case she needed me.

8. Moms Gone Wild

The next morning I slept in. Even after I woke up, I didn't get up; I lay in my frog pajamas under the dark-gold duvet in the slightly chilly attic, watching the sunlight dance through the stained-glass window and make shifting patterns on the wall.

I knew that Emma would eventually come get me for breakfast. Sure enough, about twenty minutes later I heard footsteps running up the stairs, then a burst of knocking on the door.

"Come in!" I called.

Emma rushed in, still wearing pajamas. She belly flopped onto the futon and me. "Blueberry pancakes!" she announced. "Downstairs, now!"

She rolled off the bed and rushed off, storming down the stairs with pounding feet. I put on the fuzzy navy-blue bathrobe that Jasmine always left for me, and I walked down the two flights of stairs, the smell of pancakes and fresh-brewed coffee strengthening as I descended.

I went into the little pink kitchen and took a seat next to Emma, who sat with a fork in one hand and a knife in the other, her eyes bright and her bangs askew. Jasmine looked sleepy as she wiggled her fingers at me. There was a stack of blueberry pancakes in the center of the table, along with a stick of soft butter, a bottle of organic maple syrup, and three place settings. The kitchen was full of late September sunshine, a slightly muted gold that glinted off stainless steel and glass surfaces. I looked up at the clock—nine on the dot.

"We all slept in," Jasmine said, rising to refill her coffee mug.

"I got up first," Emma said. "I went into Mommy's room to wake her up, but then I got into bed with her and fell asleep again." She was in a perky mood, no longer weighed down by the previous night's disappointment.

"My human alarm clock," Jasmine said. "Coffee?"

"Definitely."

Jasmine passed me a mug with the purple-and-yellow Naropa seal, filled three-quarters with rich brown coffee. I added sugar (brown, raw, and free trade) and half-and-half (organic from grass-fed cows). A few sips later, I felt myself start to wake up. I looked over at Emma and Jasmine. Emma was carefully placing pats of butter on top of her pancakes, and Jasmine sat with her cheek in her palm, watching Emma contentedly. I felt an inner sigh of relief; it was always so nice to be there with them.

Over breakfast, conversation meandered in several directions. Emma recounted the plot of the *Mad Men* episode, doing a good job despite a few gross misinterpretations. Then Jasmine talked about the moms' hike, which went well, although later the pizza burned and they ended up eating ice cream for dinner.

"If I did that," Emma said, "you wouldn't like it very much."

"Well, I'm not liking it much now," Jasmine said, pushing aside her hair and leaning back in her chair. "My stomach is so full, I feel like I'm pregnant."

Which led to a discussion of her pregnancy with Emma, a topic Emma always loved to discuss, especially how Jasmine used to put headphones on her belly so Emma could listen to the Beatles. As I ate and listened, I wondered if Jasmine wanted another child. She was only three years older than me, so there was still time.

Jasmine topped off my coffee for the third time, then took a sip of her own. "So you're supposed to be at your dad's at one?" she asked.

"That's right," I told her. "Can you drop us off?"

"Sure. When do you think you'll be done?"

"I don't know—four, five? I thought I'd get the bus right after that."

"No!" Emma said, her eyes wide. "Stay! Stay another night!"

I smiled. "Oh, honey, I have to be at work at eight tomorrow."

Jasmine shrugged. "It's no problem. You can get an early bus and then go right into work. I'd be happy to drive you to the bus station."

"We'll see," I said noncommittally. I didn't want to be a bother to them. I knew they were happy to have me visit, but it was such a tiny house, and I dreaded tipping over into an unwanted guest.

"Here's the thing," Jasmine said. "Before you guys go, someone needs to clean their room."

"But, Mommy!" Emma protested. "Elizabeth's here."

"Well, you promised you'd clean it before she came, and you didn't. You can't leave it like that one day longer—the health inspectors will close down the house."

Emma rolled her eyes. "That's not going to happen, Mommy. Can Elizabeth at least help me?"

"Your sister didn't come all the way from Denver just to help you clean your room. Anyway, it'll give me and Elizabeth a chance to catch up while you're cleaning."

Emma sighed, deeply and dramatically. "OK. But can she at least come upstairs for a minute and give me advice?"

Jasmine knit her brow. "Advice on what?"

"Cleaning."

Jasmine shook her head and smiled. "Five minutes. But not a second more, Elizabeth. Don't let her rope you into helping her. You're not allowed to take your coffee mug—that'll get you back downstairs quicker."

Emma and I went upstairs. Her room had looked bad the previous night, but in the cruel light of day it was a child-sized disaster area. Dirty clothes and board games were strewn over the light-blue carpet, books were precariously stacked on the dresser and night table, a pile of folded clothes was spilling off a small yellow bench, and Hello Kitty dolls were flung everywhere. It looked like the Cat in the Hat had paid a visit, only he forgot to clean up afterward.

Emma looked at me solemnly. "I don't know what to do."

"Well," I said, putting my hands on my hips and surveying the damage. "I suggest you start small."

"What do you mean?"

"You pick one small thing, and you do that. Then you pick another small thing, and you do that. You keep taking care of small things, and then one moment you're done."

Emma mimicked my pose, putting her hands on her hips and looking around. "So what should my first small thing be?"

"How about that pile of clothes on the bench? See what you can hang up in the closet, and see what you can put in your drawers."

"You could help me," she said, looking at me slyly.

"Oh no," I laughed. "I have strict orders from your mom to go back downstairs and drink more coffee."

"You drink a lot of coffee."

"I do, don't I?" I leaned over and kissed the top of her head. "Listen to music while you clean, it'll make it go faster."

"I'm not sure where my iPod is."

"Well, if you clean up, you'll find it." I blew her a kiss, then went downstairs.

Jasmine grinned when she saw me. "Five minutes exactly! Nice work."

"It wasn't easy," I said, sitting down next to her and reclaiming my coffee mug. "She's very persuasive."

"Well, it gives us a few minutes to chat. We didn't get a chance at all yesterday, what with my moms' hike."

"Emma said you guys wanted to do the empowerment ceremony to clean up bad energy?"

Jasmine rolled her eyes. "Sometimes I think 'empowerment ceremony' is just a code word for moms getting away from their kids and smoking pot in the mountains."

I laughed. "Oh, so it's like that?"

"I mean, we do have a couple squirrelly things going on in the group that need attention, and we did actually have a ceremony, but when we got to the top of Mount Sanitas, two of the moms had joints out before I'd even taken off my pack. It was Moms Gone Wild."

A thought struck me. "Is that why the pizza burned?"

Jasmine folded in her lips and nodded. Which is something Emma does as well.

"Ah ha," I said. "Was that why it seemed like a good idea to eat ice cream for dinner?"

Jasmine nodded once again. "Yep. We were like a bunch of high school kids, giggling our heads off. It was ridiculous. But also a lot of fun." She sipped her coffee. "Oh my God, speaking of pot—I was down in south Boulder at the Table Mesa Shopping Center so I could order Emma's birthday cake, and guess who I bumped into as she was coming out of a dispensary? Jill."

Stepmother One. "Did you speak?" I asked.

Jasmine shook her head. "I waved, and she gave me the curtest of nods."

"Do you still have the restraining order against her?"

"No. It ran out recently, and I decided not to renew it. Which I hope was not a foolish decision. She still hates me; I could see it in her eyes." Jasmine pushed aside her hair. "I can't blame her. I would hate me, too.

What your dad and I did to her was wrong. I see that now, of course, but back then I was too young to know any better." She shrugged sadly. "It's just something I've got to live with."

I looked at her sympathetically, but I said nothing. I know Jasmine continues to pay for what happened with my dad. Even after all these years, she is still persona non grata in certain female segments of the Boulder literary world. Jasmine once told me that Stepmother One had actually told people not to speak to Jasmine, and such was Stepmother One's influence that they obeyed, and they continue to obey to this day. These women never stopped talking to my dad, though; he was much more powerful in that world than Stepmother One, and they didn't dare alienate him, so it all fell on Jasmine.

"Do you think you'll go see her sometime?" Jasmine asked.

"I sincerely doubt it," I replied.

Not long after I moved back to Boulder, Stepmother One sought me out, which surprised me. She had heard through the grapevine that I lost my job, and she invited me out for coffee at Amante on Walnut Street. That hadn't been too bad; we actually managed to have a civilized conversation. However I was shocked at her physical transformation. I hadn't seen her in sixteen years, and she looked completely different: her honey-blonde hair, surely her best feature, was shorn into a gray crew-cut, she wore spinstery wire-frame glasses, and her face was deeply lined from the sun and, I suspect, unhappiness. Most of all it was the expression on her face that shocked me; she radiated a bitter fury, twisted and angry and suspicious. Where was that dreamy blonde, drifting around in her colorful Indian saris and gladiator sandals? This new Stepmother One made me even more uncomfortable than the old one—but she promised that she would help me find work via her wide network on the Front Range publishing scene, which was more than my dad had done, and more than Jasmine could do.

Then things got weird. She invited me over for dinner at her Table Mesa duplex, and while I was in the second-floor bathroom, I noticed that there was no garbage can. When I came out of the bathroom holding the cardboard toilet-paper roll, I saw Stepmother One's roommate, a pale, thin graduate student with short pink hair.

"There's no garbage can in the bathroom," I said. "Can I throw this out in your room?"

The woman put a finger to her lips and drew me into her room. "We're not allowed to have garbage," she whispered.

"Beg pardon?"

"Boulder is committed to eventually having zero waste, but Jill wants to do it now, so there's no garbage can in the bathroom. I'm not allowed to have one in my room, either."

"But that's insane," I said.

She looked relieved. "I'm so glad you said that. I'm moving out in a few weeks—I can't stand it here."

"But meanwhile, what do I do with this?" I asked, holding out the cardboard roll.

"Put it in your pocket and throw it out after you leave. It's just easier that way."

Sure enough, over dinner it became obvious that Stepmother One had developed some kind of Green obsessive-compulsive disorder. She talked—nay, lectured—about environmental issues during our entire meal of kale and tofu, filling me in on her role as secretary of the CU Boulder Zero-Waste Fact-Finding Commission. I really hadn't come over to talk about garbage, but I listened patiently as long as I could, and then I tuned her out. Just as I did when I was twenty and she lectured me about eating cereal for dinner.

The next and final time I saw her, she took me to a small networking gathering of her media friends at Brasserie Ten Ten, a fancy bistro in downtown Boulder. I appreciated her effort, but I was surprised at these women. They had the same bitter quality as Stepmother One, a mean middle-aged sheen, topped off by a snooty attitude that I couldn't fathom. I had met plenty of snobs in Manhattan, and it must be said that under certain circumstances, Mr. Dove could be a bit pretentious. But that was New York City, and Mr. Dove and his wife had been friends with Jacqueline Onassis, which struck me as a genuine reason to be snobby. These women, however, lived in Boulder, Colorado, and a supercilious attitude seemed way out of place. They weren't very nice to me, and they weren't very nice to each other, either. They all drank way too much wine, including Stepmother One. By the end of the night they were drunk and telling dildo stories, and I had retreated into myself completely, just waiting for the evening to end.

On the drive back to my dad's home, Stepmother One started in on me. Just like old times. "You weren't very friendly, young lady."

"*I* wasn't friendly? They were really cold to me."

"You know, I try to do something nice for you, and you don't even give me the courtesy of a thank you."

"I planned to thank you when I got out of the car."

"You always were ungrateful. You took and took from me and your father, and you never gave one thing back."

I looked at her in astonishment. I barely saw her and my dad during my summers in Boulder, and I rarely asked them for anything. I had only been a teenager—what precisely was I supposed to give back? "That's not true."

"Don't you tell me what's true." She pulled up outside my dad's house—her old house. "You're just like your father, self-centered and rude."

"Thanks a lot," I said as I unfastened my seatbelt with trembling fingers. "It's been a delight." I opened the door and got out, then I poked my head back in. "Oh, and by the way? There's never going to be zero waste, so I suggest you break down and buy a garbage can." I slammed the door behind me and marched up to my dad's house.

And that was that.

I took another sip of coffee. "No, I won't be seeing her again," I told Jasmine.

She nodded. "That's a shame. She's changed so much, hasn't she? But then, she was publicly humiliated by your dad. And by me."

"Well, she didn't have to drag out that messy court case, did she?" I shook my head. "Anyhow. That's ancient history. It's just that she's so bitter. Her Green OCD doesn't help, either."

"So tell me about Quill & Ink," Jasmine said. "Are you liking it any better? I always thought it would be a cool place to work."

I shrugged. "It's all right. I love books, but I love editing them, not shelving them. It's like if you worked at Naropa, but instead of being a professor you were a janitor."

She laughed. "I see your point. But look, one day the economy will get better, and publishing companies will start hiring again. Or maybe there'll be a start-up; lots of entrepreneurs come out to Boulder and Denver to start new businesses."

"Maybe."

"Definitely! With your skills, and eleven years at Blue Heron Books, anyone would want you." She sighed. "I wish I had more contacts. But at least I can keep my ears open for you. You should keep checking Craigslist and Mediabistro."

"You're right, I suppose. Meanwhile, at least I have a job." I smiled at her. "There's a whole Zwelland section in the poetry bay, by the way. You, my mom, dad, and Jill."

Jasmine laughed. "I see that at the Boulder Bookstore and Barnes & Noble, too. Our whole messy family, on display for everyone to read. One day Emma will join us."

I nodded. But I truly hoped that Emma would not end up like them. A poet or a writer of some kind, sure, but hopefully not one who only saw themselves. I remembered a movie I had seen for free on Hulu before my laptop died. One of the characters was a book editor, and she said something like: "Writers don't realize that although their feelings are interesting, the world is interesting, too." My great hope for Emma as a writer is that she will be able to look beyond her own nervous system.

"How's your writing going?" I asked.

Jasmine's eyes lit up. "Something really exciting has happened. I've discovered haiku." She waved a hand. "I mean, of course I've always known about haiku, and I've written a few here and there, but I was more interested in juicy, epic poems. Anyhow, the fellow who usually teaches haiku in the fall got a fellowship to Oxford, so they asked me to step in."

"So are you just reading them?"

"At first it was just reading. There's so many masters—Basho, of course, and Buson, Ikkyu, Shiki, and dozens of minor poets. Then for another class I had to reread that great *Paris Review* interview Ted Berrigan did with Jack Kerouac, and there's a whole section where Kerouac explains how to write a haiku. I don't know, it's like the two worlds just clicked together, all my Beat background and the history of haiku, and I suddenly saw an entry point. I read all Kerouac's haiku, and then I started reading Gary Snyder. I had never liked him as much as Allen or Gregory, but now I'm finally ready for him, especially his haiku."

"That's great, Jasmine."

"It feels great. I haven't had a poetic explosion for a while."

"Well, you're a mom. A single mom. It's hard to find time."

"That's another thing about writing haiku—it's much more mom-friendly. I can always dash off a few whenever I'm sitting in the car waiting for Emma. I rework them later, of course, but I'm always writing and it feels great." Her eyes twinkled. "Haiku also have another advantage."

"What's that?"

"Your dad hates them. They're much too small for him." She shrugged. "It's good for me to find a form that he hasn't explored. I feel like as a poet I've always been living under his shadow."

I couldn't disagree with that. I knew his work, and I knew her work, and her poems sounded like female versions of his. Stepmother One also wrote like my dad, although less so nowadays. Only my mom had her own voice, but sometimes it was so angry and bitter it hardly seemed worth having.

Jasmine and I talked a bit more about haiku, and she even read me a few from her clothbound notebook. I liked them; they were airy and vivid, and a few were quite funny. Then she put down her notebook and looked up at the clock. "About an hour till you go see your dad."

"How has he been about seeing Emma?"

"Like pulling teeth. Every time he's supposed to see her, I have to call him the day before to remind him. Then talk him out of whatever excuse he has for not spending time with her. I called yesterday before we went to Dushanbe, and sure enough he'd forgotten that the two of you were coming over today." She closed her eyes and sighed deeply. "Thank God I meditate. Otherwise I would have strangled him years ago."

Or ended up like my mom or Stepmother One, I thought.

Jasmine shook her head. "He only sees Emma every other Sunday, but he can hardly manage that. I try to keep her out of all this, but of course she overhears things. It's not lost on Emma that her dad forgets about her. But short of taking him to court or asking him for more money, what can I do to make him pay attention to her?" She rested a cheek on her palm. "Why is it that the only way I can get through to your father is by threatening his vanity or his wallet?"

"I worry about Emma," I said. "I don't want her to be all messed up about men."

"Me, either." Jasmine paused. "Do you think *you're* all messed up about men?"

My heart tugged. "Actually, what happened to me had nothing to do with my dad. He's caused a lot of people a lot of trouble, but he wasn't behind 9/11."

Jasmine nodded and looked at me steadily. We were silent a while; what was there to say? The story is pretty straightforward. I met Max in the summer of 1997, the same year I started at Blue Heron. We met at a bar, which sounds sleazy, but it was a nice bar on the Upper East Side and we were both there to celebrate coworkers' birthdays. He was an IT consultant, a very good one, and he also loved books and movies and art and Manhattan. He did not write poetry and he did not worship the Beats and he did not know who my parents were until I told him. He wasn't the most handsome man on earth, but he was a gentle soul, with a heart as big as a house.

My mom died on Saturday, September 1, 2001. She was only fifty-one. It was her heart, which finally gave out due to excessive drinking and poor diet and complete lack of exercise. Walking from the car to the liquor store is not a workout, even if you do it every day. One of my mom's acolytes found her slumped over the kitchen table. The woman called me, and Max and I went to New Jersey immediately. My mom was buried two days later at a small Methodist church a few blocks from our house. My mom wasn't a Methodist—her only religion was poetry—but that was the best solution we could come up with. The acolyte promised to organize a memorial at the Poetry Project at St. Mark's Church, which in fact she did about three months later.

I spent the next few days in a flurry of activity. I wanted to clean out my mom's little house as quickly as possible so I could sell it and use the money to pay off her debts. Max offered to stay and help, but he was in the middle of a huge work project, so I told him to come back on the weekend. I was also my mom's literary executor, and since she already had an arrangement with Rutgers University in New Brunswick, all I needed to do was pack everything up in boxes for Rutgers to archive. Luckily my mom kept all her papers in pretty good order, so it wasn't too difficult to sort them out, and the people at Rutgers promised to come get them as soon as I was ready.

Things got complicated when I found a literary time bomb. In a large pink box in the attic, hidden behind dusty Christmas ornaments, I found my mom's correspondence with the famous married poet. There were his letters to her, and also her letters to him, which he had bundled up in a white ribbon and sent back with a note asking her not to contact him anymore.

At first I intended to include all the letters in the Rutgers material, but as I looked through my mother's letters to the poet, I started to have my doubts. At first her letters were shy and admiring, gradually changing to loving and devoted, but by the end they were pretty damn crazy. I wanted to burn them all, but I was afraid of committing some heinous crime against American letters. On the other hand, I didn't want scholars pouring through my mom's emotional wreckage. Not to mention that the poet was still alive and still married, and even more famous due to recently winning the Pulitzer Prize. Did I have an obligation to contact him, and did the letters legally belong to him now?

I called Max and told him what was going on, and he suggested I call my dad. I was reluctant to involve my dad in my mother's chaos because I figured he could care less. But I have to say, my dad came through for me. I called and told him the whole story, and without hesitating he said, "Burn them all. That's your mother's private business; don't let anyone drag her through the mud." Then he put Jasmine on the phone so I could tell her, and she agreed: "Burn them. No question about it." So when Max came back on Friday afternoon, he burned the letters in the backyard while I took a nap.

Anyhow. Max and I worked hard all weekend, and by Sunday afternoon we were done. The next day both the Salvation Army and a team of people from Rutgers were coming to clear everything out. Max offered to stay; he said his assistant, Michi, could hold down the fort for a few days, but I knew he was in the middle of a crucial project, and I didn't have the heart to keep him in New Jersey. He wasn't the most physically strong person; he was tall, but he was a beanpole like me, and I doubted he could help the half-dozen brawny men I had hired for the day. So Sunday night, I sent him back to Manhattan.

Monday was a long, tiring day. By four in the afternoon my mom's house was empty, save an air mattress, bedding, and the coffee maker—I figured I would be coming back again for various real estate matters, and there wasn't a hotel in the little town. I had dinner at the Greek diner down the street, which was owned by my old friend Helena Papadopoulous' family. When I came home, I called Max. I told him I planned to sleep in the next day, then I'd take a bus into the city and we could meet up at my place late afternoon. Then I did something I'd never done before or since: I took a Valium. It was one of my mom's; I had saved the bottle in case of emergencies, and after the week I had just endured, I felt like I was in the middle of one.

I slept in the next morning, and when I woke up in the bare room, I checked the time on my cell phone. It was a few minutes after nine, and I had three messages. I fell asleep again, and the next time I woke it was almost eleven, and I had twenty-five messages. I was surprised; I never got that many calls.

As it turns out, Max and Michi were working near the top of the South Tower. When the first plane hit the North Tower, there was an announcement in their office to remain calm and stay put. But Max felt a deep internal punch in his gut, and a voice in his head said, "*RUN!*" He grabbed Michi's hand and, leaving their laptops and expensive equipment behind, they began a mad headlong scramble down ninety-odd flights of stairs. Because they took heed and left at once, they were below the second plane when it hit the South Tower, and by the time the South Tower fell, they were running up Broadway in a panicked sea of people.

So they made it. They ran all the way to Max's apartment on Greene Street in Soho and, oddly, fell right into bed and had sex. It could have been a one-time thing, but over the next days, that's where they stayed.

I stayed ignorant in New Jersey, relieved that Max was safe, and more than willing to avoid the painful chaos in Manhattan for as long as possible. Mr. Dove told me to stay exactly where I was. "My dear," he told me over the phone, "the greatest city in the world has been reduced to a hellhole. Be safe in New Jersey."

So I did stay, until October 1, to be precise. Hansika sent me a fat manuscript to work on, and I used my free time to deal with the realtor, a tiny redheaded lady with a snappy can-do attitude, who managed to sell my mom's house during one of the worst crises in Western history.

Max and I talked on the phone often during those weeks. He insisted I stay in New Jersey, but he refused to come join me; he was getting trauma treatment, he said, and he didn't want to leave. If I had gone back right away, things probably would have been different. If I had asked him to stay in New Jersey that Monday and help me with the movers, things definitely would have been different. As it turned out, when I came back to Manhattan on October 1—the city in shock, smelling horribly from the underground fires still burning at Ground Zero—Max sat me down and told me gently that he and Michi were in love. They had gone through something together that they couldn't explain to anyone else, and as time went on they saw that their feelings were genuine and not just a fluke.

At first I didn't believe him. I had just lost my mom, almost lost my city, and it was inconceivable that I should lose him as well. However as time went on, I had to accept the unacceptable, and in spring 2002 Max and Michi got married.

That period of my life is a black hole. If it weren't for my family at Blue Heron, frequent calls with Helena Papadopoulos and Jasmine, trips to Boulder to hold Emma, and work, work, work, I don't know how I would have survived. Eventually I came to believe that something might have been brewing between Max and Michi all along, and 9/11 was only the catalyst. But I'll never really know one way or another.

"I'm sorry I never met Max," Jasmine said. "Are you two still in touch?"

"No." I was quiet a while. Then I said, "I dream about him sometimes. It's always the same dream. Do you remember those huge escalators in the World Trade Center, the ones that went down to the PATH trains?"

She shook her head. "Your dad and I didn't get downtown during our trip, and that's my only time on the East Coast."

"I dream I'm on the escalator going down, and he's on the one going up. But he's far away and he doesn't see me, so we pass without speaking." I took a deep, shaky breath. "Do you know there's a World Trade Center in Denver? It's two towers."

"Really? Oh, wait—it's on the 16th Street Mall, right?"

"Between Tremont and Court."

"That's so weird. But they're not new, are they?"

"I think they've been there for a few decades, so it's not like they're a memorial or something. I don't like them."

"I don't blame you. Elizabeth," she said gently. "When's the last time you were on a date?"

Just then footsteps came bounding down the stairs, and Emma burst into the kitchen. "I'm done! Come see, come see. All my Hello Kittys are lined up on my bed."

As we walked upstairs behind Emma, Jasmine reached out and squeezed my hand.

9. Worth Talking To

At one o'clock exactly, Jasmine pulled her green Subaru in front of our dad's house. Emma leapt out of the car and raced to the front door. I hesitated a moment, steeling myself for the visit.

"Ready?" Jasmine asked sympathetically.

"There's no 'ready' anymore," I said. "There's just enduring."

"Good luck. Call me when you need to get picked up."

"What are your plans?"

"Go home and take a nap."

I laughed. "Moms Gone Tired?"

"Precisely."

My father has a beautiful house. Perhaps the oldest and most imposing section of Boulder is the Mapleton Hill Historic District, an exclusive neighborhood not far from the Flatirons and a short walk to the Pearl Street Mall. It's a hilly area with grand Victorian and Queen Anne houses, as well as old maple and cottonwood trees planted by settlers in the late 1800s. My dad lives on Mapleton, and his Queen Anne is a beauty, chocolate brown with gables, balustrades, fancy ivory-colored spindlework, a ruby-red front door, and a square tower on top complete with a weathervane. A City of Boulder Landmark plaque by the front door proclaims that the house was built in 1877 by Silas Grange, who was famous for organizing buffalo hunts and producing vast amounts of whiskey. There is also a small but immaculately landscaped front lawn, and a roomy garage that houses my dad's black SUV and his mint-green vintage Jaguar.

Emma was waiting for me at the front door with bright eyes, jumping up and down with excitement. Our dad got jumping just like I did, although he hardly deserved it. I could hear his booming voice from inside the house, so I opened the door and we went in. Many people in Boulder don't lock their doors, and in my dad's case, given that he has valuable artwork and rare manuscripts, this strikes me as another example of his hubris.

We entered the foyer, which like the rest of the house has polished wood floors and antique Oriental rugs. There's a narrow staircase with a gleaming banister, and the steep steps have cream carpeting with gold stair rods at each step. My dad's voice was coming from the living room, so I took Emma's hand and turned right to pass through an open arched doorway.

The living room is a tasteful space that houses the best of my dad's art collection. The room has the original tin ceiling, and the walls are a subtle light green with ivory-colored molding. The mullioned windows have half-circles of stained glass on top, and on sunny days the colors from the window dance on the fawn-colored Oriental rug. Well-organized bookshelves line most of the walls, the books interspersed with framed photos of me and Emma and my dad's famous friends. The walls are packed with stunning abstract art, and a few funky sculptures sit on elegant tables. There's also a freestanding pink oval thing in one corner; apparently it's quite valuable, but according to Emma it looks like a booger. There is a polished rectangular coffee table of dark wood, surrounded by a Queen Anne sofa and wing chairs in light-purple brocade. Sitting in one of the wing chairs, talking on an old-school black phone in his majestic, booming, confident voice, there he was: Jasper Zwelland. The Great Poet. Our dad.

When we walked into the room, he didn't even pause. He leaned over the coffee table and rapidly wrote a series of notes using one of the black Sharpies and pads of yellow legal paper that he keeps all over the house in strategic places. Then, still talking, he held up the notes one by one: INTERVIEW. SEATTLE POST. IMPORTANT. Emma and I looked at each other and sat down on the couch. We were used to our dad's poetic emergencies.

As we sat, Emma pressed up close to me, and we both stared at our dad. I don't know how she saw him, but to me he more and more resembled a walrus. He is a handsome, imposing man with vivid green eyes, olive-colored skin, and thick black-gray hair that he wears in a well-trimmed ponytail and bushy sideburns. He has an excess of chest hair—just as I have a lot of hair on my arms and legs, and one day Emma would as well. For some reason my dad always makes a point of exposing his chest hair. I'm sure he sees the rug of hair as proof of his virility, but to me it's pretty gross, and I can't believe that any woman could fall for his oozy sexuality.

But they do fall, again and again and again. Worse, my dad has a habit of playing with his chest hair, running his fingers through it while he speaks, which he was in fact doing right then as he spoke on the phone. Emma and I had christened our dad's chest hair "The Beast," and Emma once wrote an epic poem about the Beast jumping off our dad's chest and slaying a posse of cowboy ghosts roaming the Flatirons.

But what really makes our dad resemble a walrus is his weight. When I was little he was tall and lean like Emma and me, but over the years he had packed on the pounds. You couldn't call him obese, but he is at least eighty pounds overweight, most of it settled in his upper body and enormous stomach. As his weight crept up, he abandoned the jeans and dashikis he had always favored and started wearing silk pajamas and elaborate robes with rich embroidery, usually dragons. He got the idea after doing an interview with the painter Julian Schnabel, who was likewise large in size and personality. In Boulder, my dad's eccentric dress is regarded as further proof of his literary merit, a charming aspect of his artistic imperative.

So between the height, the good looks, the weight, the chest hair, the pajamas, the voice, the books, the awards, the prestigious position at Naropa, the network of famous friends, the nationwide and indeed international fame, my dad cannot be ignored. Which is how he likes it.

The interview went on, and Emma and I continued to sit and watch him speak. I could tell that Emma was impatient for our dad to get off the phone; her foot was tapping and her lips were pressed together, as if she was making an effort to hold in all the millions of things she had to tell him. Which I'm sure she was. Yet our dad didn't look anywhere near finished. He was comfortably ensconced in his favorite chair, cozy in his navy-blue pajamas and ivory-colored silk robe, his hand roaming through the Beast, his eyes looking up at the tin ceiling as he spoke.

"Boulder feeds me. The energy is essential for my creativity. If you take the Flatirons as a metaphor—and I highly suggest you do, all nature is a metaphor—then you see that Boulder represents an upthrust of energy, a paradigm of creation and renewal."

That was the sort of talk my dad could spew out in his sleep. It was also the sort of talk that could literally put me to sleep, since I had been hearing it my entire life. The journalist must have been eating it up, though, because I could tell from my dad's tone of voice that he felt safe. If the journalist had been attempting to pierce my dad's armor of words—which did happen on occasion—my dad would have sounded defensive, and he would have ended the interview as quickly as possible.

"I don't write poems, I *live* poems. Every day is a page, every hour a rhyme, every breath a comma. The entire world is a poem, pulsating and heaving and throbbing."

I looked at Emma, and she looked at me. She was biting her bottom lip, struggling not to laugh. I winked at her. Sometimes I think she's smarter than all of us put together.

"Well, naturally, given my writing and my position at Naropa, I've come in contact with all the original Beat poets. I say 'original,' since there are still many of us latter-day Beats roaming the earth. We talked about Allen earlier, of course . . . No, I didn't have the great pleasure of meeting Jack Kerouac. Both he and Neal Cassady had already died by the time I came out here and connected with Allen. I did get to know Jan Kerouac quite well, though. She visited Naropa in 1982 for a conference on her father, and we often shared a hot tub together. She was quite fond of me; I imagine I reminded her of Jack."

If there was a bullshit meter above my dad's head, it would have been straining against its topmost limit, red-hot and ready to burst. According to what I could gather, during the 1982 conference my dad (who was married to Stepmother One at the time) had followed Jan Kerouac around like a puppy, and she once kicked him out of a hot tub when his advances became too much for her.

"Williams Burroughs! I certainly did know Bill, and we were quite close up until his death. Bill taught fiction at the first Naropa Summer Writing Program, and he was a wonderful presence here over the years. We talked about writing often, and his cut-up poems were a great inspiration to me. As was his lifestyle. In fact, let me tell you a funny story. The first time I met Bill—"

I stood up. I didn't want Emma to hear the story, which involved William Burroughs holding up an enormous audience because the young man who was supposed to bring him a joint was running late. My dad was posted outside to intercept the young man, and afterward my dad got high with the Great Beat and his friends. Emma knew about lesbians and empowerment ceremonies, but I wasn't quite sure what she knew about drugs. Jasmine was an occasional smoker who never kept pot in the house, but my dad was always indiscreet, witness the roach in the alabaster Art Deco ashtray on the coffee table in front of us. If it was at all possible, I wanted to prevent Emma from growing up as I had, where the presence of pot was as normal as orange juice in the fridge.

"Let's go upstairs and look at our room," I whispered to Emma. She nodded eagerly. We stood up, and I caught my dad's eye and motioned upstairs. His eyes widened and, still talking, he picked up his Sharpie to write something. Ignoring him, I took Emma's hand and left the room.

We walked up the narrow staircase to the second floor, which has a long hallway with a plush peach-and-cream Oriental rug, and more abstract art on the wall. There is a door to the tower, which is our dad's study and strictly off limits. There are also four bedrooms—our dad's massive room at the end of the hall, two small guest rooms, and a medium-sized room that is officially known as the Daughter Room. This was my room growing up, then it was Emma's room, and when I came back she and I joined forces.

Our dad had told us that we could decorate the Daughter Room however we liked, and he even supplied us with some nice furniture. There are twin beds with hand-carved headboards, painted white with pink and yellow flowers. Above each bed is a large wooden letter E, decorated by Emma and me with feathers and beads and shiny hearts. The wallpaper is an explosion of multicolored polka dots, and the walls are decorated with our paintings and drawings as well as a few collages. Strings of small Christmas lights hang along the molding next to the tin ceiling, which is painted a rather shocking pink. Hello Kitty has managed to slink into the Daughter Room, too; three identical Hello Kitty dolls sit on top of the white antique dresser, all dressed as cowboys in pink vests, pink cowboy hats, and tiny pink boots with spurs. Best of all, the room has a spectacular view of the Flatirons. We pushed aside the white curtains with pink polka dots to reveal the mountains, which that day stood in crisp relief against a vivid blue sky.

We admired our handiwork for a while, then Emma said, "I have to go to the bathroom."

"OK," I said.

"I want to use the one in Daddy's room."

Our dad's enormous room at the end of the hall has a bathroom en suite, with a Jacuzzi tub and a white antique cabinet with glass doors, filled to the brim with oils, creams, lotions, and body butters. Emma and I love sneaking into his room and using his products, putting everything back carefully to avoid detection.

We left the Daughter Room and joined hands as we walked down the hall. The door to our dad's room was closed, so I turned the glass doorknob and we went inside. On the enormous four-poster bed, there was a young woman, early twenties at most, sitting cross-legged and reading *The Irony of the Leash* by Eileen Myles. She looked up at us and smiled. She was extremely beautiful, with long, thick auburn hair cut in layers, cornflower-blue eyes, and porcelain skin with a splash of cinnamon-colored freckles across her nose. She wore jeans and a loose green sweater, and the toenails on her bare feet glinted with silver polish.

"Hello," she said.

"Hello," we replied. Emma's hand tightened in mine.

"I'm Jane. You must be Jasper's daughters. He talks about you all the time."

"I'm Elizabeth," I said. "This is Emma."

"Well, I'm glad to finally meet you both. Is Jasper done with his interview yet?"

Just then a roar sounded from downstairs. "Daughters! I'm done! Come here at once."

Jane smiled. "Guess that answers my question. See you again soon, I hope."

"Daughters!" our dad bellowed.

Emma and I backed out of the room into the hallway. We were too stunned even to say good-bye. It wasn't a surprise that our dad had a girlfriend; he always had at least one at any given time. It's just that he never let any of them enter his lair, his precious house. Yet there was Jane, perfectly comfortable and looking right at home.

Emma used the immaculate ivory-colored bathroom in the hall, then we went downstairs. Our dad was off the phone, and Emma immediately rushed over to him. "Daddy!" she cried, jumping onto his enormous lap. He smiled, gave her a hug and patted her hair. Emma jumped off to get her notebook from her backpack, so I went over to our dad, put an arm around his shoulders, and gave him an awkward hug. He smiled and patted my arm.

I went back to the couch. Emma jumped back on his lap, talking a mile a minute about her latest poems and how he needed to see them right away. She opened her notebook, found the right page, and put the book in his hands. Our dad went through the poems quickly, but he did read them, so I have to give him credit for that. Emma snuggled into him as he read, her eyes never leaving his face.

Once I must have loved him as much as she did. In fact, I'm sure I did. I know I missed him terribly when my mom and I moved to New Jersey, but then I didn't see him again for seven whole years, and despite his occasional phone calls and gifts, he gradually faded away. When I was Emma's age I never talked to him face-to-face, and I never sat on his lap. When I did finally see him again, it was too late; we had missed our moment, and we never really got it back.

At that point in our relationship, my dad and I got along in the barest possible way. He loved me, I was pretty sure of that, but I always felt like my presence made him uncomfortable. He seemed to be genuinely fond of Emma, but even that had its limits. Emma never noticed, or if she did, she had never said anything. For her, things were simple: he was her daddy, and she adored him.

When our dad was finished with Emma's poems, he put the notebook on the coffee table with greatest respect. He said that she was an extremely talented young lady, and he was very proud of her. Emma beamed as she stared up into his face.

I let them have their moment, but finally I had to address the elephant in the room.

"Dad," I said. "There's a girl in your bedroom."

He looked solemn. "Oh. You saw her."

"We sure did."

"Was she dressed?"

"Yes, Dad. She was dressed."

"Oh, good." He gave Emma a hug.

"Dad, why don't you introduce her to us properly? She doesn't have to hide upstairs like a prisoner."

He winced. "I didn't want things to get complicated."

"Like they're not already?" I sighed. I looked at Emma; she was still snuggled against our dad, and she was following the conversation with wide-open eyes, not missing a thing. I thought that I probably shouldn't talk to him that way in front of her, so I decided to drop it.

"Anyway," I said. "Let's go get some coffee."

Emma looked up at our dad. "Elizabeth drinks a lot of coffee."

He laughed. "Oh, she does, does she? Well, I'm not quite ready yet. I still have to do yoga."

I couldn't believe it. "Yoga! Dad, you're supposed to spend the afternoon with us."

"Yes, I know that. I had planned to do yoga before you got here, but I got confused about the interview time because Seattle's in a different zone. So I need to do it now."

I narrowed my eyes. "Dad, Emma's been looking forward to seeing you all day. All weekend."

He glared at me. "Elizabeth Zwelland. Daughter. Doing yoga is part of my commitment to myself. It's very important that I keep those commitments. I would hope that you of all people could understand."

Ah, yes—the petulant side of my dad. Always a pleasure.

In other circumstances I would have challenged him, and then he would have exploded with anger. Jasmine says that my dad has anger issues, but he really only gets angry when he doesn't get his way. I looked at Emma, whose eyes were about as wide as they could go. It wasn't worth trying to make him change his mind; I had seen his angry outbursts often enough to know I didn't want to witness another one.

"Fine," I capitulated. "How long do you need?"

"A half hour," he said sniffily.

"Well, it's a beautiful day, so how about Emma and I walk over to the Idealplex? By the time you drive over, we should be there."

"If we go slow," Emma chimed in.

"If we go slow," I agreed, smiling at her and trying to rein in my fury.

"Fine," our dad said. "I'll meet you at Vic's in a half hour. Forty-five minutes."

"Fine," I said back. "But let's go to Pekoe."

"Pekoe?" He knit his brow. "But we always go to Vic's."

"All right, Dad," I said. "Vic's in forty-five minutes. Emma, don't forget your notebook."

Emma gave our dad a hug and he kissed her on the forehead, then she scooted off his lap. As she packed up her notebook, I stared stonily at the pink booger statue. I have no beef with Vic's. In fact, during the six months I lived at my dad's, I went to Vic's practically every day for coffee. Vic's also gives away free pens, and all the pens in my apartment are from there. The problem was that Vic's is my dad's hangout, so whenever we go there we are surrounded by a half-dozen people who want to talk to him. Which he always does, and in the process ignores Emma and me. This had happened so often that it had become a pattern. For myself I didn't care—I expected nothing from my dad—but Emma was little, and she needed him.

But Vic's it was. We walked outside into the lovely day. It was past two and the sun was shining, but there was a breeze from the mountains, and the sidewalks were shady from all the big trees. Emma and I walked slowly, very slowly, discussing all manner of things, including the name of the string that caterpillars hang from, how Hello Kitty's friend Keroppi got his name, and the best place in Boulder to get ice cream.

When we got to Broadway, the traffic picked up a bit, so I took Emma's hand.

"Is that OK?" I asked.

"Is what OK?"

"Me taking your hand in public. Because one day you'll be too old for that."

"Elizabeth?"

"Yes?"

"You're weird."

I laughed. "Yes, I'm weird. Thank you very much."

"Elizabeth?"

"Yes?"

"Do you think Daddy's mad at us?"

"No. I think he was almost mad."

"Because sometimes Daddy gets mad. *Really* mad."

My stomach tightened. "With you?"

"No, not with me. With Mommy." She looked up at me. "And with you."

That's because we're the only ones who stand up to him, I thought. But I didn't say it. Emma was a bright girl, and one day she would figure things out for herself. When she did, both Jasmine and I would do our best to be there for her.

We were standing on the corner of Broadway and Maxwell waiting for a break in the traffic so we could cross, when suddenly I heard a familiar sound: QUACK! QUACK! I turned my head and saw a brown hillbilly bus chugging up Broadway. Oh no—Banjo Billy's tour bus! Could I never get away from their beeping?

As the bus passed us, people stuck their heads out the window, waving wildly and yelling, "Yee-haw!"

Emma waved back enthusiastically. "Elizabeth!" she said. "Wave!"

Reluctantly I lifted a hand. "They're always beeping at me," I complained. "And it's always weird beeps, like a quack or a horse whinny."

Emma knit her brow. It always disturbed her when we didn't agree. "I like the weird beeps. I like the quacks the best."

"Well, they're funny," I conceded, "but you might not want to get beeped at every day. They pass by my apartment twice a day, and if I'm outside they always beep at me."

Emma looked up at me. "QUACK!" she yelled.

I laughed. "All right, Miss Quack. There's no more cars; let's cross over."

Although we had walked slowly, I could see by the clock on top of the Boulder Credit Union that we were still fifteen minutes early. We could have gone into Vic's right away, but I was determined to make our dad pay for our drinks, so we wandered around the Idealplex to pass the time. "Idealplex" is the name that Emma and I gave to the little strip mall by our dad's house. But the Idealplex is not a typical string of anonymous stores attached to a parking lot; it is actually quite charming, with all the stores linked by a wavy light-yellow roof with a row of small light bulbs in front. Across the street there is another row of stores, including a Whole Foods that was originally Ideal Market, an old Boulder supermarket from the 1940s. In the parking lot there's still a large retro sign with white neon letters declaring IDEAL BROADWAY SHOPS.

Emma and I peeked into Vic's on the extremely remote possibility that our dad was early, but of course he wasn't. We went next door to Jacque Michelle, a colorful store that sells clothes and cheery knickknacks. Emma and I modeled a few hats for each other, checked out the clearance shelf in the back, then examined the stuffed animals by the front window, which like all the stores in the Idealplex faced a stunning view of the Flatirons.

"Should we go to Vic's now?" Emma said at last. "Daddy might be there."

"Sure," I said, taking her hand. "Let's go."

We went over to Vic's and walked inside. Our dad wasn't there, but I spied a free table by the window, so we sat down there to wait. We both took off our jackets, and Emma unearthed her notebook and pen and started writing something. I looked around the room; the café was quite crowded, as usual. Vic's attracts all sorts of customers, but there are usually a fair number of middle-aged men like my dad holding court. Vic's is sometimes a bit of a testosterone fest, but I love it anyway: I love the colorful faux-Fiestaware cups and saucers, the splashy art on the walls, the large front windows with the Flatiron view, and the thick tables in pink, yellow, and orange. They only play jazz at Vic's; I don't know much about jazz, but according to my dad, who is a big fan and collector, the jazz at Vic's is all classics from the 1950s.

Suddenly Emma sat straight up. "It's Daddy!" she cried.

I looked out the window. There was our dad out in the parking lot, in his navy-blue silk pajamas and ivory-colored robe, hurrying toward the door. Emma waved wildly and started bouncing up and down in her seat.

When our dad walked in, the whole place exploded. A few men got up and rushed over to him, and others turned in their seats and called out his name. One man took our dad's arm and tried to get him to sit, but our dad said, "No, no. I'm over here with the Daughters."

He sat down at our table, arranged his robe around his seat, then put both hands flat on the table. "Double espresso. Please."

I held out my hand. "Money."

He sighed heavily, as if he couldn't understand a world where he actually had to use his own money to pay for what he wanted. He took a twenty out of his thick leather wallet and gave it to me, then Emma and I went to the counter to order our drinks: our dad's espresso, hot chocolate with whip cream for Emma, and a large triple latte for me.

By the time we came back with the drinks—me carrying the latte and hot chocolate, Emma carrying our dad's espresso with both hands, taking small, careful steps so she wouldn't spill a drop—three men had drawn chairs up to our table, and two others at nearby tables had moved closer, all of them staring eagerly at our dad. Apparently a friend of Frank Sinatra's once proclaimed, "It's Frank's world; the rest of us are just living in it." I often felt like that with my dad: wherever he goes, he is always at the center. Which means that you and everyone else are at the periphery.

Emma and I sat down and started our drinks. None of the men said hello to us; it was if we weren't even there. The men talked rapidly at our dad—one was a high school teacher who wanted our dad to come speak to his class, another a neighbor who asked our dad to be a special guest at a potluck fundraiser to fight climate change, another was organizing a silent auction at his ashram and hoped our dad could contribute a signed book or two. "We'd love it if you came as well," the man said to our dad. "Be sure to bring your pretty girlfriend."

Did everyone know about Jane except for us? I wondered wearily. Then I wondered if Jasmine knew. She hadn't said anything, but maybe she was just being discreet.

Emma tried to get our dad's attention. She asked him for a sip of espresso, which he gave her. Next she asked to sit on his lap, but he declined because there was not enough room. He patted her head, then turned back to his fans.

I motioned toward the notebook and said to Emma, "Want to play the Sentence Game?"

She nodded eagerly. The Sentence Game is what we usually do during excursions to Vic's with our dad, or whenever we find ourselves at loose ends. We make up a story one sentence at a time, alternating turns. The weirder the sentence, the better.

"You start," I said.

Emma put the Hello Kitty pen to her lips and looked at the ceiling. Then she smiled and wrote in a flash:

> Once upon a time there was a blue polka dot mouse.

I took the pen and wrote:

> His best friend was a green squirrel who wore a fancy cowboy hat everywhere he went, including the bathtub.

Emma took the pen back and wrote:

> One day the mouse asked the squirrel "Are you a piece of cheese?"

I wrote:

> The squirrel replied, "No, sir, I am certainly not a piece of cheese, so please don't make any plans to put me on a cracker and eat me, or I shall be most upset and cranky and cross."

Emma looked at me. "That's a long sentence."

"But it is just one sentence, Miss Sentence Police."

"Well—that's OK for now."

I tried not to laugh; that's something our dad often says.

The story flew off in several surreal directions, eventually including Sally Draper from *Mad Men,* a few space aliens, and our dad's neighbor's dog, a fat pit-bull named Nellie. Eventually we could go no further, so Emma took the notebook and held the story right in front of our dad's face, interrupting his tale about his good buddy Ken Kesey.

"Daddy, look!" she said. "We wrote a story. You have to read it."

Our dad gave another heavy sigh—imagine, when you have children you actually have to talk to them! But he did stop his story, and he started reading ours aloud to his café mates in a big, booming voice.

The man closest to me leaned in my direction and smiled. He was bald with a deep tan, probably from running or biking or hanging off a mountaintop from a skinny rope. "It must be something, having such a genius for a father."

"Oh, it's definitely something," I said.

"I'm a great admirer of your father's work. He's so courageous."

"What do you do?" I asked him.

"I'm in advertising," he said. "At Crispin Porter + Bogusky."

"Oh!" I said. "Like Don Draper."

He gave me an odd look, then turned away. I guess that was the wrong thing to say.

For the record, I don't think my dad is courageous. He doesn't write intimate details about himself in order to break internal or societal taboos. He writes about himself because that's all he cares about.

But as much as I dislike my dad's poetry, that's not my problem with him. Here's my beef with my dad: He's an artist, and I suppose he is quite good. People admire him greatly for his poems, he has edited several essential volumes of Beat writing, he excels at the occasional pieces of journalism he takes on, and he is renowned for his impassioned teaching. He's achieved a lot in his life, and I don't begrudge him that. I just don't think that all his achievements entitle him to a free pass on basic moral and familial responsibilities. None of my dad's fans care about his string of ex-wives or the two children he neglects, just as none of my mom's acolytes seemed to notice her drinking or chronic debting. None of their admirers called them on anything; instead they just basked in my parents' literary fumes.

This is something that Mr. Dove never, ever did. Over the years I saw him humor writers or even flatter them; that was part of his job, just one piece of what it took to get to the finish line—a published book. Yet he never let our authors ride roughshod over him or us. In fact, he once canceled a contract with a writer who was rude to Hansika. I never got the whole story, but I believe the man was drunk and said something cruel about her hand. I remember that day so clearly: Mr. Dove called me into his office, and I found him sitting at his beautiful oak desk, with the long windows behind him revealing a lush garden full of green leaves. He handed me a fat manuscript and told me that we wouldn't be working with So-and-So anymore, and would I be so kind to return the manuscript via media mail. Then he looked me in the eye and said: "Artists are special people. But they are still accountable to the rest of humanity."

This is a point that my dad seems to have missed. Sometimes I feel like the only reason he is accountable to Emma and me is because we force him to be. This is Jasmine's beef with our dad, and it's a battle she has been fighting on Emma's behalf since the day Emma was born.

We sat with our dad and his cronies for about an hour. Eventually our drinks were done, and all our story ideas were depleted. Then Emma rubbed her eyes. From the time she was an infant, this has been her code for "I'm tired."

"Dad," I said, raising my voice in order to be heard above his. "Dad! We're going."

He looked shocked. "Already? I just got here! I didn't even have a chance to ask you about your job."

I stood. "Jasmine is giving us a lift home. We'll call her from the courtesy phone."

Our dad held out his arms. "Daughter Emma, come here. Say bye to Daddy."

Emma flew onto his lap, wrapped her long skinny arms around his bulky shoulders, and pressed her cheek against his. Then she moved back to look at him. "You're coming next Sunday, right?"

He looked puzzled. "Next Sunday . . ."

Emma widened her eyes. "My birthday party! I'm going to be nine."

"Oh, yes, yes! Of course I'll be there. But tell your mother to call and remind me, all right?"

"I will." She kissed him, then slid off his lap.

My turn. I wedged between the men, leaned over and gave our dad one of my awkward half-hugs. "Bye, Dad."

He patted my shoulder. "Bye, Daughter."

I took Emma's hand and we went up to the counter to use the phone. Jasmine answered right away and said she would pick us up in ten minutes in front of Breadworks. Emma and I left Vic's and walked a few stores down to the large bakery and café, where we sat outside at one of the black-iron tables.

We sat in silence and stared at the Flatirons, which were wrapped in a late-afternoon glow from the impending sunset. Then Emma said, "Elizabeth?"

"Yes?"

"Daddy doesn't talk to us much."

My stomach tightened. I always knew this moment would come. I also knew that there would be many more of them. I got off my chair and I kneeled in front of Emma. I took her little hands in mine and looked her straight in the eye.

"You're right, Emma," I said slowly. "Daddy doesn't talk to us much. But that doesn't mean we're not worth talking to."

Emma looked at me in surprise. Not because of what I had just said, but because of how I looked, on my knees on the sidewalk of the Idealplex.

"Please hear what I'm saying, Emma, because it's important. I want you to always remember this."

"All right," she said. "I'll remember." Then she grinned. "I think your knees hurt."

"A little." I put her hands together and gave them a kiss, then I stood up and got back in my seat. "I just want you to know how cool you are. In fact, I'd say you're one of the coolest people I've ever met."

"Really?"

"Nay—you *are* the coolest person I've ever met."

"Cooler than Daddy?"

"Definitely."

She thought a moment. "My mom's cool, too."

"Yes, she sure is. That's true."

"She's here!"

Emma jumped up and ran over to the green Subaru, which was just pulling up at the curb. "Mommy!" Emma said as soon as Jasmine leaned over and opened the doors for us. "Daddy has a new girlfriend. Her name is Jane."

Emma was never one to bury the lead. "Did you know?" I asked as I got into the front seat.

Jasmine nodded. She looked well-rested, fully recovered from her Moms Gone Wild interlude. "As if it's possible to keep a secret at Naropa. I never mentioned anything because I figured it wasn't serious."

"She was at the house," Emma said. "*Upstairs.* We saw her sitting on Daddy's bed."

Jasmine looked at me. "Was she dressed?"

I laughed. "That's just what Dad asked. Yes, she was dressed. She was even reading a book—Eileen Myles."

"At least she has good taste," Jasmine said, driving carefully through the Idealplex parking lot. "If she was at the house, and upstairs at that, it's definitely serious."

"Do you know her?"

Jasmine turned left onto Broadway and headed toward downtown. "I know who she is. She's a grad student in poetry. She just started her first year."

"She's pretty," Emma said. "But not as pretty as you, Mommy."

Jasmine looked at Emma in the rearview mirror and smiled. "You're a flatterer, just like your dad."

Emma tapped me on the shoulder. "Was your mom pretty?"

I turned to look at her. "My mom? Yes. Yes, she was. My mom had beautiful hair."

Emma looked at me solemnly. I know she felt bad for me because my mom was dead. I patted her hand, then turned to Jasmine. "So," I said. "If Jane just started her first year in grad school, she must be around twenty-two?"

Jasmine nodded. "I believe so."

"That's about halfway between me and Emma."

"So she's young enough to be his daughter—"

"—but not as young as his youngest daughter."

Emma leaned forward, constrained by her seatbelt. She looked at us worriedly. "Didn't you like her? I thought she was nice."

Jasmine put out a hand and touched Emma's head. "Oh, honey, I'm sure we'll like her very much once we get to know her. And I'm sure she'll love you." Jasmine turned to me. "Do you want to pick up your things and get the bus? Or do you want to hang out with us and go tomorrow?"

"Tomorrow!" Emma said. "Tomorrow, tomorrow!"

"OK," I gave in. "Tomorrow."

Back at the house Jasmine put on water for tea, and Emma announced that she had to go upstairs for a moment because she had something important to show me. As soon as she was gone, Jasmine said, "I suppose I should invite Jane to Emma's birthday party."

I raised my eyebrows. "Is that a good idea?"

"I think it is, actually. I always promised myself that if Jasper got serious with someone, I'd make it an easy transition for Emma. I don't want her to feel guilty for liking Jane." Jasmine's eyes twinkled. "You never had that problem. You hated Jill, and you hated me."

I felt myself blush. "Oh—I'm sorry. I didn't know you."

"Well, I was only three years older than you, and I was having an affair with your married father. Plus I was living in your house. I think it's pretty normal that you hated me."

Suddenly Emma was in the doorway, holding a Hello Kitty doll. "What are you talking about?" she asked.

"We're talking about your party, sweetie," Jasmine said. "What do you think about inviting Jane?"

"I think yes!" She came over and sat on my lap, carefully putting the Hello Kitty doll on the table. I kissed the top of Emma's head and put my nose in her hair. "A lot of people are coming," she said. "I don't think we have enough chairs."

"Oh, we have a few folding chairs tucked away in the basement. We can get them out the day of the party."

Emma shook her head. "No," she said firmly.

I laughed. "No? You don't want more chairs?"

"No, I want more chairs. But I don't want to go down to the basement."

"But why?" I asked. "I don't get it."

"I'm scared."

"Why are you scared?"

"You know why," she said.

"No, I don't, actually."

Puzzled, I looked at Jasmine. She looked up at the ceiling, then back down to me. "JonBenét Ramsey," she said.

"Oh." I looked at Emma. Her face was pale, and her lips were pressed together tightly. I had never seen her look like that. "I'm sure your mom can do it herself," I said hurriedly. "Right?"

"I guess," she said slowly.

"So," I said, turning the Hello Kitty doll on the table to face me. She was white and plush, with a purple-plaid jumper and a matching bow on one of her ears. "Hi Kitty."

Emma laughed. "Elizabeth! It's 'Hello Kitty.'"

"Hi Hello Kitty."

"No! It's just 'Hello Kitty.'"

"But that's her name anyway. What do you say when you say hi to Hello Kitty?"

"You're *always* saying hi to Hello Kitty. So you don't have to say hi."

"What about when you say good-bye?"

"Then it's 'Good-bye Hello Kitty.'"

"So you say 'Hello' even when you say 'Good-bye'?"

"Yes. That's just how it is with Hello Kitty. You better get used to it, because *this* Hello Kitty"—she thrust it in my hands—"is for you!"

"For me?" I looked up at Jasmine. She was leaning against the counter, trying not to laugh. She knew how I felt—or didn't feel—about Hello Kitty. "But won't you miss her?"

"When I was cleaning my room this morning, I found one just like her. This is her twin, and she wants to come live with you in Denver."

"Oh, she does, does she?" I held up the Hello Kitty doll and looked at it. I think what weirds me out the most about Hello Kitty is that she has no mouth. I find that creepy. But nevertheless I gave her a big kiss on her no-mouth and said, "Hello Kitty! I think you're really going to like Denver."

Emma hugged me. I looked up at Jasmine, who gave me a wink. The things you do for love, I thought, clutching my new Hello Kitty doll to my chest. The things you do for love.

10. The Goof of Terror

The next morning I caught the express bus from Boulder, arriving at Market Street Station with plenty of time to spare before my shift started.

I walked over to Quill & Ink, eager for some coffee. I had a little spending money because Jasmine had slipped me a twenty before I got on the bus. I protested, but she said, "It's your dad's money. Consider it payment—ten dollars for staying an extra night, and ten dollars as compensation for finding your dad's new girlfriend in his bed." That sounded fair to me, and to reward myself further, I planned to get a triple latte.

As I pushed open the door to Quill & Ink, my stomach sank a little, as it always did when I came to work. But I distinctly remember noticing the smell of the store that morning, that unique scent of citrus and wood and coffee, and I remember I found it comforting. I was never going to be entirely happy there, but maybe I was finally adjusting to my new life.

The first person I saw was the Wolf Man. He was sitting in one of the easy chairs by the door, wearing his wolf hat and nursing a cup of coffee. His stuffed wolf was resting on the armrest of his chair, and as I passed by, both the Wolf Man and his wolf stared at me with empty blue eyes.

Bree was behind the counter at the café. I said good morning and ordered my triple latte. While she fixed my drink, I looked up at the chalkboard. Hadley's quote for the week was:

> THE GOOF OF TERROR TOOK OVER MY THOUGHTS
> AND MADE ME ACT PETTY AND CHEAP
> JACK KEROUAC, *ON THE ROAD*

"That quote isn't very uplifting," I said as Bree handed me my drink.

She rolled her eyes. "I told Hadley the same thing. I think he likes the word 'goof.'"

That's because he is one, I thought but didn't say. I thanked Bree and went back to the break room. With any luck, Ruby would not be there. Hadley, either. Or Stacie, or Fat Bob, or anyone. With any luck, I could have a little time alone with my thoughts and my triple latte.

I pushed open the door, and there was Hadley sitting on the flowered couch, as usual in one of his oddly contorted postures, this time with one knee askew on the couch and the other bent close to his mouth. His eyes brightened when he saw me. "Good morning, Elizabeth Zwelland!" he declared.

"Hi, Hadley."

"Did you have fun in Boulder?"

Had I told him I was going? I couldn't recall. "Yes, I did." I knew this was the place where I was supposed to ask him about his weekend, but I didn't. I set my latte on the table and went to my locker.

Hadley filled the void, as usual. "I got in at five thirty to open, so I'm taking my break now. Also because I knew you were coming in, and I wanted to tell you the news."

I opened my locker and stuffed my knapsack inside. "What news?"

"About London. She's gone."

I turned to look at him. "Gone? What do you mean?"

"She quit Saturday morning."

"But—why?" I was stunned. I took a seat at the table and pried the lid off my drink.

"Well, it's good news for her. She got a plum decorating job. She got hired to do up Kyle Orton's LoDo loft."

I frowned. "Who's Kyle Orton?"

Hadley laughed. "Ha HA ha! Elizabeth Zwelland! You're the only person in Colorado who doesn't follow sports. He's the Broncos quarterback, silly. Apparently he just bought a gi-normous loft in the Sugar Cube."

The Sugar Cube is a fancy building just a block from Dixons. Maybe that's why London was having dinner there.

"But is she gone already?" I asked. "Didn't she give two weeks' notice?"

"Nope," Hadley said, stretching his arms above his head and intertwining his fingers. "Kyle called her Friday night, and he wanted her to start right away. His mom and dad were in town for the game, and he wanted London to meet them for a powwow. Hilda was cool about it; she doesn't want to hold London back."

"Wow." I sipped my latte and pondered. I felt very sorry that London was gone. Who would I chat with behind the bookshelves? Who would laugh with me about Ruby's non sequiturs during book club? Still, maybe this meant it would be easier for us to get together outside of work. I didn't have London's number, but she could always call me at Q&I. Or just stop by; surely she would be filling Kyle Orton's home with pricey coffee-table books.

Then it occurred to me: If London was gone, there were now thirty free hours on the schedule. That meant I could go full-time. Which meant a bigger paycheck and health insurance. Which meant no more King Soopers—or not as much, anyhow—and no more stale sandwiches for dinner. It meant buying a cell phone, and maybe a new laptop; if I saved up half the money, I could reasonably ask my dad for the rest. Maybe I could even buy a hardcover book or two, and start rebuilding my home library.

"Is Hilda in today?" I asked Hadley. I wanted to talk to her right away.

"Yep," he said, rising from the couch. "She got in when I did. Well, I better get back to the café." He pointed at my latte. "Did you pay for that?"

"Yes."

He frowned. "Totally unnecessary. You should've just waited until I was behind the counter."

"Oh, that's all right. I came into a little money."

"An inheritance?"

I thought of Jane sitting on my dad's bed reading Eileen Myles. "You could say that."

"Ah, the mysterious Elizabeth! But that's why we love you." As he left the room, he reached out a hand and patted my shoulder. I rolled my eyes. I looked forward to the day when some new woman started at Q&I, and Hadley transferred his work crush to her.

I drank the rest of my latte, my head full of numbers. Ten more hours a week multiplied by four weeks—even after taxes, I'd be pulling in at least $260 more a month, which was around $3,100 a year. I wondered what kind of apartment I could get if I paid $100 more a month; small, surely, but not in a basement. If London had walked in that moment, I would have given her a huge hug. Without a doubt, my life was about to change for the better.

I put on my name tag and went over to the time clock to punch in. To my delight, there was a yellow Post-It note on my time card: E—SEE

ME AS SOON AS YOUR SHIFT STARTS—HILDA. I punched in and quickly left the break room.

Down the hall is a door marked OFFICES, with a drawing of the Q&I gnome wearing glasses and adding 2 + 2 on a sheet of paper. I opened the door and went in. There's one room for cashiers to use when they count out their drawers, and the other room is Hilda's office. The door was slightly open, so I poked my head inside. Hilda was at her desk, looking down at her hands and frowning.

"Hilda?" I said.

She looked up, her expression blank.

"You wanted to see me?" I asked, opening the door a little wider.

She nodded. "Yes, I do. Please come in and shut the door behind you."

I closed the door and sat in one of the soft orange chairs opposite Hilda's desk. London always called this room "Office of the Dead," because it's filled with Hispanic cultural artifacts, including some of those creepy Day of the Dead panoramas where skeletons in bright colors and fancy headgear pose in regular human activities. Hilda has a whole shelf of these, including one with a family of skeletons gathered around a table for an elaborate meal, and another with a couple sitting on a bench and holding hands. London told me that the latter was a gift from Hilda's boyfriend. Like I said: creepy.

There are also two large framed Frida Kahlo prints on the walls, one where Frida is sitting next to another Frida and appears to be getting a blood transfusion, and another with a deer that has Frida's head and is shot full of arrows, the wounds dripping blood into the fur. I have enormous respect for Frida Kahlo, but let's face it: creepy.

Last but not least, Hilda has an enormous statue of Our Lady of Guadalupe. By "enormous" I mean three, maybe four feet tall, complete with golden rays behind her head, a purple robe dotted with stars, and a mournful expression with downcast eyes. There was no way Guadalupe could fit on the neatly arranged wall-to-wall bookshelves behind Hilda's desk, so she had her own bright-red table in the corner.

I perched on the edge of my chair, a small smile on my face. I hoped I looked eager and chipper and ready to get promoted. The latte had been strong and I felt good, energetic and mildly buzzing.

Hilda took a deep breath, then looked over at the statue of Guadalupe. Her mouth moved briefly, and she appeared to be saying a quick prayer.

Oh, for God's sake, I thought. Just tell me about London and the extra hours.

Hilda looked at me. "Elizabeth, I brought you in here to talk about what happened at the book club on Friday afternoon."

I knit my brow. "The book club?"

She nodded, her expression stern. "About you and London making fun of Ruby."

"I'm sorry," I said. "I don't know what you're talking about." Was this some kind of weird segue to telling me about London's departure?

"On Saturday morning, Rebecca came into my office. She said that after book club, she found Ruby crying in the ladies' room. Apparently Ruby was upset about you and London teasing her. I asked Rebecca if she had seen anything, and she told me it was true, that you and London were laughing at Ruby."

Rebecca from Dinosaur. What the hell was her problem?

"So I called Ruby in to ask her about it, and she started crying. Apparently you and London have been making her life miserable here for months."

"Hilda!" I said. "That's just not true. Sure, maybe we kid her a bit, but we don't make her life miserable." Anyhow it was more London than me, but I didn't want to say that; it felt like ratting out London.

"Elizabeth, I don't tolerate bullying in my store—"

"Bullying!" I laughed. Then I stopped: I had never seen Hilda look so serious, her eyes steady and her thick brows drawn together.

"Yes, bullying. I don't tolerate it. I particularly don't tolerate it where Ruby is concerned."

I felt hot sweat on the back of my neck. Was I about to get fired? Suddenly it was hard to breathe. I put a hand on my stomach to steady myself. "Hilda, I'm so sorry. I never meant to—it's just, well, Ruby's not a very good worker. Plus—and I hate to say this—I think she drinks before work, or even at work. Sometimes I smell gin on her."

Hilda snorted. I backed up in my chair; I suddenly realized that she was extremely angry. "You think I don't know that about Ruby?" she said. "Elizabeth, have you noticed the sign in the front window of the store, the one that says 'C Heart C'?"

I blinked. "No. Yes." I did know what she meant. It was a white sign about four times the size of a bumper sticker, with red writing that said: C ♥ C.

"That stands for 'Colorado Loves Colorado.' It's a state-funded program that's been around for about ten years. They give jobs to people who need help for whatever reason—former drug addicts, people with intellectual disabilities, people who've suffered severe trauma, lots of things. The state government pays two-thirds of the person's salary, and the store pays the rest. If you see that sign in a store's window, it means they're part of the program. It's a sign of pride for the store, and it's also kind of a heads-up to customers so they know they might encounter someone a little different."

"Oh," I said. "I didn't know."

"Exactly," she practically spat. "You don't know."

I could see pretty clearly where she was going with this. "And Ruby is—"

"Ruby is a person suffering from severe PTSD. The reason, Elizabeth, that Ruby has severe PTSD is because of her last job. Do you know what her last job was?"

"No," I said helplessly. "I don't."

"Ruby worked in the cafeteria at Columbine High School."

My stomach turned into a sheet of ice.

"Do you know much about Columbine?" Hilda asked.

"I—I wasn't here then. Just the two boys, and they had guns—"

"Yes, they had guns. An entire arsenal. When they started shooting outside the cafeteria, almost everyone in the cafeteria ran away, but a bunch of people ended up in a storeroom off the kitchen. A small room, without a lock. They were all crammed in there, listening to all the shooting and screaming, and at one point the two shooters even tried to get into their room. Because the school is so big, it took the SWAT team three hours to get to them. Ruby was in that storeroom."

I sat perfectly still. I couldn't breathe.

"She had counseling, lots of it, and she tried to go back to work three times." Hilda held up three fingers. "Three times. The first time she lasted a day, the next time a week, and the third time she made it to a month. Then she didn't work at all. She just sat in the dark in her house in Littleton. Finally some people got her help, and about five years ago she got a place in Denver and started working with us. She's doing a damn fine job, all things considered."

I said nothing.

"Then there's Stacie."

"Stacie!" I practically shouted. "There's no way Stacie complained about me. I never even speak to her. I—she's scary."

"Oh, for God's sake, Elizabeth! Stacie isn't scary; Stacie is scared."

"Did she—"

"Stacie used to live in Grand Junction. About four years ago she was gang-raped, and her eye got damaged by the broken bottle they used to threaten her. She has severe migraines because of her head injuries." Hilda pursed her lips. "That's Stacie's story."

"Hilda," I said, my voice and hands shaking. "I didn't know. No one told me. You can't blame me for something I didn't know."

"Well, Elizabeth, here's the thing. Everyone from Colorado Loves Colorado has the right to tell their story or not. The situation with Ruby and Stacie is not something we tell our new staff right away, out of respect for Ruby and Stacie's privacy. But as a person works here longer, as they get closer to the group, eventually someone will let them know. It's not an official policy, exactly, but it's sort of an unsaid rule so Ruby and Stacie don't become stigmatized." She knit her brow so strongly that her eyebrows almost touched. "I didn't think anyone would need to know all this in order to behave like a decent person toward them. Apparently, though, you do."

I tried to swallow, but my mouth and throat were completely dry. "Hilda, I'm sorry. But London—"

Hilda held up a hand. "Forget about London. London's gone. The only reason she'll be back is to buy stacks of coffee-table books for her rich clients. I'll keep her away from Ruby. But quite frankly, Elizabeth, as bad as this is, there are other problems with you."

Now I knit my brow. "Like what?"

"A customer complained about you just last week. She wanted to know which translation of *The Tibetan Book of the Dead* she should get, and apparently you were quite rude to her."

"I—I wasn't rude to her."

"You were rude enough that she came back to the store the next evening and asked for a manager. I wasn't here, but Rebecca spoke to her."

Rebecca. Again. "I wasn't rude to her. She didn't know what she wanted, and I just—"

"But most of all," Hilda interrupted me, "you're not a team player. You're just not part of the family here."

I sat back in my chair, stunned. I flashed on Blue Heron for a moment, remembering sitting with Hansika and Gerard at the office in the wee hours of the morning, pulling together the final files of a book while New York City slept outside.

"I do my job," I protested. "I do it really well, in fact. You even gave me more hours a few months ago! I'm quiet and I keep to myself; I shouldn't get punished for that. It has nothing to do with Ruby."

"But it does go back to Ruby," Hilda insisted. "It does, because if you'd made an effort to speak to your coworkers instead of just looking down on them, they would have felt comfortable with you, and they would have told you about Ruby and Stacie. Elizabeth," she said, leaning over her desk and folding her hands, "do you know why I hired you out of all those dozens of people? It's because I could see how much you loved books, and you had all that great New York City publishing experience. I thought you could bring some East Coast sophistication to the store. But instead all you've done is add negativity and bitterness. I don't need that. Neither does Quill & Ink."

A red-hot chill went down my back. She *is* firing me! I thought. I had never been fired from a job in my entire life.

Hilda looked over at Guadalupe, then back at me. "You've had a hard time, I know. You lost your job at Blue Heron, and now you're stuck in this cow town with all of us hicks. I get that. But why did you have to take it out on Ruby? Why did you have to take it out on the one person who absolutely could not handle it?" She pointed a finger at me and said quietly, "You have a black heart."

At that moment, something happened. It was unlike anything I had ever experienced before or since. There was a painful kick in the center of my chest. It came from deep inside, and it felt like a horse hoof slamming against the wall of my chest. I actually gasped and bent over slightly. Looking back, I think of that iconic picture of Lee Harvey Oswald when he got shot, or even Ronald Reagan, his lips clutching as the bullet entered his lung.

Hilda didn't seem to notice my reaction. She said, "So here's what we're going to do. I'm not going to fire you, but I'm going to send you home now, and you won't be on the schedule for a week."

I looked at her. "You're not firing me?"

"No. But I want you away from the store for a week. I think you need a break from Quill & Ink, and I think Quill & Ink needs a break from you. You'll be back on the schedule a week from today, same time as today, so there's no need for you to phone and get your schedule."

I nodded. I felt immensely relieved, but I also felt that searing pain in my chest.

"When you come back, I don't want even the faintest whiff of bullying. If I witness anything or if someone reports something to me, you're fired. Do you understand?"

"Yes."

"That's it," she said curtly. "You can go."

I stood. I wanted to say something else, but what could I possibly say? Hilda was done with me. I looked over at Our Lady of Guadalupe; her expression was sorrowful, and her eyes downcast.

☼ ☼ ☼

I don't recall my journey home. I must have gone to the break room, taken off my name tag and collected my things, left the store and got on the Mall Ride, and walked home from the Civic Center Station. I must have done all that, but I don't recall it.

But there is one thing from my walk home that I've never forgotten. As I was walking up the stairs to the Sketchy Park, a guy who was clearly drunk or homeless or both passed me on his way down. He wore a filthy brown coat, and his hair was wild and smelly. As he passed by me, he said loudly, "Hi there."

I didn't answer him, I just kept walking up the stairs.

He called out again, louder this time. "Hey there, lady! I said hello to you."

By that time I was almost at the top of the stairs. I ignored him again and walked a bit faster.

"You know what?" he called out after me. "I hope you have an ugly life!"

His words slammed into that crack in my chest. As insults go, that has to be one of the worst. Don't you agree?

Part 2

After

1. The Necessity of Shame

Monday

I spent the rest of Monday in bed with a fever. Not a terribly high fever, but enough that I felt hot and disoriented, and all I wanted to do was sleep. I have vague memories of waking up and drinking glasses of water, and I must have eaten saltines because the empty box was on the counter. But the specifics escape me.

Tuesday

The next day I woke up a little after nine. I opened my eyes and blinked a few times. My lids felt heavy and swollen. I looked at my lemon-yellow walls, my red table and chairs, my microscopic kitchen, the big window with the drawn Venetian blinds. My fever was gone, but the searing pain in my chest was not.

I was ravenously hungry. I went to the bathroom, then I opened my kitchen cabinets and tiny refrigerator. People say, "I have nothing to eat," but I actually had nothing to eat. Just a tin of anchovies, a box of baking soda, a bottle of Italian dressing, and Lipton tea. My cabinets were rarely full anyway, but I hadn't shopped in a few days because I had been in Boulder all weekend. I had planned to make a King Soopers run Monday after work, but of course that never happened.

I sat down on my bed, weary to the bone. It must have been raining outside, because my studio was filled with soft gray light. Colorado is famous for having three hundred days of sunshine a year, but that day was not one of them. I was still wearing the long-sleeved T-shirt I had worn to work on Monday, but at some point during my feverish sleep I had kicked off my jeans. My hair felt tangled, my face swollen, and I was so hungry I was ready to eat anchovies with Italian dressing.

I needed some help. A little, not a lot. I didn't want to ask Jasmine to come all the way from Boulder, and my dad—forget it. But I did need help.

Just then I heard Trixie's door open and her voice call out, "See you next week!"

All right, I thought. You can do this.

I put on my jeans and ran a hand over my ratty hair. I went out into the hall, careful to undo the button on the doorknob so I didn't lock myself out. I walked shakily to Trixie's apartment and knocked.

Trixie opened the door immediately. She was wearing white sweatpants and a Kelly-green muscle T-shirt, her red hair pulled back into a ponytail, her fair skin glowing. Just behind her, I could see a massage table set up on the shiny wooden floor, and the smell of lavender oil drifted into the hallway.

"Elizabeth!" she said. "You're sick! Come in, come in."

I walked over to her fat pink couch and sank heavily into the cushions. "I'm not so sick, not really," I said. "I just had a little fever yesterday."

Trixie sat down beside me and put a hand on my forehead. Her palm was cool and smelled of roses. "You're not too hot now, but you don't look so good." She tilted her head. "Did you have some kind of emotional setback?"

Ah. She thought it was a man. I couldn't possibly tell her what had really happened, so I just went with it. "Yes. Yes, I did." I put a hand on my chest. "I have a pain right here. I feel like I weigh three hundred pounds."

She nodded sympathetically. "I know how that is. Do you have to work today?"

I shook my head. "I'm off schedule all week. Trixie, the thing is, I have no food. I mean, no food. Is there any way—"

"Absolutely. In fact, I planned to go to King Soopers this afternoon, but if I leave now I can do it before my next client. What do you need?"

I smiled weakly. "You know what I really want? I want graham crackers and milk. Two boxes of graham crackers and a gallon of milk. Also a large bag of plain, milk chocolate Hershey's Kisses. Not the fancy kinds with the stripes."

She laughed. "OK. How about I also get you some peanut butter and whole wheat bread?" I nodded. "Anything else? Do you need toilet paper?"

"I—you know, I don't know."

Trixie patted my hand. She was so pretty and together, so comfortable and cozy with her lovely smelling apartment and smushy pink couch. "I'll figure it out. Why don't you go back to bed?"

I nodded. "All right. Trixie—thanks. Thanks so much."

She looked at me. "You know, when you moved in, I told you to let me know if you needed anything. And I meant it. Now, go back to bed. I'll knock on your door when I get back."

I shuffled back to my room and fell right into bed. I must have slept again, because the next thing I knew I heard a light knocking, and Trixie's rosy smell filled the room. "Elizabeth? I'm back."

I watched in gratitude as she came into my little world, quickly and quietly unpacking a grocery bag. Then she came over to my bed and sat on the edge, looking at me in sympathy.

"You should have enough food for today and tomorrow. I also got you a pint of Ben & Jerry's Coffee Heath Bar Crunch. They're the only two men in the world who will never let you down."

I smiled. "Thanks, Trixie."

"You'll be all right," she said. "I know what it's like. I've had some messy breakups in my day."

I nodded.

"Well, I have a client coming in a few minutes. I'll check on you later, OK? Don't hesitate to knock if you need me."

"Oh," I said. "Money . . ."

"We'll settle later. It wasn't much, anyhow; King Soopers is so cheap."

The minute she was out the door, I got up and went to the kitchen. I poured a full glass of milk, then opened the box of graham crackers and took out a whole pack. I put the glass on my bedside table and rested the graham crackers on top of a throw pillow, then I took off my jeans and slipped under the duvet. I ate the graham crackers like I did when I was a little girl and spent hours in my room reading Nancy Drew: break the cracker into quarters, dip each quarter in the glass of milk, let it get wet enough to soften but not so wet it falls into the milk.

Slowly and steadily, I worked my way through the entire pack. I put the empty glass and the wax paper on my bedside table, then I burrowed in my bed, pulling up the duvet so it covered most of my head.

I think the primary emotion I felt in Hilda's office was fear. I was afraid she was going to fire me, and some kind of horrible, clammy adrenaline had shot through me. I have been scared, really scared, only a handful of times in my life, and that was one of them. Even after my chest did that weird kick, and even after Hilda said she wasn't going to fire me, that adrenaline was still coursing through me. In fact that must be what fueled my walk home, and what caused my fever.

But finally the adrenaline was gone. It had worked its way through me, and I was no longer afraid. I had my job. Even though I was off schedule for a week, I still had my job, and I clung to that.

In place of the fear, though, there was another feeling, a feeling I didn't want to touch. When I think back on that Tuesday—that sad, gray, late September Tuesday—it was a day of extremes. There was the thing I didn't want to feel, and there was anger. Lots of it. I was so angry! Lying in bed, sitting up occasionally for more milk and graham crackers, once in a while going to the bathroom, my mind was churning furiously. I blamed Hilda and everyone at Q&I for not telling me about Ruby. I particularly blamed Hadley, who spoke to me more than anyone else. I blamed London for sucking me into her negativity. I blamed c ♥ c for not having bigger signs. I blamed Ruby for not standing up to London and me. I blamed Stacie, although I wasn't sure why. I blamed Bernie Madoff—oh, how I blamed Bernie Madoff! I think Dante should have invented a special circle in hell for that evil, greedy man. I blamed my dad, I blamed the publishing industry, I blamed Stepmother One. I would have blamed the Wolf Man and the Snuffler, too, if that had made any sense.

These blaming operas churned through me all day, loud and blustery and bombastic. I even talked out loud at times, and I think I might have shouted on occasion. The Snuffler passed outside my door, as did a few Swiss Arms residents doing their laundry, but I didn't care if they thought I was the crazy lady in the basement studio. I had been wronged! Someone had to pay!

I finally settled down by early evening. After a quick visit from Trixie—who thankfully did not arrive mid-shout—I lay down on my bed, clutching a throw pillow. I was all out of anger and bluster, and I was physically exhausted.

Then in a sudden harsh flash, I saw the truth. I was to blame. It was my fault. No one else, just me. I had made fun of a person who had PTSD from the Columbine shooting. I did that. Me.

With that realization, the other thing flooded in. The other thing was shame. Deep dark-red shame. It was the oddest, most unpleasant sensation, like thick gritty lava flowing through me. It was awful. As it passed through my heart, through that fissure from the kick, the feeling was just about unbearable. It was so painful, so raw, that I didn't think I could hold it together. I actually didn't think I was strong enough to feel what I was feeling.

It was a long night. I slept in pieces, harsh broken pieces, waking up each time to find that I felt exactly as I did before. I sweated profusely, I know because I got up and changed at one point. While I was awake, I lay in bed taking small breaths, riding out—waiting out—that dark-red sensation. I have never been a suicidal person, but that night I understood why people kill themselves. I think it's because you feel such an enormous amount of pain, more pain than you can bear or even adequately express. The pain doesn't seem like it will ever go away, and the only way to make it go away is to make yourself go away altogether. I think it's like that.

Ruby probably felt this kind of pain. Also Stacie. My mom, too.

Wednesday

When I woke up, I was shocked to see that my clock said two. Two p.m.? I wondered. Yes, it had to be. Colorado sunshine, clear and bright, was pushing through the thin crevices in the shuttered Venetian blinds.

I lay perfectly still on my bed. I put a hand to my heart and took stock. The feeling of shame was still there, but it seemed to have lodged in the fissure in my chest. I felt heavy and exhausted, and my mind felt terribly weak, as if it could be broken by a complex multiplication problem—49 x 37, say. But the dark-red beast from the previous night was no longer in charge. I was back. There wasn't much of me, and what there was felt awfully fragile, but I was back. I would have cried, but I was too tired.

It seemed like the perfect moment for ice cream. Trixie had shown great foresight in her purchases. I took out the carton, pried off the top, and put the carton in a patch of sunlight on the counter. After a few minutes the top had softened, so I took it back to my bed and I slowly ate every single bite.

I had just put the empty carton on top of the graham cracker wrappers on my bedside table when I heard a gentle knock on the door. I pulled on my jeans, then got up and turned the knob without even looking through the peephole. It was Trixie, tall and fit in blue sweatpants and a pink tank top. Her pretty face moved from tension to relief.

"Oh, thank God you're OK!" she said. "I knocked three times this morning."

"I think I had another fever," I said, leaning weakly against the doorframe.

"How are you now?"

"Better. I just polished off the Ben & Jerry's."

She laughed. "That's a good sign! You'll see," she said sympathetically. "You'll get through this."

I nodded. "I'll be all right."

"You need anything else?"

"Not right now."

"Okeydoke. I'll pop by later. Is that all right?"

"That's fine. Trixie—"

"Yes?"

"You've been so nice to me."

She smiled sadly. "I can see you're in trouble," she said, "and I know what that's like."

I nodded. She patted my cheek, then turned and walked down the hall. Somehow she reminded me of Jasmine, only taller.

The ice cream had helped, and I felt a little stronger. I couldn't bear the mess in my apartment, so I decided to clean until I ran out of steam. I pulled up the blinds and opened the window, letting a fresh breeze blow through the studio and dissipate my sick, stale air. I threw out all the food wrappers from my bedside table, and I cleaned off the kitchen counter and wiped it with citrus spray. I went into my closet and found a fresh pair of sheets—pink flannel, on sale at Ross for $9.99—and changed my bedding, hanging my duvet over my closet door to air it out.

Next was me. I took off my clothes and stuffed them in the hamper in my closet, along with my old sheets and all the other dirty clothes from the past few days. Then I took a long, hot shower and washed my hair. When I came out of the shower I felt a little wobbly, and I had to sit on the toilet a few moments to get steady. You're OK, I thought. Keep going.

I realized that I desperately needed caffeine. I didn't have a coffeemaker but I did have Lipton teabags. I made a strong cup of tea using two bags and a little milk, then I sat on my bed and drank it. When my mom wasn't drinking gin, she drank tea; she said it was bracing. I thought of her while I sat and sipped, looking across the room through the window at people's legs occasionally passing on Ninth Avenue, just like a François Truffaut movie I had seen long ago.

My burst of activity had drained my energy. I wasn't up to going out that day. The only thing I really wanted to do was lie in bed and read Jane Austen and eat Hershey's Kisses. When I sold my books before I left New York, there was one I could not part with: a leather-bound Jane Austen omnibus that my mom had given me on my twelfth birthday. It was the only thing I owned from her and my old life, and it sat on my red table under the two Simone de Beauvoir novels I had borrowed from the library. Reading that book and eating Hershey's Kisses was my go-to comfort activity. I had done it often as a teenager and young adult, and I sometimes did it as an adult: at my mom's house after she died, in New York when Max broke up with me, and during my six unemployed months in Boulder.

I finished my tea and was about to go back to bed with my book and Kisses when I realized that I hadn't brushed my teeth. I went into the bathroom, but my toothbrush wasn't there. I frowned; where was it? Then I realized I had never unpacked my knapsack after my Boulder trip. I went into the main room and saw my knapsack on the floor under the table, where it was partly concealed by a chair.

I sat on the multicolored rug and unzipped my knapsack. I felt a small shock when Hello Kitty popped out and landed in my lap. I shook my head and smiled; I had forgotten about her. When I packed up my things in Boulder, I had stuffed in Hello Kitty at the very top. Which I could do because although her head was large, almost ten inches across, it was quite soft and smushy.

Sitting on the rug with Hello Kitty on my lap, I suddenly had a strong sense of Emma. It was as if she were in the room, leaning against me with her bony elbow in my side, the smell of her clean hair in my nose. Just the thought of her—her eager smile, her beloved notebook, the way she jumped up and down when she saw me—and I started to cry. Isn't that odd? I hadn't cried once since everything happened, not in Hilda's office and not afterward, but suddenly I was weeping helplessly.

I moved onto the bed, still holding Hello Kitty with her big white head, her mouthless expression, her purple-plaid jumper with the matching bow on one ear. I cried because of Emma, because of her goodness, because of her love for me and all the faith she had in me. Is there anything as pure and good as a little girl's love? No matter what I had done, there was one person who still loved me, one person who would never say that I had a black heart. She was only eight and she didn't know any better, but still. Still.

If only I could be a little bit good, I thought. If only I could be good for Emma's sake.

Then it all came crashing back, all the feelings and thoughts I had been staving off with my burst of housecleaning: Ruby, Quill & Ink, and that horrible, horrible talk in Hilda's office. But the difference was that I was able to say the words to myself almost right away: I teased someone who has PTSD from the Columbine shooting. Me. I did that. The words sent a dark shiver through my heart, but so be it. That was the starting point, somehow, just admitting that and letting the words stand plain and bare.

I didn't really know where to go after that. I hadn't figured anything out; I hadn't been strong enough. But the thought of going back to work again, the thought of walking through those doors and seeing Hilda and Rebecca and, my God, Ruby—I felt weak to the core. Thank goodness I still had a few more days. I counted on my fingers: Thursday, Friday, Saturday. Three days, and then Sunday I had to go to Boulder for Emma's party. Jasmine and Emma had wanted me to sleep over Saturday night, but I told them no because I was scheduled to close at Q&I. Now that I was suspended I wasn't closing anymore, but I didn't need to tell them that. As it was, I could hardly imagine going to Boulder midday Sunday. But I knew what it was like to be eight years old, and someone missing your birthday party was not a forgivable offense. I had to go. Even if I needed to put a hundred-dollar taxi ride to Boulder on my lone credit card, I could not miss Emma's party.

Which gave me three days. Three days to somehow glue myself back together so I could walk into work on Monday. So I could face all those people and what I had done.

I spent the rest of the afternoon reading Jane Austen. I started right at the beginning of the omnibus with *Sense and Sensibility.* I sucked slowly on Hershey's Kisses as I read; usually I could make a Kiss last almost two whole pages. I slept, too, fifteen minutes here and there, and I had a short chat with Trixie, who stopped by late afternoon. Thank God for Trixie.

Then around seven, I put down the book and rested my cheek on Hello Kitty, whose big white face provided the perfect headrest. I felt better; the book had worked its magic, the Austen universe lulling me into quietude. I was up to the part where Willoughby is feverishly courting Marianne, but of course I knew already that Willoughby was bad news. One could say, in fact, that Willoughby had a black heart.

A black heart! I shifted restlessly in my bed. What a thing to say to someone! Was that part of Hispanic culture, or even just Catholicism? I had never heard anyone use that expression before. There was something so damning about it, something so final.

Then I found myself wondering: Is it true? Do I actually have a black heart?

Well, I had to think about that. I had to think about it very hard. I did something then that I had never done before: I went over my life. I'm sure I missed some things, but I really did my best to flash on each period, recalling where I had lived and the people around me and my general state of mind. Early life in Boulder, then to New Jersey at five, grammar school, middle school, high school, each year at Barnard, and all my summers in Colorado. Then the literary agency, my many years at Blue Heron, moving to Colorado and six months unemployed, then my job at Q&I—but I wasn't ready to think about Q&I, not yet.

It took me over an hour, and concentrating that hard tired me out. I must admit I did remember some mean things I had done, as well as some flat-out stupid things. It's probably impossible for anyone to avoid those behaviors altogether. But I felt that despite those incidents, I could definitely conclude that I had not been moving through the world as a malevolent force. I had never killed anything, or hurt anyone physically, or even chased anyone after school—if anything, I had been chased on a few occasions.

So what did Hilda mean? She certainly knew that I was not a murderer or part of some evil organization. I think she just meant that I didn't care about people. But that wasn't true! I cared about lots of people. Emma, Jasmine, Hansika—Hansika! She was handicapped, and I never, ever made fun of her or did anything to hurt her. I cared about Mr. Dove, Gerard, Eileen. I cared about my grammar-school buddy Helena Papadopoulos, who I was still in touch with sporadically. I cared about my mom tremendously, even when she was drunk and garrulous. I cared about my old boyfriend Max. And despite everything, I did genuinely care about my dad. Hilda didn't know about any of those people; she thought I was only the side I showed at Q&I.

I'm not a bad person, I thought. I don't have a black heart. Hilda is wrong.

I felt a great sense of relief. I turned on my side, moving Hello Kitty and holding her in my arms. What Hilda had said simply wasn't true.

Yet—I had to admit that I had teased Ruby, and I had scorned just about everyone else at Q&I. Maybe that wasn't a black heart, but it was definitely something.

I sighed. I was tired. I couldn't do anything else that night, so I didn't. I took a long bath, then I spent the rest of the evening reading Jane Austen, slipping into that long-ago world while I leaned my head on Hello Kitty and rested a hand on that strange pain in my chest.

Thursday

The next day I woke at eight. I made a peanut butter sandwich for breakfast, which I ate at the table like a civilized person—my first meal there in days. I made my bed, smoothing out the white duvet and propping up the turquoise throw pillows, then I fixed a cup of tea and put it on my nightstand. I sat against the pillows and put Hello Kitty in the crook of my arm. My window was open a few inches to let in some fresh air, but my blinds were down and only partially open so no one could peek in.

I knew that I had more things to look at. I didn't particularly want to think about Q&I and what had happened. But clearly something was wrong, and clearly something had to change. I had hurt someone very badly and I had nearly lost my job. In some significant way, I was off course, off balance, and that had to be righted before I went back to work. Otherwise I would lose my job, and that just could not happen.

I have to admit, I didn't think of anything important for a while. My thoughts flitted over Jane Austen, Emma's party, the brand of peanut butter that Trixie had bought, which was actually better than my usual. Then my thoughts moved to the life review I had done the day before. What surprised me, I suppose, was the different times I had been—well, not bullied, but outcast. All through school, including college, I had never really fit in anywhere. I was also surprised to realize how few people had really been part of my life. When I thought of my childhood, I saw that I had spent most of my time alone. Where was everyone? Really it was just me and my mom, and a few friends here and there. We lived on the edge of downtown, so I had no idyllic group of friends who played together on suburban lawns. I saw me at school, me on my bike, me at home doing schoolwork or reading. Where was everyone?

Then I remembered something, something I hadn't thought about the day before. It was the silliest thing, really. In my town, high school starts in tenth grade; the two middle-schools join up, so there is a whole new crop of people to know, or more likely to avoid. In my first year in high school I took biology, and my lab partner was from the other middle school. She and I became friends, bonding over the hellacious dissections we had to perform and the lengthy lab reports we wrote together.

Her name was Marilyn. She was a bouncy girl, blonde and a little plump, full of enthusiasm and good cheer. We used to work at her house; I never invited her to mine. Her home was big and clean, and she had a stay-at-home mom who seemed to like nothing better than to make brownies and sit with us at the kitchen table, asking about our day at school and really listening to what we said. Marilyn also had a black Labrador named Prudence, two younger blonde brothers who played soccer and roared through the house at regular intervals, and a handsome dad with a fetching smile and an important job in New York City. Every time I stepped into that house, I felt like I was visiting another planet.

Marilyn had the same group of friends all through grammar school and junior high, and they were still friends in high school. There were six of them altogether, and they called themselves the Roosevelt Six, after their grammar school. Due to my budding friendship with Marilyn, they all started saying hello to me in the hallways, sometimes even stopping to chat. Looking back, I'm sure they didn't know what to make of me, a tall, shy, slightly sullen girl who always wore black. I suspect I was a bit of a fixer-upper for Marilyn, but only in the nicest way.

Anyhow. One Saturday afternoon in spring, Marilyn had her Sweet Sixteen party at her house. There were about thirty guests in all, including several sets of parents and, of course, the Roosevelt Six. After the song was sung, the candles blown out, and the yellow cake with white icing distributed to all, Marilyn started working her way through an enormous pile of presents. She opened my gift first, the CD *Meat Is Murder* by the Smiths, my favorite band but one that none of the other guests had ever heard of. In her kindness and enthusiasm, Marilyn wanted to put on the CD right away, but I told her we could listen to it later. How would Morrissey and his ironic anguish ever fit into such a cheerful party, with its pink balloons, picture-perfect cake, and wholesome sixteen-year-olds?

It wouldn't. And there was me, all in black, eating too many M&M's and drinking too much Coca-Cola, watching it all from the sidelines.

When Marilyn picked up a gift from a Roosevelt Six girl named Whitney, she let out an excited squeal. It turned out that the Roosevelt Six had a tradition stemming from grammar school: They had a particular piece of wrapping paper that they used again and again for their birthday parties. Six times a year, they passed along this paper, writing the name of the birthday girl and the date. It was a rather large piece of paper, light pink with a blue-and-white birthday cake, interspersed with names and dates in different colored ink. Despite the years, the paper was in good shape, and it was passed around the party for everyone to admire. Finally the paper came back to Marilyn, who carefully folded it and handed it to her mother for safekeeping.

Two months later in June, Marilyn threw a surprise birthday party for me. I was stunned, not only because I had never had a surprise party before, but because my birthday is in July. Turns out Marilyn wanted to celebrate my birthday before I left for Boulder, so she and her mom had concocted a little get-together for me. All of the Roosevelt Six were there, as well as Helena Papadopoulos and her mom. Not my mom; I suppose they didn't invite her, and in my heart I knew it was better that she wasn't there. To my even greater surprise, Marilyn had wrapped my present—a bright-pink hoodie that I would never, ever wear—in the precious Roosevelt Six wrapping paper.

"But—" I said.

"You're one of us now," she said cheerfully. "Just pass it on the next time."

I found the whole afternoon rather overwhelming, but I was deeply touched as well. They all knew that my dad was far away, and they all knew about my mom's drinking since she taught at our school. Basically they knew that I was pretty much on my own, and they wanted to help me.

A few weeks later, I went to Boulder for the summer. When I came back in September for eleventh grade, Marilyn and I didn't have any classes together, and we both had new responsibilities: she became head of the Key Club, and I was voted assistant editor of the literary magazine, and I had also started working at Burger King. Marilyn and I hung out a few times, and I still waved to the Roosevelt Six in the hallways, but our bonds faded as they often do at that age, and I suppose at all ages.

But I still had the wrapping paper. It was in my closet; I was always surprised when I spotted it on my top shelf, but otherwise I didn't give it a moment's thought. Later, packing for college and cleaning out my closet, thinking I would never again live in my hometown if I could help it, thinking it was too late to give it back, I tossed the pink sheet of paper in the trash.

Now there I was eighteen years later, lying in bed in a basement studio in Denver, clutching a Hello Kitty doll to my chest, and at the thought of that wrapping paper I had tears rolling down my face. Why did I do that? Why didn't I just get in the car and drive it to Marilyn's house? None of the Roosevelt Six had ever asked me for the paper, but I can't believe they forgot about it. They were probably too polite to ask, or they were embarrassed because they didn't invite me to their parties anymore. It was nobody's fault; we just lived in different universes. By the end of high school, these girls were all standing on lawns in their pastel prom dresses, excited to make the next stop to Lehigh or Bucknell or Georgetown, while I was on my hands and knees scrubbing grease off the floors at Burger King, about to head into Barnard and gritty New York City. Our lives had totally diverged. But still—I should have returned that wrapping paper. I could have mailed it; my mom and I only lived a block from the post office. Instead I just tossed it out.

As I dug further into my life review, I saw that I frequently did those sorts of things. Not flat-out mean things, but careless, neglectful things.

Just like my dad.

Ouch. *Ouch.*

Once I saw things from that light—from the word "careless"—something clicked. But not in a good way. Suddenly everything dropped to another place, a darker place, and I realized that I needed to be perfectly honest with myself. It wasn't just carelessness: I actually didn't like people very much. I was not a people pleaser. In fact I think it's safe to say that I didn't care one bit about pleasing other people. That's not to say I didn't care about certain people; there were people I cared about with all my heart. But otherwise, no—I didn't really care about other human beings.

That's what Hilda saw. That's what my coworkers saw. And that's what made me utterly unsuited to work in retail.

Underneath that realization, there was an even darker place. I saw, and I saw it so clearly, that I did get some sort of weird pleasure out of disliking people. I did. And at Q&I, there was London, and London voiced her thoughts, which as it turned out were nearly the same as my thoughts. I was just as negative as her, but normally it was all on the inside so no one knew. But the truth was, my insides were churning with mean thoughts. Not all the time, but often enough. I guess Ruby seemed weak to me, and that made me dislike her most of all.

Oh, fuck! I thought, putting my face into Hello Kitty's. So was Hilda right? Did I have a black heart?

It was a long moment, sitting on my bed and turning that question over and over. A very long moment. But then something broke through: I realized that no, I did not have a black heart. At my core, I did not. But the good heart I had was covered over by my carelessness and scorn.

That was another bad day. Maybe not as bad as Monday or Tuesday had been, but still bad. All I could do was lay in bed; it was as if the pain in my chest was nailing me to the mattress, as if the heaviness of my shame would not allow me to move. No, that day did not go well at all.

☼ ☼ ☼

But the evening was better. Around six, there was a knock on my door. I opened my eyes and I heard Trixie's voice. "Elizabeth? Elizabeth, it's me."

I crawled out from under my duvet and opened the door. Trixie's eyebrows raised at the sight of me. "Bad day?" she asked.

"Very."

"Can I come in?"

I waved her inside, then went back to bed and slid under my duvet. Trixie sat on the edge of my bed, looking at me worriedly.

Suddenly I laughed. "Trixie, you're wearing a suit!"

And so she was, a two-piece, navy-blue suit in a demure cut that made her look like an accountant. Her glossy red hair was pulled back into a matronly bun, and she even wore stockings and sensible navy-blue pumps.

She sighed. "I know. Scary, isn't it?"

"Do you do this often?"

"God, no. I had to go deal with a legal thing."

"Is it serious?"

"Hmmm—it's at the manageable stage. Today I had to meet someone downtown. As soon as it was over, I went to Diego's and had two enormous strawberry margaritas."

I laughed. "That sounds like a normal reaction."

"I'm about to get in my pajamas, order a pizza, and watch a stupid movie on Netflix. You in?"

I smiled. "Only if it's a really, really stupid movie."

She raised a hand. "I guarantee that we will find the stupidest movie in existence."

"*Booty Call* is good," I said. Hansika and I had watched that once. "Or *Caddyshack.* That's a classic."

"Sounds like you're something of an expert," Trixie replied. "Change into your pajamas and come on over."

We had a nice evening. It was good to be out of bed and out of my apartment. Trixie's place was much different from mine, a warren of small interconnecting rooms, full of flowery smells and mellow pastels. But it was still in the basement, and it still had low ceilings and bars on the windows.

We ate the pizza while watching the movie—*The 40-Year-Old Virgin*—then we split a pint of Ben & Jerry's Phish Food. Afterward Trixie said, "That was as good as therapy—and cheaper."

I looked at her. Like me, she was wearing flannel pajamas and sprawled on the smushy pink couch under a soft pastel throw. "Do you go to therapy?" I asked.

"I have. Not now, though; I can't afford to. You?"

"No."

"Ever?"

"No. Although it's probably not a bad idea."

"If you get a good shrink, it's a lifesaver. But speaking of therapy, I have an idea. Have you ever been to the Botanic Gardens here?"

"No. Where are they?"

"They're superclose to us, about a half-hour walk. Which is nothing by car. The point is, I'm a member, and as a member I get free passes. So you know what I was thinking?"

"What?"

"Well, tomorrow I have to work at my new gig—I'm doing massages every Friday morning at National Jewish Hospital—and on my way I could drop you at the Gardens and then pick you up on my way home."

"Don't I need you to get in?"

"Nope. I had a friend from Boston staying with me a few weeks ago, and she used one of my passes while I was seeing clients. You can just go on your own."

I bit my lip. I'm not much of a nature person, and I had never been to a botanic garden.

"There's a café," Trixie teased.

"Well—I suppose so." Why not? I had to get out of the house sooner or later, and this would be good practice. I could always bring my Jane Austen omnibus and read in the café.

"Great! You'll love it. No matter what kind of mood I'm in when I go there, I always feel better when I leave."

"Do you go a lot?"

She nodded. "Usually once a week. Sometimes more. Depends on the week."

"Dress code?"

She grinned. "Colorado casual; what else?"

Friday

Friday was a lovely day, midfifties with a blue sky and puffy white clouds. Still, it was a bit of a shock to be outside again, face-to-face with all that fresh air and space and sunshine. Trixie told me that her car was parked in the big municipal lot behind our building, and I must say I was rather surprised when she led me to a fire-red Porsche. I whistled when I saw the car, and she smiled apologetically.

"I got it secondhand. Thirdhand, actually. I paid in cash, so it's all mine."

I nodded. I didn't know masseuses made that much money, but maybe Trixie had an inheritance or a trust fund. Or she used to have one, because otherwise why would she be living in the basement with me and the Snuffler?

As she drove up Ninth Avenue, Trixie said, "You'll be shocked by how close the Gardens are. They're just past the park above King Soopers."

I looked at her. "There's a park above King Soopers?"

She laughed. "Cheesman Park! You've never been? It's like maybe four blocks from King Soopers. Short blocks."

"I guess I just always walk to King Soopers and come right back."

"Well, you haven't been here that long. When did you move in?"

"June. So four months ago."

"That's right. I remember when you came. Well, my dear, it's time to learn the neighborhood."

We passed King Soopers on our left, and a few blocks later we were at Cheesman Park. Ninth Avenue stops abruptly at the park, so we took a right and drove along a curving road, passing a few cyclists and dog walkers. The park is a huge stretch of sloping green lawn with a stately white-marble pavilion at the top. It was only about nine thirty so there weren't many people on the grass, just a couple with a black puppy and a few walkers here and there.

"I can't believe this is so close to our building," I said, craning my head to look.

"Well, before you get too excited, I have to tell you a little history." Trixie stopped at a crosswalk to let an old woman using a walker creep past. "This used to be an enormous cemetery. There's probably about two thousand bodies lying under that lawn."

I widened my eyes. "You're kidding me."

"It's true," she said calmly, resuming driving. "But you get used to it. I say a little prayer for them, when I remember."

"Is this common knowledge?"

"Oh yeah. They even talk about it on the Banjo Billy tour."

"Banjo Billy! Every time I see them, they always do one of their annoying beeps."

"Oh, Banjo Billy is fun. I always take my out-of-town guests for a tour."

We drove through the rest of the park and then we picked up Ninth Avenue again. On either side of us were gorgeous homes, stately mansions of red brick and white stone with ornamental pillars and exquisite landscaping.

"I can't believe how beautiful this neighborhood is," I said, again craning my neck.

"The Gardens are just here," Trixie said, turning left. "I'll drive through the parking garage and drop you off at the entrance."

On the other side of the parking garage was a one-story gray building with benches in front. "That's where you go in," Trixie pointed. "Let me get your ticket." She opened her teal purse and pulled out a green ticket with a pink flower. "I have a three-hour shift, so I'll be back here a bit after one. You can stand right here and I'll swing by and get you."

"Will you come in then?"

"No. I wish I could, but I have a client at my place at two." She shrugged. "It's one of those days. But I need the money."

"I know what that's like. Trixie—thank you. For everything."

She waved. "My pleasure. I'm always happy to bring people here."

I got out of the car. I waved at Trixie as she drove away, and then I had a moment of doubt. I was at a place I didn't know, about to look at plants. But I'm still in Denver, I told myself, only a thirty-minute walk from the Swiss Arms. I have my book, so worst comes to worst I'll just curl up in the café and read.

I walked into the entrance. There was a ticket counter and an extensive gift shop that smelled like fancy candles. The woman behind the counter took my pass and gave me a map. "Or you can just wander," she said. "That's fun, too."

"Is it possible to get lost?"

She laughed. "No. It's not a jungle in there. Actually, compared to other cities, this botanic garden isn't so big; it's only two blocks by four blocks. You can always look at the mountains to get your bearings."

I nodded, embarrassed. I sounded like a tourist, not like someone who had been born there. "And the café?" I asked.

"On your right." She turned around and pointed out another low gray building. "From there you can get to the Tropical Conservatory. But otherwise the plants are all outdoors."

"Thanks a lot," I said. I put the map in my knapsack and went over to the big glass doors that led outside. All right, I thought. It's not possible to get lost, and there's a café. You can do this. I pushed against the glass doors and went outside again.

Then I just wandered. I started by taking a left down a red-brick pathway, which was surrounded by thick groupings of plants on both sides, including some purple and gold flowers. Then the pathway opened up: there was a courtyard with a few benches, to my right another long pathway, and to my left something very cool, a wall with water flowing down into a pool with a funky swordfish sculpture. The wall was light purple, and the color shimmered and shifted behind the sheet of water. There was a bench in front of the wall for sitting and looking, but I didn't feel like resting just yet.

So that's how it went, me walking, meandering really, and coming upon one beautiful thing after another. The layout was not uniform, but it didn't feel chaotic, either; there were just dozens of little universes, all peacefully coexisting. I saw plenty of trees, both short and tall, and even though it was almost October, I came upon more flowers than I expected.

There were also dozens of benches in a range of sizes and materials, marble, iron, stone, and wood.

I fell into a pattern of walking a bit, sitting on a bench to rest, then getting up and walking again. It was nice to just sit and look at whatever was in front of me—sometimes a sweep of lawn, sometimes densely packed plants, sometimes well-tended flowerbeds. Water flowed all through the Gardens, in many forms—fountains, little ponds, narrow waterways, and one huge vertical sculpture with water pouring down it that created a cloud of mist.

When I sat, I also smelled. I'm not a big olfactory person—I don't believe I've ever bought myself a bottle of perfume in my life—but as I sat, I breathed in deeply. Mostly the scent was light and lovely, or the rich tang of fallen leaves, but sometimes I got a hit of pond water or some unknown pungent flower.

What struck me most was how quiet it was. Surely they had visiting school groups that made a lot of noise, and weekends were probably packed, but on a Friday morning in late September, the Gardens were very still. The only noises I heard were the flow of water, breezes rustling the leaves, an occasional voice from the volunteers working here and there, and once the mournful drone of an airplane passed by overhead.

The place I sat longest was the Japanese Garden. It had a square wooden gazebo, nice and shady with a view over a small pond. Twisting pine trees leaned over the pond, and I watched a smattering of yellow leaves float on the surface. It reminded me of the Chinese Garden Court in the Metropolitan Museum of Art, which was my go-to spot in Manhattan whenever I felt stressed or sad. In one of my college art-history classes, the teacher hipped us to the fact that the Met has a "pay what you will" policy, so it was possible to get in with just a quarter. I used to go there and sit in the Chinese Garden Court, then wander a bit in the rest of the museum. Did the Botanic Gardens have a "pay what you will" policy? I could certainly use a regular place to de-stress in Denver. Which Trixie had known. Thank you, I told her silently.

I decided it was time to find the café. As I walked out of the Japanese Garden, I looked up at the beautiful white high-rise standing just outside the Gardens' gates. I imagined what it would be like to wake up and look down at the Botanic Gardens while drinking my morning coffee.

Up ahead was the Tropical Conservatory, which led to the café. I went inside; the air in the high-ceilinged room was moist and warm, and the stone paths slick with condensation. Tall trees with massive leaves loomed overhead, with thick growths of ferns and bamboo underneath. Waterfalls spilled over large rocks, and dark-green plants mingled with bright flowers, including some stunning orchids. It was like strolling through a rain forest, lush and heavy and redolent with scent, and as I walked I pretended I was in a jungle in the Amazon.

Then the jungle stopped, and there was a door to the lobby. I opened it and saw the café to my right. A pretty, open space, the café had windows for walls and was decorated in earthy sages and browns. Tea was the cheapest thing on the menu, so I got a cup and sat on the brown banquette behind a little square table. There was a water sculpture in the café as well, with clear sheets of water pouring up and over a glass pane that caught the light in tiny bright sparkles. I didn't feel like reading, so I didn't. I sat and drank my tea, taking it all in.

At one point I asked an older woman passing by what time it was, and she said it was noon. So I had an hour and a bit until Trixie came to get me. I finished my tea and went outside again, meandering in no particular direction.

Eventually I found a section that I had missed on my first walk, a shaded area with an Oriental theme, including a bamboo grove, a wooden moongate, and a charming wooden pavilion. There was also a path composed of small black rocks, all sticking up about two inches. I thought this was terribly odd, but then I watched the Japanese couple in front of me. They were both wearing bucket hats like the one favored by Reni, the drummer from the Stone Roses, and they were walking barefoot on the stones, giggling happily as they slowly stepped on the upright rocks. In a flash I had my sneakers and socks in one hand and was right behind them. I walked to the end of the path and back, treating my feet to a rocky mini-massage. I thought about Emma and Jasmine and how much they would love this, too.

I sat on a wooden bench in the pavilion and put my socks and sneakers back on. Then I wandered along a dirt path, and before long I found myself in a rose garden, with a few autumn roses still in bloom. I found a white-marble bench under a shady patch of trees, and I sat down to rest. A breeze flew by and ruffled the leaves above me, moving dappled shadows over the bench and tickling the waters of the man-made pond.

I felt calm, but I also felt that searing pain in my chest, the place where the weird kick had occurred. The previous day had been a bad day. A very bad day. To realize how mean I could be, to realize that I had picked on Ruby because she seemed weak—that was bad. That was really bad.

But what could I do about it? I couldn't just wave a wand and change myself. I couldn't instantly become a people-pleaser who baked cookies for my coworkers. But I could at least try to be nice. Or—a better word, a less sappy word—I could try to be kind. I could try to approach my fellow human beings with a modicum of kindness.

There! That was it. I could treat people with a modicum of kindness. I could definitely do that. I was sure of it.

And it wasn't only Ruby that I had to treat differently. I had to be kinder across the board: Hadley, Bree, Fat Bob, Stacie, all my coworkers. Also the customers, who got under my skin like no one else; I hated their indecisiveness, their lack of purpose. But I had to be kind to them too, because I would lose my job if I wasn't. I could not, under any circumstances, lose my job.

All right, I thought, standing up. A modicum of kindness. My new motto.

I wandered around a bit more, then found myself back in the main building. I saw a big green-and-pink sign that I had missed earlier: LAST SATURDAYS FREE AT THE GARDENS. Someone had put a yellow banner on top of the sign that declared: TOMORROW!

I went up to the young lady behind the counter. "Excuse me. Is tomorrow free for everyone?"

"Yes, it is. The last Saturday of every month is free, all day long." She smiled at me. "Of course, if you're a member, it's always free."

"How much is membership?"

"Are you a student?"

"No."

"An individual membership is forty-five dollars."

Forty-five dollars. It might as well have been a thousand. But at least I could come back the next day. "Thank you," I said. "A regular admission is—?"

"Ten dollars."

"Thanks."

I went outside to wait for Trixie on York Street, musing over the money. Maybe I could get a membership as a Christmas present. I could ask my dad to get it for me. But he would forget; better to ask him for the money and then do it myself. Meanwhile there were the free Saturdays, if I wasn't working.

A few minutes later, Trixie pulled up in her sporty red car, and I hopped in the front seat. "Hi," I said.

"Hi there," she replied, pulling into the road. "How'd it go?"

"Trixie, how can I thank you? It's such a wonderful place."

She laughed. "You got zapped, huh?" She made a right onto Ninth. "It's the plants. They're healing."

"I can't believe this has been so close to me all these months and I never knew it. I'm going back again tomorrow for the free day."

She looked at me. "I'm so glad. I could tell you needed . . . something."

I told her about the Chinese Garden Court at the Met and how it used to be my go-to destination when I needed to decompress. "If you live in a city, you have to have that," I said. "Or no matter where you live, I guess. Can you imagine the people who live in that white high-rise next to the Gardens? They can just walk out the door and they're right there."

"Actually," Trixie said, stopping at the red light in front of King Soopers. "That's the Cheesman Club Apartments. That's where I used to live."

I raised my eyebrows. "You're kidding me."

"Nope. I had one of those corner balconies that face west and south. I could look over the Gardens and I could see the Rockies. During nice weather, I used to live on my balcony."

"I bet," I said. I wanted to ask more, but I left it at that. Clearly Trixie had a story. Maybe a rich boyfriend who dumped her? A gambling problem? I was curious, but it wasn't my place to pry.

"The thing about the Gardens is, you can use them how you like," Trixie went on. "People have picnics there, they bring their laptops and work—you can really make yourself comfortable."

"I'm going to spend all day there tomorrow," I declared.

She laughed. "I'll take a detour and show you where to get the bus. It's really close to our building."

Back in my studio, I lay down in my bed and slept deeply for several hours, waking up around four when the Snuffler passed by my door with an unusually loud expulsion of phlegm. I was hungry and I had energy, so I walked up to King Soopers to buy some real food—no chocolate for dinner that night. As I approached the store, I thought about how Cheesman Park was just a few blocks up, and the Botanic Gardens just a few blocks more. This is where I live, I thought.

I walked back in the cool early evening, fixed tuna fish salad for dinner, then lay in bed and read Jane Austen. I had finished *Sense and Sensibility* and was about halfway through *Pride and Prejudice.* My namesake, Elizabeth Bennet, was just telling Mr. Darcy that he was arrogant, conceited, and full of selfish disdain, when my eyes grew heavy and I fell asleep.

Saturday

I woke up Saturday morning just after eight, eager to start my day at the Gardens. For breakfast I had a cup of tea and a day-old croissant from King Soopers, then I tidied up my studio and took a shower. I dressed in jeans, a dark-purple long-sleeved T-shirt, and a black cardigan with fat white buttons. I packed up a peanut butter sandwich on whole wheat for lunch, filled up my water bottle, and was about to put my Jane Austen omnibus in my knapsack when I chose Simone's *She Came to Stay* instead—much lighter for walking around. I dug through my bowl of spare change and counted out enough money for the bus, and I also took my lone credit card so I could buy Emma's birthday present at the gift store. I had intended to buy a book for her at Quill & Ink with my employee discount, but for obvious reasons that wasn't going to happen.

It was another lovely day, midfifties with a blue sky and cheerful breeze. I walked over to Twelfth, and only waited a few minutes before the bus lumbered up the street. The ride was pretty; there weren't stately mansions like the blocks between Cheesman Park and the Botanic Gardens, but there were plenty of trees and nice brick apartment buildings, some old like the ones on my block. The bus curved left through Cheesman Park, and I looked out the window at the pristine green lawn, thinking of all those dead bodies. I wondered what sort of prayer Trixie said for them. I hopped off the bus just past York Street and walked over to the Gardens. Easy—the whole thing took no more than twenty-five minutes.

As I entered the main building, a pink-and-green sign declared: FREE ALL DAY! COME IN! Hooray, I thought. I walked right through the building and out into the Gardens.

I wandered around just as I had the day before, only this time I meandered along the south side of the Gardens. That particular section bordered the rear of the fancy mansions on Ninth Avenue, and sometimes I could see the houses and their backyards through the black-iron and wooden fences that enclose the Gardens. The south side was a remarkable stretch of greenery, one small, thoughtful oasis after another—the Herb Garden, the Scripture Garden, the Woodland Mosaic, the Birds and Bees Walk, the Rock Alpine Garden, with courtyards and trellises and benches and fountains and statues. I could hardly believe my eyes, it was so lovely. I did the same bench-hopping as before, just sitting and looking and smelling, occasionally drinking water from my canister.

The Gardens were definitely more crowded that day, and the numbers increased as the morning went on. Most people were quiet and respectful, although a few were loud and commented on absolutely everything that crossed their vision. Don't hate them, I told myself. Don't hate them. The good thing was that they always moved on, leaving me in relative peace.

I slowly worked my way around the perimeter of the garden, discovering along the way a cactus sanctuary and a really cool Plains Garden with sage bushes and sweetgrass. Then I bumped into the Japanese Garden where I had sat the day before. Truly the Gardens were not all that big. But I didn't mind; I loved Central Park in Manhattan, but sometimes it felt so enormous and unwieldy, and you never knew when you would suddenly find yourself in some semi-deserted nook, face-to-face with a homeless person or someone doing drugs. Once when Hansika and Gerard and I were taking a walk, we came upon a couple having sex in the bushes. You could maybe do that in the Gardens, but it would have to be very early in the day, and you would have to be quick.

I sat on a slatted wooden bench in the Japanese Garden and looked up at the white high-rise. It was so white and elegant, like a tall, skinny wedding cake. I looked at the huge balconies wrapping around both sides of the building, and I could see a few umbrellas from patio sets peeking above the balcony walls. The rent must be phenomenal—three thousand a month, maybe four? It was the sort of place that London would decorate for an obscene amount of money.

London. I wondered how it was going for her and the Broncos' quarterback. She was probably ecstatic to be out of Q&I and once again working in the field she loved. Well, good for her.

I ate my peanut butter sandwich on a bench in the rose garden, then walked to the gift shop. I figured I should get Emma's present right away and not rush at the end when I was tired. Emma was extremely easy to shop for: books or Hello Kitty. Or both, if they somehow overlapped. I was happy to see a children's section in the shop, and even happier to see so many books. I assumed that there wouldn't be a Hello Kitty section; this place was much too sophisticated for that, with its blown-glass vases, exquisite textiles, and top-quality gardening gear. Still, I thought as I collected a few books to look through, Hello Kitty could find a niche there. I imagined her in flowered overalls and a little straw hat and a miniature spade in her paw, her mouthless expression utterly unfazed by the task of gardening.

I sat in a quiet corner and looked through the books. I finally settled on one about the Japanese tea ceremony, complete with lovely drawings and easy-to-follow instructions on conducting a ceremony at home. I knew this meant that one day soon I would be kneeling on the floor of Emma's room, wearing a bathrobe in lieu of a kimono, with a fair bit of tea splashed about. But I didn't mind. The book was twenty-five dollars, way over my nonexistent budget. I hated to put anything on my credit card—I was poor, but at least I was debt-free. The book was for Emma's birthday, however, so I made an exception.

I took my time looking around the rest of the store, lingering over a table with gorgeous coffee-table books on flowers and plants. Q&I had a decent gardening section, which I had shelved many times, but this shop had at least two dozen titles I had never seen before. I didn't care much about gardening per se, but I could always appreciate a well-made book, and as I looked through some of the titles I was impressed by the high quality.

I moved onto the ceramics section and examined the mugs, then I tried on a few hats and eyed the tasteful jewelry. I went over to the wall to examine a display of framed flowers in thin gold frames. I was just thinking that the display reminded me of the wall of framed flowers in *The Girl with the Dragon Tattoo,* when I heard a voice behind me say, "Don't you love Columbine?"

My eyes flew open. I turned around to see who would say such a crazy thing, but by the time my eyes landed on a short gray-haired lady with a Denver Botanic Gardens name tag, I realized my mistake: in this universe, Columbine is a flower.

"I do," I said. "It's my favorite."

I looked back at the wall and there it was, a Rocky Mountain Columbine, the state flower of Colorado. When I was in hippie preschool in

Boulder before moving out East, we used to draw Columbine, and Emma also drew it for her school. It's such an unusual flower, with creamy white petals upright in a circle, bluish-purple spurs stretching out underneath, and long yellow stamen in the middle. Columbine bloom in early summer, and I remember when I came back to Colorado as a twelve-year-old, I saw Columbine at Rocky Mountain National Park and had such a strong feeling of nostalgia, of home. And that moment, as a thirty-six-year-old, I had that feeling still. I never learned about New York or New Jersey's flower, but this flower I knew.

I was about to buy Emma's book when my eye fell on a CLEARANCE sign. I went over to a corner bookshelf with items that were chipped or had somehow missed the mark. I saw a flat gray rock with writing on it; I picked it up and read:

> I GIVE THANKS FOR HELP UNKNOWN,
> ALREADY ON ITS WAY
> —NATIVE AMERICAN PROVERB

I'm not much of a crier, as I've said, but when I read the inscription my eyes filled with tears. I turned it over—there was a splash of red paint on the back and a sticker that said: DAMAGED—$5. I decided to buy the rock for Trixie. Maybe she wouldn't like it, but I pretty much thought she would.

The young woman behind the counter wrapped my gifts with precision, using sparkly red-gold paper and thick white ribbon. I smiled to myself as I thought of Fat Bob at the front desk of Q&I, fumbling over a roll of gift wrap. Elizabeth! I told myself sternly. No more Fat Bob. Just Bob.

I asked if I could pick up my gifts on the way out, and the young woman said, "Sure. People do that all the time." I thanked her and walked over to building with the café. I spent a fair amount of time wandering around the library and art exhibit and other public rooms, then I went to the café for a cup of tea. The clock on the wall said two o'clock on the nose; the Gardens closed at five, so I still had plenty of time.

I settled into a soft chair in a corner, in front of the large windows that look into the Tropical Conservatory. I sipped my tea for a while, not thinking of anything in particular, then I pulled out *She Came to Stay.* For a moment I imagined that this lovely sage-and-brown room with floor-to-ceiling windows was my home. I used to do that at the Metropolitan Museum of Art, wandering around the museum and pretending that it was my home. I once told my old boyfriend Max about that, and he laughed so hard he snorted.

I read for a while, an hour at least, but as I read I kept fighting back a sour feeling in my stomach. It wasn't the tea, or the milk I had put in it. Eventually I realized it was the book. I had no problem with the prose: even in translation, Simone's language was exquisite. It wasn't the ideas; I found the characters' exquisitely nuanced discussions quite thrilling. No, it was the dreadful plot, which concerned a couple named Françoise and Pierre—Simone and Sartre, let's face it, since the book is largely autobiographical—and their weird romantic triangle with an unstable but desirable young girl named Xaviere. This included Françoise's machinations to make the unsavory situation work out in her favor, which she finally does. I won't reveal the book's ending, but I will say it is not pretty.

I realized something at that moment. It pained me to admit it, because I'd loved Simone so much for so many years. But it was time to face the truth: Simone was kind of a bitch. She was cold and calculating, and when she turned her brilliant, incisive language on someone she disapproved of, the results were devastating. Jane Austen could be snippy, but Jane was a pussycat compared to Simone, who was often flat-out eviscerating.

This was not news to me. In fact, Simone's clever cruelty was something I had always rather enjoyed. Over the years I had read almost all of Simone's considerable literary output—her novels, memoirs, and letters, as well as many biographies. And although I had lied to Hadley Barr about it, I had read that terrible memoir by Bianca Lamblin. In the years before World War Two, Lamblin had been both Simone and Sartre's lover, and she had enjoyed a weekly lunch with Simone up until Simone's death in 1986. When Simone's letters were published posthumously, Lamblin had been stunned to read the petty and vengeful things Simone had written about her, and so Lamblin wrote her own book to set the record straight. It wasn't just that Simone had been catty; she had pooh-poohed Lamblin's fears about the Nazis, although Lamblin was Jewish and in grave danger. As it turned out, some of Lamblin's family did die in concentration camps. On Simone's part, this was beyond callous; it was downright cruel, and emotionally ice-cold.

I knew all that, but I never cared because I loved Simone so much as an artist. As I sat in my cushy chair in the café at the Denver Botanic

Gardens, I saw with a shock that I had done with Simone what so many people did with the Beats and my dad: I gave her a free pass for her bad behavior because she was an artist. I didn't care that Simone hurt people, because I liked her art.

I thought about this for quite a while. Clearly, if you only let yourself read books, see paintings, and hear music by morally impeccable people, your life would be pretty empty. The point was more that Simone had been a role model for me. I thought she was so fabulous and intelligent, living in hotels and writing in cafés and exercising her formidable intelligence. All that was true, and it was genuinely compelling. But some of her behavior—particularly the way that she and Sartre used young women—was despicable.

Restless, I finished my tea, put Simone in my knapsack, and went outside to wander through the Gardens again. By now the paths were quite full, but I barely noticed the other people. I wandered all the way to the Rock Alpine Garden in the southwest corner and sat on a wooden bench that was practically invisible behind a weeping willow. I took out my canister and had a long drink of water, and suddenly I thought about *Washington Square.* What was that one line? Something about how it was better to be clever than to be good. Before I would have agreed with that wholeheartedly. But now? Now I wasn't so sure. Simone was clever, but Simone was not good.

I needed a new role model, someone or something good. Oddly enough, Hello Kitty popped into my mind. I laughed out loud, but I didn't dismiss it. Maybe that's why Emma liked Hello Kitty so much, because she was good. I had seen unwholesome depictions of Hello Kitty—Hello Kitty straining on a toilet, Hello Kitty on all fours wearing black-leather chaps—but overall Hello Kitty had an air of harmless, no-mouth innocence. For me, of course, what really lay behind Hello Kitty was Emma, her goodness and her kindness and her pure love for me, which included her simple faith that a thirty-six-year-old woman would appreciate a plush Hello Kitty doll in a purple-plaid jumper and bow.

Good-bye Simone. Hello Kitty.

I laughed and shook my head. I was tired; I wasn't thinking straight. Probably it was time to go home.

When I stopped at the gift shop to pick up my presents, the woman behind the counter was busy with a difficult customer. I knew what that was like, so I waited patiently, twirling a rack of postcards and looking at them idly. There were postcards of the Botanic Gardens throughout the four seasons, and there were also beautiful close-ups of flowers. There was even a Rocky Mountain Columbine, in all its elegance and gorgeous colors.

When the woman at the register called me over, I took a Columbine postcard out of the rack. "I'm here to pick up my presents," I said. "And to buy this."

She put my gifts into a small shopping bag and rang up my postcard. I put the bag in my knapsack, and I tucked the postcard carefully within the pages of *She Came to Stay.*

Sunday

Emma's party was from two to four, and I showed up at one. A few purple balloons were tied to the white fence, and a Hello Kitty doll had been squeezed into the heart-shaped carving on the gate, her big head popping out to greet everyone as they entered.

I rang the doorbell. I heard running feet, then the door flew open. Emma stood before me, resplendent in her birthday attire: pink long-sleeved T-shirt, pink leggings, a royal-purple shift, hair in two braids with Hello Kitty barrettes at the ends, and last—but not possibly least—lime-green cowboy boots.

She threw herself into my arms. "Sister! Look at my cowboy boots!"

"I see them!" I exclaimed. "They're beautiful."

"They're my present from Mommy."

Jasmine emerged from the kitchen. She looked pretty in a loose flowered dress, her thick hair in a disheveled bun. It occurred to me that I should have dressed up and not just shown up in my usual jeans, but after the week I had been through, it was enough that I was there.

"Hey," Jasmine said. I leaned down so she could kiss me on the cheek.

"Hey there," I said. "You both look so nice."

"Thanks. Do you want some coffee? I have a fresh pot."

"I desperately want coffee."

She grinned. "Well, follow me."

Holding Emma's hand, I walked to the kitchen. The little house looked good, full of balloons and streamers and bowls of candy and chips, plus a card table set up in the corner with soda for the kids and wine for the adults. The kitchen table was almost covered by a magnificent sheet cake that had a huge Hello Kitty head floating in a sea of pink frosting. I admired the cake, then sat down and drew Emma onto my lap.

"I know it's the style to rent ponies and psychics for birthday parties," Jasmine said while she fixed my coffee, "but we're doing this old-school. Lots of sugar and bright colors, everyone in and out in two hours."

"Last year," Emma said, "I went to a party and we all had our horoscopes done."

I nodded. "That's very Boulder."

"At another party, we rode ponies. But one girl broke her collarbone."

"See?" Jasmine said, putting my coffee on the table and taking a seat. "Much safer this way."

Emma tapped my knapsack, which I had put on the floor by my seat. "What's in there?"

"Oh," I said, sipping my coffee. "Nothing much."

"Nothing? Are you sure?"

"Well, now that you mention it, there might actually be something in there. I don't remember."

"Just so you know, we have a special rule for this birthday."

"And what's that?"

"I'm allowed to open family gifts early. I don't have to wait for dinner tonight like we usually do. That's how come I have my boots."

"Is that so?"

"Yep. So if you have something in there, it's OK to give it to me now. I'm just sayin.'"

"Well, I'm just sayin' that I do, so why don't you open my knapsack and see?"

Emma immediately leaned over and unzipped my knapsack, her eyes widening when she saw the shiny red-gold paper. In the blink of an eye, the present was out of the knapsack, the wrapping torn off, and Emma had the tea-ceremony book open on her lap. She carefully turned the pages and we read through it, with Jasmine standing and looking over our shoulders. I could tell that Emma loved the book, and I felt happy. I hugged her to me and put my nose in her sweet-smelling hair.

"You got this at Quill & Ink, of course," Jasmine said.

"No, I actually got it at the Denver Botanic Gardens. Have you ever been?"

"You know, we haven't, which is ridiculous. We're so Boulder centered."

"My friend Trixie from the building is a member, so she gave me a free pass. And yesterday was their free day, so I went a second time."

"Oh, so you're hanging out with Trixie? That's great."

"We're hanging out a bit. She's really nice." I hesitated. No point elaborating on my bad week; I didn't want to kill the party buzz. "I think I'm going to ask Dad for a membership for Christmas. If you're a member, you can go as often as you like."

"Is it close to your apartment?"

"Very close. Just a short bus ride, or a half-hour walk."

"Emma," Jasmine said. "Everyone's going to be here soon, so why don't you run upstairs and put the book some place safe in your room?"

"OK." She slid off my lap, then turned around and gave me a hug.

"Happy birthday, other daughter," I said, kissing her cheek.

"Thank you, *other* other daughter."

As soon as Emma left the room, Jasmine turned to me. "Someone had a little meltdown this morning."

I laughed. "You?"

"Believe me, I was right behind her."

"What happened?"

"We had to go down to the basement to get the card table and a few folding chairs, and she wouldn't go. I told her we'd be together, but she started crying."

"Because of JonBenét?"

Jasmine shrugged. "Apparently. Emma's never acted like this before; I don't know why it's gripped her so strongly. Anyway, that's why I let her open her present early. It was the only way to make the day move forward."

"Bribery?"

"Completely." She looked at me worriedly. "Am I a bad mom?"

I laughed. "You're a great mom. And a great stepmom, to boot."

Jasmine smiled broadly. She was so pretty. "Well, thank you, ma'am."

"Speaking of parents, is Dad coming?"

"I left him two messages, Emma left him three, I spoke to him twice at Naropa, I spoke to Jane once, and on Friday I left a huge note in his office. So no, I don't know if he's coming. I'll kill him if he forgets." The doorbell rang. "That must be Peach and her mom. They said they'd come a little early. Oh well," Jasmine said, rising from her chair and heading for the door. "Let the madness begin."

And madness it was. Within a half hour, the tiny house was packed with about twenty children and just as many adults—moms, dads, moms and dads, moms and moms, dads and dads, the full range of the modern family. There was also the usual slew of poets, including Jasmine's mentor Beatrice Woolster, who stopped by on her way to the airport to give Emma a kiss and drop off a present. Emma was in her element, whirling around like a tornado in her lime-green cowboy boots, accepting gifts, giving hugs, running upstairs to put her presents on Jasmine's bed, which was the only free space available. She was excited but she was gracious, and I was proud of her. As usual.

As for me, I drank far too much coffee and ate way too many M&M's, which have been a weakness for me since childhood. I wasn't up for adult conversation, particularly with some earnest Boulderite who wanted to discuss my vision for the planet, so I stuck to the kids. Emma's hairstyle had set off a rash of copycats, so for a while I was in charge of braiding hair. Then Emma needed me to go upstairs with her and Boy Dylan to rearrange the presents, which were teetering in a precarious arrangement. After that I had a surreal conversation with Famous Peach and Girl Dylan about the difference between Hello Kitty and Chococat, during which Girl Dylan revealed the shocking truth that Hello Kitty was not supposed to be Japanese but was in fact British.

An hour into the party, it was time for cake. Jasmine didn't dare try to lift the massive sheet cake from the kitchen table, so everyone squeezed into the kitchen and the back porch in order to watch Emma accept the Happy Birthday song and blow out all nine candles in one concentrated swoosh. I helped Jasmine cut and distribute pieces of cake, and when everyone had been served I went out to the back porch with my own plate, hoping for a little peace and quiet. Unfortunately a group of Moms Gone Wild were smoking a joint in a corner of the tiny backyard, and since I can't stand the smell I went back inside and took my cake up to Jasmine's room. There to my surprise was Jasmine, sitting on the edge of the bed beside the tower of presents, thoughtfully working her way through a slice of pink-and-white cake.

"I'm hiding from my guests," she explained.

"I'm hiding, too," I said, perching next to her. "Look at this stack of presents!"

"We have nowhere to put any of it. Thank God for regifting. Are you having fun?"

"I am, although I'm a victim of too much caffeine and too much sugar. Speaking of which, this cake is delicious."

"I know, right? Usually I give away the leftover cake at the end of the party, but not this time."

"We can have seconds tonight," I agreed.

We ate in silence a bit, then I said, "So—Dad?"

Jasmine shot me a look. "Not here, clearly. There's only a half hour left."

"Has Emma said anything?"

Jasmine shrugged. "She wanted to wait to cut the cake until he showed up. I didn't have the heart to tell her that he might not come at all."

But he did show up, finally. Jasmine and I had just ventured back downstairs, relieved to see that a few of the guests had cleared out, when the front door opened and there was our dad. Also Jane, who looked shy and nervous and absolutely lovely in a lacy white dress.

"Daddy!" Emma shot like a bullet through the crowd and threw her arms around him, pressing her cheek to his big stomach.

"Happy birthday, Daughter," he said, bending over and kissing the top of her head.

Emma looked over at Jasmine. Jasmine nodded, so Emma released our dad and threw her arms around Jane, who blushed prettily and laid her cheek on Emma's head.

From that moment on, it was our dad's party. He started off with a bang by turning around and displaying the enormous Hello Kitty head on the back of his red-silk robe. Then he took a seat in the center of the couch with Emma on his lap and Jane next to him. I brought them coffee and cake, and we all watched as Emma opened her present from him. It was a medium-sized rectangular box with Hello Kitty wrapping paper, and inside was a Hello Kitty waffle iron, in the shape of Hello Kitty's head. Emma was delighted, and our dad looked happy, too. It always amazed me how he pulled it off: he was unforgivably late, but he had managed to redeem himself, and once again his misconduct faded away like mist.

As Emma clung to our dad, he proceeded to work the crowd, telling charming tales about Emma's childhood and her burgeoning gift with words. All the adult guests sat enthralled, hanging on his every utterance. At one point Jane got up to refill our dad's coffee, and I saw her and Jasmine talking in the kitchen. I remembered my modicum of kindness and went to join them. I could see that Jane was nervous, but Jasmine was kind and welcoming, and the three of us had a nice chat about Boulder and Naropa—that is, until my dad bellowed out, "Jane! Coffee!" She smiled at us apologetically and went to bring coffee to the Great Poet.

I listened to my dad for a few minutes longer, but then something snapped. It had been an awful week, what with being banished from work and then spending all those painful hours in my bed. Trixie had been great, I loved the Botanic Gardens, and I was always happy to see Emma and Jasmine, but the moment arrived when I was just done. I edged past the guests and went upstairs to Jasmine's meditation room, where I lay down on the futon and wrapped the duvet around my body and over my head.

I must have fallen asleep, because when I woke up the room was dark. I heard the sound of the door creaking open; I peeked out of the duvet and saw Emma's little face in the doorway.

"Can I come in?" she asked.

"Of course." I held open my arms, and she dropped onto the futon and snuggled next to me. "Is the party over?" I asked.

"Yep. Boy Dylan threw up, then everyone left."

"That's usually a sign it's time to go. Is Dad still here?"

"He doesn't like throw up, so he left. Him and *Jane.*" She said the name in italics.

"Did you talk to her?"

"A little. She said she helped Daddy pick out my gift."

Undoubtedly. "Well, it's a really cool present. Next time I come over, we can make Hello Kitty–head waffles."

"What about tomorrow?"

"Tomorrow I have to get up early and get the bus to work." I sighed heavily.

Emma peered at me in the half-dark. "Are you sick?"

"No, not exactly."

"Is something wrong?"

I don't know why, but it always broke my heart to see how vigilant Emma was whenever anyone was upset. "It's just that I messed something up. I really hurt someone's feelings. I didn't mean to, but I did."

Emma looked at me, her eyes big and solemn. "Was it Daddy?"

"Oh no." As if anything I did would ever penetrate him. "Someone at work."

"Who?"

"A woman named Ruby."

"What did you do?"

"I said some things that hurt her feelings. I want to make it right, but I don't know how."

Emma took my hand, and we lay in silence. Then she said, "Remember what you told me about cleaning my room?"

"What was that?"

"You said to start small. To take one little part, fix that, and then pick something else."

"I did say that, didn't I."

"So maybe you could do that."

I smiled. She was so kind, just like Jasmine. "That's a good idea. Speaking of cleaning—"

"Yes?"

"Why don't we go downstairs and help your mom?"

"Boy Dylan's mom already mopped up his throw up."

"Now, that's good manners. But there's probably a bunch of other stuff we can help your mom with."

"Well, before we help Mommy, can I show you my presents? I unwrapped them all when you were sleeping."

I laughed. "Sounds like a plan." I remembered the huge sheet-cake on the kitchen table, and my plans to have seconds. Thus inspired, I got up to rejoin the world.

2. Start Small

I returned to Quill & Ink the next day. My intention was to start small, but honestly, walking into the store that Monday morning was one of the most enormous things I have ever done.

The early-morning bus trip from Boulder to Denver was a continuous internal pep talk. I told myself that I was not a bad person. I had messed up, and yes, sometimes I was a little mean, but from now on I could do better. I *would* do better. I couldn't take back what had happened with Ruby, but at least I could ensure that it never happened again. My relationships with my other coworkers wouldn't change overnight, but I was returning to work with a modicum of kindness, and that would take me forward.

The bus pulled into Market Street Station at seven thirty. During the walk to Q&I, my stomach twisted into a knot, and when I touched the ornate brass doorknob at the Wynkoop Street entrance, my hand was shaking. I swallowed hard and went inside.

The first person I saw was the Wolf Man. He was sitting in an easy chair by the door, wearing his wolf cap and stroking his pet wolf, a cup of coffee on the small table at his side. He looked at me with his ice-blue eyes, then turned his head away.

Great, I thought. Even the Wolf Man is snubbing me.

I turned right and went to the café. Hadley was behind the counter, and when he saw me, he broke into a huge smile. I smiled back. I had never been so happy to be on the receiving end of his boundless enthusiasm.

"Elizabeth Zwelland! Back! I missed you."

"Hi, Hadley. How's it going?"

"Good, very good. You punching in at eight?"

"Yep."

"You need some coffee?"

"I do. Just a regular."

But Hadley made me a latte anyway, and he didn't charge me. As he passed me the cup, I had an unbearable moment of paranoia. Did he know? Of course he knew. Did everyone know? Of course they did. That feeling of shame came back full force, and I put my hand on the fissure in my chest.

I looked up at the chalkboard and read Hadley's weekly Kerouac quote:

> HOLD STILL, MAN, REGAIN YOUR LOVE OF LIFE
> JACK KEROUAC, *DESOLATION ANGELS*

I smiled. "Nice quote."

"I know!" Hadley said. "Jack as positive life-coach. I like it."

"Well, I better punch in. Thanks for the latte."

"See you later!" He gave me one of his goofy-awkward waves, and I wiggled my fingers back.

I walked slowly to the break room, taking a cautious look around as I moved through the store. I saw Fa—I saw Bob standing at the register, Juniper sashaying up the stairs, Rebecca working in the stationery section. So far, so good.

But when I went into the break room and looked at the schedule, I had an unpleasant shock. As promised, Hilda had put me on the schedule for that day, but only for a four-hour shift instead of my usual eight. I had another four-hour shift on Thursday, then I was working six hours on both Saturday and Sunday.

The first problem was that my hours had been cut. I had started at Q&I working twenty hours a week, then moved up to thirty, and now I was back to twenty. I was also working both Saturday and Sunday. Hilda always gave people at least one weekend day free, but suddenly I was on the schedule for both days. It felt like a slap in the face—as it was intended to be, I'm sure.

I took a deep breath. Steady, I told myself. Steady. I looked at the schedule to see who had gotten my extra hours, and I saw two new names on the schedule, two people who were each working twenty hours a week. Hilda had taken London's thirty hours, added ten from me, and hired—whoever they were—Rich and Debbie.

I sat down and drank my latte. I felt deeply hurt. And scared: How could I go back to living on twenty hours a week? And if I was now working both weekend days, when would I ever see Emma and Jasmine, or go to the Botanic Gardens on free Saturdays? I could only hope that the situation was temporary. Maybe I was just working Saturday and Sunday that particular week; maybe it was a one-time occurrence intended to teach me a lesson.

A four-hour shift is very short, especially when you have a mandatory fifteen-minute break, so my day was practically over before I knew it. I shelved travel and photography books most of the morning, and thankfully both sections were quiet. About an hour into my shift, I saw Hilda rushing by with a stack of Stieg Larsson books. She nodded to me curtly, but otherwise didn't speak. Rebecca passed me several times without even bothering to make eye contact. But I have to say, everyone else was pretty normal, and by the end of my quick shift, I felt OK. Not great, but OK.

One thing I did notice was how I felt around customers. An older man with bright white hair and equally bright white sneakers came over to me when I was in the photography section to ask about buying a present for his son-in-law. As he hemmed and hawed and hesitated, it was all I could do not to pick up an enormous Ansel Adams book and bop him on the head. I saw how I immediately got impatient with customers. All they had to say was, "Excuse me," and suddenly my whole body was burning with irritation. It was such an unpleasant feeling; no wonder I wanted them to go away. But it was interesting to observe, and I felt it happen each time someone came near me. Wow, I thought. I really don't like people.

I did see Ruby that day, but just barely at the end of my shift. In fact, that was probably part of the reason for my truncated hours: I worked eight to twelve, and Ruby was on from eleven thirty to six. I was returning my cart to receiving when I saw her in the hall outside the break room. When she saw me she flinched, as if she was scared of me. Then I realized: she *was* scared of me.

My heart sank. I had a long, long way to go.

I went back to work on Thursday for another mini-shift from ten to two. I had a new resolve: every day I worked, I would do one nice thing for a coworker. I still hadn't figured out how to deal with my antipathy toward customers, but I could at least start small with the people I worked with.

Bree was at the café when I came in, and I decided it was her turn that day. I had already figured out what to say to her, but I wasn't sure when I would get the opportunity. So after she handed me my morning coffee, I cleared my throat and said, "Bree, remember you were asking me about the New York City publishing world? I'd be happy to talk to you about it. I'm pretty out of the loop these days, but I can tell you what I know."

Bree blinked. "Oh! Well, yeah, sure. When's your break?"

"I'm only working four hours today, so I just get fifteen minutes. Probably at eleven thirty or so."

"Hadley comes in at eleven, so how about I find you at eleven thirty? We can sit outside in the alley."

In the alley next to the receiving room's rolling door, there was a little platform with a railing and a roof. The smokers went out there on breaks, as did other staff. I never hung out in the alley, but of course I knew where it was.

"Sure," I said. "See you then."

We only had time for a short chat, but it went well. I told Bree in a nutshell what Blue Heron was like, and how it folded due to Madoff and not the economy per se. I didn't want to discourage her, so in addition to telling her about the deep cutbacks in the industry, I told her that eBooks and self-publishing were booming.

"The whole industry is in flux," I said. "The old order is still in place, but the gatekeepers don't have the money or the power that they used to. It's a good time for little publishers and self-published authors to do something new."

I could tell that Bree was grateful to hear what I had to say. She thanked me profusely, and as we walked back inside, she shyly asked if I could take a look at some of her writing.

"I'd love to," I said firmly. "I'm working both days this weekend, so why don't you bring something in for me then."

Which meant that on Saturday, I did two nice things. When Bree came in midday, I went to the café and she handed me a short story, about forty pages in a plastic maroon binder with a neat label on the front that said: FOR ELIZABETH ZWELLAND. I went to the break room to put Bree's manuscript in my locker, and I saw Stacie lying on the flower-patterned couch with a hand flung over her head and her toothpick sticking straight up in the air. Suddenly I realized: Stacie's toothpick was a weapon. It protected her.

I cleared my throat. "Stacie, are you all right? Do you need anything?"

Stacie took out her toothpick, raised herself up on one elbow, and looked at me. It wasn't a hostile stare; she just looked puzzled. She stared quite a while, then reinserted her toothpick and lowered herself back down.

Oh well, I thought. At least I tried.

Then suddenly, Stacie spoke. She didn't speak often, so it was always a surprise to hear her clear, girlish voice: "No, thanks."

Great, I thought happily as I left the break room. That's a start.

Sunday was the day for Bob. I was sitting on the platform in the alley during one of my breaks, and Bob came out to have a smoke. He looked surprised to see me, but he sat next to me and pulled out a lighter and a pack of cigarettes.

"How's your day going, Bob?" I asked in a friendly voice.

He cocked his head and looked at me, his thick glasses shifting slightly to one side. "Elizabeth, can I tell you something?"

My heart blanched. "Sure," I said bravely. "Go ahead."

He blinked. "I prefer to be called Robert."

"Oh!" I laughed. "I'm glad you told me."

Then we had a funny chat about nicknames. I told him about all the nicknames that people had tried to pin on me over the years: Liz, Lizzie, Eliza, Betty, and the dreaded Betsy. Bob laughed and told me that when he started at Q&I, there was a part-timer in receiving who was also named Robert. The store couldn't have two Roberts, so he was christened Bob. However, Robert in receiving had just quit, so Bob was trying to reclaim the name before another Robert was hired. We had a laugh, and then I went back inside. It was a nice moment, and I was surprised by how funny he was.

Monday went well. Bree and I made plans to meet during her break on Thursday to go over her short story, Robert offered me a piece of chocolate that I accepted with great enthusiasm, and Stacie nodded to me when I was on line at the café to get coffee. Also it was my day to be nice to Juniper. She and I had always gotten along well enough, but I knew I had walked away from her several times when she was speaking to me about the Lord, her sex life, or—the worst—some combination of the two.

I knew that if I really wanted to make Juniper happy, I could tell her that I had found Jesus in my heart, but I didn't want to lie to her. I was starting small, after all. So when I stopped by her desk to drop off some reshelves, I decided to give her a compliment. That day Juniper was working her seventies disco look, complete with dark-purple jumpsuit, sparkly eye shadow, fake diamond earrings, and her trusty Afro wig.

"Juniper," I said. "You look great in purple." Which was true; it set off her chocolaty skin to perfection.

She jerked her head back a little and looked at me. "Slim! You sweet talker. Thank you very much, skinny lady."

After that I didn't even have to try anymore, to zoom in on one person and check them off my list. I was speaking to everyone, everyone was speaking to me, and I was always careful to be kind and not scornful. I was even nice to the two new people, despite the fact that they had taken my hours. First I had a long talk with Rich, a short, half–Native American guy who was getting a master's in education at Metro State. He told me about his hometown, Leadville, which was ten-thousand feet above sea level and the place where John Sayles had filmed his movie *Silver City*. Another day I got to know Debbie; she was a single mom who like me lived in Capitol Hill. After she bragged about her eleven-year-old son, Joseph, I bragged about Emma. Then we talked about King Soopers, and she told me that the Capitol Hill Whole Foods had special sales every Wednesday, which was good to know.

With Hadley, I was careful. I was nice but not too nice, because I didn't want to encourage him. I couldn't tell if Hadley had a crush on me or my family. I suspected it was the latter and therefore not very serious, but I still didn't want to give him the wrong idea. In any case I behaved better with him: I didn't cut him off when he talked to me, I sidestepped his questions about my dad with a little more grace, and I didn't inwardly or outwardly grimace when I saw him in the break room.

I was grateful to Hadley, because I think he noticed the change in me before anyone else. After I read that initial story by Bree—which was quite good, actually, about a transsexual who lived in her building—I read a few more, and one day in the break room Hadley told me how much it meant to Bree that I was taking an interest in her work. Then Hadley patted my shoulder and gave me a kind look. My eyes filled with tears, and I turned my head away.

So those were my successes. But it wasn't all successes. Because as those first weeks passed, I saw that Hilda wanted nothing to do with me. She spoke to me when she had to for work, but otherwise she just nodded curtly. One day I came up beside her as she was talking animatedly with a customer, and when I entered her field of vision, I saw her face freeze and harden. That was a bad moment for me. I realized that her heart was set against me; sparkly comments and offers to buy coffee would not make a dent. With Hilda, it was going to happen on her terms. If it happened at all.

Worse was Rebecca. She made no secret of her dislike for me, and if Hilda reduced me to curt nods, Rebecca just walked by as if I wasn't there. I guess I really hurt her when I blew her off all those weeks ago, and now her hatred was in full fester. As assistant manager she had to speak to me on occasion, but she did it in the coldest possible tone, and she avoided eye contact as we spoke, which was particularly demeaning. But despite all that, I held out an odd ray of hope. Once upon a time, Rebecca had liked me, so maybe one day she would like me again. Or at least look me in the eye.

But the worst, the very worst, was Ruby. How I wanted to make up with Ruby! I wanted that more than anything else. But whenever Ruby saw me—if she walked into the break room when I was there, if she happened to come into the receiving room as I was loading up a cart, or if she passed the café when I was chatting with Bree or Hadley—she looked scared. That look, that frozen and anxious expression, always sent a piercing pain in my chest. It reawakened my shame at its deepest level, and I was right back where I was during the week I was suspended, lying in bed with that agonizing fissure in my chest.

Several times it was on the tip of my tongue to apologize to Ruby. She was often in an obscure corner of the store, polishing shelves or sorting out some small project, and it would have been easy and private to go over and speak to her. But I couldn't do it; what had happened to her was too big, and I just didn't know what to say. I didn't have to apologize for what she had been through, I knew that, but I could apologize for what I had done. But each time I was on the brink, my shame was too great and her fear too palpable. One time when she was in the knickknack section organizing bookmarks, I took a few steps toward her, and I saw her flinch. As I turned and walked away, I realized that I was now part of Ruby's PTSD. Some days the shame of that was almost too much to bear.

Yet there was another success, and that was with the customers. It didn't happen overnight—the kindness thing was an uphill climb—but there was a real shift, and I have to say it made my life much easier.

It happened the first weekend I was back. There was an older woman who simply could not decide which Charles Dickens novel to buy for her niece. She had laid out the novels in two rows on a large table and was reading the back covers again and again. Then she spotted me shelving in the psychology section and drew me into her tortured decision-making process. She gave me a brief synopsis of each book, explaining how it might or might not suit her niece, who was laid up with a broken ankle from rock climbing and wanted to use her convalescence to read the classics. The whole situation was a migraine in the making.

As the woman explained her situation to me, every fiber of my being was trembling with hot irritation. It was excruciating. Then, almost like you would speak to a puppy, I told myself: "Stay. Just stay with this." Somehow that helped; all I had to do was stay with her, listen to her, then offer my opinion. If she started up again—and she did, several times—I just stayed again. All I had to do was stay.

To my surprise, it worked. Or at least, I didn't bite off some mean comment and make the woman feel bad. She walked away with a copy of *Our Mutual Friend* and no toxic fallout from me.

I used the method with the next customer, and the next, and it really worked. Once in a while I forgot, but basically whenever a customer approached me—particularly if they had a gleam in their eye, or that most dreaded object, a list—I just thought: This person probably doesn't know what they want. This will probably take forever. Just stay with it. I would envision myself missing my break, remaining after the store had closed for the night, standing and listening to the customer until both of us had died and turned into skeletons, which subsequently turned into piles of dust. Bring it on, I thought as the person eagerly flagged me down. Just bring it on, and I'll stay with whatever it is you dish out.

As the weeks went by, I got better at staying, and eventually I got bold and started applying the method to noncustomers. One day I was sitting on the platform in the alley with Juniper and Bree, and I actually said, "Juniper, tell me, how was your date last night?" She was off in a flash, with more details than a story could possibly bear, and I just stayed with it. I expected her story to last forever and it just about did, or at least until Juniper's break was up. But Juniper loved talking about her dates, and my listening made her happy: she walked away with a smile on her face and a promise to find me later so she could finish.

It's not that the hot, sticky irritation went away. It didn't. But now I expected it and I stayed with it, no matter what.

Another change that first month was all the free time I suddenly had. My schedule never varied: Monday I worked eight to noon, Thursday ten to two, Saturday and Sunday twelve to six. So every week I had two big chunks of time to fill, and little or no money with which to fill it—because now that my hours had been cut, I was poorer than ever. Less hours did mean that my feet hurt less, but sore feet and an extra sixty dollars a week was preferable to happy feet and poverty.

During my first free day, I spent the morning reading, and I also did a fair bit of thinking about my situation at work and how I could improve things. But eventually I got restless, and so in the afternoon I found myself walking up Ninth Avenue to Cheesman Park. I walked home along Eighth Avenue, and I was surprised to discover that I lived only two blocks from the Governor's Mansion, a gorgeous Georgian Revival building with imposing columns. Next to the mansion was Governor's Park, a small patch of green that was basically a big hill with a few benches and a playground at the bottom. So I sat there a while as well, watching dog walkers, a few high schoolers sitting on swings, and a clump of homeless men sitting by a tree and passing a bottle. The latter was a bit sketchy, but mostly the park was a calm oasis just a stone's throw from the Swiss Arms, and I decided to go back soon with a blanket and a book.

In my next free block of time, I left work at two on Thursday and took the express bus to Boulder, arriving early enough to spring Emma from her afterschool program. I bought us ice cream at the Ben & Jerry's store on the Pearl Street Mall, then we went back to the house and I helped out with her homework, which gave Jasmine a chance to run a few errands. Afterward we ordered Chinese food, and the three of us had a leisurely dinner and played a game of cards. There was no question of seeing my dad because he taught on Thursday nights, so I didn't have to face that stress.

I slept over, and in the morning we all had breakfast and I took Emma to school. Emma and Jasmine wanted me to stay another night, but I didn't want to wear out my welcome, which meant that by noon on Friday I was back in my apartment with an empty day in front of me. I walked to Cheesman Park and the Governor's Mansion again, and when I got back to the Swiss Arms I ran into Trixie by the mailboxes, and we ended up having another stupid-movie night. Saturday morning I slept in, then started my shift at Q&I at ten. So I managed to get through that first week, but still I wondered how I was going to fill so much free time.

The next week threatened to be the same. Monday, though, was a bad day. I was determined to make some inroads with Rebecca, and so I approached her when she was in the Children's department. I knew that Rebecca had a particular fondness for children's books; before she was promoted to assistant manager, she had been in charge of that section of the store. I saw her looking at a book with a shiny silver cover, so I said, "Wow, that's a cool cover. Who wrote that?"

Rebecca turned her head slowly and looked at me. Her eyes were completely dead, utterly expressionless. She closed the book, put it on a shelf, and walked away without saying a word.

I felt like I had been stabbed. Fortunately my shift ended soon after, but I felt miserable on my Mall Ride and walk home. So that's how it is, I thought. That's how it's going to be from now on. I was trying so hard, I really was, but maybe Rebecca—Rebecca and Hilda—were never going to budge.

My thoughts were very dark by the time I got home. The mailman was just leaving the building as I entered, so I opened my box, expecting at most a menu or a supermarket flyer. But I had a letter, and it was from the Denver Botanic Gardens. I opened it on the spot in the hushed, carpeted foyer. I was stunned to see that it was a membership card, and the pink-and-green letter that came with it announced that my membership was a gift from Jasmine and Emma Zwelland.

I could hardly believe my eyes. I ran downstairs to my studio and called Jasmine on my GoPhone.

"Hey," Jasmine said. "You all right?"

"Yes, I'm fine. I'm calling because I got something in the mail from the Denver Botanic Gardens?"

She laughed. "Oh, did you?"

"Jasmine. Thank you. I can't even—thank you."

"Oh, Elizabeth. I know you haven't been too happy in Colorado, and now that you've found something you like, I want to be sure you have access to it."

"It's the best gift I've ever gotten. I'm going first thing in the morning."

"And we'll see you Thursday afternoon?"

"Yes. Absolutely."

I hung up and looked around my tiny studio. It was only quarter to one, and my feet felt fine. Why wait until the next day? Why not go right away? I quickly ate a peanut butter sandwich, then I collected a few precious dollars from my change dish and went out the door with my membership card and water bottle.

So thanks to Jasmine, I ended up at the Botanic Gardens on many of my free days. Sometimes I took the bus, sometimes I got a lift from Trixie, and sometimes, if my feet were up to it, I walked. My experiences at the Gardens were never as dramatic as my first two visits, but I always experienced a shift, some kind of small emotional realignment.

I also started going to art galleries. Denver has plenty of museums, but museums cost money, and galleries are free. Unbeknownst to me, the Swiss Arms was on the edge of a section of Denver called the Golden Triangle. It was golden due to the amount of money needed to live in one of the neighborhood's swank high-rises, but it was also golden because of the culture. In fact the Denver Art Museum and the main branch of the public library constituted the wide end of the triangle, with the bottom point not too far from me. Trixie hipped me to all that, and she also told me about two galleries on Cherokee Street just a ten-minute walk from our building.

So one day I went. The two galleries—the William Havu and the Walker—were not large, but they were filled with beautiful, interesting art. At the Havu, I sat and looked for a long time at canvases filled with thick, boldly colored horizontal lines by an artist named Monroe Hodder. I must have sat there for a half hour, and when I finally roused myself I felt that shift again. It had something to do with beauty, something to do with forgetting myself. Whatever it was, I liked it.

As I strolled around the Walker, which had a group exhibit of local artists that included abstract sculptures in shiny silver steel, I realized that wandering in galleries was not new to me. I had always loved the museums in Manhattan, but it was my old boyfriend Max who introduced me to galleries. After we got serious, I started staying at his place in Soho every weekend, and we often spent our free time walking around and looking at art. He was an IT geek but he had a strong visual sense, and he liked to feed his eyeballs, as he put it. We even went a few times to galleries on Madison Avenue, supersnooty places that sold Picassos and Pollacks. Max was a good person to be silent with, a good person to walk beside and look at beautiful things. But after we broke up I stopped doing all that, because it reminded me too much of him.

So between my trips to Boulder, the Botanic Gardens, my gallery visits, occasional hangouts with Trixie, not to mention all my reading, I did fill my time, mostly. I definitely got lonely—of course I was lonely, I was so often alone. But between Emma and Jasmine and Trixie and my new buddies at work, I was OK. Not great, but OK.

I also had another activity. I guess you could call it a research project. The first week I was back at work, I was passing through the New Release section, and my eyes fell on a book: *Columbine* by Dave Cullen. The cover was stark, a gray sky looming over a flat building. I must have seen the book before, but it hadn't registered. Or to be honest, I hadn't really cared; it was the sort of book I would never, ever read.

An hour or so later, I was in the receiving room chatting with Hector, and my eye fell on the book again. "Does that sell well?" I asked, pointing to a stack teetering on a cart.

He snorted. "You kidding me? We can hardly keep it in stock. It's been out a few months, but it still moves quick. Littleton is only a twenty-minute Light Rail ride from where we're standing, Miss E."

There was no way I would have bought the book in the store even if I could have afforded it, so the next time I was at the library, I went to the information desk on the first floor and asked if they had a copy.

The woman checked her computer and laughed. "We have fifty altogether in all our branches."

I raised my eyebrows. "So many!"

"Well—of course. We have several copies in this branch, and at the moment there's one on the shelves. I suggest you check it out now, before someone else grabs it."

I found the book and checked it out, then I immediately went to a chair in a corner of the magazine section. I read for almost two hours straight, until my stomach started rumbling in hunger; I had forgotten that I was on my way home to eat lunch.

As I walked through the plaza in front of the Denver Art Museum, the book in my knapsack, I thought back to where I was on Tuesday, April 20, 1999. At Blue Heron, for sure. We always worked on our fall catalog in spring, so I was undoubtedly up to my eyeballs in book blurbs and deadlines. The Blue Heron catalog was a work of art in itself, and it was always all-hands-on-deck to make it as gorgeous as possible, with some very late nights toward the end. So the Columbine shooting was just a blip on my radar, something in the headlines of the newspapers and magazines that I glanced at as I rushed to and from work. I met Max in the fall of 1999, so it wasn't something that he and I ever talked about. And although it happened in Colorado, the state where my father lived, Littleton was over an hour away from Boulder. I wasn't close to Jasmine then, and Emma hadn't even been born, so the shooting had nothing to do with me.

As I read the book over the next week—taking breaks here and there, because I often found it overwhelming—I realized that the shooting was a complicated story. My initial understanding was woefully incomplete: I thought that the two boys had shot and killed some of their classmates and then killed themselves. I didn't know that they had actually intended to blow up the whole school and kill as many people as possible, and that in addition to guns they had a slew of homemade bombs that, thankfully, didn't detonate as intended.

The day of the shooting was a complicated web of crisscrossing events, starting from the moment the two boys parked outside the school, and ending when the SWAT team evacuated the last of the survivors many hours later. Not to mention what happened in all the years leading up to that day, and all the repercussions for years afterward, up until the present day. It was a tragic, multifaceted story with many layers, and reading that book was the first time I had really entered it.

I went to Boulder that Thursday and spent time with Emma and Jasmine as usual. I put Emma to bed, then went downstairs to join Jasmine in the living room. She was curled up on the couch grading papers, so I got out my copy of *Columbine* and sat next to her.

She glanced at my book. "A little light reading?" she said.

"Well—" I shrugged. I hadn't told her about Ruby. I knew that Jasmine loved me, and I knew she would do her best to support me, but I was too ashamed to tell her what had happened. "You were here then, right?"

She nodded. "I sure was. It was a sad day. A scary day."

"I bet."

"You know, a few years later I had a student from Columbine High. He was a junior there when the shooting happened."

"Really?"

"Yep. He was an amazing guy. He's at Stanford now, he's getting a PhD in psychology. The people who went through that are special. It's like they're marked somehow."

"Yes—but I would imagine that not everyone is doing as well as him," I said cautiously.

"That's true. Being marked isn't always an easy thing. But they're special anyhow. They know something the rest of us don't."

Jasmine turned back to her papers, and I returned to the book. But after that conversation, I sometimes found myself watching Ruby surreptitiously, looking at her as she put stickers on used books or sorted out the postcard rack. She was someone who knew something, someone who had been through history. Like the cashier at the Mill Luncheonette, one of my hangouts during college: when he rang up your bill on the old-school cash register, you could see the numbers tattooed on his forearm. Or my old boyfriend Max, for that matter. Jasmine was right: These people were special. They were marked.

I finished *Columbine.* But I somehow needed to know more. It's almost as if piling on facts and information was the best way to get close to what happened. Also I was looking for Ruby, looking for her name and her story. But that book didn't mention her, nor did the two that I read immediately afterward: *Columbine: A True Crime Story* and *Comprehending Columbine.* After reading all three books I knew quite a bit, but I still hadn't found what I needed. It was like some restless drumbeat inside was driving me, pushing me to something I hadn't yet reached.

When I left work at noon the next Monday, I stopped by the library to return *Comprehending Columbine,* then went up to the fourth-floor technology center to check my e-mails. The technology center is a big, bright room with dozens of computers organized in circular pods, manned by cheerful library staff at a central desk. Plenty of people use the technology center to work on resumes or noodle on the Internet, but it also serves as a hangout for homeless and almost homeless people. I had even seen the Wolf Man there on occasion, slowly tapping a keyboard while his stuffed wolf looked on.

I had a few e-mails: Barnard wanted to know if I had something to contribute to the alumnae magazine's class notes (nope); the permissions department from Shambhala Publications asked if they could reprint one of my mom's poems in an upcoming book (yes); an e-mail from the Botanic Gardens provided a list of upcoming events; and Jasmine had forwarded an article about someone in Nederland who found a bear in their car ("This is one of my former students," she wrote). That got me thinking about her student from Columbine High, and I would have Googled him if I had his name.

Then it struck me: the Internet. Hello! There must be a wealth of information on Columbine on the Web. I went to Google and tapped in "Columbine," and then I was off.

I guess I got pretty obsessive the next few days. The library has a daily maximum of four hours on the computer, and I used up every minute that afternoon, reading furiously as a rainstorm blew outside. I came back the next two days as well. I went pretty deep, diving into a deep stream of facts and images. YouTube was the real mother lode: they had the movie *Bowling for Columbine* broken into segments, as well as news reports, interviews, documentaries, tributes—hours and hours of footage.

To me the most haunting images were the films from the Columbine High School cafeteria on the day of the shooting. The school had been having a problem with students leaving trays on tables, so cameras were installed that took footage at regular intervals. Someone had posted a montage of the cafeteria films from the day of the shooting, and as I watched I felt myself chilled to the core. It was one thing to hear or read about the shootings, and quite another to see the grainy black-and-white images: the students eating lunch on a typical Tuesday, then suddenly everyone hiding under the tables, then a panicked rush of running, including a clip of the lone teacher who was shot as he raced up a staircase, and afterward the empty cafeteria, full of abandoned trays and overturned chairs. Finally I saw the shooters themselves, black-and-white ghosts roaming through the deserted cafeteria with their weapons hoisted on their shoulders, one of them pausing to sip a half-finished drink, the other throwing a Molotov cocktail and starting a fire. It was deeply chilling.

Finally I found Ruby. It took quite a while, and her name wasn't even mentioned explicitly. Her experience was just one story in a day of many stories, but the information was there. I read a few accounts, and the facts didn't always line up exactly, but from what I could gather there was a small storeroom off the kitchen, filled with bags of flour and sugar. In that panicked moment when the two shooters—the two boys, the two teenagers—opened fire just outside the cafeteria, eighteen people ended up in that storeroom. As they huddled together, they could hear the gunfire, the screaming, and the running, all going on just outside the storeroom door. There was no lock, so one boy planted his feet against the door to keep it shut. The girls got on their knees and bent their foreheads to the floor, putting their hands on the backs of their heads, and the boys formed human bridges around the girls to protect them.

After the students ran out of the cafeteria, the shooters roamed through the school, shooting at random and throwing homemade bombs. The massacre in the library occurred right above the heads of the people in the storeroom. The shooters eventually came back to the cafeteria and partially detonated a propane bomb, which caused an explosion and a blazing fire. About fifteen minutes later they came back to the cafeteria once again, and this time they went into the school kitchen. The people in the storeroom could hear the shooters reloading their weapons, and one of the shooters even tried to open the storeroom door.

The shooters killed themselves in the library about ten minutes later. But the eighteen people stuffed into the storeroom didn't know that. The SWAT team didn't reach them until three hours later. When the SWAT team finally led the group out of the school through a broken window, they passed pools of blood and dead bodies lying on the ground.

There was also a 911 call made from someone in the storeroom, and that was online, too. Apparently there were hundreds of 911 calls from people inside the school, and at one point all the calls were released to the public. I listened to a few minutes of the call from the storeroom, but then I had to stop. The terror in the young man's voice—it reminded me of the calls people made from the Twin Towers just a few years later.

I took off my headphones and looked around me. I was on the fourth floor of the main branch of the Denver Public Library. It was three-fifteen on a Wednesday afternoon, October 2009.

I picked up my knapsack and wandered across the street to the Civic Center Park. It's a beautiful park, with large stretches of green lawn and a white-marble Greek theater, which has a few out-of-sight nooks favored by pot smokers. I sat on marble steps by a defunct fountain. I had a lot to think about, a lot to digest. Strangely enough, even after all the research I had done, all the facts and images I had piled up, that internal drumbeat was stronger than ever.

So I started small, and the weeks went by. Eventually a month passed, and it was time once again for the Short Novel Book Club.

That was a bad day. It was a Monday, and I came to work for my usual four-hour shift. Hadley gave me a latte that he had accidentally made, then I went into the break room to put away my knapsack and sweater, and chat with whomever else might be there. The break room was empty, so I sat on the purple couch and sipped my drink, waiting for my shift to start.

The door opened. It was Hilda, wearing khakis and a soft bright-red shirt, her thick black hair in a plait down her back. As always when she saw me, her face hardened and her lips pursed.

"Elizabeth," she said. "Do you have a moment?"

My stomach dropped. Surely she wasn't going to fire me in the break room! She would take me to her office to do that.

"Of course." I gestured at the couch. "Would you like a seat?"

"No. I'll stand."

Well, she wasn't going to fire me standing up. Nevertheless I felt nervous. "How can I help you, Hilda?" I asked, trying to keep the note of desperation out of my voice.

"I need to apologize to you."

The heart is a funny muscle, because at that moment I actually felt my heart lift up with joy. It was such a strange feeling; I put my hand on my chest and swallowed. "All right," I said.

"This morning I overheard Debbie on the tail end of a phone call. It turns out that someone called and asked if you were working today and what your schedule was, and Debbie told them."

I blinked. "I'm sorry, Hilda. I don't quite follow."

"Well, that's not information we're supposed to give out about fellow employees. So I just want to say I'm sorry. Even if this person is someone you want to see, it was a violation of your privacy. Debbie's still pretty new, so she didn't know."

There was my heart again, only this time it was sinking. "That's all right, Hilda. Thanks for telling me. But—do you know, was it a man or a woman?"

"A woman."

"OK."

"I have to get back on the floor. But again, I'm sorry." She nodded curtly and left the room.

I sat back on the couch. I didn't give a fuck about getting my privacy violated. What I did want was Hilda and Rebecca to treat me like a human being, and not like the lowest life-form on the planet. Hilda was a reasonable person; she had to know that she couldn't continue treating one of her staff this way. She had to see that I was making an effort, a strong effort. But now Hilda and Rebecca were doing to me what I had done to everyone else—they only saw a slice of me, and they assumed that's all there was to see. It was like being trapped in a tight little box.

The day got worse. I overheard Bree and Hadley discussing refreshments for the book club, and I saw Ruby sitting at a café table frowning over a copy of *St. Mawr,* a book that I had read my junior year in college and dearly loved. When I went to the break room for my fifteen-minute break, the new fellow, Rich, was at the table leafing through *St. Mawr.* He smiled at me and asked brightly, "Are you coming to book club this afternoon? I'm not sure which one you're in."

I smiled weakly. "I'm in the Short Novel Club. But I'm not going. Not this month."

"Oh." He looked puzzled. "That's too bad. Well, I'll let you know how it goes."

"Please do."

I walked out to the platform in the alley to spend my break there. I closed my eyes and breathed in deeply—which wasn't much help, since the alley smelled like garbage from all the dumpsters. No one had actually told me that I couldn't go to the book club, or shouldn't go, but I knew that if I asked Rebecca about it she would give me one of her cold no-stares, and maybe walk away without speaking. If I just showed up as usual—well, that would make Ruby uncomfortable. I didn't want to do that anymore than I already did.

It was so painful not to be welcome. I wished with all my heart that I could take back what had happened. But I couldn't. Although I was doing pretty well with my modicum of kindness and staying put with customers, it wasn't enough. It couldn't undo what I had done, and it couldn't make things right with Hilda and Rebecca and, above all, Ruby. Now that I knew all that I knew about Ruby's past, how could I even try to speak to her? Not to mention that just the sight of me made her cower.

I couldn't foresee where or how the situation would end. Eventually something had to give, but I couldn't imagine what. Or who.

I comforted myself by thinking of the phone call that Debbie had taken earlier, where she committed the faux pas of revealing my schedule. Because as I was shelving the Black History section, I realized that the caller could only be London. I really wanted to talk to her, to find out if she knew about Colorado Loves Colorado, and to ask if anyone had spoken to her after the book club. I thought she might be able to fill in a few gaps for me, and it would also be nice to see a friendly face. London was maybe mean to some people at Q&I, but she had always been nice to me.

However, when my shift ended at noon, it wasn't London waiting for me by the front doors, reading the big calendar of events with a scowl on her face. It was Stepmother One.

What fresh hell was this? I didn't want to see her on the best of days, and particularly not on a day like that when I felt so low. I started to turn around so I could sneak out through the receiving-room door, but then she saw me and it was too late.

"Elizabeth!" she called out in an imperious tone.

"Hello, Jill," I said, inwardly tensing.

She strode up to me. "I'm here to see you."

I lifted up my hands. "Well, here I am."

"There's a restaurant on the corner, Dixons. Let's go there and eat lunch. I need to talk to you." She saw me hesitate. "I'm paying," she said.

Since moving to Denver, my restaurant meals had been few and far between. I've always been pretty skinny, but those days I was eating so little that I was losing even more weight. It's not true that you can't be too rich or too thin; if I got much thinner, I would need new jeans, and I couldn't afford that. I had been to Dixons once and it was delicious. I made a flash decision: I would go, eat a lot, and if Stepmother One got crazy—when she got crazy—I would tune her out. Like I always did.

"Well?" she demanded.

"Let's go."

As we walked in silence out the store and down the wide sidewalk on the 16th Street Mall, I remembered my modicum of kindness. Surely it didn't apply to Stepmother One as well? I had to conclude that it probably did, given that somewhere inside that sturdy, angry body, she was a fellow human being. Elizabeth, I told myself sternly. Try. Just try.

To the right of Dixons' front door, I saw a red-and-white sign: C ♥ C. Now that I knew about it, I seemed to see C ♥ C practically everywhere I went.

Dixons has a bar right in front when you walk in, with a large dining area to the left and a smaller one to the right. There was a hostess behind a podium in front of the bar, but before she could even open her mouth, Stepmother One barked, "Table for two. Somewhere private."

The hostess smiled, unperturbed, and led us to a small booth next to a raucous party of eight.

"This isn't very private," Stepmother One complained.

"Ma'am, it's lunchtime," the hostess said easily. "This is the only free table we have. Enjoy!" She left menus on the table and hurried away. I envied her escape.

We sat down at the not-particularly private table. I was grateful for the large group next to us; I thought I might need witnesses, if the tense look on Stepmother One's face was any indication of what was to come. I hadn't seen her since our blowout the previous winter, but she hadn't changed a bit: supershort gray hair, small wire-frame glasses, round face, angry expression. Even though it was a fairly chilly autumn day, she wore layered sleeveless T-shirts that showed off her muscular arms. She was the most resolutely unglamorous woman I had ever met in my life. Even my mom put on a pair of earrings now and then. Stepmother One's poems were the same: plain, direct, and unsparing. At first she had written in my dad's voice, florid and confessional, but after he left her, she kept the confessions and developed a blunt, biting style that I found hard to take. A few months before, Jasmine and I had sat down on the floor of the Boulder Bookstore and looked through Stepmother One's latest book, *The Straight Dyke,* and the language nearly singed our eyebrows off. Yet Stepmother One was quite a popular poet, and beloved in certain sections of the Boulder and indeed national literary community.

I opened my menu, as did Stepmother One, and we studied them in silence. I resolved to order as much food as possible, and when the waitress came over I asked for a strawberry lemonade, a Caesar salad with extra dressing, and the salmon and chips with extra tartar sauce. Stepmother One ordered a spinach salad and steak and fries, but only after subjecting our waitress to an interrogation about where the beef had come from and whether or not the farming methods were sustainable.

"So," Stepmother One said as the waitress walked away. "I've had a busy semester so far. And a great year." She proceeded to tell me about all the grants, awards, and publishing accolades that had come her way since I had last seen her. Apparently *The Straight Dyke* had been on the long list for the National Book Award, and *Poets & Writers* magazine was featuring Stepmother One on their December cover. As I worked my way through my blissfully dressing-heavy Caesar salad, using bread to mop up the thick sauce, I wondered why she was bothering to tell me all that. She had to know I didn't care. But in the interest of kindness, I pasted an expression of friendliness on my face and tossed out an occasional, "Wow, that's great!" or "Good for you!"

After the waitress took away our empty salad bowls, Stepmother One went in for the kill. The recitation of her thriving career was just a way to establish dominance. Typical.

"So." She folded her hands on the table and peered at me. "You're at Quill & Ink."

"Yes, I am."

"Supervisor?"

"Bookseller. How did you find out?"

"Your father told me. He didn't tell you that he told me?"

"No." My dad and I never discussed Stepmother One.

"With all your publishing experience, it's a shame you're stuck in a bookstore."

"I like it," I said simply. Which was true. By that point I did like my job, except for being shunned by the manager and assistant manager, and not earning a decent wage.

"Liking it is not the point. The point is that you had a bright career in publishing, and now it's totally stalled."

Oh, the evil words that were dying to fly from my tongue! Instead I shrugged. "It's the economy." Stupid.

"No, Elizabeth. It's you. You have absolutely no networking skills. I introduced you to some of the most powerful women in Colorado publishing, and you acted like a mute."

"Quill & Ink is a great place to work," I said placidly.

"But not a great bookstore. Only two of my books are on the shelves; you're obviously not well-stocked."

I knit my brow. "There's a whole Zwelland section."

"Yes, but it's mostly books by your dad and Jasmine." She practically spat out Jasmine's name. "And of course, your mother's books."

I looked at her. She had a lot of nerve mentioning my mother, no matter what the context. "Well," I said, as calmly as I could, "your books probably sold out. Maybe they just need to be restocked."

"You could do me a favor and keep an eye on my titles. I think you could manage that much."

"Sure," I said. "Of course." I took a sip of my strawberry lemonade, my modicum of kindness stretched so tight it was screaming.

The waitress brought our entrees. Stepmother One made the woman wait while she cut the steak to ascertain if it was in fact medium-rare as requested. I shot a sympathetic look at our waitress, a woman in her early thirties with a big blonde ponytail. She caught my glance and rolled her eyes, and we exchanged a smile.

My plate was overflowing with three breaded-and-fried salmon filets on a bed of thick fries, and a side of crisp, creamy coleslaw. I broke the crust of a filet with my fork, and savory steam wafted out. My usual dinner was a three-day-old café sandwich; from a culinary point of view at least, I was in heaven.

"So," Stepmother One said as she plunged her serrated knife into the thick slab of steak. "Do you know about your father's new girlfriend?"

"Jane?" I chewed a French fry and watched her warily. "Sure. Why?"

"She's very young," she said, sawing into her steak. "Very, very young."

"Dad's girlfriends are always young."

She shook her head in disgust. "It's criminal."

"No, actually, they're all over eighteen, so it's perfectly legal." Look at me, defending my dad. "I'm not sure why you're so upset."

Stepmother One put down her utensils with a clang. "I'm not sure why you're *not* upset. I hear she's practically living with him."

Ah, I thought. Now I get it. Stepmother One was on a fishing expedition. She came all the way to Denver to find out about Jane. But why? She couldn't possibly still be in love with my dad, not after all the hell they'd been through. But then I saw that it was true: she still loved my dad. Despite the public betrayal, despite the horrible divorce, despite the many years that had passed—how many now, ten, fifteen?—she still loved him. My mom had been the same way; I know, because she admitted it to me not long before she died. I'll never understand why my dad inspires such devotion, especially among the people he hurts the most. I for one refuse to join the club.

"Dad is Dad," I said, poking a fry into my dish of tartar sauce. "He does what he does. You can't change him."

"He preys on young women. His students. This Jane is just a plaything for him."

"Actually," I said tersely, "this is the first serious relationship my dad has had since Jasmine left."

"So I take it you approve?"

"I don't care what he does. I'm just saying."

"Do you know why your father hasn't gotten serious with anyone since Jasmine?"

"No," I said, taking a bite of coleslaw. "And I don't really care."

"He's still in love with her. That's why."

I put down my fork. Now, that surprised me. Was it even true? And how did she know? "How do you know?"

"Because I asked him. Several times."

"When do you see Dad?"

"Oh, I still see your father," she said coyly. "Or I did, until this Jane came along."

I looked at her. Oh no. Had my dad and Stepmother One started sleeping together again? I shook my head and picked up another fry. I felt like I was living inside an Ingmar Bergman film.

Stepmother One pointed her fork at me. "The only reason your father can't forget Jasmine is because *she* left *him*. She's the only one who did. It's like Picasso and Françoise Gilot."

I raised an eyebrow. "You're comparing my dad to Picasso?"

"Yes. It's not an absurd analogy."

"I kinda think it is. Dad may be a talented poet, but he's no Picasso."

"Well," she said, making a particularly brutal incision into her steak. "You've never been on your father's side."

I laughed. "Oh! You have been?" I wasn't in Colorado during their epic court battle, but Jasmine filled me in years later. Apparently Stepmother One's language got so foul that the judge had threatened to throw her out of court several times.

"I am the only woman who truly understands your father. Not like Jasmine; Jasmine is nothing but a little vixen."

"Can we change the subject?" I asked.

"A vixen. Not only for stealing your father from under my nose, but for getting pregnant. Your father was adamant about not wanting children, so I took care of the birth control. Unlike Jasmine, who said that she was taking care of it, but somehow managed to get pregnant anyway." She smiled a false, brittle smile.

I shrugged. I always figured that Emma was an accident from my dad's point of view. I turned to my food, and we ate in silence for a bit. Then Stepmother One burst out, "That child is spoiled. I saw her and Jasmine at Whole Foods a few weeks ago, and I could tell she has Jasmine wrapped around her little finger."

I set down my silverware with a bang. "Jill. Say what you want about my dad, say what you want about Jasmine, and say what you want about me—you always have. But don't you dare say a word about Emma. You don't have the right."

"I most certainly do," she retorted. "I'm her stepmother, in a sense."

"In what universe is that? I don't think Emma even knows who you are. Which may have something to do with the fact that Jasmine has had a restraining order out against you for the past decade." My modicum of kindness was gone, and it was not to be seen for the rest of the conversation. "And you have some nerve saying anything about Jasmine stealing my dad from under your nose, when that's exactly what you did to my mom. My mom—remember her? Your friend? The one you used to drink tea with? The one who helped you with your poetry? My mom, who slunk off to New Jersey and spent the next twenty years drinking herself to death?"

Stepmother One stared at me. As did the formerly raucous party of eight at the next table.

"You know what?" I said, picking up my knapsack and wrestling it on. "Leave me alone. Forever. Don't ever seek me out again."

I was about to walk away, but then my glance fell on my half-finished meal. I put the small dish of tartar sauce on the fries, then I picked up the plate and walked to the front door. I stopped at the bar and set my plate on the shiny wood. The bartender tilted his handsome bald head and looked at me curiously.

"Can I help you?" he asked.

"Yes, you can. I just had a fight with the person I was sitting with, but I still want to eat this. Can I have a to-go container?"

"Sure," he said slowly. "Just let me—"

"I got this," a voice said behind me. I turned around; it was our waitress. "I'll go find one. Don't you work at Quill & Ink?"

"I do."

"I thought I recognized you. Here, let me take that." She picked up my plate and went through the kitchen doors. I tried to act nonchalant as

I stood there waiting, but my heart was racing with anger and I could feel that my face was deeply flushed.

The waitress came out quickly with a white bag in her hand. "I also put in a slice of cheesecake. On her." She winked and gestured to the big dining room.

I smiled. "Thank you. I'm sorry I'm crazy."

"No worries. Just go before Broomhilda comes to get you."

I walked out and started stalking up the 16th Street Mall, so blind with rage that I didn't see or hear a thing from the busy streets around me. I walked for blocks, angry and oblivious, fueled by my fury and my desire to put as much space as possible between me and Stepmother One.

Eventually I slowed. I was still hungry, and my food would be cold if I didn't eat it soon. I looked around and saw that I had walked almost to the end of the Mall and was in fact right in front of the squat World Trade Center buildings. I sighed in frustration. There were benches in the plaza in front of the buildings, so I walked up the steps and sat down to finish my lunch. The waitress had thoughtfully included a plastic fork and knife and several napkins, so I was able to eat the rest of my meal without making a complete mess of myself or the bench.

When I was done, I put my garbage into the white bag and brushed off my jeans. I had to laugh: Could the day have been any worse? First there was Hilda's nonapology, then the Book Club snubbing, and to top it off, a visit from Stepmother One. I felt bad that I had lost my temper, especially in public a half-block from where I worked. But I couldn't bear to hear Stepmother One slagging Emma. I could stay with a customer agonizing over which bookmark to buy, I could stay with Juniper describing how to do a Kegel, and I could stay with Robert recounting the entire plot of the Lord of the Rings trilogy. But I could not stay with Stepmother One disrespecting Emma. There was a limit, after all. I should have told Stepmother One that she had a black heart; that would have really brought things full circle.

I walked home slowly. When I entered the Swiss Arms, I checked my mail—nothing, not even a menu—then I went downstairs. I knocked on Trixie's door; she answered right away, looking as frazzled as I felt. But she smiled when she saw it was me. "Hey there," she said.

"Hey," I said. "You with a client?"

"Someone's coming in a few minutes. How's it going?"

"I had the crappiest day in the history of humanity. I think it's a stupid-movie night."

She laughed. "Oh, after the morning I've had, it's most definitely a stupid-movie night."

"Legal stuff?"

"Yep. Why don't you come over around five? We can get pizza."

"Sounds good."

Trixie shut her door, and I went to my studio. I shut the blinds, took off my jeans, and fell into bed for a deep, dark nap.

3. Columbine Is a Flower

One morning—Veteran's Day, actually—I got a wild hair, and I decided to go to Columbine High School.

The thought of going had crossed my mind many times. It was so close, after all. But that morning I woke up and I knew I would go. It was that strange inner drumbeat, that persistent something that would not let me go, no matter how many books I read or how many videos I watched. I needed to go; it didn't even feel like a choice.

I had tea and a day-old bear claw for breakfast, then I gathered up my lone credit card and all the quarters from my change bowl. I filled up my Naropa water bottle and put it in my knapsack. Otherwise I took nothing.

It had snowed lightly the night before, and the previous days had been quite cold as well. I dressed warmly in a thick navy-blue pullover, jeans, hiking boots, my gray wool coat, and matching dark-purple hat, scarf, and gloves, a Christmas present from Jasmine. When I stepped outside it was only a little after seven, and the sun had risen just a few minutes earlier. The day felt new and raw and cold.

I walked my usual route downtown, and as I stepped onto the Mall Ride I saw the typical assortment of Denverites, bundled up against the cold and on their way to work, or who knows where. I got off at Stout and crossed over to the Light Rail. As I waited for the D Line, I looked up at the heavy gray sky and felt the cold seep through my jeans. Hopefully it wouldn't snow, or at least not until I was safely home again.

The D Line arrived soon after. At that time of day most people were traveling from Littleton to Denver and not vice versa, so there were only a few of us in the car, each looking out a window and enclosed in our private worlds. As the Light Rail pulled away from the station with a cheerful clang, I felt a strange mixture of excitement and fear. It was as if I was about to touch something—well, not holy, certainly, but something important. Or as if I was going to finally, at long last, solve a mystery.

It was a clean, fast ride. We went through parts of Denver that I had never seen before—nothing spectacular, just warehouses and a few factories, some abandoned with broken windows. The Rocky Mountains were a constant on the right-hand side, but when we passed through Englewood they suddenly got much closer. The snow-covered peaks had low white clouds in front and a ribbon of blue on top, with a brooding steel-gray sky above that stretched up into infinity.

I got off at the Downtown Littleton stop. As I stood on the outdoor platform, I took a deep breath of frigid air. The platform had a wall with a colorful folk-art mural, a detailed depiction of a small town full of cheerful residents, happy shopkeepers, and charming buildings, the very image of American energy and wholesomeness. I walked up the steps and saw a bus stop, complete with an idling bus. I stepped over to the bus and tapped on the door. The middle-aged bus driver opened up and looked at me expectantly.

"Hi," I said. "Can I take this bus to the Columbine Memorial?" I knew that the memorial was close to the high school, and I figured it was better to ask about the memorial than the high school. I didn't want anyone to think I was a creeper.

"We-ll," he said. "I don't go directly there. That would be the 60, but it's not running today 'cause it's a holiday. No school."

"Can you drop me close enough to walk?"

"Sure, close enough. It's maybe a half-mile walk."

"Great."

As we passed through Littleton's downtown and into its residential section, I saw again how much closer the Rockies were to Littleton than Denver. I was also struck by how ordinary Littleton was. It was a plain, bland town. Nothing special; anonymous, even. It struck me as a place to disappear.

The farther we traveled west, the more spread out the homes became. I even saw a farm, complete with a white house, red barn, and silver silo. Again, ordinary, except for the gorgeous mountains that got closer and closer with each block. Looking out the window I saw a few Black-Billed Magpies, a striking black-and-white bird that you don't see back East, but which I remembered vividly from my childhood.

The bus turned left, and we were on a wide street with big American mall stores. We pulled into a large parking lot and stopped in front of Chili's. I had never been inside a Chili's.

"This is it," the driver called out to me.

I got up and stood next to him, stooping to peer out the wide front window. "And I go—?"

"It's real easy." He turned slightly and pointed south. "Walk to the end of this block, take a left, and walk a few more blocks. You'll pass a reservoir, and then you get to the public library. That's where you go into the park. The memorial's there."

"Great. Thanks so much. Where do I get the bus back to the Light Rail?"

"Right here. Same bus, the 59."

I stepped off the bus into the cold parking lot. All right, I thought, looking around to get my bearings. Walk straight, then left, look for the library. I was getting close.

As I walked I noticed several flocks of geese hanging out on the snow-crusted grass. The picturesque image was quickly replaced by the reality of geese poop on the sidewalk. It was an unpleasant blackish-green mixture, and it practically covered the sidewalk. The combination of the previous night's snowfall and the carpet of geese poop made the sidewalk quite slippery, and it took all my concentration not to end up in a pile of snowy droppings.

I was still cold, even with the walking. Usually by now the sun would have started warming things up, but I glanced at the sky and saw that the sun was just a blurry white circle surrounded by gray. The Rockies were behind me at that point, and I was walking on a completely flat surface. That's the odd thing about Colorado: it's flat until it isn't, and there isn't much variety between the two extremes.

I walked several very long blocks. God bless the bus driver, but that was no half-mile walk. Finally I saw the reservoir, a small body of water covered by ice and snow. Just past the reservoir was the library. I turned into the parking lot in front of the library, then crunched over the snow to get to a green sign with white letters: ROBERT F. CLEMENTE PARK. Looking ahead a little ways into the park, I could see a sign with a map. I turned around and looked across the street to orient myself: there was a Red Robin Restaurant, another chain I had never entered, but Hadley often raved about their food. That would be my landmark when I walked back.

I suddenly felt an anxious chill in my stomach. But it was too late to turn back; I had traveled a long way to get there.

I turned around and walked into the park. As I walked over the icy snow to look at the map, my feet sinking into the crust of snow, I passed another gaggle of geese. I studied the map: if I skirted the reservoir and went more or less straight, I would end up at the memorial. According to the map, Columbine High School was east of the memorial.

I stepped onto the snow-covered asphalt path closest to me and started walking into the park. I saw a few other people, mostly bundled-up women in bright colors and fat white sneakers. Now and then bits of their cheerful chatter floated my way, but I couldn't understand what they were saying. The geese were back with a vengeance, radiating intense displeasure at my presence. One goose even started honking at me and flapping his wings menacingly. I took off my mittens and clapped loudly several times. The goose got off the path and glared at me as I passed, highly affronted by my noise.

The view as I entered the park was gorgeous. The Rockies loomed above the reservoir, still with a few white clouds floating around their peaks. Despite the heavy gray skies, there was a glare from the icy snow on the reservoir and the flat meadow behind it. I wasn't wearing sunglasses, and I scrunched my face against the blinding white gleam.

Suddenly I felt disoriented. I knew I was going in the right direction, but there were several paths and the layout was unclear. I stopped a moment and breathed in the icy air. You're fine, I told myself. You're going the right way.

I went left and cut through a parking lot. Just beyond a few gazebos, there was a brown sign with a white arrow and white letters: COLUMBINE MEMORIAL.

I turned right and followed the arrow. The geese had thinned out, but occasionally one let out a lone cry. Up ahead there was a hill, and to the left in the distance I could see the back of a low white building. That had to be Columbine High School.

I paused a moment. I felt like I was about to do something that I could not go back from. But I had no choice, not really, so I trudged on through the cold.

The hazy white sun seemed closer to me as I walked south. I passed a playground and more gazebos, a small parking lot with an idling car, then a baseball field. I could see the back of a sign up ahead, and as soon as I was close enough I stepped in front of it. This time the arrow to the memorial pointed to a path going straight up the hill.

This path was also covered in a thin layer of snow, which made the uphill climb quite slippery. I leaned forward as I moved slowly up the path. My nose was running a little, so I wiped it with the end of my thick purple scarf, the wool scratchy on my nose.

I got to the top of the path, and the memorial was on my left. At the entrance was a brown-and-white sign that spelled out rules for ensuring the appropriate atmosphere: no smoking, no dogs, no cell phones, and so on. I could understand why the sign was there—the memorial was behind a high school, after all—but personally I had never encountered such a solemn place. The ambiance was thick and still, and not easy to break even if you wanted to.

I went into the memorial, which was essentially an outdoor sculpture garden. The design was simple and elegant: a reddish stone wall built into the curving hillside, and then a smaller stone wall about ten feet in front. The ground was covered in multicolored marble, with a large carving of a ribbon, like the type people wear on their lapels to show solidarity with a particular cause. In the tails of the ribbon were the words NEVER FORGOTTEN.

The lower wall had a plaque for each of the victims. Each one had a name and a short remembrance. A thin coating of snow covered the plaques, and I carefully wiped the snow off each one. But I didn't read the remembrances; I somehow couldn't bear to. I stepped back and looked at the wall. I stood perfectly still.

After a while I walked to the wall that was built into the hillside. Plaques of various sizes were set into the wall, all in freckled gray marble with white lettering, each one containing a quote. I walked slowly in front of the wall and carefully read each plaque. The quotes were not quite what I expected, I think because they were so informal and conversational. But that was OK; this was a high school, and this was about kids. They had their own way of expressing things.

I didn't cry until I read this one:

> WE DEDICATE THIS GROUND TO THE MEMORY OF THE 13; WE DEDICATE THIS GROUND TO THOSE WHO SUFFERED PHYSICAL HARM; WE DEDICATE THIS GROUND TO THE STUDENTS AND STAFF WHO WERE AT COLUMBINE HIGH SCHOOL; WE DEDICATE THIS GROUND TO ALL OF THEIR FAMILIES; AND WE DEDICATE THIS GROUND TO THE COMMUNITY THAT IS COLUMBINE; WE ARE . . . COLUMBINE.

It was the last line that got me. I knew from my reading that "We are Columbine" was the school's war cry for sports and important events. I also knew how the word "Columbine" had changed since April 20, 1999. Columbine is a flower, but the word has forever become synonymous with death and destruction. The people in the town, however, had not abandoned the word or the war cry. This community had been broken, broken right down to the core, but they were able to stand up and say their own name. Their courage moved me in a place I didn't know I possessed.

I wiped my nose on my scarf. I continued walking in front of the wall and finished reading the rest of the quotes. Then I walked out of that magic, haunted circle and went back to the path on the hill. I was hungry, I had to pee, and my feet were cold, but I needed to go to the high school. There was no turning back because of a little discomfort. Deeply chastened, I walked slowly down the slippery path.

I knew the general direction of the high school; it was east of me, but once again there was no clear path. I weaved my way through various sports fields, and finally I reached the main entrance to the park. Three flagpoles stood at the entrance to the park, the wind whipping the flags in a frantic cacophony.

Now there was a wide paved street in front of me, and to my right was Columbine High School. Suddenly it occurred to me: What on earth was I going to do there? The school was closed, the parking lot empty; it was as if the whole place was sleeping. I didn't want to be a creeper. But in my heart I knew that I was sincere, and that I was just there to soothe my desperate internal drumbeat.

I kept walking, slowly. A few cars passed me, but I saw no one else on foot. Again, everything looked absolutely ordinary, but even that was starting to unravel a bit. I think certain events create a kind of psychic shock that reverberates. I've never been particularly sensitive to such things, but I did feel something there, a sort of displacement of air. A few times I even shivered. But maybe it was just me; maybe I was just cold.

Then I was in front of the high school. I stood before a gray marble sign with brick edges. There was an etching of a Columbine flower, and blue letters that said:

> COLUMBINE HIGH SCHOOL
> HOME OF THE REBELS

The school was a low building made of sandstone, with shimmering green windows that were difficult to see through. I tried the front doors—locked. But that was better; if I had no business being outside, I certainly had no business inside.

I turned right and started walking around the school. Behind the school there were tennis courts, yellow buses, and a few maintenance vehicles. It was a big school, much larger than my old high school. I arrived at the corner of the building and turned left. I saw a concrete semicircle of steps, and beyond that was a big parking lot.

Suddenly I knew exactly where I was. This was the Commons, the place outside the cafeteria where students eat, study, and hang out. This was where it all started. The shooters brought two duffel bags with homemade bombs into the cafeteria, then went back to the parking lot and waited. If things had gone according to plan, the bombs would have demolished this part of the school. The surviving students would have fled into the parking lot, and the shooters would have killed the fleeing students as they ran.

That was the plan, but it didn't work. The bombs never went off, and so the two shooters got out of their cars and started firing in the Commons. One of them briefly entered the cafeteria, and after that they both entered the main part of the school.

I walked over to the big windows. This was the cafeteria, a large room with a soaring atrium. Originally there had been no atrium. That was where the library had been, which was where the two shooters killed ten students and injured others. That's also where they killed themselves. Eventually the school gutted the second floor and built the atrium. Now there was only space and light, and there was a new library somewhere else in the building.

I slowly walked around the perimeter of the cafeteria. It had pale green windows, like old Coke bottles, which slightly distorted everything inside. Yet it was still possible to see through them, and at one point I stopped and looked in. It was spooky to see the quiet, still room, the many empty tables and chairs. I shifted my gaze to the right, and I saw a staircase. I recognized the staircase from the video; I remembered the image of the teacher who got shot tearing up the stairs. I remembered the images of the shooters on the staircase, one of them kneeling there to shoot at one of the undetonated bombs. All that—the students hiding under the tables, the panicked running, the shooters roaming through the desolation—all that happened here. It was one thing to read about it, another to see photos, another to see videos, and then there was this, standing right at the window in the cold November wind, looking in.

Somewhere inside—I peered harder, but it was impossible to see—there was the door to the kitchen, and beyond that a ten-by-ten storeroom where Ruby and seventeen others had been packed inside for almost four hours. I put my forehead to the glass and closed my eyes. Oh, Ruby, I said. Ruby, I'm sorry. I'm so, so sorry.

When at last I lifted my forehead, I was startled to see somebody looking at me. But it was just me. It was just my reflection, just my sad, puzzled face with red nose and cheeks, with eyes in slits from the cold and the white glare. It was just me.

I tore myself away from the cafeteria and walked around to the front of the school. Eventually I reached the main sign. I was back to where I started from, and now it was time to head home.

A few steps in, I turned around for a last look at Columbine High School. The sun was starting to come out, and the slice of blue sky above the Rockies was now wider. It was going to turn into a nice day, eventually.

Journeys always feel quicker on the way back. I walked rapidly through the park, and it was not long before I saw Red Robin. I stepped out of the park and crossed the wide street. As soon as I touched the sidewalk on the other side, I felt a palpable relief. Columbine High School was finally behind me.

I smelt fries as I approached Red Robin. A young man in a uniform was sweeping the front steps. He told me they were opening in fifteen minutes, and I guess I must have looked pretty pitiful, because he smiled and told me I could wait inside.

Once inside, I blinked rapidly and realized how snow-blinded I had become. I also desperately needed to pee. There was a bathroom right by the entrance, so I scooted inside. It was such sweet relief to finally pee and let go of that tension. As I sat on the toilet, I put my hands on my bare thighs, which were red and cold. Washing my hands, I looked at my reflection and saw my chapped face, small eyes, and messy hair. I felt as if I had been far, far away, somewhere cold and distant and forlorn, a stark frozen place like Iceland or Antarctica.

I went out into the restaurant and sat in a booth. I ordered a coffee and a veggie burger with fries. Hadley was a big Red Robin fan, and he had often mentioned their special French fry topping, which he called "crack." He wasn't too far off; I ended up drenching my fries and burger with the spicy brown powder. As I was about to take my first bite, I suddenly flashed on my startled reflection mirrored in the green glass of the Columbine High School cafeteria. I felt a piercing sadness, but I also felt intense relief.

I had more coffee, and then it was time to go. I walked back quickly to Chili's. I was in luck; my bus had just pulled up, and it was even the same driver. Fifteen minutes later we were at the Light Rail station, and soon afterward the Light Rail pulled up to take me back to downtown Denver.

☼ ☼ ☼

I remember two things from the journey back. The first is that I thought of the final line from one of my favorite books, Jay McInerney's novel *Bright Lights, Big City:*

> You will have to learn everything all over again.

The second thing is that I saw an eagle. A full-on, white-headed, noble-beaked American eagle. One of my fellow passengers started craning his neck to look out the window, so I looked, too. My body gave a quick shock at the sight of the huge bird with its white head, majestically soaring above our little train. I knew that there were plenty of eagles in Colorado, but I had never seen one. I figured you had to go deep into the mountains for that, and since I'm allergic to hiking and camping, I never imagined I would see one. But there I was on the Light Rail heading to downtown Denver, and I saw an American eagle.

Was it possible? Anything was possible.

4. One Heart

The last Monday of November the entire staff of Quill & Ink gathered for an early morning meeting to discuss the upcoming holiday season. When I walked into the store at 6:45 a.m., I was less bleary-eyed than I expected. I was even looking forward to the meeting, because Juniper had told me that Hilda would be giving out the holiday schedule, and I was sure to get more hours.

Bree was at the café. "Hey!" she said. "Good morning."

"Hey there. How's it going? Are you coming to the meeting?"

"Nope. They need someone at the café. It's all right; Hadley will fill me in. Would you like some coffee? It's free."

I raised my eyebrows. "Really?"

"All coffee and tea is free for the meeting. Just drip coffee, though; no lattes or cappuccinos."

"In that case, I'll take a large free coffee."

As Bree poured my coffee, I looked up at the chalkboard. Hadley had already written the quote for the week:

> THE MAD DENVER AFTERNOON
> JACK KEROUAC, *VISIONS OF CODY*

"Shouldn't that be 'The mad Denver morning'?" I said as I took my cup.

"I don't think Kerouac saw too many mornings," Bree replied. "At least, not in his later years."

I laughed. "Thanks, Bree. See you later."

I fixed my coffee with three sugars and cream, then headed up the staircase. The meeting was in the event room, and I was one of the first people to arrive. Hilda was behind the podium on the little stage, and she and Rebecca were looking through a stack of papers. Stacie was sitting a few rows back, so I went to sit next to her.

Oddly enough, Stacie, Bree, and I had formed a bit of a trio. It started one Sunday afternoon when Bree and I were heading out to Dazbog for an after-work coffee. Stacie was leaving at the same time, and on impulse I asked her to join us. She barely said a word, just chewed on her toothpick and listened as Bree and I talked about books and writing, but when we were ready to leave Stacie said, "That was fun." Since then we had all gone out once more, and a few days previously on Black Friday—the retail hell day after Thanksgiving—Stacie got a ferocious migraine, and Bree and I joined Stacie on the bus to make sure she got home safely.

Stacie raised one corner of her mouth as I sat down. She was wearing, as usual, her green camouflage jumpsuit and khaki eye-patch. Her bristly blonde hair was standing straight up, and her ever-present toothpick was in place.

"Hey, Stacie." I nodded at my mug. "Free coffee!"

"Yep," she said. That was all. But I knew she didn't mind me sitting there.

The rest of the staff slowly joined us, and soon the air was buzzing with happy, chattering voices. Juniper sat down on the other side of me, appropriately dressed in green satin pants and a red sweater with white fur trim around a plunging neckline. Her hair was a mass of corkscrew curls with strands of tinsel woven in, and a pair of gold Christmas-ball earrings provided the finishing touch.

"You look amazing," I said.

"Slim, these are my clothes from last night! I crawled out of a man's bed this morning to get here so damn early. No time to go home and change, you dig me?"

I laughed. "Juniper, I do dig you."

I asked Juniper where she got her sweater, and I listened carefully as she told me about a recent shopping trip to Ross. Then Hilda called out, "Good morning, everyone!"

"Good morning!" we called back. I looked around; there were about twenty-five of us altogether. I saw Hadley on the other side of the room, sitting next to Ruby. He gave me one of his wild awkward waves, and I wiggled my fingers back at him.

Hilda stood in front of the podium, not behind it. She wore loose black slacks, a crisp white shirt, and a forest-green cardigan with a big

Santa pin. Her thick black hair was held back with a wide red hair band, and like Juniper she had gold Christmas-ball earrings, although hers were considerably smaller. Rebecca was sitting in a chair behind Hilda, wearing her usual jeans and flannel shirt, her hands folded on her lap and her gaze turned up at Hilda.

"Thanks for coming in so early," Hilda said. "And on a Monday!" She held up her mug. "There's free coffee and tea in the café. If you didn't get any on the way in, be sure to get one on the way out."

Juniper called out, "Hilda, what's your policy on refills?"

Everyone laughed, but I was glad that Juniper asked because I had been wondering the same thing. Hilda grinned and said, "Refills are free, of course. Thanks for asking, Juniper. So—I really appreciate everyone coming in. It's great to have us all together, we don't get to do this very often."

Hilda was warm, but she was to the point and efficient, as I would have expected her to be. She started by saying that in retail, stores make about 40 percent of their annual earnings in the six weeks from Black Friday to January 1. All the extra sales were great, but it also meant extra work and lots of traffic in the store.

"It's important that we treat everyone well, no matter how rushed and crazy it gets. Some of these people are new customers; they're only here because someone else asked for a book. But if we treat them well, and if they see that we're not just a bookstore but a café with great coffee and merchandise, they might become regulars, or at least stop by whenever they're in this part of town. So we need to be extra attentive. I've bumped up the part-timers' hours a bit, and I've hired our regular holiday temps, so we should have sufficient staffing. Rebecca's going to pass out the schedule at the end of the meeting. I know you don't all have your datebooks and calendars with you, but if you know of a conflict, come see either me or Rebecca right away, or definitely by tomorrow morning. We'll have the final schedule ready for everyone by tomorrow afternoon. This way we can all go ahead and make our holiday plans."

Juniper called out, "Hilda, when's the Christmas party?"

"Thanks, Juniper. As usual, we're having our holiday party mid-January. The date is Sunday, January 17th. Details to follow, but again as usual it'll be at my place. And yes, Juniper, you can bring a date!"

Everyone laughed. Juniper turned to me and raised her eyebrows knowingly. "You too, Slim," she said.

"Two other points. Next Monday and Tuesday are our Employee Appreciation Days. Anything you buy—and I mean anything, even from the café—is 40 percent off. You don't have to buy all your holiday gifts from us, of course, but it's definitely possible. Robert has cleared a shelf behind the register for employee holds, so feel free to start putting things back there. It's a good idea to stake your claim now; you don't want your gifts sold out from under your nose.

"Lastly, I know that the pressure gets intense during this time, and I want to encourage everyone to take good care of themselves. Sleep as much as you can, eat well, try not to party too hard if you have an early shift the next day. If the store gets crazy—and it will get crazy—take a few deep breaths. If you really feel stressed, just leave the sales floor for a few minutes. I'd rather you do that than get impatient with a customer.

"That's it from me. Rebecca will hand out the schedules now. Any questions or comments? Managers, if there's something you need the whole staff to know, this is a good time to say it."

Hadley was the first one to raise his hand, and during his rather rambling comment about the holiday goodies available at the café, Rebecca—with pursed lips—handed me my schedule. As I read it, my stomach dropped. My hours were exactly the same. Exactly. I worked 8 to 12 on Mondays, 10 to 2 on Thursdays, and 12 to 6 on Saturdays and Sundays. I wasn't working one minute more than I usually did.

I folded the schedule carefully and tucked it inside my knapsack. I took a few deep breaths; I needed them now, never mind the holiday rush. What a slap in the face. Even during a time like this when the store needed all the help it could get, Hilda and Rebecca didn't want to see any more of me. As I sat there, feeling the rest of the staff buzzing with excitement, vaguely conscious of Hadley discussing gingerbread men and peppermint lattes, I realized that Hilda and Rebecca were freezing me out. They wanted me to go, and they were just waiting for me to get the message.

There were a few more questions, and then the meeting finally ended. I had about twenty minutes until my shift started at eight, so I went back to the café for a refill. Then despite the cold, I took my coffee outside to the alley so I could digest what had just happened.

I sat down on the concrete platform and sipped my drink, staring into the empty, smelly alleyway. I had hoped, really hoped, that I could fix things at Q&I. I was trying so hard to do better. And I was doing better: I had developed friendships with my coworkers, and my customer service had improved so much that twice customers had come in and asked for me specifically.

But despite all that, Hilda and Rebecca could not forgive me. To them I was a toxic person, and I needed to go. They would always minimize my role at the store, and they would never give me my ten hours back. I could live with that, although my financial situation was close to desperate. I definitely had to get another part-time job, if I could.

The deeper problem, though, was Ruby. She was still so scared of me; she still flinched at the sight of me. A million times I had wanted to apologize to her, but the minute I came near her for any reason whatsoever, her eyes would flash and her body stiffen. At those moments, that fissure in my chest flared, and I left her in peace. But she would never have any peace until I left Q&I.

I finished my coffee and returned the mug to the café, then I went to the break room to punch in. As I walked over to receiving, I knew it in my bones: I was finished at Q&I.

Yet I couldn't just leave. It was my job, my only source of income.

Something has to give, I thought as I loaded up a cart with cookbooks. *Something has to give, and preferably soon.*

☼ ☼ ☼

Curiously enough, something did give. A few hours later, in fact.

It was just after eleven. The café was lively but the rest of the store was dead; the shoppers were exhausted from their holiday weekend and Black Friday shopping frenzy. I was on my way to the receiving room with an empty cart, and I had stopped by Juniper's desk for a quick chat. Although it was never a quick chat with Juniper. As she was in the middle of telling me about her date the previous night, with details so vivid I actually blushed, the phone on her desk rang.

"Hang on, Slim. I'm just gettin' to the best part." She picked up the phone. "Information. How can I help you?" She listened a moment, then raised an eyebrow and looked at me. "She's right here, Robert." Juniper put a hand on the receiver and said, "You got a phone call. Want to take it here? I need to go pee anyhow."

"Sure. Thanks, Juniper." I never got phone calls at work. As Juniper waited for the transfer to come through, I realized that it had to be London. It would be nice to finally speak to her.

But it wasn't London; it was Jasmine. "Oh, Elizabeth! Thank God you're there."

"Jasmine? Is everything all right? Is Emma—?"

She laughed. "Oh, I'm sorry! I didn't mean to scare you. Everyone's fine. But Elizabeth, listen: I have a lead on a job. For you."

I was slow to respond. This was the moment I had been waiting for since I moved back to Colorado almost a year before, but I had stopped hoping it would ever come. "A job? In publishing?"

"Yes, in publishing! I'm on my way to class so I have to be quick. I ran into one of my old students just now—I may have mentioned him at some point, his name is Seabourne, he's from New Zealand. He was just about to post a note on the job board and I asked him what the job was, and when he told me I made him promise not to move a muscle until he talked to you."

"What's the job?"

"Seabourne has worked for years at a transcription company called One Heart; they focus on dharma talks and spiritual teachings. Apparently the owner—I know him too, he's a Naropa grad—apparently he got a big inheritance a few years back, so they're going to start publishing books. They need someone who can do developmental editing and book production, and chip in with copyediting and proofreading."

My heart lifted. "I can do that. I can do all of that."

"I know! Which is why I told Seabourne I'd call you at work and you'd call him right back. He's in the student lounge now, waiting for your call."

"I don't have my GoPhone, Jasmine. And I can't call from the store phone."

"Can you maybe borrow someone's cell?"

I saw Juniper walking toward me, her Christmas ball–earrings swinging back and forth. I could borrow Juniper's phone, but bless her heart, she was not the world's most discreet person. Bree—I could borrow Bree's phone. "You know what, I can."

"Great. Do you have a pen?"

"I do." I picked up a purple marker from Juniper's desk and grabbed one of her many Post-It notepads. "Go ahead."

Jasmine read out the phone number, I wrote it down and then repeated it to her. "That's right," she said. "And Elizabeth, best of all? They've been located in Boulder for years, but they're just now getting offices in Denver. In Capitol Hill, no less."

"Wow."

"Look, I have to go, but call him right away. Then leave me a message and let me know how it goes."

"Oh, Jasmine! Thanks so much."

"Fingers crossed."

I put down the phone. OK, I thought. Deep breath.

"Bad news, Slim?" Juniper asked as she took her seat.

"No, not at all," I said, putting Seabourne's number in the back pocket of my jeans. "I better go and put this cart back."

"We'll finish up our chat later, don't you worry."

I brought my cart into the elevator and went down to the first floor. But instead of going to receiving, I parked the cart in a discreet corner of the magazine section and went over to the café. I caught Bree's eye, and she came over to me. I leaned on the counter and said, "Bree, I have a favor to ask. Can I use your cell phone? It's an emergency. A good emergency; I'll explain later."

"Sure." She reached under the counter and handed me a sparkling pink phone. "I have unlimited minutes, so talk all you want."

"Thanks, Bree. I owe you."

"No, Elizabeth," she said seriously. "I owe you. It's the least I can do."

I wasn't sure where to make the call, but then I realized that the event room was probably empty, so I hurried upstairs. Thankfully Juniper was busy with a customer so she didn't try to stop me. I walked down the hall, then made a left into the large empty room. I sat on a chair, took a deep breath, and with trembling fingers dialed Seabourne's number.

He answered immediately. "Seabourne here," he said in a lilting Kiwi accent.

"Seabourne? This is Elizabeth Zwelland."

"Oh, hello, Elizabeth! That was quick. Jasmine said it might take you a bit to sort out a phone."

"One of my coworkers came through."

"Excellent. So—Jasmine said you might be interested in this job?"

"I would," I said. "I would be interested in this job."

✩ ✩ ✩

After I punched out at noon, I took the Mall Ride and walked through the Civic Center Park to the library. My interview was the next day at ten, and I needed to freshen up my resume and do research on One Heart. I spent about two hours getting everything together, then I went home and knocked on Trixie's door—no answer. I went to my apartment and wrote a note asking Trixie to come by when she got home, then I went out into the hall and slipped the note under her door.

I ate lunch and tried to take a nap, but I was too excited to just lie around my apartment, so I took a precious two dollars out of my change bowl and hopped on the bus up to the Botanic Gardens. It was a nice afternoon, cold but sunny, and I walked aimlessly around the Gardens, mentally rehearsing answers for my interview. When the Gardens closed, I walked home along Ninth Avenue, stopping at King Soopers for peanut butter and tea bags.

As I rounded the corner on Sherman Street, I could see lights in Trixie's apartment. I went downstairs and knocked on her door, and we spent the evening making spaghetti and picking out an interview outfit for me. Trixie and I had gotten quite close over the previous few weeks, and I think the deal was officially sealed the evening she told me that her dad was an alcoholic, a quiet one just like my mom. We spent several hours sitting on the smushy pink couch and exchanging horror stories, and I saw that we were more alike than I had ever imagined.

Trixie was considerably curvier than me, but we nevertheless found the perfect ensemble among her extensive wardrobe: boot-cut black pants, a trim black jacket that closed with one gold button, and a bright white collarless shirt. I contributed a gold chain, small gold hoops, black knee-high stockings, and low-heeled black shoes. Even to my own eyes I looked wildly professional, and we celebrated our success by splitting a pint of Ben & Jerry's Chubby Hubby.

I slept well that night. I was afraid I would be too excited to sleep, but I had worked four hours and walked in the Botanic Gardens all afternoon, so I fell asleep immediately and didn't wake until eight. My interview was at ten o'clock at City O' City, a soulful vegetarian café a few blocks from my apartment. I lay in bed and rehearsed interview questions in my head, then I took a shower and dressed carefully. At nine thirty I left the Swiss Arms and walked slowly down Sherman Street, giving myself an internal pep talk the entire way.

City O' City is on the corner of Thirteenth and Sherman, right next to the Jack Kerouac and a block from the Capitol building. It was renovated not long after my interview, but at that time both outside walls were painted black and filled with poems in large white letters, poems by E. E. Cummings, Dorothy Parker, Charles Bukowski, and of course Walt Whitman. I told the tattooed fellow working at the host station that if a man with a New Zealand accent came in looking for Elizabeth, that was me. He winked and said he would send all Kiwis my way. I went to the dark back room and took a table by the window, which had a view of the front door and the host's podium.

I ordered a cup of coffee with cream, which the efficient waitress topped off twice. I was dressed sharp, I had my resume in a dark-brown faux leather folder (courtesy of Trixie), I was sufficiently caffeinated, and I had no stray food on my teeth. I was ready.

At exactly ten the front door opened, and a tall, thin man in glasses walked in. The host turned and pointed at me. I stood, and when Seabourne came over to the table, I held out my hand.

"Hello," I said. "I'm Elizabeth."

He took my hand and gave it a gentle shake. "Seabourne. Nice to meet you."

Seabourne took off his gray wool coat, then neatly folded it and placed it on the back of an empty chair. He sat down and opened up his navy-blue cloth satchel, pulling out a pad of paper and a black pen. "This is one of my favorite places in Denver," he said. "They have great tea. Do you come here often?"

No, because I'm broke. "Surprisingly not, even though I live just a few blocks away."

"Well, tea is why we're moving our offices here. A few months ago I was here having a cup when one of the waitresses told me about the space for rent upstairs."

I raised my eyebrows. "Your new offices are here? Above City O' City?"

"Yes—or they will be, once we finish a bit of construction and electrical work. Then painting. It's a brilliant location, eh? We're right by the Capitol Building, and there's fresh tea and coffee for miles."

The waitress came over, and Seabourne ordered a Hibiscus Cooler. We made small talk as we waited for his tea, and when the waitress delivered an elaborate tea-making device and a large glass, I looked at Seabourne as he fixed his tea. He had a bony, elfin face and small wire-frame glasses; he wore jeans and a white button-down shirt with small blue stripes, tidy but not too formal. As he carefully spooned sugar into his tea, I looked at his long, elegant fingers. His movements were economical and elegant, and altogether he seemed quiet and centered. I could definitely imagine him working in publishing; he probably wouldn't be much good in retail, either.

"Just let me sop up these bits of water—all rightee." He grinned. "I have my tea, so now we can start."

"Here's my resume," I said, opening up Trixie's snappy folder and handing him a crisp resume.

"Brilliant." He looked it over slowly, nodding to himself as he read, now and then making a brief note on his pad of paper. I sipped my coffee and watched him, willing myself to keep my mind blank.

"All right," Seabourne said at last. "Jasmine told me that you worked at Blue Heron, but this gives me a better picture. Tell me about working there."

As we sat in the weak light coming from the windows, surrounded by the chatter from other tables and the low hum of cars passing on Thirteenth Avenue, I told Seabourne about my time at Blue Heron. Posture erect, Seabourne folded his hands on the table and breathed slowly in and out as I spoke. He didn't seem to be in any hurry, so I described Blue Heron in some detail, telling him about Mr. Dove, Hansika, the authors, the many books I had worked on, the actual tasks that I carried out on any given day. I loved talking about Blue Heron, and I didn't stumble once. Then I told him about the end, and to my horror my eyes filled with tears. But Seabourne was unfazed; he handed me a napkin and watched me sympathetically.

"So I landed here," I said, lifting my hands. "I looked for a job in publishing for six months, then I got my position at Quill & Ink. It's been great," I lied confidently, "but I'm an editor. Shelving books is just not what I'm meant to do."

"That Madoff was a right bastard, eh?" Seabourne said, taking a sip of tea.

I shook my head and pursed my lips. "You know, it wasn't just individual people like Mr. Dove, he also wiped out a few charities. The whole thing was a tragedy."

Seabourne nodded. "I've always loved Blue Heron's books. We had them in New Zealand, as you no doubt already know. It's always a shame when a good publisher goes under."

We sat in silence a moment, then he said, "All rightee. Why don't I tell you about One Heart? Have you heard of us?"

"I read your website yesterday," I said. "Twice."

He laughed. "So you've seen our resume, have you? Well, I'll go over it again and fill in some details."

The waitress came by and topped off my coffee. Seabourne took a sip of tea and then breathed in and out audibly. I knew that mindfulness practice and meditation were part of Naropa's curriculum—that's where Jasmine started her practice—and it seemed part of Seabourne's life, too. But I didn't mind; there was something so measured and peaceful about him. I could picture him reading for hours on end, sitting in a comfy armchair, sipping his tea and breathing.

He started at the beginning, telling me how One Heart was the vision of a man named Devon Michaelson. Devon had been a seeker since childhood, and during his undergrad years at Naropa he got heavily involved with the Shambhala community founded by Chögyam Trungpa. After graduation Devon went to Nepal and India and studied with various masters, and when he returned to America he spent a few years traveling to spiritual centers, doing retreats at Tibetan, Japanese, and Korean Buddhist monasteries, as well as a long stint at one of Thich Nhat Hanh's centers. Devon also spent time at a number of Vipashyana, Christian, Hindu, and Sufi organizations. As Seabourne talked, I realized that Devon was not only a seeker, but a seeker with a trust fund or a rich girlfriend—all that travel and study had to cost a small fortune.

When Devon turned thirty, he came back to Boulder, hoping to set up a business that was congruent with his values. He decided to start a spiritual transcription center: teachers give lots of talks, and these talks need to be transcribed, copyedited, and proofread. Spiritual centers usually get students and volunteers to do this kind of work, and during Devon's years at various centers, he discovered that he had a knack for transcription and editing. He was able to accomplish miracles with poor recordings and teachers with heavy accents, and he was also skilled at cleaning up other people's bad transcriptions.

"Do you know about 'one-paragraph-itis'?" Seabourne asked me.

I laughed. "No. Actually, wait—we had an author like that at Blue Heron. He was incapable of breaking his prose into paragraphs. We had to do it for him, and you would have thought we were breaking his bones."

"Exactly. In transcriptions, it's when transcribers don't shape the material at all. Or they have 'um-and-you-know-itis,' where they put in every utterance that the speaker makes. It's a shame, because many of these transcriptions from spiritual centers get Xeroxed and distributed, or even put up on the Web. They give an altogether wrong impression of some quite prominent teachers, not to mention skewing the meaning of the teachings themselves.

"But when transcriptions are done well, they can eventually become books; in fact, that's where many spiritual books have their origins. That's where Devon is a real visionary, because he thought, why not offer a service that provides top-notch transcription at a reasonable price? Fill the staff with seekers who are devoted to the material and who also have a firm grasp of the English language, and then teach them the fine art of transcription. That's how One Heart was born. It started small, but eventually word spread, and Devon was able to realize his vision."

I nodded. The words "vision" and "visionary" were all over the website, mostly in reference to Devon. In fact, the heading of his bio was: OUR VISIONARY. The site was sprinkled with photos of Devon, a dashing man in his late thirties with faraway eyes. In one photo he was wearing a Patagonia hat and perched atop a treacherous mountain range; in another he was standing bare-chested in the tree pose, his brown hair long and tangled, his neck weighed down by thick-beaded malas. There was also a shot of him holding Mother Teresa's hand and gazing earnestly into her eyes, and one with him wearing a white scarf around his neck and sharing a raucous laugh with the Dalai Lama. Modicum of kindness or not, I thought Devon looked like he was pretty full of himself—and as the daughter of a man who is supremely full of himself, I was in an excellent position to judge.

"At first our customer base was spiritual centers, both domestic and international. They usually got sponsors to pay for our services, so it worked out pretty well. But eventually publishers caught onto us, and we started working with Shambhala, Wisdom, Snow Lion, Sounds True, and HarperOne. Then Devon realized, why do all this work and pass it on to someone else? Let's start our own publishing company. Also Devon finally finished his autobiography, so that was another impetus." Seabourne shrugged. "So here we are. We're right on the ground floor, and we need an experienced editor to get us started."

"What's your vision for the company?" I asked. There had been nothing on the website except a mysterious teaser: BIG NEWS SOON! ONE HEART IS BRANCHING OUT!

"It's taken us a year to get our business plan in place. Basically we're going to have two imprints: One Heart and Many Mountains. One Heart will be run the old-school way; it'll be a traditional publishing house where we pay authors and edit their books and take care of marketing and distribution. Many Mountains will be new-school—it's our self-publishing arm, where people hire us to put out their books and pay for services like editing, proofreading, marketing, and so on. We'll screen out the books if they're not up to snuff; we want to keep the quality pretty high."

I nodded. "That's a smart plan. And eBooks?"

"Oh, eBooks for miles. Devon is quite excited about eBooks; they're the future, eh? The present, actually."

I smiled. "Yes. They are."

"The way Devon sees it, we have a good shot at making a go of it. For decades—a century, really—the New York City publishing world has had all the power. But now everything is up for grabs; the big companies are scrambling due to the economic downturn, and all the new technology like eBooks and self-publishing have them whirling. The whole industry is in flux, but that's where little publishers like us can pop up. There's no reason why Denver or Portland or Austin can't be the new center of publishing, or at least get a foot in the door. What New York sees as a disaster, we see as an opportunity."

Now I was the one breathing in slowly—inhale, exhale. I had to contain myself. I wanted this job so badly I could feel the red pen in my fingers and the weight of the manuscript on my knees. Suddenly I had a flash of panic: What if Seabourne didn't like me? What if he thought I had a black heart? But there he was, so calm and sincere and centered. Everything's fine, I told myself. Calm down. Just stay.

"So basically we're starting small, and we're starting slow. We have two manuscripts ready to go: one is Devon's autobiography, and one is from Dzigar Kongtrul Rinpoche, a great Tibetan teacher who has a center up in the mountains in Ward. We also have a half-dozen manuscripts ready to get started. We just need an editor, other than me."

"What's your role in the company?" I asked.

"Well, I studied poetry undergrad at Naropa, and during those years I transcribed part-time for One Heart. Then when I graduated I kept working part-time for them, but I also got another part-time job copyediting and proofing for Sounds True. They're in Louisville, just a stone's throw from Boulder."

I nodded. "I contacted them during my job search, but they didn't have any editorial positions open."

"It's a terrific company, and I learned quite a lot there. I worked both jobs for almost five years, then Devon offered me a full-time job, half-transcribing and half-administrative. Plus part-time computer techie. Many hats. But now I'll just be the managing editor. I'll oversee the editorial department and the graphics, and maybe have a hand in editing as needed. We'll see."

So I would be working under Seabourne. I imagined us drinking our respective hot beverages and peering at manuscript pages spread out on a desk. Just like me and Hansika.

"For the last months I've mostly been setting up the company," he went on. "We already have transcribers and an accountant. We're bumping up one of our transcribers to editorial assistant, a really nice young woman named Campbell. She ended up at Naropa grad school for poetry, by way of undergrad at Harvard. You'll like her; Jasmine knows her fairly well, I believe. I already hired a fellow for IT who'll also be in charge of our eBook production, and we have a part-time designer and a part-time sales and marketing person. Our vision is to eventually bump all the part-timers up to full-time and hire more staff. But this is good for now; as I said, we're starting slow."

"And, if I may ask—your funding?"

"Devon. He's always been independently wealthy, and he's recently inherited assets that allow him to expand what the company offers. So that's our deep pocket. But we certainly hope to be profitable. Our transcription arm has been in the black for years now; we don't use Devon's money at all. But to set up the publishing imprints, it's down to Devon. The new offices, in particular. I'd take you up to see, but we have a bunch of workmen in there now."

"It's a great location," I said politely.

Seabourne looked at me intently. "So, Elizabeth. How does all this sound to you? We're a start-up and it's bound to be bumpy for a while, but all of us are 110 percent committed to making it work."

I looked Seabourne in the eye. It wasn't the high-end fiction I was used to, but so what? It was publishing, and I would be editing. "Seabourne, it sounds wonderful. I'd like to give 110 percent as well."

He beamed. "Brilliant. So now I suppose it's time to get down to tin tacks. We can offer you $40,000 annually. It's not as much as a New York City salary, I know, but we think it's fair for Denver. You'd be expected to work thirty-five hours a week, maybe a bit more when there's a deadline. You get health insurance, three weeks of vacation to start, and all the City O' City coffee and tea you can drink—we're working out an arrangement."

Inwardly I raised my eyebrows. Wow—$40,000 a year! At most, I thought it would be $35,000. I tried not to whimper; at the moment I made less than $10,000 a year, which definitely put me at poverty level. With $40,000 a year, my whole life would change. No more day-old pastries, for one thing.

"That sounds fair," I said calmly.

"Excellent." Seabourne took a sip of tea and smiled at me. He had been pretty chilled-out all along, but at that moment he visibly relaxed. Maybe he thought I was going to argue about the salary, and he was relieved that I had agreed so quickly? I didn't care; I was in no position to haggle over money.

"You're fine with the subject matter of our books?" he asked. "It'll be predominantly spiritual nonfiction, at least on the One Heart end."

"That's fine."

"Do you have a spiritual life? It doesn't matter in terms of the job, but I'm just curious."

I thought a moment. I thought of the Denver Botanic Gardens, I thought of Hello Kitty sitting on my bed, I thought of my face reflected in the window of the Columbine High School cafeteria. "I do," I said at last. "Yes, I do."

He nodded. "Cool. Are you all right working with new authors, particularly on the self-publishing side?"

"I love new authors," I said honestly. "Mr. Dove always talked about how important it is to cultivate new writers."

"Excellent. I guess I should also say that we're a pretty close-knit staff. We often go out for drinks, and everyone's birthday is a big deal. Devon is really into bonding."

"That sounds great," I said firmly. "I love working at a place like that. That's how we were at Blue Heron."

"I'm sure Quill & Ink is like that, too. You can feel it when you walk into the store."

I sipped my coffee. "That's true. It is."

"It's great that you have a foot in there. That will help us a lot."

"Sure," I said brightly.

Then we just started chatting. He told me that Jasmine was one of his favorite teachers, and he had enjoyed her classes immensely. He had also met Emma a few times; he told me about the evening Jasmine had students from her Alice Notley seminar over for a potluck, and Emma performed a free-form interpretive dance for the group.

Then he said, "I also took a class with your dad, actually."

I wasn't prepared for that, and for a moment I was speechless. I didn't want my dad spilling into the interview. I wanted the discussion to be about me and my experience as an editor, and I wanted the connection to Seabourne to come just from Jasmine. When I could speak, what came out of my mouth was, "Indeed."

Immediately I felt like an idiot; I sounded like someone out of a George Eliot novel. Seabourne just laughed. "I don't think he liked my poems. Too quiet for him. So then I took a class with Jasmine, and she became one of my mentors. But your dad is a brilliant teacher; he really ignites a fire in people."

"Do you still write poetry?"

"Oh, yes. In fact I plan to self-publish my first book with Many Mountains. It'll be Many Mountains' first book as well; I'm the guinea pig." He took another sip of tea. "My vision is that we become a resource for poets. We'll give them a decent price, and who knows, maybe we'll publish some poets on the One Heart side as well."

"That sounds great," I said. And I meant it. From the moment I was born, it had been my fate to be surrounded by poets. This would be just another piece of that destiny.

"Elizabeth," Seabourne said suddenly, putting his palms flat on the table. "I've never done this before, but I honestly can't see a single reason why we shouldn't hire you."

I beamed. "Me either."

He laughed. "I have to run everything by Devon, of course. But it's really just a formality; he trusts my judgment. He knows Jasmine as well, and her word means a lot to both of us."

"That sounds fine," I said, doing my best not to sound giddy.

"Oh, and I forgot—we won't need you to start until early January. We're getting the offices together this month, and what with the holidays, everything's pretty mad."

"That's actually better," I said slowly. "Quill & Ink is superbusy now, and I'd feel bad if I left them in the lurch. So the beginning of January would be fine." Except for the fact that I had absolutely no money for Christmas gifts. Thank God for Employee Appreciation Days.

"Perfect. So can I call you later today?"

"Actually, e-mail is better. It's on my resume."

"Brilliant. I'll call Devon right after I've had a chat with the workmen, then I'll shoot you an e-mail."

Seabourne paid the bill, and we talked a bit more, just odds and ends about our living situations, the differences between Boulder and Denver, and the Naropa Summer Writing Program. Then we walked outside, where we shook hands and said our final good-byes. Seaborne went left, and I went around the corner, where I stood in front of Dorothy Parker's poem and took out my GoPhone to call Jasmine.

She answered immediately. "Well?"

"It went great," I said. "Just great. He needs to check with Devon, but it's pretty much a formality."

Jasmine let out a happy squeal, which was identical to Emma's happy squeal. "Oooh! I'm so happy, Elizabeth. When is he getting back to you?"

"He's going to e-mail me today. So I figure I'll just wait an hour or so, and then go to the library to check."

"Isn't Seabourne cool? He's a terrific poet. But you'll have to watch out for Devon; he makes passes at everyone."

"I figure he's the same type as Dad. I can handle him."

Jasmine laughed. "I just bet you can."

Emboldened by my success, I decided to bring up something that had been on my mind for several weeks. "Jasmine, I want to run something by you. I've been doing a lot of thinking, and I'd like to take Emma to JonBenét Ramsey's house."

"Really!" She was quiet a moment. "Did Emma put you up to this?"

"Not at all. It's just that I think going to the house might help her. If she can touch it somehow, then maybe she'll be able to let it go."

Jasmine said nothing.

"We'll make it a ceremony," I went on. "A pilgrimage. We won't be creepers. We'll just go and pay our respects."

Jasmine stayed quiet, then she said slowly, "I'm inclined to say yes, since it seems like you genuinely want to do it. Maybe you're right, maybe she does need some kind of ceremony. How about we talk about it when you come over Thursday night, once Emma's in bed?"

"That sounds good."

"You better go, you're eating up your minutes, and you need to have a few left so you can call me later and tell me that Seabourne offered you the job."

I laughed. "Right you are. Jasmine—I can't thank you enough."

"Oh, this is entirely selfish on my part," she said cheerfully. "I want you to stay here. For my sake, and for Emma's sake."

Tears pricked my eyes. "Well—fingers crossed."

"Fingers *and* toes! Call me later. Love you."

"Love you, too."

I put the phone in my—in Trixie's—bag, then thought a moment. I wanted to go to the library at once so I could log on to a computer and stare at the screen until Seabourne's e-mail appeared. But no; better to walk around a bit and burn off some of my excitement and nervousness.

I decided to go to the Denver Art Museum, which was only two blocks away. The museum costs money to get in, but the gift shop is free. The museum is an extremely modern structure, all angles and silver surfaces, and part of it looks like a ship's prow, a big triangular section that juts across Thirteenth Avenue. I had grown to love this part of town; it's a large plaza with enormous public art, including a blue dustpan and broom that's sweeping up two huge pieces of crumpled-up paper. In front of the library is my favorite statue, a red chair two stories high with—why not?—a brown-and-white horse standing on the seat. The plaza is right next to the Civic Center Park, which is laid out like a grand European park with swathes of green grass and white marble. I found this combination of old and new immensely pleasing, and the plaza had become another one of my go-to spots for peace and beauty.

I entered the museum. The ground floor is a large, cool room with soaring ceilings; there are no walls separating the ticket booths and the gift shop, which makes the shop feel like an exhibit of its own. I moseyed around the artfully arranged shelves and counters, ending up at the extensive jewelry counter. I picked up a pair of dangly earrings made of light-green stone and held them to my ears so I could examine myself in the mirror. If I get the job at One Heart, I thought, I'm going to become a member here, and then buy some earrings with my membership discount. But no, if I got the job at One Heart, the very first thing I needed to do was get a cell phone.

When I was done with my imaginary shopping, I walked out into the plaza again. I stood and thought a moment: Was it too early to check my e-mail? Then to my surprise, I heard someone call out my name: "Elizabeth!"

I looked behind me. "London!" I cried.

There she was, skinny and elegant in black leggings, black boots, a butter-yellow leather jacket, and a fabulous cream-and-navy scarf draped on her shoulders. I bounded over and gave her a hug, which she accepted awkwardly.

"London! It's been so long since I've seen you. I was just thinking of you yesterday."

"What are you doing right now?" she asked. "Do you have time to grab a coffee?"

"Sure. I'm completely free."

She gestured at Novo, a fancy coffee shop on the plaza that's part of a sleek modern apartment building with many angles and large glass windows. "Let's go here. These days it's practically my second home."

We went inside and stood at the counter, looking up at the minimalist menu on the wall. I had just enough money to afford a small coffee, but London said, "Have whatever you want. We'll put it on my tab."

She ordered a large cappuccino, so I ordered the same, and then we headed over to the seating area. The place has a sleek Euro vibe, full of bright colors and interesting shapes; I felt like I was in Milan or Stockholm or some other city with über-modern design. I had never been to Novo because I figured I couldn't afford it, but if I got the job at One Heart I would surely be back; it was perhaps one of the most striking cafés I had ever been in, even by Manhattan standards.

"Oh, U2," London said, motioning at the air as we settled into low-backed, lime-green sofas. "They have great music here."

I wrinkled my nose. "U2 was always a bit tame for me."

She laughed. "I bet in high school you smoked clove cigarettes and listened to the Smiths and the Cure."

"Morrissey was my first love," I confessed with a grin.

"I'm a Bono girl. Although these days he's a little too peace-and-love for my tastes."

A young man dressed in black came over and put two exquisitely prepared cappuccinos on the low glass table. He fawned over London a bit, admiring her chunky cream sweater and amber jewelry. When he walked away, I picked up my drink and said, "A tab at Novo! What's going on?"

"I have a client in the building. He and his wife bought a two-bedroom condo here, and they hired me to decorate it before they move in." She held up her thumb and rubbed it along her fingers, the international symbol for piles of money.

I whistled. "That's a great gig. This has to be one of the fanciest apartment buildings in Denver. Imagine looking out your window and having the art museum as your front lawn."

"And the Rockies in the distance," she said. "You can't believe their view."

"How did it go with the quarterback?"

"Oh, God, that was a few jobs ago. I've been so busy, it's been great. Economic downturn or no, there's still plenty of rich people."

London proceeded to tell me several anecdotes about her Denver clientele. It was so good to see her, and so lovely to be relaxing with a cappuccino in this ultra-modern café with huge windows and a view of the museum just across the plaza. London looked great, and she seemed happy and energized in her new—or, actually, old—lifestyle.

But London was still London, so it was a conversation with plenty of barbed wire. I found myself inwardly wincing a few times at her sharp—nay, bitchy—comments. I pasted a smile on my face and kept listening, nodding on occasion when I actually agreed with what she was saying. London was so sophisticated and stylish, but she could be so mean and catty. She even looked like a cat, with her narrow eyes, pointy cheekbones, and mane of sleek golden-brown hair.

"What about you?" she said finally. "What's new?"

"I just had a job interview," I said. "With a small publisher. It went really well, so . . ." I held up crossed fingers.

"Oh, that's great news, Elizabeth. Neither you or I belong in that hellhole Quill & Ink."

"It's not so bad there. I've actually grown to like it."

She arched an already arched eyebrow. "Then it really is time to go! Before you turn into one of them."

"The people there aren't so bad."

"What's happening at the store? What's the latest gossip?"

I gave her an abbreviated rundown of the store and its employees, keeping it short and positive. "Robert's good," I said at the end. "He's writing some great poems. He even lost a bit of weight, which is helping his sleep apnea."

She frowned. "Robert? The guy in receiving?"

"Not that Robert." I waved a hand. "Bob. Fat Bob."

"Oh, so he's Robert now?" She rolled her eyes.

I took a deep breath. We were having a nice time, mostly, but I really had to ask her a few things. "London, do you know about Colorado Loves Colorado?"

"No. Wait, it's that grant program, right? I think one of my clients is on the board. What about them?"

"Well, turns out a few people from the store come from that program. Stacie, for one. And Ruby."

"Stacie, clearly. What, is Ruby brain damaged? I always thought so."

"No," I said slowly. "She's not brain damaged."

I told London, haltingly, what had happened to Ruby. Then I said, "That last book club, when we were laughing at her? Apparently she was really upset afterward, and she was crying in the bathroom. Did anyone talk to you about it?"

"No. I think I left the next day." She laughed. "I didn't even come in, I just quit over the phone. The only time I want to step foot in that store is with a big fat credit line from one of my clients."

"Well, they talked to me. Hilda, that is. I got in a lot of trouble. I was suspended for a week, and my hours were cut." I felt ashamed to talk about it, but I also felt relieved. Up until that moment, I hadn't told a single soul what had happened.

"Hilda did that? Hilda the pushover? I'm surprised."

"And now," I went on, "it's still pretty awkward. The worst thing is, Ruby always cowers when she sees me. She has such bad PTSD, and I guess we—I guess I kind of retraumatized her."

London snorted. "Oh, for God's sake! Columbine was, what, ten years ago? Time to get over it."

"But PTSD doesn't work that way. It can last for years, or even a lifetime. It's like the wiring in your nervous system gets blown out, and you can't fix it."

"Why do you know so much about PTSD?"

I shrugged. "I did a little research."

"But it's not like Ruby got shot at Columbine or lost her kid or something." London rolled her eyes. "She just doesn't want to work hard."

I looked at London. Was she trying to be tough, or did she genuinely lack empathy? Either way, it was chilling. Either way, her callousness made me ill. And either way, I didn't have to sit there one second longer.

"London," I said, pushing away my cup and gathering my purse and jacket. "I have to go."

She leaned back against the stylish couch in surprise. "Already? I thought you had nothing to do."

"Turns out I was wrong," I said as I stood. "Thanks for the cappuccino. Good luck with your decorating."

"Thanks," she said. As I walked away, she called out, "Don't be a stranger!"

I waved, so upset my hand was shaking. Blind with anger and shame, I stalked across the plaza, past the library and the horse on the chair. I entered the Civic Center Park through the Greek Theater, and I didn't slow down until I was halfway around the circumference of the park, by the fountain with statues of little boys clutching sea lions. I sat on the low steps in front of the fountain to catch my breath, facing into the park with a view of the Greek Theater, and the library and art museum behind it. I could smell someone smoking pot behind me, but I didn't care.

Slowly my feelings evened out. I didn't like London. There was no reason to ever hang out with her again. I felt ashamed that I had ever considered someone like her a friend, or worth admiring.

Oddly, I also felt a splash of joy. For weeks I had been feeling like I was such a bad, broken person. But no matter what I had done, no matter how careless and bitchy I had been over the course of my life, I was not like London. Unlike her, I could actually feel something for people. Thank God, I could feel.

Elizabeth Zwelland, I told myself. You do not have a black heart. So there.

I sat for a while, awash in that good feeling. The park sparkled before me, all green lawns and white marble, the gold-domed Capitol Building on my left, the majestic City & County Building on my right. It was a crisp, beautiful December afternoon in Denver.

5. Softest Creature in the World

Emma and I did go to JonBenét Ramsey's house. We committed to a date—Wednesday, December 23—and everything unfolded from there.

On the Monday before, I worked at Quill & Ink. It had been a crazy weekend due to all the holiday mayhem, but that morning was peaceful. I mostly restocked the shelves, with only a little customer service. A snowstorm was brewing outside, and people were hunkering down at home to wait it out.

I punched out at noon and headed toward Market Street Station, walking through the first drifting snowflakes to get the express bus to Boulder. By the time I reached Boulder, there was an inch of snow on the ground, and the Flatirons were blocked from view by white sheets of falling snow. Normally Jasmine and Emma would have picked me up, but because of the snow I had told them not to bother. I transferred to the JUMP bus, which moved slowly through the snow and dropped me off a block from the little blue Victorian.

Both Jasmine and Emma were off from school for the holidays, and they were waiting for me with grilled cheese sandwiches and tomato soup. After lunch Jasmine made hot chocolate for everyone, and we had a powwow at the kitchen table.

"If you're going to do this," Jasmine declared, "you have to do it right. Let's make a plan."

We decided to go first thing Wednesday morning, as soon as the sun was up. Jasmine would fix us a hearty breakfast and then drive us over. But rather than dropping us directly in front of the house or doing some kind of creeper drive-by, she would let us out a few blocks away so we could walk and collect our thoughts. I had the exact address, so the three of us gathered around the kitchen computer and figured out our route. We would bring a few offerings—a card, flowers, and one of Emma's Hello Kitty dolls. We would put our gifts on the front stoop or wherever possible, and have a moment of silence. Meanwhile Jasmine would drive around and deliver a few Christmas presents. When Emma and I were done, we would meet Jasmine at Buchanan's Coffee Pub on the Hill, and we would continue our day from there.

Jasmine volunteered to clean up the lunch dishes so Emma and I could go upstairs to choose a Hello Kitty doll. We didn't know if JonBenét had been a Hello Kitty girl, but we imagined that she probably was, or perhaps would have been one day. Our eyes traveled over the range of dolls, then the choice became obvious to both of us: Beauty Queen Hello Kitty, complete with sparkling tiara on her big head, miniature gold scepter in her paw, and a pink sash that said, of course, HELLO KITTY. She was the one.

We took Beauty Queen Hello Kitty up to my room for safekeeping, putting her on a pillow and sitting her in front of the altar. The Dylans, boy and girl, were due to arrive any minute for a playdate, so we decided to leave the flowers and card for Tuesday afternoon. Emma wanted to include a poem in the card, and she told me in all seriousness that she needed time to let it marinate. That was a Jasmine expression through and through; I suppressed a smile and told Emma that marinating was an excellent idea.

As the snow fell steadily outside, Emma and I played a never-ending game of Monopoly with the Dylans. They both stayed for dinner—homemade pizza and more hot chocolate—and due to the storm it became clear that a sleepover was safest for everyone concerned. Jasmine usually tries to limit Emma's TV intake, but that evening she gave up completely, and the five of us watched every single retro Christmas video they possessed: *Rudolph the Red-Nosed Reindeer, How the Grinch Stole Christmas, A Charlie Brown Christmas,* and finally *It's a Wonderful Life,* which made all three children fall sound asleep.

Tuesday morning I woke to a snow-covered world. There was almost a foot of snow on the ground, and Boulder had the hush it always takes on after a storm. Laying snug inside my attic bedroom under the warm duvet, I could hear the scrape of the neighbors' snow shovels and the strange way their voices echoed outside in the snowy world.

We had French toast for breakfast, then I went back to bed for an early morning nap. The children went outside to play in the snow, and by late morning the front yard was filled with a range of snow creatures, everything from snowmen to snow dogs, and even a snow alien with five charcoal eyes. Then we all piled into the car so Jasmine could take the Dylans home and we could go to King Soopers to buy flowers.

The store had a decent range of bouquets, and everything seemed pretty fresh despite the previous day's storm. As Jasmine went looking for cookie tins, Emma and I discussed the merits of each bouquet. Finally we settled on a simple arrangement with six yellow roses, sprigs of baby's breath, and a few green leaves. On the car ride back home, Emma held the bouquet in her lap to keep it safe.

While Jasmine fixed whole-wheat pasta and seitan wheat-balls for lunch, Emma and I decided to snazz up the bouquet. We covered the King Soopers' paper with pink Hello Kitty Christmas wrap (Hello Kitty in a Santa hat, offering up a smartly wrapped gold present in one paw). We put the flowers in a vase with a touch of water at the bottom, then brought the vase up to my room and put it in front of the altar next to the meditating Beauty Queen Hello Kitty.

After lunch it was time for the card, so Emma and I set up shop in the living room. The place was a cheerful disaster, with a small, overloaded Christmas tree in one corner and an explosion of brightly wrapped presents underneath. The coffee table was covered with art supplies, including a pink plastic box full of miscellaneous decorations, everything from glitter to sequins to stickers to feathers. I must admit that Emma did the heavy lifting; she chose the materials while I lay on the couch, drinking coffee and nodding approval at her choices.

We decided that Emma needed to write the poem in the interior of the card before she decorated the outside. She wanted to write the first draft in her notebook, then transfer it to the card. She squeezed her notebook onto the coffee table, picked up her favorite purple pen, and stared at the open page, frowning slightly in concentration.

I decided to give Emma some space, so I went into the kitchen to top off my coffee and check on Jasmine, who was making an endless stream of chocolate chip cookies. We chatted a little as she put dollops of dough on greased baking sheets, then I drifted back into the living room and sat down on the couch.

Emma looked up at me, her expression solemn. "Elizabeth," she said. "I don't have any words."

My heart melted. "Oh, Emma, that's OK. Words don't always come."

She looked close to tears. "But I marinated all yesterday and this morning."

"Well, that's just how it is sometimes. Look, why don't you fix the front of the card, and you can just write a simple message inside and we'll sign it. I think that's good enough."

"Really?"

"Really. You always make such beautiful cards." Which was true, she did.

"I'm going to tell Mommy." Emma raced into the kitchen, then a minute later raced out. "She said it's a good idea."

"So it's unanimous. What's your plan for the front?"

"I'm thinking of a lot of feathers and a lot of sequins. Like a beauty-contest costume. But not an actual design."

"Free form," I said. "Abstract."

"Yes," she said decisively. "Abstract."

Emma set to work, and I kept up my coffee-drinking post on the couch. I watched Emma as she carefully chose feathers, glitter, and sequins from the magic pink box, which always seems to be full of supplies no matter how often we delve into it. I pulled a purple afghan from the foot of the couch and wrapped it around my shoulders, leaving my hands free for the coffee mug. I was rested and content, happy to watch Emma, happy to smell Jasmine's baking and hear her cheerful off-key singing from the kitchen.

I was also ready for the next morning. I had visited the library the previous week to get a little background. There were a surprising number of books on JonBenét—or I suppose it wasn't so surprising, given how obsessed the nation was with the case and how long it dragged out. I do recall reading about the murder all those years ago; it happened in Boulder, after all, the place where I had grown up and where my dad and two stepmothers lived. When JonBenét died, she was only six years old, just a year older than I had been when I left Colorado; she was a little girl in Boulder, just like I had once been. At Christmastime 1997 I was twenty-four years old, just starting my job at Blue Heron and moving into my Morton Street apartment. I have a distinct memory of myself at a CVS in Manhattan, standing in front of the magazine rack and reading an article on the case.

Of all the JonBenét books on the library shelves, I chose just one, mostly because I liked the title: *Perfect Murder, Perfect Town.* I sat at a table next to one of the big windows overlooking the Civic Center Park and went through the book. I read the description of how the body was found,

I skimmed through the parts about the Boulder police and the many procedural disasters that occurred, and I skipped the forensics altogether. What interested me most were the short oral-history sections, the first-person accounts from people who had known JonBenét, and eventually I just searched for those sections. I liked reading about what JonBenét was like when she was alive; she seemed to have had a healthy dose of mischief.

One story in particular struck me. JonBenét was at a lake for a day of swimming with some relatives, and when someone told her to put on her shoes, she refused. The relative insisted, but JonBenét held her ground, saying, "I want to feel the earth's life under my feet." I read that several times, and then I got up and put the book back on the shelves. I felt like I had found what I came for, somehow.

Then I went upstairs to the Technology Center to check my e-mails. I had one from Seabourne asking for my Social Security number and setting my start date; I had two requests from publishers to quote my mom's work; and last but not least, I had a spam e-mail from my dad, who had apparently been hacked. I answered all my e-mails, and then I wondered what the Internet might have on JonBenét.

Turns out there was quite a lot, including several documentaries, and I was immediately sucked in. Once again, it was one thing to read about something, and quite another to see images. Two of the documentaries had extensive tours of the house's interior; apparently it had gone through a few owners since the murder, and these people had willingly opened up the property for inspection. The house was currently for sale, with no one living there, which would make our pilgrimage that much simpler. I also discovered the bizarre fact that the house number had been changed, and I noted down the new address. How could anyone imagine that changing a few numbers would erase the house's history?

As I dug deeper, I was surprised to see that there were quite a few clips of JonBenét herself. But then she had been a minor celebrity during her short time on earth: she was Little Miss Colorado for a year, and she once had her own float in the Colorado Parade of Lights. The videos were fascinating, but one made my stomach turn: JonBenét was dancing in a pageant in a fancy black dress, made up and trussed up like one of those horrid stuffy dolls that people collect and never touch. I thought of the back cover of *Perfect Murder, Perfect Town*—in that photo, JonBenét is on a boat in a normal swimsuit, her hair wet and plastered to her head, a happy smile on her face. She looks like a typical little girl, which is what she was underneath all those costumes. I suddenly understood why the author had chosen that shot, undoubtedly wanting to offer some contrast to the artificial fantasy that JonBenét had been stuffed into, and that years later is still the image most people have of her.

But the worst image, the most haunting image, was the basement. There was a short segment from a documentary that showed the basement storage room where JonBenét's body was discovered, a room that is now sealed up. In contrast to the rest of the airy plush home, the basement room was small and dark, with a gray stone floor and concrete walls, and not a single window or hint of warmth. To think of that vibrant little girl lying in such a cold, harsh place—I got chills, and tears pricked my eyes. I closed the video. I had seen enough.

As I walked slowly down the three flights of stairs to the main floor of the library, it struck me: Was this what Emma had seen? Was this the image that was haunting her?

Jasmine's cell phone rang. Her ringtone was the first bars of a Parliament Funkadelic song, and it was coming from the general vicinity of the front door.

"Mommy," Emma called. "Your phone!"

Jasmine came out of the kitchen, smudges of flour on her cheek and jeans. "It's in my purse, which is—where? Behind the coat rack, of course." She unearthed the phone and answered: "Hello? . . . Oh, hi . . . Yes, we're all here . . . Now? Well—all right. Sure . . . Be careful driving. You know you're terrible in the snow . . . Yep. Bye."

I looked up at Jasmine. "Dad?"

She nodded and took a seat on the couch by my feet. "He's on his way over. He wants to talk to all of us."

I frowned. "That can't be good."

"I don't imagine it is. But let's see what he has to say for himself."

Emma looked at Jasmine eagerly. "Daddy's coming over?"

"That's right, honey." Jasmine reached out a hand and distractedly ruffled Emma's hair. "He's on his way right now."

Twenty minutes later, our dad walked in without knocking. He wore a black fur hat and his enormous winter coat, a floor-length maroon down jacket. He dropped the coat on the staircase—there was no room on the coat rack for that behemoth—and underneath he was in his customary sleepwear: a black robe with a red-and-gold dragon on the back, and black pajamas with red piping and a monogram. As usual his hair was in a ponytail and his huge sideburns were carefully groomed, but he had a serious expression on his face that did not bode well.

He sat down in the purple armchair. Emma immediately tried to sit on his lap, but he gently pushed her away and said, "Not now, Daughter. In a moment."

"Jasper," Jasmine said. "Do you want some coffee and cookies?"

"In a bit. First I want to say what I came here to say." He took an enormous breath, then clapped his hands on his knees. "Jane's pregnant."

I felt rather than saw Jasmine's eyebrows shoot into the center of her forehead. I know that's where mine went.

"Yes, she is," he said, more to himself than us. "She's pregnant. To say this is a surprise is the understatement of the century. But we'll get married, and soon."

"Wow," Jasmine said slowly. "Congratulations. When is the baby due?"

"Well, Jane's two months pregnant, so that makes it—" He looked puzzled.

"July," Jasmine said. "That makes it July."

"She's moving her things in tomorrow morning," he said. "My house is about to get very crowded and very messy."

"Emma!" Jasmine said suddenly. "Honey, what's wrong?"

I was still on the couch wrapped in the afghan, although I was now sitting rather than reclining. Emma was on the floor at my feet, and I leaned over to look at her. Emma's eyes were brimming with tears, and her lower lip was trembling. She was looking at our dad. "B-but, Daddy," she burst out, "there's no more space in the Daughter Room!"

Our dad sighed heavily. He opened his arms. "Daughter. Come here."

You didn't have to tell Emma twice. In a flash she was sitting on his lap, her arms wrapped around his large chest and her gaze pouring into his eyes.

"Apparently," our dad said, "Jane has some sort of aunt who's some sort of psychic, and this aunt woman is 100 percent sure that Jane is having a boy."

"A little brother?" Emma asked.

"That's right. So he'll have his own room. I bet Jane will need your help with the decorating."

Emma's eyes lit up. "Hello Kitty!"

"We-ll," our dad said. "Do you think Hello Kitty is right for boys?"

"Maybe Keroppi," I said.

"Keroppi!" Emma agreed. "I bet he'd like Keroppi."

Our dad frowned. "Who's Keroppi?"

"Daddy!" Emma cried. "I've told you a million times. He's a frog."

"Oh, a frog. Frogs would be fine."

Emma looked at me, then back at our dad. "Is Jane going to give him a Jane Austen name?"

"You know, I hadn't thought about that. Why don't you and Elizabeth make up a list of names and bring them over to the house tomorrow?"

"Tomorrow?" Jasmine said. "I thought Emma and Elizabeth were going over in the evening on Christmas Eve."

"Well, that's the other reason I'm here," our dad said. "The Daughters are still coming over Christmas Eve, but Jane was hoping all three of you could come for dinner tomorrow night. To get to know each other, and to celebrate, I suppose. Is everyone free?"

I looked at Jasmine. "We have plans tomorrow morning," I said slowly, "but dinner would work."

"Jasmine?" Our dad looked at her. "You'll come, too?"

"Sure," Jasmine said. "That sounds great." She paused. "Are you also inviting—?"

"Jill? Lord, no. She had a public scene with Jane last week when we bumped into her at the Kitchen. The management had to ask her to leave."

I looked at our dad. He was sitting with his chin resting on Emma's head, and he seemed absolutely despondent. He hadn't wanted children the first time, nor the second, and not this time, either. And if what Stepmother One had said was true, if he was still in love with Jasmine, then he really wasn't where he wanted to be. Seeing him so sad and unhappy, I almost felt sorry for him.

Almost.

"Jasper," Jasmine said. "Why don't you let Emma show you her new poems, and Elizabeth and I will bring out some coffee and cookies?"

"Yes," he agreed. "That sounds just fine."

Emma jumped off his lap, grabbed her notebook from the coffee table, and in an instant she was back on his lap and ruffling through the pages of her notebook.

Jasmine and I went into the kitchen. She put fresh grounds in the coffee pot and set it to brew, then she leaned against the counter and looked at me. "Well?" she asked.

I shrugged. "Well—I don't know. I think I'm going to have to let this one marinate. Do you think Emma will be all right?"

"Oh, sure. Once she realized that the baby wasn't taking her room, it was a whole new ballgame."

"I just feel so sorry for the baby, being born into all this Zwelland mess. Emma, too."

"You survived it. They'll survive it, too. With your help, of course." She turned toward the coffee pot, and I couldn't see her face. "That is, if you're staying. I'm always so afraid you're going to tell me that you're moving back to New York."

My heart melted all over again. "Don't worry. I'm staying."

She turned to look at me. "Really? You're sure?"

"Yes. I'm sure." I had a new job in Colorado, not to mention my entire extended dysfunctional family. There was no reason to live anywhere else. "What about you? Are you all right with dinner tomorrow night?"

"Definitely. I want to get to know Jane better. After all, she's going to be Emma's stepmother." Jasmine's eyes twinkled. "Yours, too."

"Stepmother Three." My dad's life was now officially as complicated as his Beat heroes.

Jasmine sighed. "I'd like to befriend Jane sooner rather than later. Because the truth is, Elizabeth, one day she's going to need us."

I nodded. I am not a person with any psychic powers whatsoever, but even I could see what the future held.

☼ ☼ ☼

To my surprise, our dad stayed quite a while, eating cookies and chatting with Emma and me. It was my first chance to tell him the details about my position at One Heart, and I could tell he was immensely pleased for me. After he left, Emma finished the card: it was an explosion of glitter and feathers and sequins in a design that could only be called abstract. It was gorgeous. Then she opened it up and showed me what she had written in lieu of a poem:

> DEAR JONBENNET,
>
> WE LOVE YOU.
>
> LOVE, EMMA AND ELIZABETH (E^2)

We both signed our names, then Jasmine helped us wrap the card in tinfoil—no envelope on earth could possibly contain it. We brought it upstairs to the altar to leave it with the flowers and Beauty Queen Hello Kitty, for safekeeping and perhaps to pick up a little spiritual mojo from the Buddha statue and Chögyam Trungpa's photograph.

While Jasmine fixed lasagna for dinner, Emma and I snuggled together on the couch with the afghan and opened the notebook. It was time to choose a name.

"All right," I said. "There are six Jane Austen novels, so there's six heroes. Do I have your permission, madam, to write them on a page of your notebook?"

"Yes," Emma said. "You have my permission."

I picked up the purple pen and wrote a list:

JANE AUSTEN NAMES FOR NEW BROTHER

SENSE AND SENSIBILITY: EDWARD FERRARS

PRIDE AND PREJUDICE: FITZWILLIAM DARCY

MANSFIELD PARK: EDMUND BERTRAM

EMMA: GEORGE KNIGHTLEY

NORTHANGER ABBEY: HENRY TILNEY

PERSUASION: FREDERICK WENTWORTH

"Let's take them one by one," I said. "Edward?"

Emma wrinkled her nose. "It's kind of formal. Like a king's name."

"Fitzwilliam?"

She looked at me in horror. "I don't even know what that means."

"Me either. Let's skip it. Although, maybe we could get funky and use a last name. We could call him 'Darcy.'"

"That's a girl's name."

"This is Boulder. No one cares about that kind of thing here."

"What's next?"

"Edmund."

Emma shook her head vigorously. "I don't like the 'mund.'"

"Fair enough. George?"

"Curious George. No."

"Henry?"

"Peach's dog is named Henry."

"Frederick?"

She grimaced. "Too fancy."

We looked at each other.

"What do you like?" she asked me.

"I like Edward. A lot. It's a nice name: Edward Zwelland. It's an *E* name, after all."

Emma's eyes lit up. "You're right." She took the purple pen and wrote in the margins: E^3.

"Exactly," I said. "And king names are good. There's Queen Elizabeth, right?"

Emma bit her lip. "That's true. OK—yes!"

"So it's final? Edward?"

"Let's go tell Mommy."

Jasmine approved. Upon further discussion over dinner, we realized that Edward Ferrars was not exactly the most spunky Jane Austen hero. And of course there was his deception with Lucy Steele, which was not his finest hour. But Edward was basically a good guy, and by the end of the novel he had straightened himself out, which was all one could really ask from any protagonist. I decided that I would not mind having him as a little brother. In fact, I looked forward to it.

☼ ☼ ☼

The next morning, Emma woke me at six. She had somehow slipped into my room without me noticing, because when I opened my eyes she was lying next to me, fully dressed and staring into my eyes.

"Elizabeth," she whispered. "It's today."

I dressed quickly and we went downstairs. Jasmine had already fixed our breakfast—chocolate chip pancakes and strong coffee, and the special coffee drink she makes for Emma, half-coffee and half–hot chocolate. We ate in silence, and when we were done Jasmine informed us that it was only ten degrees outside, and we needed to bundle up carefully. I looked out the window; it was still dark, but a weak light had started to break through just above the neighbor's rooftop.

Emma and I went upstairs to get our offerings. In order to carry everything, we had a large bright-red gift bag that Jasmine had found the night before. We took the flowers out of the vase and dried the damp ends with a towel that Emma got from the bathroom, then we packed up the bag and brought it downstairs. Jasmine was outside warming up the car, and Emma and I began layering for the cold: thick sweaters, coats, scarves, big woolly hats, Thinsulate gloves.

Jasmine came inside, her cheeks and nose bright pink, and told us that the car was ready. We were about to leave when she told us to wait. She ran upstairs and came back down with a jar of coconut-rose oil from Rebecca's Apothecary. She rubbed some on Emma's nose and cheeks, then mine, then her own. She adjusted Emma's scarf a few inches so it covered her mouth and nose, then waved a hand toward the front door: it was time to leave.

The bitter cold hit us as soon as we stepped outside. We hurried over to the green Subaru that was silently chugging white puffs of exhaust into the street. We put the red gift bag on the passenger seat in front, then Emma and I got into the back. She took my hand at once, and I gave her fingers a gentle squeeze.

We drove in silence through the dark, empty streets. Even though the streets had been plowed they still had a layer of snow, muffling the sound of the car on the road. It was not a long drive, maybe ten minutes at most. When we arrived at Eighteenth and Cascade, Jasmine pulled over to the curb but didn't turn off the motor. Emma and I got out, and Jasmine reached across the passenger seat to open the door. Emma took out the red bag and clutched it to her chest.

Jasmine leaned over the empty seat. "See you at Buchanan's," she said.

"See you there," I replied.

She drove off and we were alone, standing on the sidewalk in the biting cold. The Flatirons were closer now, and the residential neighborhood was silent and asleep. The sun was just coming up, revealing a white-gray sky that threatened more snow.

Holding hands, we started to walk. We knew exactly where we were going: three blocks west, then turn left onto Fifteenth Street.

The day before had been cold, but that day was bitter. There was no wind at all, just deep, penetrating cold. I looked over at Emma: with the thick pink scarf over her mouth and nose, and the pink woolly hat pulled down over her bangs, all I could see were her big green eyes, steady and serious.

There was about a foot of snow on the ground, and the sidewalks were icy in spots, so we moved slowly. I felt an odd wince in my stomach—fear, maybe, or sorrow. I also had a strange sense of anticipation: we were finally doing this. We had talked about it, we had planned it, and finally we were there. I imagine Emma felt the same, only for her the anticipation—the desire—had been going on for months.

As we walked along the Boulder streets, the perfectly normal Boulder streets, we saw a few signs of life: a car passed, a woman came outside to call her dog, and since it was Boulder we saw a jogger and even a cross-country skier, both so bundled up I couldn't tell if they were male or female. But overall the streets were empty, and the silence complete.

We reached Fifteenth Street. We crossed over and made a left, walking slowly on the sidewalk. The corner house, then the next house, and another house—and there it was.

I was struck by how close the house was to the street, and how close the houses were to each other. In all the still photos and documentaries I had seen, the red-brick house had seemed so isolated, so large and looming. It was in fact a big house—as we approached, I could see how far back it went—but the facade was not wide, and the front lawn was fifteen-feet deep at most. It was a cozy little neighborhood, not isolated at all.

But unlike all the photos I had seen, there was now a black-iron fence in front of the house, tall and imposing with square red-brick pillars and a door with an intercom. We stopped and looked through the fence. Snow was piled on the front stoop and small lawn. No one had been there since the storm, and who knows how long before that. The house didn't have an air of neglect; it was more that it felt empty and still. Eerily still.

I figured the door on the fence was locked, but I tried it anyway, just in case. Locked. The bars of the fence were fairly close together, but there seemed to be enough room to push all our offerings through.

I let Emma do it. She gave me the red bag, then she took out the foil-covered card and put it through the fence, bending her hand to the left so the card could rest against the brick pillar, making it invisible from the street. Then she took out the bouquet of roses. They were a tight fit, but Emma pushed them through and leaned them on the card. Beauty Queen Hello Kitty was last. Luckily she had a smushy head, and with a little help from me, Emma was able to squeeze her through, too.

We stood a moment on the sidewalk, our cold breath puffy and white. I looked at the house again. Icicles were hanging from the eaves, and there were large patches of dead ivy on the facade.

I looked down at Emma. She looked up at me and nodded. I took her hand, and slowly we walked away. I allowed myself one last look at the house, and as I turned my head, I saw that Emma was doing the same.

On the corner, there was a low brick wall bordering the sidewalk. I sat down and Emma sat next to me, fitting her body into mine. I put my arm around her and rested my chin on her head. I had a strange feeling of relief and release. It was as if we had accomplished something, as if we had taken care of something. I wondered if Emma felt the same.

I want to feel the earth's life under my feet.

We sat for a while. Then Emma moved her head and looked up at me.

"Elizabeth," she said. "I think I have some words now."

"All right," I said softly. "Let's walk to Buchanan's. We'll get hot chocolate, and you can write down your words."

We walked slowly up Fifteenth Street, holding hands and taking care not to slip on the ice. A few blocks later, it was a tremendous relief to see the red-tile roofs of the University of Colorado campus. We were coming back to the world. We were leaving those cold, still streets behind us.

6. I Don't Have Any Words

My first day at One Heart was scheduled for Monday, January 11. Trixie wanted to treat me to dinner that evening to celebrate, but then one of her clients had to move their appointment. We decided instead to go out for breakfast on my last day at Quill & Ink. Jasmine and Emma were also coming to Denver that day for a late lunch at Dixons, so I would be eating out twice.

"We'll go to Snooze, of course," Trixie said.

"What's Snooze?" I asked.

She widened her eyes. "You've never been to Snooze? My dear, how can you call yourself a Denverite?"

So early that Thursday morning, I knocked on Trixie's door, and we set out in her fire-red Porsche for the mythical Snooze.

Winter in Denver is a strange beast. There are days of cold and snow and storm, and then there are lovely days in the high fifties with plenty of sunshine. Even if Denver gets a foot of snow, it usually melts within two days. That morning was already looking like a beauty, with plenty of sunshine and a pleasingly crisp chill. Trixie and I both wore jeans and sneakers and thick sweaters in lieu of coats, and her red hair was done up in a complicated white turban.

Snooze wasn't far at all. Trixie drove up to Cheesman Park, then took a right onto Seventh Avenue. The street was a revelation to me. It was extremely wide, wide enough to accommodate sizable islands in the middle with full-grown trees and slumbering gardens, as well as bike lanes on both sides. The houses lining the street were gorgeous; some were old, and some were intended to look old, but for the most part they were regal homes of red brick or white stone, with elegant iron fences and superb landscaping.

"This street is amazing," I said, craning my neck.

"It's great for biking," Trixie replied. "If you bought a secondhand bike for cheap on Craigslist, you could get to Snooze in twenty minutes."

Seventh Avenue ended at Colorado Boulevard, a busy street with plenty of early-morning commuter traffic. As we waited for the light to change, Trixie pointed across the road to a low brick building with an orange neon sign. "Snooze," she said with reverence.

We parked behind the restaurant and went inside to give our names to the perky hostess, who said it would be about a fifteen-minute wait. To my delight, a small coffee bar was set up inside for those who were waiting. Trixie and I each prepared a cup with milk and sugar, then we sat on a bench outside, chatting and sipping happily.

"This coffee—" I said.

"I know," Trixie agreed. "It's organic. From Guatemala."

"I wonder if they would mind if I sat on this bench all day and set up an IV line to the urn," I mused.

Fifteen minutes later, the waitress seated us in a booth in a corner, next to a large plate-glass window looking out onto Colorado Boulevard. I loved the décor, which was a kind of stylized fifties space-age look, with unusual colors like burnt orange and pea green. The booths and the counter had curving lines and stainless-steel bottoms, and sprinkled throughout the store was the Snooze icon, an eight-pronged atomic snowflake. The place was packed to the brim with chatting diners, and altogether it had a fun, cheerful vibe, brimming with life and the smell of that rich coffee.

Our waitress, a pretty blonde with colorful snake tattoos coiling up each arm, brought us thick yellow mugs of coffee and then came back to take our order. I got the crab cake Benedict, Trixie the veggie Benedict, both with hash browns. The food came fairly quickly, and as we ate we chatted about my new job and Trixie's position at National Jewish Hospital, where she had just been given another five hours a week.

We also marveled at Trixie's first face-to-face encounter with the Snuffler. Two days earlier she had a bout of insomnia, so she decided to do a load of laundry in the middle of the night. As she approached the machines, she came upon a little man in a large green overcoat who was unloading a dryer. He looked at her in panic, then frantically snatched up his clothes and ran down the hall.

"But how do you know it was him?" I asked, lifting up my coffee cup and nodding to the waitress that it was fine to take our empty plates.

"Because he snuffled! I'd know that snuffle anywhere."

"It's like seeing Big Foot; no one's going to believe you."

"But it's true, it was him. When I walked back to my apartment, I heard a snuffle as I walked by his door. He must have been watching me out the peephole."

"I think he does that a lot; I often hear him snuffle when I pass. What did he look like?"

"Short, which I knew from the time I saw him from behind. And bald. A round head, clean shaven, big blue eyes, dead-white skin, which is not surprising. He wore a striped scarf, quite possibly cashmere. He had a bit of a Truman Capote thing going."

"Age?"

"Indeterminate. Not thirty, but not sixty."

I scrunched up my face. "Why won't he say hi to us? We're such harmless neighbors."

Trixie shrugged. "Who knows why anyone does anything?"

I put down my mug. "Speaking of which—there's something I've been wanting to tell you. But I've been kind of scared to bring it up."

"Oh, go ahead," Trixie said cheerfully. "You can't shock me."

"Well—maybe I can. I'm not leaving Quill & Ink just because of my new job. I mean, that's a huge part of it, but I knew I needed to leave even before I got hired at One Heart."

"Why? I thought you liked it there."

"I do now. But I didn't at first. You know that week when I was at home, when you brought me graham crackers and took me to the Botanic Gardens? I was home because I'd been suspended."

"Suspended! Why?"

I told her. Slowly, and not making much eye contact. Trixie was only the second person I had told, other than London.

When I was done, I looked up and met Trixie's eyes. I could have cried when I saw how kindly she was watching me.

"Oh, Elizabeth! You didn't know. No one told you."

I wrinkled my nose. "That's true. But ultimately that's not even the point. I was just mean. Angry and mean."

"It happens," she said sympathetically.

"I let you think that I was upset about a guy because I was too ashamed to tell you the truth. I'm sorry."

"That's OK. You're human. We humans do stupid things all the time." She sighed. "Well, since it's true-confession time, there's something I've wanted to tell you. You know how I've mentioned my legal problems?

And you know how you've always been far too polite to ask me what's going on?"

I grinned. "I give my mom credit for any good manners that I actually do possess."

"Well—I was arrested."

Now it was my turn to be surprised. "Arrested! For what?"

She closed her eyes. Then she opened them and looked directly at me; she started to speak, slowly and carefully. "Well, as you know, I'm a masseuse. A dancer turned masseuse, to be exact. One day I was carrying my table into a fancy hotel downtown, a hotel which shall remain nameless. One of the bellboys—a bellman, really—asked me if I was interested in making some extra cash."

She looked out the window. "It was just hand jobs. A regular massage, but always with a hand job at the end. Sometimes oral, but rarely. If I did do that, I made them pay through the nose. So to speak."

I said nothing. I just gazed at Trixie steadily and let her talk.

"At first I worked at that hotel exclusively, but eventually I got in at a few other places downtown. I charged $500 a pop, and during the annual Western Stock Show I usually made around $10,000. I had so much money I literally didn't know what to do with it; I had envelopes of cash stuffed under my mattress." She sighed. "I got used to living pretty large. I ate at all the fancy Denver restaurants, I bought my Porsche, and I took a few Hawaiian vacations, the highest of the high end.

"It went on for about five years, then that bellman got busted." She shrugged. "Oddly enough, it's worse to procure sexual services than to be the one actually providing them, so he got jail time whereas the other girls and I just got fines. It was a huge deal; it was in all the local papers. They wanted me to name names, but I wouldn't do it. That's why my fine is so high."

She took a sip of coffee with a trembly hand, then looked out the window again. "I didn't lose my massage license, thank God, but it was suspended for six months. I'm also banned from every hotel in downtown Denver. All my cash is gone, but I did keep my car and my clothes. Not much else, though. I held on to my apartment for as long as I could, but finally I let it go and moved to the Swiss Arms. Now I'm rebuilding my clientele from scratch. I'm still paying off my fine."

I finally found my voice. "How much is your fine?"

"A lot. A whole lot. I paid off half right away, and I can pay off the rest in increments. But I can't be even a day late, or it's all due at once. So I'm really scrupulous about it. I also have to meet with a sort of parole officer every month, and I'm really scrupulous about that, too." Trixie looked at me, her blue eyes fragile. "You must be pretty shocked."

"Well, yes," I said slowly. "I am a little shocked. But like you said—we're all human."

"So it's not a deal breaker?"

I smiled and shook my head. "No. It's not a deal breaker."

Trixie leaned back into the booth, an expression of relief flooding her face. "I'm glad to hear it." She laughed. "We're a fine pair. You harass survivors from the Columbine shooting, and I give hand jobs in fancy hotels."

I laughed. "Yep. That about sums it up."

"You want to know another secret about me?"

"Go ahead. Shoot."

"You're not the only one named after a literary heroine. My mom named me after Trixie Belden."

"Who's Trixie Belden?"

"How can you not know about Trixie Belden? She's a girl detective, she has a whole series of books. She's like Nancy Drew, but with more soul."

I held up a hand. "I'm sorry, but that's just not possible. Nancy is nothing but soul."

"You can't speak knowledgeably about this subject until you read one of Trixie's books. I have the whole set; I'll lend you one."

"All right," I said. "You're on."

We finally left at nine thirty, so full of caffeine we could have run the city of Denver singlehandedly. As Trixie drove me to Quill & Ink, we passed through Cheesman Park. I looked out the window at the wide expanse of grass with the thousands of bodies underneath.

"Why doesn't it bother me that the park used to be a graveyard?" I mused. "I don't know why, but it just doesn't."

"It's a Denver thing," Trixie said. "Just part of its quirky charm."

"What prayer do you say for them?"

"Nothing fancy. I just think: 'May they move forward. May they be happy.' Simple."

"Maybe they are happy. Maybe they don't mind people playing Frisbee on top of them."

"Could be," Trixie laughed. "Could be."

☼ ☼ ☼

I had already reconciled myself to the fact that there would be no happy ending for me at Quill & Ink, so I didn't have any false expectations for my last day. I knew there would be no friendly farewell chat with Hilda, and no last-minute forgiveness from Rebecca. They were set against me, and that wasn't going to change. When I first told Hilda about my new job and said that I would be leaving in early January, she barely reacted, except to ask a few questions about One Heart. But about a half-hour later, I happened to spot her and Rebecca in the Military History section, talking happily and laughing. I'm not a paranoid person, but I could pretty much guess the source of their good mood.

So on that last day, those final few hours, I'd say my primary emotion was—wistful. Obviously I was glad to be going back to publishing, because obviously that's where I belonged. But Q&I is a great place to work. It's a caring environment with cool people, and it's located in the heart of downtown Denver. It's busy and bustling and fun, and what with all the lectures and book clubs and author appearances, it's one of the city's cultural hubs. I saw all that by the end of my time there, but it was too late. Because of everything that had happened, I would never feel comfortable at Q&I, not even as a customer.

As usual, I came in and got a coffee. As usual, I chatted with Bree and read Hadley's weekly Jack Kerouac quote:

> IT WAS OUR LAST NIGHT IN HOLY DENVER
> JACK KEROUAC, *ON THE ROAD*

And as usual, I shelved.

There was one bright spot, though. When I went to the break room at noon to punch out for my fifteen-minute break, the room was full: Hadley, Bree, Juniper, Stacie, Hector, and Robert. On the table was a tray of chocolate cupcakes, each with white frosting and a pink letter, which spelled out: GOOD LUCK ELIZABETH!!!!!!!

"I made two dozen," Juniper explained. That day she was dressed as a Catholic schoolgirl, complete with knee socks, plaid skirt, and a white blouse straining at the buttons. "That's why you got so many exclamation points."

My eyes filled with tears. They even had a card for me, a stylized drawing of a group of cats in black leather jackets that said: GOOD LUCK FROM THE GANG. I opened it up and saw that everyone had signed it and written a little something. I told them I would read the card later, and I put it in my locker. To this day, I have the card hanging on my refrigerator with a magnet.

Hadley and Juniper had to run back to their posts, but everyone else hung out for a few minutes. I nervously ate two cupcakes, an *E* and a *!*, feeling a bit shy from all the attention. But then everyone started talking about Stacie's new eye-patch, which was a Christmas present from Bree and me. Her khaki one had obviously been on its last legs, so Bree and I had gone to a costume store and found a black silk patch with a row of pink and purple sequins around the edges. When we gave it to Stacie in the break room on Christmas Eve, she smiled and said the longest sentence I had ever heard her utter: "This eye patch is bad-ass."

Then the party was over. Juniper packed up a *!* cupcake for her newest boyfriend, and everyone went back on the floor. Bree lingered behind; her shift was over and she was leaving for the day. She gave me a hug, and I was surprised to see how sad she looked.

"I hope we can stay in touch," she said. "I know people say that and they don't mean it, but I really do."

"When I get my first paycheck, I'm buying a cell phone," I said. "As soon as I get my new number, I'll stop by and give it to you all."

She gave me another hug, and I felt how tiny and bony she was, like a delicate little bird. Then she punched out for the day, and I went back on the floor for the rest of my shift.

At one thirty, a half hour before I was scheduled to leave, I was doing reshelves in Fiction when I heard a familiar squeal. I turned around, and there was Emma running toward me full force. She threw her arms around my waist and burrowed her head in my stomach. Jasmine trailed behind her, waving happily at me as she approached. I buried my nose in Emma's hair; it was so good to have them there.

"We're early," Jasmine said, kissing me on the cheek. "I hope you don't mind. It's pathetic that we've never visited you here, so we're making it up in your waning moments."

"That's all right," I said. "Although I don't know how I'm going to work with a little monkey wrapped around me."

"Jasmine Zwelland?"

We turned around. It was Hadley, standing with his arms intertwined in that awkward way he had, a gleam in his eye that I recognized very well.

"Hi there," Jasmine said. She looked at me quizzically, as if to ask: Do I know him?

Hadley strode forward and took both her hands in his. "My name is Hadley Barr. I work in the café and I run the Beat Book Club here at the store. I'm an enormous, enormous, *huge* fan of your poetry."

Jasmine smiled and lifted her shoulders. "Oh—thank you. That's sweet of you."

"I recognized you from your book covers. I also saw you walk in just now with Elizabeth's twin. A short twin, with bangs."

Emma, her arms still wrapped around my waist, leaned back her head and looked up at Hadley. "We're sisters," she said. "We have the same daddy."

"That's right," he said. "Elizabeth told me."

"Our mothers named us after Jane Austen heroines. And in the summer we're going to have a little brother, and his name is going to be Edward, like in *Sense and Sensibility.*"

"Very cool."

"His mom is Jane. She was our daddy's student, then she was his girlfriend, then she got pregnant, and now they're getting married next month."

Discretion has never been Emma's strong point. But Hadley was unfazed. "That's awesome. So you'll have a brother from another mother."

Emma looked puzzled for a moment, then she beamed. "*Exactly,*" she said.

"I have a sister from another mister." Emma knit her brow, so Hadley explained, "I have a stepdad, and he and my mom had a girl."

"Oh!" Emma said. "I get it."

"I didn't know you had a half-sister," I said.

"Elizabeth Zwelland," Hadley replied, looking at me seriously. "There are many, many things that you don't know about me."

I blushed. Luckily Emma wasn't done spilling family secrets, so the attention shifted back to her. "We asked Jane to name our brother 'Edward,'" she said. "We were scared she'd say no, but it turns out she had a grandfather named Edward, so she said yes. He's getting his own room," she added.

"Well, isn't he a lucky guy. Jasmine," Hadley said, turning to her. "Since you're here, would you mind signing a few books?"

"Sure. Elizabeth, do we have time?"

"Oh, definitely," I said. "I have to bring this cart back to receiving, I'll see if we have any more of your books down there."

"I'll get a Sharpie from the information desk," Hadley said. He put out his two large palms and moved them up and down. "Do not move! I'll be right back."

I dropped the rest of the reshelves at Juniper's desk, then I took the empty cart down to receiving. I went over to the poetry shelves, and sure enough I found a half-dozen of Jasmine's books waiting to be shelved. I carefully took the books in my arms, then I went over to Hector to say good-bye.

"How you gonna hug me if you're carrying all those books?" he asked.

I put down the books and gave him a hug. His head fit just under my chin, and I could feel the taut muscles under his T-shirt, which was still white and crisp even after a busy morning.

"Stay cool, Miss E," he said, looking up at me. "You got that?"

"Hector," I smiled, "no one can stay as cool as you. But I'll try."

I went back upstairs with the books. I headed to the poetry section, where I figured Hadley had set Jasmine up at a table. But as I rounded the corner, I saw that Jasmine had plopped down cross-legged on the green carpet and was signing the books on her lap. She's such a hippie, I thought with a smile as I sat down next to her. Emma, who had been leaning against Jasmine and talking to Hadley, crawled onto my lap and put her arms around my neck.

Jasmine finished signing a book and put it facedown on the carpet. Emma looked at the back cover and frowned. "Mommy," she said sternly. "Your shirt is really low here."

Jasmine's first book, *Hot and Holy Love,* had an author photo that showed Jasmine at the height of her lusciousness, leaning forward in a low-cut peasant blouse that revealed a substantial amount of cleavage.

Jasmine sighed. "Yes, dear. I know."

"What were you *thinking*?" Emma asked.

"In those days? Not much, and not often." Jasmine looked at me and winked.

"So, Jasmine," Hadley asked. "Do you have a new book coming out anytime soon?"

"As a matter of fact," Jasmine said, "I do."

I frowned. "You do?"

She nodded, unsuccessfully trying to hide an enormous smile. "I just found out this morning. I got an e-mail from Coffee House Press; they want to put out a book of my haiku."

"Jasmine!" I cried. "That's great!" They were a good publisher, and getting a book accepted during an economic crash was no small thing.

"So this lunch is a double celebration," she said. "We're celebrating Elizabeth's new job and the new book, too." She smiled at me. "I planned to tell you at lunch. I bribed Emma with gummy worms so she wouldn't tell you the second we walked in the store." She turned to Hadley. "Aren't I a good mom?"

He laughed. "I love haiku. Kerouac wrote awesome haiku; have you ever read his *Book of Haikus*?"

Jasmine's eyes lit up. "Oh, I love that book! Did you ever read *The Paris Review* interview Kerouac did with Ted Berrigan? He explains how to write a haiku. I think I've read that section a hundred times."

"People think of Jack as being so verbose, but he was a very economical writer as well. When he chose to be."

"He could do whatever he chose to do," Jasmine agreed. "He was a genius. A true genius."

I felt someone staring at us. I glanced up and saw Hilda in front of the Fiction section, her head tilted to one side. I felt a squeeze of fear and started to rise, but she waved a hand, telling me to stay. Probably she recognized Jasmine, and also figured out why I had a little girl on my lap who looked just like me.

"I actually live at the Jack Kerouac," Hadley said. "It's an apartment building a block from the Capitol Building."

Jasmine laughed. "The Jack Kerouac! I love it."

"There's also the Jack Kerouac Lofts in another part of town, but they're much more upscale. My building is more true to Jack's spirit. He and Neal and Allen used to hang out in Capitol Hill, back in the day."

"That's really cool. My ex knew Jan Kerouac."

"I know! In the hot tub at the Naropa conference in 1982."

"Wow, you really are a Zwelland fan. Do you write?"

"Nope. Not a drop. But I love good writing."

"Same as Elizabeth. Although she has a tremendous talent with words. It's her inheritance from her mom and dad."

"These are our daddy's books," Emma said to Hadley, pointing at the shelves.

"That's right," Hadley said. "I love his poems, too. Does Mr. Zwelland have any books coming out?" he asked Jasmine.

"One in the summer. He also edited a Beat poetry anthology for Oxford University Press that's coming out in the fall." She turned to me. "And guess who's writing haiku now?"

I raised my eyebrows. "Dad?"

Jasmine folded in her lips and nodded. "Yep."

"Wow. He's pretty transparent."

She gave me another wink. "Emma writes poetry, too," she told Hadley. "She's very talented."

Hadley laughed. "Another Zwelland poet! Do you know any of your poems by heart?"

Emma took off her backpack and pulled out her notebook. "I can show you some. If you want."

"Oh, I do. Hello Kitty! Excellent taste."

Emma beamed. Clearly Hadley had excellent taste, too. She slid off my lap and crawled onto his.

"Well," I stood. "I better take these books downstairs and punch out."

Jasmine stood as well. "I need to buy a copy of *The Girl Who Played with Fire.*"

"We have about a million copies downstairs," I told her.

"Emma," Jasmine said. "We have to go, honey."

"It's cool," Hadley said. "I have about another half hour on my break."

"You're sure you don't mind?"

"Not at all. I'm getting a sneak peek at a great poet."

Emma smiled broadly as she leafed through her notebook. At the rate Hadley was going, she was never going to leave his lap.

"All right," Jasmine said. "If you're sure. I'll come back up and get you when I'm done."

The minute we were out of earshot, Jasmine looked up at me, her eyes in a major twinkle. "So—that Hadley guy is nice."

I shrugged. "He's OK. Yeah, he's nice."

"He likes you."

I sighed. "He likes the Beats and he likes Dad."

"Maybe so," Jasmine said as we descended the stairs. "But there's a big difference between liking them and liking a flesh-and-blood female."

"My point exactly. I don't think he sees me like that. All he sees are the Beat connections."

"Oh, you think that's all he sees?"

I rolled my eyes, then pointed to the front of the store. "Your book, madam, is over there. That big orange stack on the table by the window. I'll meet you in the poetry section in a few minutes."

I took Jasmine's books to receiving, put an AUTOGRAPHED COPY sticker on each one, then put them back on the shelves. I went to the break room to punch out and clean out my locker—there wasn't much, just Chap Stick, my copy of *Washington Square,* and the farewell card I got that day. I wrapped up a *!* cupcake in three napkins and put it carefully in the front compartment of my knapsack, then took a last look around the little windowless room. Despite the mess, I saw how hard Hilda had tried to make it homey, and I felt that wistfulness once more.

Before I went upstairs to fetch Emma and Jasmine, I swung by the cashier's desk and said good-bye to Stacie and Robert, giving them both hugs and promising to stay in touch. As I walked back to the staircase, I glanced at the fancy notebook section. There was Ruby on the floor with several piles of notebooks in front of her, a confused look on her face.

I hadn't seen much of Ruby during the previous month. On weekdays she was always scheduled to come in right before I punched out, and the weekends had been so crazy with the holidays that I barely had time to breathe. I stepped behind a wooden pillar where I knew she couldn't see me. This was my chance, maybe my last chance. But looking at her, in her lime-green pantsuit, her dyed black hair with the white stripe at the part, her pale skin and perplexed expression—I didn't have any words. My eyes filled with tears. I wanted, more than anything, to have a few words. But I just didn't.

Then I remembered Trixie's prayer. So I said it on the inside: May you move forward. May you be happy.

I watched Ruby a moment more, then went on my way. It was time to go.

7. Mad Denver Afternoon

On a Friday afternoon in early April 2010, I was sitting in the plaza outside the World Trade Center, drinking a large latte from Dazbog. I had an appointment at the Colorado Convention Center at three, but since it was a nice day, sunny and breezy, I decided to spend a little time on the 16th Street Mall before I walked over.

I was free on a Friday afternoon not because I had lost my job, but because I had worked so much overtime that Seabourne asked me to take a day off. I had grown fond of sitting in the World Trade Center plaza because, as it turned out, the plaza was a good spot to have lunch. It took me just under fifteen minutes to walk from our offices above City O' City to the World Trade Center, then a half hour to eat and dawdle and people watch, and another fifteen to walk back—the perfect lunch hour. I usually socialized with people from work in the evenings, so I didn't join them for lunch; I took that time for myself to stretch my legs and clear my head a bit. Also it saved money if I brought my own sandwich. I made a generous salary by Denver standards, but I still kept many of the thrifty habits from my retail days. I never wanted to be caught as unaware as I was when Blue Heron went under. Bernie Madoff was responsible for many disasters, but it wasn't his fault that I didn't have a savings account and that I spent all my money on rent and eating out.

I really like the World Trade Center plaza, an oddly shaped space between the two buildings and a perfect place for aimless hanging out. The long benches are modern, made of light-brown wooden slats with no arm or back rests. One long length of bench curves in front of a bumpy marble wall, and that's where I like to sit, drawing my feet up on the bench and resting my back after hours of sitting and editing. During midday this spot is always shady, and it gives me a full view of the plaza and the people coming in and out of the buildings.

I have even grown fond of the buildings themselves. They are fat and squat, about thirty floors each, with facades of dark-gray rectangular mirrors separated by black piping. They seem secure to me, and I like that; they aren't going anywhere.

I was not alone in my fondness for the plaza. The first day I sat there, I was halfway done with my sandwich when I felt someone looking at me. I lifted my head, and all the way at the end of the long bench was the Wolf Man, sitting peacefully with his little stuffed wolf on his lap. I raised a hand and wiggled my fingers, and he nodded at me, briefly and formally. That became our routine, because I saw him just about every time I went to the plaza.

As expected, he was sitting in the plaza that Friday. We had already exchanged our wave and nod, and we sat at a distance in companionable silence. I was musing over the Wolf Man's schedule—Quill & Ink in the morning, the WTC plaza midday, sometimes the library, but what did he do the rest of the time? Suddenly I heard my name ring out across the plaza: "Elizabeth Zwelland!"

I looked up. Hadley Barr was striding toward me, waving his large hands wildly.

"It *is* you!" he said, flopping on the bench next to me. He looked exactly the same: long limbs, unruly curly hair, large nose, nice brown eyes, happy expression on his face. He was wearing jeans and a T-shirt that I had seen in the window of the Beat Book Shop in Boulder, a white shirt with a black drawing of Jack Kerouac's face, and underneath it the query: DIG?

I smiled. "Hi, Hadley. How's it going?"

"Great! I just got off work. How are you? I haven't seen you since you left! You work right next door to my building, I just figured I would run into you all the time."

I had thought so too, but it hadn't worked out that way. Our schedules were different, for one thing, and although I worked above City O' City, I usually just popped in and out for coffee. Devon liked to hold some of our meetings there, but I spent most of my time at my desk in the quiet office I shared with Campbell, the Harvard gal.

The fact is, I had seen Hadley. Several times. But always from behind, or across the street, and I never called out to him. I still felt pretty embarrassed about what had happened at Q&I; I still had that sliver of shame in my chest, and I was afraid that talking to him would reawaken that feeling. But suddenly Hadley was sitting right beside me, and it felt fine. I was actually really happy to see him.

I was deciding whether or not to admit that I had seen him from afar, when suddenly Hadley said, “Look, it’s the Wolf Man! Hey!” he called out. “How ya doin’?”

The Wolf Man turned his ice-blue eyes toward us. When he saw Hadley, he lifted his stuffed wolf and tipped its head.

I looked at Hadley in astonishment. “You got a wolf nod! I never get a wolf nod, and I see him here just about every day.”

“Oh, the Wolf Man’s my guy. My first day at Quill & Ink, he was there. I went to Joanne—she was the manager before Hilda—and I asked if it was OK to give him a free coffee, and she said go ahead. So we’ve been tight right from the start.”

“Does he ever speak?”

“Nope. But we’re still tight.” He looked at me and grinned enormously. “So here you are, Elizabeth Zwelland! Tell me every last thing. How’s Emma and Jasmine? Did your dad get married? How’s your new job?”

“They’re doing fine. The wedding was pretty fun, all things considered. The job is great. I really love it.” Which I did. On my first day, the moment I was finally alone at my desk with a manuscript in front of me, I leaned over and kissed the first page. I was home.

“So what’s it like?”

Hadley seemed genuinely interested, so I told him all about One Heart. Since we were a start-up, things were sometimes a bit ragged, but with every passing week the company felt a little more cohesive. So far I got along great with everyone: Seabourne, Campbell the Harvard gal, Cameron the IT and eBook dude, the designer guy, the marketing gal, the accountant, the transcribers—everyone. Even Devon, who as predicted made a pass at me. I turned him down firmly, and after that we were fine; he was just one of those men who always had to try. Also as predicted, Devon was immensely full of himself, but he had been surprisingly amenable when we went over his autobiography and I gently suggested toning down the florid language that described just how wonderful he really was.

Most importantly, Devon was a great boss. He was generous and enthusiastic and very focused on bonding. In fact the previous Saturday, he had treated the entire staff to a group outing: first we had breakfast at Dozens, then we piled into taxis and headed over to the Black American West Museum in Five Points. Devon was also generous when it came to the business. Our offices were beautiful, with gray walls and black carpeting, sensitive lighting, ergonomic furniture, and the very latest in IT. I had loved working with Mr. Dove, but he didn't have a clue about computers, whereas Devon was right on top of the latest developments, and was in fact eager to get there first.

Best of all, I was enjoying the work. In my three months at One Heart, I had edited Devon's autobiography, a compilation of transcribed talks by Dzigar Kongtrul Rinpoche, a memoir of a woman's spiritual journey through cancer, and a trekking journal from Nepal. I worked on a few Many Mountains projects—Seabourne's poems, a memoir by a man who lived in a Theravada monastery in Australia, and even a novel about a dysfunctional family. There was a lot of variety and a lot of work, and I felt completely at home.

I told Hadley all that, leaving out the part about Devon's pass. He listened carefully, and when I was done he said, "That sounds really cool. I'm happy for you."

"Thanks. How have you been? How's—how's Quill & Ink?"

"Oh, it's great. The Beat Book Club's going great. Next month David Amram is coming to Denver for a concert, and he agreed to come by the store and talk about making *Pull My Daisy* with Kerouac and the gang. I can't wait." He looked at me carefully. "You said you'd stop by, but you never did. We miss you. Bree misses you; she keeps asking me if I've seen you around the neighborhood."

I looked down at my latte. Hadley, Bree, Stacie, Juniper, Robert, Hector . . . "I miss you guys, too," I said finally. "But I just don't feel comfortable going to the store." I looked up and met his eyes. "Because of Ruby."

Hadley folded in his lips and nodded, just like Emma and Jasmine do. "Gotcha."

"Not my finest hour."

Hadley shrugged. "It happens. But don't worry about ol' Ruby. She's doing fine. Her son's moving down here from Craig. So she's pretty happy about that."

"Oh, that's great! I'm glad she got some good news." I sighed. "I really wish someone had told me. About Colorado Loves Colorado and all that."

"Well, that's part of the Colorado Loves Colorado philosophy," he said. "People have to find their own way to tell about it. That includes the store's management. Me, I just tell everyone straight out."

I knit my brow. "You're part of it?"

"Sure," he said cheerfully. "That's how I got my job. After my arrest I went through rehab, and when I came out I couldn't work in a pharmacy again, for obvious reasons. So they got me a job at Q&I. Best thing that ever happened to me."

"Wow. I didn't know."

"Yep. But the point is, Elizabeth, we miss you. Did you ever get a new cell phone?"

I nodded. As planned, the moment the direct deposit from my first paycheck showed up in my bank account, I got a new phone at the Sprint store. It felt like a gift from heaven, and suddenly I was back in touch with the world. First I called Jasmine and Emma, then my dad, then my old friend Helena Papadopoulos. Last but not least, I called Hansika. She was just about to step into a meeting, but she called me back that night and we spoke for two hours. She caught me up on everyone: she had landed on her feet at Random House, Gerard was unemployed for a while but then he was hired at Penguin, and Mr. Dove was in New Jersey writing his memoirs. He came into the city once a week to see Eileen, who was enjoying early retirement, and about once a month he went out to lunch with Hansika and Gerard. So everyone was doing fine.

Hansika and I had talked frequently since then. In our most recent phone call she told me that Random House was developing a book with a woman who had run away from a freaky Christian cult in Montana; the woman lived in Colorado Springs, and soon Hansika would be coming out to work with the woman on her manuscript. I could hardly wait to see Hansika, and I was looking forward to introducing her to Emma and Jasmine and showing her all around Denver.

"I love my phone," I said. "If I give you my number, can you give it to Bree?"

"Sure." He took a deep breath. "The thing is, Elizabeth, I really missed you, too. I knew you were working right next door to me, and I've thought a million times about going up and saying hello, but I didn't want to stalk you." He paused. "Well—I *did* want to stalk you, but only in the nicest way."

I laughed. "A gentleman stalker."

"Exactly." His eyes roamed over my face. "So what about right now? What are you doing the rest of the day?"

"I have an appointment at three."

"Tomorrow's Saturday. I'm not working; do you want to hang out?"

I looked at him. Hadley Barr, tall and awkward and more than a touch goofy. But he was a gentle soul, with a heart as big as a house. Why not? I thought. Why on earth not?

"All right," I said. "Tomorrow. Let's do something together tomorrow."

"Really?"

"Really."

He beamed. "Elizabeth Zwelland! I knew you couldn't resist the Hadley Barr magic forever."

I laughed. "Apparently not."

Then I looked down at my lap. I felt shy. But I also felt happy. Then something occurred to me: I had never introduced any of my old boyfriends to my dad, because I was always afraid they would run away in terror at my dad's oversized personality and torrent of words. But Hadley already loved my dad. And my dad would love Hadley, because they could talk about my dad's favorite subject—namely, himself. I could picture my dad in his pajamas and robe, his hand roaming through the Beast, rambling on about his life and his poems and his famous friends, and Hadley bobbing his head eagerly as he soaked up every word like manna from heaven. It was certainly something to ponder.

We discussed what we should do the next day. Hadley suggested that we take the Mall Ride to its western end at Union Station, then walk over the Millennium Bridge to LoHi, the Lower Highlands. He said we could eat at a cool breakfast spot called Mona's, then head down the block to My Brother's Bar, which in a previous incarnation was known as Paul's Place and was a favorite watering hole for Neal and Jack. In fact, Hadley told me, Paul's Place was mentioned in the first line of a famous letter that Neal wrote from the reformatory, asking his benefactor to pay off his tab there (of course). It sounded like a plan to me, and I told Hadley I'd love to go.

We took out our cell phones to exchange numbers—Hadley's cell black and functional, mine white with a Chococat head—and I jumped when I saw the time.

"Wow, I have to go," I said, standing up. "Why don't we just meet in front of City O' City at ten?"

"Okeydoke." Hadley stood, too, then leaned over and gave me an awkward kiss on my cheek. "Tomorrow!" he exclaimed.

I laughed. "Tomorrow!"

Hadley raised himself to his full height and saluted me. "Elizabeth Zwelland, good-bye for now."

I wiggled my fingers. "Bye."

I needed to be at the Colorado Convention Center at Fourteenth and California a little before three, and it was quarter of. I would make it, but I would have to walk fast.

☼ ☼ ☼

I walked briskly over to California, where I made a left. I passed the restaurant Bubba Gump's, where someone in a pink shrimp costume with a black top hat was passing out coupons and luring people inside. I love shrimp, even ones in top hats, so I took a coupon and briefly touched the fuzzy pink costume.

Ahead of me was the Colorado Convention Center, an enormous building that stretches for two whole blocks and has a facade of windows that reach from the sidewalk to its modern, triangular roof. As I reached the corner I looked across the street and saw two things of note. One was Denver's most famous public artwork, a towering bright-blue bear standing on its hind legs, its paws leaning against the Convention Center and its snout close to the glass. The second thing of note was parked at the curb in front of the blue bear: the Banjo Billy tour bus.

The tour was due to leave at three, and I was just in time. I crossed over to the bus and got in line behind a few people. The bus had always been in motion when I saw it, so this was my first chance to look at the details. It was the size of a regular school bus, but it was tricked out to look like a Western hillbilly cabin. Split logs lined the sides of the bus, a rusty iron roof balanced on top, and jaunty letters on the side announced BANJO BILLY'S BUS TOURS. On the front of the bus just under the roof eaves, there was a yellow rubber chicken surrounded by multicolored Christmas lights.

The people in front of me were checking in with a middle-aged man with a clipboard and a big white cowboy hat. They got on the bus, and then it was my turn. The man gave me a big smile and said, "Howdy! Welcome to Banjo Billy's!"

I smiled. "Howdy!"

"What's your name?"

"Elizabeth Zwelland. I bought my ticket online."

"All rightee, let's see . . . Yep, gotcha right here. Elizabeth, where are you from?"

"Denver."

"Denver! Well, all right! I thought you looked familiar. Hop on board, we're starting in a minute."

I stepped cautiously onto the bus. To my surprise, the conventional seats had been replaced with mismatched easy chairs, and there was even a couch in the back. The bus was full of happy, chattering people, both adults and children. There was an empty spot right up front, so I sank into a gold easy chair and wedged my knapsack on the floor. I smiled shyly at the couple next to me, then I looked around the bus. The decorations were gleefully over the top: there were plastic yellow flowers on a green vine wrapped around the dashboard, a blue pompom fringe tacked up above the front window, all intertwined with Christmas lights. Strewn across the dashboard and fastened to the wall above the front window were an assortment of mismatched objects—a small mirrored disco ball, a miniature pair of red cowboy boots, several Hawaiian leis, and a cowboy bobblehead doll. There was also a garbage can covered in red gingham cloth, and a small fan next to the driver, a big man in a black cowboy hat. Instead of the usual sign listing do's and don'ts, a white sign with rickety brown letters announced:

TIPS AIN'T SPECTED
BUT ALWAYS PRECIATED

I looked behind me. More Christmas lights lined the roof of the bus above the seats, the walls were covered in dark denim cloth, and the floor was a springy bright-green Astroturf. There was a denim cup holder tacked to the wall next to my seat, and I stored my Dazbog cup inside. I noticed that people had taken their shoes off and gotten comfy, so I slipped off my sneakers and pulled my feet onto my chair.

The tour guide came in, and the door shut behind him. In front of me was a trunk with a fat purple cushion and a microphone. The guide picked up the mike and turned it on, then he boomed out, "How-dee! How y'all doin'?"

Everyone cheered loudly—except me, because I felt shy. Then the guide asked everyone to call out where they were from. There was a heavyset middle-aged couple from Iowa, an Asian family from Delaware, a few businessmen from Chicago, a group of friends from Oregon, and even a family from Lebanon, who had a baby wrapped up like a burrito in a yellow blanket. I was the only one from Denver, which seemed to charm everyone on board; they looked at me as if I were the luckiest girl on the planet.

The guide introduced himself as Skylar, and the driver as Rudy. He asked us all to give Rudy a big "Yee-haw!" I couldn't quite find it in myself to call out "Yee-haw," but everyone else did, causing Rudy to tip his black cowboy hat in our general direction. Then Skylar explained that these buses didn't have a horn quite like other buses, and he had Ruby display the litany of beeps: a duck quack, a dog bark, a horse whinny, a cash machine clinking, and a wolf whistle.

"Sometimes our beeps annoy the locals," Skylar drawled, "but we don't pay no mind. If someone flips you the bird, just flip it right back!"

We spent the next few minutes sitting in place while Skylar gave us a quick rundown on the founding of Denver. I've never been much of a history buff, but Skylar kept it lively, telling us in a casual fact-filled way about Denver's rootin' tootin' past, which included plenty of gold, silver, whiskey, brothels, cowboys, millionaires, and corrupt politicians. He also said that Denver was known as the Queen City of the Plains, and the Crown Jewel of the Rocky Mountain Empire, and to my enormous surprise I felt a burst of pride. Well, well, I thought.

The bus revved up, and we were soon moving up Fourteenth Avenue toward the gold-domed Capitol Building. We received a tremendous amount of attention from pedestrians; no one flipped us the bird, but people waved and called out to us, and a few took photos with their cell phones. Rudy let loose a beep whenever someone reacted to the bus, and thus we quacked and whinnied our way up to the center of the city.

Skylar called out whenever we passed a place of note, telling us charming, goofy, and sometimes naughty stories. The bus also stopped at various points of interest: our first stop was the Capitol Building and the Civic Center Park, and next we idled in front of the stately Brown Palace Hotel, which apparently was chockfull of ghosts, not to mention the hotel where the Beatles stayed when they played at Red Rocks in 1964. Then we chugged up Colfax Street, where Skylar confirmed Hadley's factoid that Colfax had indeed been christened "the longest, wickedest street in America" by *Playboy* magazine. We stopped at the Molly Brown House on Pennsylvania between Thirteenth and Fourteenth; Skylar told us the story about Molly and the Titanic, then gleefully informed us that this house was haunted as well. Apparently they gave tours of the house, and I made a mental note to ask Devon if we could have a staff outing there someday.

Our next stop was the Botanic Gardens, much to my delight. Turns out the Gardens had their fair share of ghosts as well: the grounds used to be a Catholic cemetery, and according to Skylar it was practically impossible for the Gardens to keep night guards for any length of time due to the numerous ghosts on the premises—ghosts that were, apparently, always naked. I couldn't wait to tell Trixie about that. Skylar told us that Capitol Hill used to be called Mansion Hill, and although only one out of thirty of the original mansions were still standing, the area was renowned for its gorgeous architecture. I realized that due to either good luck or dumb luck, I was living in one of the coolest, oldest sections of Denver.

As the bus turned down Ninth, Skylar called out, "Rudy, pretty girl at three o'clock!"

I looked out the window. A tall blonde with tight jeans and a swing in her walk was moving down the sidewalk with a Great Dane in tow. Rudy let out a big horse whinny; the woman laughed and gave the bus a cheerful wave.

It suddenly dawned on me: That's why they always beeped at me. They beeped at me because they thought I was pretty.

Our next stop was Cheesman Park. Skylar said it was originally an Arapahoe burial ground, and then it morphed into the city of Denver's cemetery, with over thirteen thousand bodies at the height of its use. When the city decided to turn the land into a park, people were asked to move their dead, but a few thousand corpses still remained. He said that recently the city fixed a sidewalk in the park, and they had to stop work fifty-three times in order to remove body parts. I was curious to hear all Skylar's facts and stories, but I still felt unfazed: this was my neighborhood park and I felt a great loyalty to it, corpses and all.

We traveled and beeped our way to the Grant-Humphreys Mansion on Pearl Street, then stopped in front of the Governor's Mansion. We turned onto Ninth, and I saw the back of the Swiss Arms. I guess I got carried away by all the rootin' tootin' fun, because I called out to Skylar, "Hey, that's my building!"

"The Swiss Arms?"

"Yes! I live there."

"Well," he said. "Stick your head out the window and give 'em a yee-haw!"

I hesitated. Would I really do that? Would I really stick my head out of Banjo Billy's tour bus and yell "Yee-haw"?

The bus started turning onto Sherman Street. The moment was passing, and it had to be seized. I stood, moved quickly across the aisle, stuck my head out the window, and yes, dear reader, I yelled, "Yee-haw!"

To my surprise, it felt great, so I did it again. "Yee-haw!"

Skylar and the rest of the passengers burst into applause. I went back to my seat, my face beet-red, my heart pounding with glee.

THE END

Acknowledgments

Several friends read this book in its early stages and gave important feedback. Immense thanks to Daisy Diaz-Granados, Maggie Howard-Heretakis, Kasey Jueds, Debbie Liong-Leach, Geoff Moore, Patricia Seminara, Rachel Shirk, Britt St. John, and Joanne Wilke. Thanks also to Uwe Stender for reading. Also thanks to Patricia and Rachel for advice on the cover design. Special thanks to Kasey for providing a thoughtful blurb, and special thanks to Maggie: a wonderful stepdaughter is a blessing, and a wonderful stepdaughter who is also a terrific editor is a double blessing.

Elizabeth Zwelland does not particularly like Boulder, Colorado, but it is a beautiful city, and some of the nicest people I know live there. Here's to Kristina Czimar and Zoe Scott, Laurel Kallenbach and Ken Aikin, Jaime Schwalb and Jaime Rodrigues, and Rachel Shirk and Nate Foster, who used to live there. This is also a good time to mention Denverite Marcella Saxton, a stalwart friend.

Also thanks to:

Ann Erickson, a kind person and a good listener.

Hersch Silverman, for general support and inspiration, as well as discussions about Neal Cassady and the Beat life.

Alexander Sugarman and Flora Sugarman, for always providing support and enthusiasm. Particular thanks to Flora for keeping early copies of the book under her bed for safekeeping.

Jelly and its wonderful staff, who always had smiles, encouragement, and fresh coffee during my many mornings writing there. Elizabeth Zwelland would definitely have gone to Jelly, but this book takes place from 2009 to 2010, and the first Jelly location opened in 2011. If you go to Denver, you must go to Jelly. Check out: www.eatmorejelly.com.

The Denver Public Library, the Boulder Public Library, the Westfield Memorial Library, and libraries everywhere.

Last but not least, the wonderful cities of Denver and Boulder. Most of the places listed in this book are still in existence (except Dixons, alas), so if you are in Colorado, you can enjoy them in person. A few names have been changed: for instance, there is no bookstore called Quill & Ink in LoDo, but there is the Tattered Cover, one of the great American independent bookstores and a wonderful place to shop and dream—and work, I'm sure.

Selected Bibliography

The following were either mentioned in this book or used for research.

The Beats

Cassady, Neil. *The First Third.* Rev. ed. San Francisco: City Lights, 2001.

Johnson, Joyce. *Minor Characters: A Beat Memoir.* New York: Houghton Mifflin, 1983.

———. *Missing Men: A Memoir.* New York: Penguin, 2005.

Johnson, Joyce, and Jack Kerouac. *Door Wide Open: A Beat Love Affair in Letters, 1957–1958.* New York: Viking Adult, 2000.

Kerouac, Jack. *Book of Haikus.* New York: Penguin, 2003.

———. *Desolation Angels.* New York: Riverhead Books, 1995.

———. *The Dharma Bums.* New York: Penguin, 1991.

———. *On the Road.* New York: Penguin, 1999.

———. *The Subterraneans.* New York: Grove Press, 1994.

———. *Visions of Cody.* New York: Penguin, 1993.

Kerouac, Jan. *Baby Driver.* New York: St. Martin's, 1981.

———. *Trainsong.* New York: Henry Holt, 1988.

Kerouac, Joan Haverty. *Nobody's Wife: The Smart Aleck and the King of Beats.* Introduction by Jan Kerouac. Berkeley, CA: Creative Arts, 2000.

Mukpo, Diana, and Carolyn Gimian. *Dragon Thunder: My Life with Chögyam Trungpa.* Boston: Shambhala, 2006.

Nicosia, Gerald. *Jan Kerouac: A Life in Memory.* Corte Madera, CA: Noodlebrain Press, 2009.

Plummer, William. *The Holy Goof: A Biography of Neal Cassady.* 2nd ed. Cambridge, MA: Da Capo Press, 2009.

Columbine

Cullen, Dave. *Columbine.* New York: Twelve, 2010.
Kass, Jeff. *Columbine: A True Crime Story, a Victim, the Killers and the Nation's Search for Answers.* Denver: Ghost Road Press, 2009.
Larkin, Ralph W. *Comprehending Columbine.* Philadelphia: Temple University Press, 2007.
Moore, Michael. *Bowling for Columbine.* United Artists, 2002.
Prendergast, Alan. "The Columbine Effect." *Westword* 35, no. 30 (March 20, 2012): 14–19.

JonBenét Ramsey

Schiller, Lawrence. *Perfect Murder, Perfect Town: The Uncensored Story of the JonBenét Murder and the Grand Jury's Search for the Final Truth.* New York: HarperTorch, 1999.

Miscellaneous

de Beauvoir, Simone. *The Mandarins.* New York: Norton, 1999.
_______. *She Came to Stay.* New York: Norton, 2013.
James, Henry. *Washington Square.* New York: Modern Library, 2002.
Lamblin, Bianca. *A Disgraceful Affair: Simone de Beauvoir, Jean-Paul Sartre, and Bianca Lamblin.* Translated by Julie Plovnick. Boston: Northeastern University Press, 1996.
McInerney, Jay. *Bright Lights, Big City.* New York: Vintage, 1984.
Seymour-Jones, Carolyn. *A Dangerous Liaison: A Revelatory New Biography of Simone de Beauvoir and Jean-Paul Sartre.* New York: Overlook Press, 2010.
Stokes, Donald. *A Guide to Observing Insect Lives.* Boston: Little Brown, 1983.